Dissolution

Dissolution

NICHOLAS BINGE

RIVERHEAD BOOKS
NEW YORK
2025

RIVERHEAD BOOKS
An imprint of Penguin Random House LLC
1745 Broadway, New York, NY 10019
penguinrandomhouse.com

Book design by Daniel Lagin

LIBRARY OF CONGRESS CATALOGING-IN-PUBLICATION DATA
Names: Binge, Nicholas, author.
Title: Dissolution / Nicholas Binge.
Description: New York: Riverhead Books, 2025. |
Identifiers: LCCN 2024048997 (print) | LCCN 2024048998 (ebook) |
    ISBN 9780593852163 (hardcover) | ISBN 9780593852187 (ebook)
Subjects: LCGFT: Thrillers (Fiction) | Science fiction. | Novels.
Classification: LCC PR6102.I53 D57 2025 (print) |
    LCC PR6102.I53 (ebook) | DDC 823/.92—dc23/eng/20241021
LC record available at https://lccn.loc.gov/2024048997
LC ebook record available at https://lccn.loc.gov/2024048998

Printed in the United States of America
1st Printing

The authorized representative in the EU for product safety and compliance is
Penguin Random House Ireland, Morrison Chambers, 32 Nassau Street,
Dublin D02 YH68, Ireland, https://eu-contact.penguin.ie.

For Allys, without whom, nothing.

JULIET   I have forgot why I did call thee back.

ROMEO   Let me stand here till thou remember it.

JULIET   I shall forget, to have thee still stand there,
Remembering how I love thy company.

ROMEO   And I'll still stay, to have thee still forget,
Forgetting any other home but this.

—*ROMEO AND JULIET*, ACT II, SCENE II

Dissolution

1

TRANSCRIPT NO. 273: Margaret Webb

DATE STAMP: 11 AUG. 2021

11 Hours, 0 Minutes, and 0 Seconds Until Dissolution

You've got eleven hours until reset. You need to tell me exactly what happened.

> Where am I?

We've been over this, Maggie. It's not important. The only thing that's important is that you focus on me.

> What do you mean "it's not important"? I don't know where I am. I don't know who you are. How can that possibly not be important?

I'm Hassan. Do you remember me?

> No . . . I mean, yes. I think. The name rings a bell.

Take a second. Breathe. You're in a daze.

| Have we . . . ? We've met before, haven't we?

We have.

| Where is Stanley? Is he okay?

That is precisely what we are trying to find out.

| What do you mean? Oh God, has something happened to him? Is he safe?

Calm down. We don't have time. I need you to focus—to remember what's going on. Let's start by focusing on the present. Tell me about your surroundings. Talking it through will help. Tell me where we are.

| We're in a . . . Is this an empty swimming pool?

Of sorts. Describe it to me.

| What the hell is going on?

You're disoriented. Your brain is recovering from the shift. Describe to me what's going on around you—the small details. What do you see? What does it sound like? What time of day is it?

I'm . . . we're inside. Is that right? The light is artificial, and there are no windows, like we're underground. The pool is empty—totally drained— and I'm starting to question if it's even a pool. It's too blank, too clinical. More like a giant bath basin.

Where are we, the two of us?

Surely you can see it as well as I can. Oh God, the sunglasses. Are you blind?

I'm not blind. We're just establishing a cognitive baseline. Think of this like a sobriety test; I need to check you're properly focused, like counting how many fingers are on my hand.

Okay. Well, we're set up at this desk right in the middle of the basin. You and me, and no one else, facing each other. It's deserted. My arm is hooked up to an IV. Why? Am I sick?

What can you hear?

Right now? The only sound is our voices echoing through the room.

Good. That's very good, Maggie. More. What's on the table?

There's . . . a small cylindrical container, like a pill bottle, as well as a glass of water. There's a pen and paper and a recording device, as if I'm in some kind of interrogation room. But I'm not. I'm in a pool. Why am I in a pool? Why am I hooked up to whatever is in that IV bag?

The *why* is not important. You don't need to worry about that right now.

Oh really? Well, young man, what *do* I need to worry about?

We need to know exactly what happened that led you here. It's absolutely crucial, for all of us, that we know this. You need to tell me, in as much detail as you can, about the first time you saw me.

I can't . . . remember. I can't remember anything. What are you doing with that container?

This pill will help jog your memory.

I've not taken pills from strangers in a good few decades.

If you don't start remembering soon, we will run out of time, and this will all be for nothing. The pill is not dangerous, I promise. It will just help clear the fog in your brain. Please. It's very important that we understand what took place. We don't have much time. We have to find Stanley.

Okay, okay. Fine. Keep your socks on. Jesus. If I weren't eighty-three, I'd think you were up to something.

Urgh, that's awful. I can feel that right in my throat. It stings. What the hell was that? And, at the risk of repeating myself, what the *hell* is going on?

Stanley isn't safe. None of us are safe. Something happened, and I need your help to find out exactly what. Think back: When was the first time you saw me?

What?

We have to go from the beginning. We have to see every moment. It's the only way we can know for sure. Close your eyes. Let your memories come back. Go to the first time you see me.

Okay, I'll try, but I don't know what you expect is going to . . . Wait. What on earth?

What is it?

I can *see* it. It's as though . . . This is strange—this isn't like a normal memory at all. I can see the whole room in front of me. It's like I'm there.

That's the pill starting to work. It's a memory enhancer.

> This is more than just an enhancer. I can hear the kettle boiling. I can taste the dryness on my tongue from the glass of wine I had last night. I'm not remembering, Hassan. I'm *there*.

Good—that is exactly what we need. The first time you see me, where are you?

> I'm . . . I'm at home. I think. Or what used to be home. I don't like calling it that anymore.

Why not?

> Because it was only home when Stanley was there. Now it's just a house—big, too big for me, with too many bedrooms and an open-plan kitchen I used to love. I guess I still call it home when I'm talking to other people. Or when I'm thinking to myself, *Okay, it's been a long day, I should head home,* or something similar. But that word's just a sound now—it doesn't carry the meaning it once did when Stanley and Leah were here. Because it isn't *ours* anymore, it doesn't feel like *mine*. Does that make sense?

Am I in the house?

> No. Not yet. It's just me and Sandra, the lady from Sunrise—the care home. She's talking to me about Stanley's condition, but to be honest, I've stopped listening. Halfway through the conversation, I get up to make a cup of tea. Not because I want tea but because I can't stand sitting opposite her anymore. She gives me a sympathetic, condescending look, like she finds it cute that I'm so old and still boil my kettle on the stove. I hate that ageist nonsense—obviously I have an electric kettle, and obviously

I know how to bloody use it—but boiling the kettle on the hob gives me an excuse to put my back to her. It allows me to pretend to listen, even while I'm drowning her out.

Do you always ignore people you don't like?

Oh, it's not her. It's the mundanity of it: the back-and-forth about all the kind of nonsense I've never wanted to care about—Stanley's bowel movements, food intake, medication. I used to *hate* those kinds of routines when I was young, feeling like I was trapped, like I was on a wheel. That feeling's been growing in me more and more these days. I wasn't always this callous, you know? At first, when Stanley went in, I obsessed over all that stuff. It was the only way I could establish any kind of control. But now? After the thousandth conversation, I just can't face it anymore. Frankly, I pay enough to that place that I have earned the right to ignore them when I want to. God, saying that out loud makes me sound horrible. What am I doing? Why am I telling you all this?

The drug I gave you—it encourages verbalization of your inner monologue, stimulating the pathways between your memory and your speech center. This is all good, all these details. Don't skip over anything. Is Stanley in the care home now? When did you last see him?

He is. I visited him at Sunrise just that morning. He didn't recognize me, which wasn't a complete surprise. That's been happening more and more often recently.

It began several years earlier. When I'd visit, I'd sit by his bed and talk to him about what was going on in my life. Well, I'd invent things, because I never wanted him to know how dull my life had become. I used to tell him how Leah was doing—off traveling the world, making her mark—but she doesn't talk to me anymore, and I haven't the faintest idea why.

But Stanley, he just . . . wouldn't respond. He would stare off into the distance, occasionally mumbling something I couldn't quite catch, and I thought, *This is it. This is the moment when my husband forgets me.*

But it wasn't. Not then. I know that because it actually happened two years later. For all my fuzziness, that's one thing I know I'll never forget. I walked into his room to water the plants on his windowsill—I like to water them on Tuesdays—and the look on his face, oh God, it was one I'd never seen before. The confusion and the panic. The fear. It makes total sense when you think about it. It's the same look any of us would give a complete stranger appearing in our bedroom.

He gave me the same look this morning, the morning I met you, but I'm used to it. It happens now and again—sometimes a couple of times a week, sometimes not for a whole month. It always makes me think about something Stanley said when we were younger, though, in our sixties. We'd just finished calling Leah after her first term at university, and the house was emptier than we'd thought it would be. For eighteen years, we'd been half-joking about the freedom we'd have once she left home to do anything we liked, but the truth was, we just missed her.

Stanley turned to me after she'd said goodbye, and he said, "It occurs to me that at some point, you pick up your child for the very last time. And you don't know. At the time, you don't know that it's the last time you'll ever do it." He was right, of course: Endings don't announce themselves. They sneak around you; they shuffle their way past unnoticed until, on some cloudy day, you look out on an empty street and realize everything ended some time ago.

I worry about that with Stanley now. That one day will be the last time he recognizes me. That one day will be the very last time he knows who I am, and for some stupid, silly reason, I want to make an ending of it. I want to tell him it's okay. God, I almost want to pop open a bottle of champagne just to, you know, mark the moment. To say: If this is the end of fifty-two years of marriage, then that's okay. I can accept that.

But it really hit me that morning that there won't be an ending. I'll just notice at some point that he hasn't recognized me in months. And that will be that. It will be over.

Go back to the house, with Sandra. What's happening?

She's still talking. I've finished making my tea, and I'm realizing that I'll have to sit opposite her again. Is this right? Am I covering the right things?

I can't say. We'll only know from certain very specific details. Keep going.

She's not talking about Stanley anymore. She's telling me about her work at the care home, about Sunrise. She hasn't been there very long—just transferred over from another owned by the same company down south.

"Who's humoring who here?" I ask. She's becoming dull, and I've almost finished my tea.

"Excuse me?"

I put down my cup. "Are you still talking because you figure a lonely old bat like me needs the company, or am I the one pretending to care about your life out of social nicety? I only say because I think it might be both."

"Oh," she says, staring at her hands. "Oh, I see. I should be going." She gets up and bustles her scattered things together, like a bird gathering twigs for a nest. When she gets to the door, she says, "There was no need to be rude."

I roll my eyes. After eighty-three years on this planet, I've found that, actually, there's no need to be polite.

I close the door and turn around. In front of me, there's a corridor, a stairway to the right that leads up to two empty bedrooms and an attic. There are no pictures on the walls—I moved the ones that meant anything to Stanley's room, to try and help him remember. The others I donated to the charity shop or the skip.

I move from the door and go into the living room. There's a breeze coming through the windows, a gap in the insulation that I haven't got fixed. It chills me.

Looking at the sofa, the coffee table, the curtains, I see flashes of my life inscribed upon them: Stanley rolling around on the carpet with

Leah, tickling her; her running away, then rushing back for more; Stanley crying on the sofa after she left home and me hiding behind the doorway, not wanting him to see that I have seen him; two glasses of wine and a half-empty bottle on the coffee table, the TV on behind them. The images are there, but they aren't there—pieces of the past superimposed upon one another, like a canvas that's been painted over a hundred times. The last coat of paint doesn't have any color to it. Just an off-white hue. Barren.

I don't know why Leah doesn't answer my calls. It's deliberate, I know that much. I know she's an adult now, I do, even if I have to pinch myself and remember that she's in her forties, but when Stanley started forgetting, she was all I had left. She doesn't even give me the courtesy of letting my calls ring out, of pretending she's not available. She just hangs up on me. I've sent her pleading text messages. I still send her long emails, hoping that she might read them. Recently, I've stopped calling, because I can't deal with the physical pang of despair—like a wound in my chest—that stabs through me every time she turns me down.

She won't even tell me what it is I've done. I think that's the worst part. She's just cut me out of her life like an unwanted piece of gristle.

My sister told me I should sell the house—move in somewhere smaller with fewer memories. One of those little one-bedroom flats where I can live out my days alone eating ready meals and doing "Seniors Yoga with Morganne" on YouTube. But that feels like a betrayal. If there's one thing I have left, it's a sense of duty. A sense that if one of us is going to forget all about our family, then the other has to hold on as hard as they can. Every time I find myself forgetting something, anything at all—what birthday cake we made for Leah when she was eleven, what film Stanley and I went to see on our thirty-second anniversary—I feel an intense sense of guilt.

Sometimes I feel like I'm holding a hundred thousand balloons, all pushing to be released, to disappear up into the sky, but I can't let any of them go. They're all I have.

There's a knocking at the door. I remember that clearly because it takes me a second to realize what the sound is. Nobody actually knocks anymore.

Who is it?

It's you. It's the very first time we meet. You seem friendly. The first thing I think is how young you look, how rested and fresh. Nothing like you do now. Now you look awful.

What do I say to you?

You're not going to react to that? You would have smiled before. I remember liking your smile, finding it intriguing. Anyway, when I open the door, you say:

"How much do you know about Sunrise?"

I blink, taken aback. You're tall, with a dark complexion and a certain sharklike look to your face. Not predatory, exactly, but there's a hint of danger underneath it. I like that. I've always liked that in a man.

"Who are you?" I ask.

"My name is Hassan." You step through the front door, right past me, and leave me standing there staring out into the street. By the time I've managed to turn around, you're already in the living room and sitting on the sofa.

I follow. Twenty years ago, I probably would have called the police. Ten years ago, I would have screamed at you to get the hell out of my home. But this doesn't feel like my home anymore, and you're the most interesting thing that's happened to me in months.

"What did you say about Sunrise?"

"The care home, where your husband is. How much do you know about it?"

I'm standing in the middle of the room, staring down at you. In films, they use this shot to make one person look powerful and dominating, the other weak. It doesn't work that way here. You put your hands together in a relaxed clasp and rest them on your crossed legs. I doubt you've ever looked weak in your life.

"It's a care home. My husband is in the memory ward there. They look after him. Who did you say you were?"

What are you thinking at this moment?

Is that important?

I can't be sure.

There's a little bubble of worry, because you're talking about Stanley, and it feels like there's something wrong. And beneath that, I feel a strange flutter of excitement, like butterflies in my stomach. Isn't that odd? Like I've just bumped into a high school crush. And the moment that I recognize it, it gets swept away by a wash of guilt.

Guilt?

That I should be excited about something potentially worrying. That I should be getting excited at all. That's not my job. My job is to take care of Stanley.

"Why are you here?" I ask. You cock your head slightly sideways, as if you've seen a squirrel darting up a tree. From out of your pocket, you pull a gold cigarette case and a packet of matches. Before I process what you're about to do, you light one, taking a deep puff as it rests between your fingers. You glance at me, and your eyes look like they've been crafted from mahogany. But . . .

But what?

Now you're wearing sunglasses, even though we're inside this pool. You're hiding your eyes from me. Why? What happened?

That's not important. You need to focus on what happened to you—that's what matters.

You lean forward and say, "Let me tell you a story." And at that moment, I feel like I haven't got a choice. I feel like from the moment you opened the door, I've been swept up in something, and I don't have the power to change its course. There's too much inertia. I'm too old. My legs hurt.

I think about taking a seat in the armchair opposite you. I don't.

"Three years ago, I met a man. Let's call him K."

"Is that his name?"

You give a slight chuckle. "No. He was a young man—early twenties. He'd just come out of university and had managed to get himself an internship at a prestigious news agency in London. For him, this was it: a straight career path to high-flying journalism. Traveling the world. Seeing the sights. All the frills. After a few days of getting people coffees and being introduced to HR routines, he attended his first major briefing led by the editor in chief. He sat there, intently listening for the entire thing, and left with some great ideas for stories he might be able to chase down as soon as he found a spare moment. Ten minutes later, the editor called him into the big office. 'What the hell was that?' he was asked. He shook his head, unsure. 'Look,' the big editor said, 'you get an internship like this, you should be thankful. You should appreciate it. I work damn hard, and so does everyone else in here. We certainly don't expect some jumped-up kid to come in, sit down, and ignore all our hard work.' Now, K didn't understand what the guy was talking about and told him as much. The editor got even angrier. 'You didn't take any fucking notes. You didn't even have a pen or a slip of paper. It's like you couldn't care less what was being said!'"

I still haven't sat down, and I'm not entirely sure why. I'm still perched over you like a bony old hawk, enraptured. I'm reminded, for a second, of that scene in *The Jungle Book* where the snake makes Mowgli look into his eyes just as his tail starts curling around Mowgli's neck. Before I can really process the thought, you're continuing.

"K frowned at this, rubbed his chin, and then proceeded to recite every single word said at the briefing from beginning to end. The editor was dumbfounded. Turns out, K never forgot a thing. Most strangely, he didn't realize until just then that other people *did* forget things. He'd grown up pretty secluded, thought everyone could do what he did. It had never seemed like a big deal, and no one had ever questioned him like this."

You pause, as if for thought. I take advantage of the break in words and manage to quickly utter a sentence in a single burst of breath. "What has this got to do with Stanley?"

You reach over and ash your cigarette into a bowl. I don't remember getting it out of the cupboard.

"The thing about K is that he didn't go unnoticed. Some people were jealous, others merely interested. He agreed to take part in a research study later that year for big money. He didn't know what they were doing, exactly—apparently, that was part of the study. He'd just go in and get his brain scanned, then do some simple tests, word games, number skills, that sort of thing. Then he'd go home.

"One day, he goes to work and doesn't recognize anyone. He recognizes work. It's the place he's been going to for the past year. He knows where his desk is and where the office is, but all the people are different. They act like they know him. They nod at him and greet him. Someone hands him a coffee. He's never seen a single one of them in his life. So what does he do? He calls up his friends, his family—doesn't recognize any of them either. His mother's voice on the phone doesn't sound like any voice he's ever heard before. A complete stranger is telling him that it's okay, that she loves him. He panics. Three days later, he hangs himself."

"Jesus! Did that actually happen?"

You give me a single slow nod. "Absolutely. And what was the one thing in his life that changed before he forgot who everyone was?"

I look out the window at the street. A woman jogs past in full running gear. She doesn't look at us, but for some reason, it occurs to me that nobody should be seeing this interaction at all. That it should be clandestine. It feels ridiculous, but I walk over to the window and close the curtains. "The research study?" I ask.

"Run by a group called Sunrise Medical. Of course, outside of a few very well-hidden paper trails, there's no evidence that it ever took place."

I'm pacing, trying to work out what the hell you're saying. My heart is in my chest, beating hard. For some reason, I'm taking this personally. Too personally.

You finish your cigarette as your eyes track me across the room. "I think Stanley was involved in a similar experiment. I think he still might be."

I stop dead. "You think they're experimenting on him? You think . . . Wait, wait, wait. Are you actually saying that Stanley's Alzheimer's is . . . what? That they've done that to him?"

"Yes."

My whole body tightens. This is crazy. This is absurd. You've just walked into my house and started telling insane stories, and I have no idea who you even are.

But you believe me.

Yes.

Why?

I don't know. As you're speaking, I suppose, the idea occurs to me that if whatever's happening to Stanley isn't natural, if it's being done to him, then it might be reversible. You've not mentioned that. You've not even hinted at it. But the minuscule chance that it might be within the realm of possibility is enough to make me want to believe you.

"I should get him," I say. "Go sign him out. Bring him back here."

"That might not be as easy as it sounds."

You stand up, and I notice how tall you are, and how intimidating. I swallow the spit that's building up in my mouth.

"What do you mean? It's a care home, not a fucking prison. I'm his wife."

"When's the last time you remember signing him out?"

"I . . ." I stare up at you, losing focus. "I don't know."

"Since he was admitted, do you have any specific memories of taking him out of that care home? For any reason?"

I look down at my hands, and for a moment, it's like I'm seeing them for the first time. I turn them over, looking at the wrinkles on the back, the curvature of the bones. I can feel your eyes on the top of my head. "I don't know. But I know that I can. Take him out, I mean. In a general sense."

"Then why do you have no actual memories of doing so?"

I look back up at you. I am lost. I feel like a balloon has just slipped out of my hand and is floating up, up into the sky, never to return.

"But that's why I chose Sunrise. Because I wanted him close by. It's just down the road. So I could . . ."

You put a hand on my shoulder, and I can feel its weight all through my body. "Do you actually remember choosing Sunrise? Do you specifically remember admitting him there?"

I turn away. I can't take it anymore. I stumble over to the kitchen to try and make another cup of tea so that I can get some kind of handle on reality. I'm trying to think about the day I came to the decision that I couldn't care for him full-time anymore. I can see myself flicking through brochures downstairs while Stanley's in the bedroom because I don't want to do it in front of him. Memories of staying up after Stanley had gone to sleep to read reviews on my laptop. And then . . . he's at Sunrise. I'm trying to picture what it was like when I found their brochure or their website, or when I first called them. I'm trying to remember our first visit there and what the weather was like.

But I can't.

It's not there.

"What the hell is going on?" I whisper.

You appear behind me, closer than I would expect. I remember feeling both comforted and scared, all at the same time.

"That's what I'm trying to find out. I need you to listen closely to me: Something very strange is happening in that building, and I don't think anyone is allowed to leave. And I think Stanley might be the key to working out why." Then you say: "Will you help me?"

What happens then?

I say that I will. I've already decided there isn't any other choice. Something's happening to Stanley. Something's being *done* to him. I ask you what you need me to do.

And what do I say?

"I need you to break him out."

2 | Stanley
1950

THE SCHOOL GATES WERE HUGE. WROUGHT IRON. AT LEAST TWENTY FEET tall. He didn't know how long he'd been standing beneath them as they loomed over him, imperious and forbidding.

Everything in his life up until that point had been small and inconsequential—a fusty bedroom, a tiny kitchen, a cowering mother. The biggest thing he'd encountered in his daily life was a fist.

His father didn't know he'd applied to Whelton College or even that he'd sat for the exams. As far as he knew, fathers were not the sorts of people you told these sorts of things to. They were creatures to be placated, to be avoided, to be feared. Stanley had never understood why anyone would need, let alone *want*, a father.

From a young age, he would look at that slurring, red-faced bully and he would tell himself: *That is not where I came from. It can't be. I won't let it be.*

He whispered it to himself at night, under the covers. He repeated it to himself in the shower. He ran it through his mind like a mantra when he walked through the streets of Ryhope Colliery. Boys from mining towns did not go on to do anything with their lives except follow in their father's footsteps, join them down at the pit. But with each repetition, Stanley added links and chains to a promise that he kept tight in his heart: his story would not be the story of where he came from but, rather, the story of where he went.

And so despite a hostile and unwelcoming home—screaming, hiding, cleaning up messes—he managed to pass the entrance exams. He was now a student at one of the most prestigious boarding schools for boys in the country. With a full scholarship, no less.

But when he stepped onto the train platform with little more than his acceptance letter and a patched-up secondhand uniform, he expected to feel guilt—for leaving his mother behind to deal with that brute, for abandoning her. He thought he would be drowning in it. But he wasn't. The truth was, he couldn't picture her anywhere else but with his father. She'd been around that man so long it felt like she belonged there now, like a rat belongs in a cage.

As for himself? He felt freedom. He tasted it in the wind, acrid with railway fumes, that lifted his hair and blew hard into his face. He saw it on the horizon, across untold miles of green fields. He heard it in the screech of the brakes as his train pulled into the station.

There was shame too—at feeling so free, at being so happy to escape, and at the lack of guilt. Though he supposed shame was a form of guilt. Emotions tended to layer themselves like that: sets nested deep within supersets, like circles in an Euler diagram.

Before him now lay four centuries of imposition and expectation. Beyond the gates, stone archways and twisting turrets framed pristinely gardened courtyards; students bustled in groups, tightly knit, weaving among teachers clad in gowns. He was stepping into a new world, and he knew he should have felt intimidated—terrified, even.

To Stanley, it was *electric*.

Joining third form at the age of thirteen, he found that the intake was tiny—the only other boy starting in the same year quickly got lost in the hubbub of the first few days, in the whirlwind of new experiences. Everything had its own name—lessons were "orations"; teachers were "professors"; classrooms were either "halls" or "towers." Periods that he had never seen before appeared on his timetable: Greek history, Latin, philosophy. This was a universe in which distant possibility became probable, in which dreams became something waking, not sequestered in the recesses of sleep.

This, he thought as he settled into a front-row bench in the Third Tower for an oration on calculus, *is where I belong*.

But it slowly dawned on him that few people spoke to him. Not properly. There was the beaming fifth-year who showed him around the school on his first day, but he had not seen him since. The first few days had been such a flurry of new ideas and thoughts, he'd barely been able to keep up. His English professor referenced books that every child his age *must* have read, except his house had never had books; his house had never had the safety needed to read one. He found science tricky and Latin trickier. Only maths offered a welcome break from the intensity—a comfort that it had always offered him. It was just numbers and shapes, lines and intersections. It made sense. It always had.

But by the time he was back in bed for the night, when other boys were chatting and playing, he was so tired that he just collapsed onto his mattress and fell fast asleep. By day four, he had seeped into the background—the new kid who didn't speak, a ghost, a pattern on the wall.

There were odd people here too, particularly among the staff. One lunchtime, when he was sitting alone on a bench with his water bottle and a sandwich, one of the professors approached him. An old lady with silvery hair.

"Excuse me, young man," she said, approaching him. Stanley glanced around him, unsure why he was being spoken to.

"Y-Yes?"

"I'm going to need that bottle of water."

Stanley blinked, baffled. "My water bottle?"

"Yes," she said, and held out her hand. "Now."

Not willing to make a fuss, Stanley handed it over. She smiled at him and disappeared without another word. This kind of strangeness seemed almost a staple at this old institution, and Stanley found it a little intimidating.

But Whelton was a place of opportunity, not cowardice. He'd seen too much cowardice from his mother, too much acceptance of the brutalities of life. No—he had come here to leave cowardice behind. And so after a particularly challenging oration in the Lesser Hall on Plato's *Republic,* he attempted to approach the three boys who had been sitting in front of him. Though only one of them was tall, all three felt towering in a way that Stanley couldn't quite identify—a confidence in the way they held themselves, a certainty in the way they spoke.

"Hello?"

The tall one—a boy with striking blond hair that flickered just above his eyes—turned.

"Yes?"

"I'm Stanley."

The other two turned with him, like cogs. "Oh, look, Barty," one of them said. "The runt can speak."

Barty laughed. "What do you want, runt?"

"My name's Stanley," he repeated.

"Oh dear," the third boy jeered. "I think you've broken him. He's stuck."

"That's what happens when you come from cheap stock," Barty replied, his voice matter-of-fact, as though he were explaining a maths problem or a chemical equation. "Think about it, Charles. Like when people buy cheap foreign stuff and it falls apart in a day or two. If the raw materials are subpar, you're never going to make anything with any quality."

Stanley's face bloomed red-hot. He opened his mouth to retort, but it came out as a breath of air. They weren't even talking to him. They were talking *about* him, like he was a thing. A discarded object they were trying to decide what to do with.

"Well?" The boy called Charles leaned into Stanley, lowering his voice so that a passing professor couldn't hear. "What the fuck did you want?"

Confronted by the immediacy of the demand, Stanley let out a quiet reply: "I wanted to make some friends."

He curled inward as soon as he said it, cringing at the pathetic words that had weaseled their way out of him.

All three of the boys burst out laughing—a cruel, uproarious cackle. They embraced the mockery of it. They took pleasure in it.

"Listen, runt," Barty said, cruel anger twisting the lines of his face. "I don't know what begging your parents, if you even have parents, had to do to get you in here, or what charitable bullshit you're meant to represent, but seriously, look at you." He roughly grabbed Stanley's uniform and pulled at the secondhand fabric. "You don't belong here. You're never going to belong here. And it won't be long before the school realizes and then sends you back to whatever shithole you came from. I wouldn't bother wasting your time making *friends*."

Stanley's insides were burning. His fists clenched. But all he could do was stand there, frozen and speechless.

Barty leaned in, inches from Stanley's face, and his cruelty suddenly flickered into a kind smile. "I'm sorry, little runt. I really am. But it's not about you or me. It's about quality. When you come from good stock, it's not really fair to have to mix with people from bad. You know what I mean?"

He gave Stanley a little slap on the cheek, like he was inspecting a farm animal, then turned around and walked away, the other two boys following in tow.

It was all Stanley could do not to cry—both then and later in the dorm. He'd had practice bottling up his emotions, keeping them well under the surface so that he didn't get punished for them. But this time felt different, because despite how angry he was at being spoken to that way, he knew they were right.

Stanley pictured the town he grew up in, its coal-blackened residents and ice-cold winds. He pictured his father, face red and puffy, drunkenly stumbling about the house.

If the raw materials are subpar, you're never going to make anything with any quality.

Pressing his face deep into the pillow, he let the tears flow silently— so silently that no one would possibly hear him—until, at some point, he finally fell asleep.

It's a strange phenomenon that a single event can completely define one's perception of a place. For Stanley, Whelton College deteriorated almost overnight. The stone corridors and spiral staircases, once brimming with life, melted into a gray-brown sludge that stuck against his feet as he walked. The friendly faces of the professors held frowns and sneers behind their well-positioned smiles, knives behind their eyes.

As the weeks turned into months and the colors turned to grays, Stanley dwindled further.

He continued to attend all his orations but no longer sat at the front, where he was visible, where everyone could see his defects, his poor quality. He sidled into the back rows and was quietly forgotten.

It was easier, he told himself. It was easier if he wasn't seen.

Once Friday came and he was no longer in class, he would go full weekends without saying a single word. He hid in the library or checked out books to take back to his dorm—on mathematics, on logic and chance. There was a certainty to those pages, with their balanced equations and measured proofs, that he no longer felt elsewhere.

Even during the week, he found himself speaking only once in lessons, just a sullen "Here, sir." In many ways, that exemplified his new existence: He was there in name only. The rest of him—his hopes, his dreams, his searching soul—was elsewhere. Or perhaps nowhere at all. Perhaps those parts were dead.

But just as a single event can change the course of a life, so can a single person.

It was a Thursday morning and toward the end of early lunch, when the younger students were allowed to eat while the older ones remained in class. Stanley was trudging his way up to the Second Tower for a dull lesson on ancient Roman emperors when he came to a stop outside an open door.

"Well?" a deep voice boomed out mid-lesson. "Are you all *mute*? Or do you perhaps think I stand here for your pleasure, like a clown?"

Through the doorway, a short, hunched man stood leaning on his cane. The front rows of the class were visible to Stanley—much older students, sixteen or seventeen, he thought. They watched the man before them quietly and intently. He spun around and whacked the board with his cane.

"If we accept that e^{ix} is equal to cos x plus i sin x, then what happens when x is pi?"

The class stared at him, wordless.

"Come on, come on." He waved his cane—not at the class but at the window. "Think! Work the problem!"

"You get zero and minus one," Stanley said, then immediately put his hand over his mouth.

"Yes!" the man shouted gleefully. He did not turn to look at Stanley but instead started scribbling on a board that was just out of view. "Exactly! If cos pi equals minus one and sin pi equals zero, returning to our original equation, it follows that . . . ?"

"That $e^{i\pi}$ equals minus one plus zero i." Stanley didn't know why he was still speaking. Students were leaning forward to look at him through the doorway now, to examine him. He was no longer in the background. He was exposed.

"Indeed! Or, seeing as the i is canceled out by the zero, we can write this as—" He scrawled out the equation, $e^{i\pi} + 1 = 0$, then turned back to the class. "Now, why is this important? Why do we care?"

Stanley didn't want to answer this time, all too aware of the attention that was on him. His heart accelerated in his chest. His palms dripped sweat. But still, as though compelled by fate, he spoke.

"Because those are five of the most important constants in all of mathematics, and they're all there in the same perfectly balanced equation. It's the language of the universe, and it makes sense."

The man frowned, turning slightly toward Stanley. "Why do you sound like you're not in my classroom, boy?"

"I . . ." The professor now glared searchingly across the room—the gray hair, wrinkled brow, and large round glasses. "Because I'm not *in* your class, sir."

"Well, you'd better come in, then."

The very thought of actually walking into the room and standing in front of a whole host of Whelton College boys—boys like Barty, like Charles, only older and meaner—horrified him. His feet froze in place. "I really think I should be getting on to . . ."

"What is your name, boy?"

"S-Stanley."

"Come to this classroom after the end of the day," he said, looking vaguely in Stanley's direction. "At six o'clock on the dot. I do not tolerate tardiness. Is that clear?"

"Yes, sir."

"Good!" Spinning back to his whiteboard, he continued as though Stanley had already left. "If you turn to a new page in your exercise books and ready your pens, you will find . . ."

Dumbstruck, Stanley backed away, trying to escape what felt like a trap reeling him in, as he knew too well what happened if you got caught. As soon as he was out of the eyesight of the class, he sprinted, darting down the corridor and round the corner.

Sinking to the floor, he hugged his knees and took a few deep breaths. He was back in his room at home, hiding under the covers, his father's angry footsteps shaking the stairs. He had been close—too close—to being seen again. He had promised himself that he would not let that happen. As his pulse slowed to a normal pace, he analyzed the encounter. What had just happened? Was he in trouble? Why had he felt so obliged to speak?

These thoughts plagued him through Roman history and Latin, through the long corridors and hallways, and when he finally went back to that classroom, a good fifteen minutes before he was supposed to be there, he found the door closed.

He waited. And he waited.

With nowhere to sit, five minutes felt like an hour. Ten was an eternity. Eventually, at precisely six, he knocked.

The door pushed open as he did, creaking backward like it had only been held closed by the lightest of cobwebs. There were two other boys in the room, each sitting behind a desk. One was a boy about his size—a dark-skinned boy with black hair, leaning back in his chair with his feet up on the table. The second was taller—a slim and excessively lanky Asian kid with black hair that flopped over his eyes. He hunched over his desk, his knees pressed into the top of it and his elbows at sharp angles.

"Hello," the smaller boy said. "I'm Jacques. What's your name?"

"Stanley. I was told to be here."

"Yes—that happens. Professor Waldman does that once in a while. To be honest, since Theo graduated, I've wondered when we'd get a new one. It's just been the two of us for a good year." He cocked his head toward the older boy. "That's Raphael."

"Raph," the tall boy murmured. He didn't look at Stanley. His eyes darted all around the room.

Jacques smiled. "He prefers Raph."

Stanley looked around, confused. He had only been just outside the door before, but now he could see the full shape of this room, and it didn't look like any other in the entire school. Every single wall was a bookcase, and unlike the clinical organization elsewhere, each case was covered in a messy array of books, trinkets, board games, and ornaments. A human skull sat on one of the shelves. There was a huge sword propped up by the window and an ant farm tucked into the corner.

"Is this . . . not detention?"

Jacques burst out laughing, and Raph let out a few little chuckles. But it was not mean laughter—not like the mockery that had pushed its way into his brain and scarred him. It was warm, like honey.

"Come take a seat," Jacques said, motioning to the chair. "And no— you're definitely not in detention. You're in third year too, right? I feel like I've seen you in a class somewhere."

Stanley nodded as he crossed the room. "I'm new."

The second his bottom touched the wood of the seat, the door slammed open. Professor Waldman barreled into the room, his cane clicking furiously against the floor.

"Good evening!" he said to the window. "So, our newest recruit has made it."

"How can you tell?" Jacques asked. Stanley blinked, taken aback by the boldness of such a question. Leaning forward, he noted the way Waldman gazed not at them but slightly off-center. The tight grasp on his cane. The cloudy white eyes.

He'd been so petrified earlier that he'd completely missed that the man was blind.

"It's the smell," Waldman replied, setting his cane against the desk. "I remember it clearly, Stanley. You have a very distinct smell."

"That's rude," Raph murmured, looking down at his hands. "Some people might find that offensive."

"Can't see why!" he blurted, his old hands fumbling at his desk. "Ha! Get it? Can't *see* why?"

Raph groaned.

"I'm consistently amazed," Jacques said, "that even after all these years, you still manage to make blind jokes."

"Blind jokes?" he cried, dramatically throwing his hands in the air. "Blind jokes? Nothing blind about them—I think you'll find they're very in*sight*ful. Ha!"

Jacques shook his head. "You know, the jokes would probably be funnier if you didn't stress the punch line each time."

Stanley stared at him. No one had spoken to a professor like that in his entire time at Whelton.

"Oh, look at that!" Waldman muttered to himself. "The great Jacques Bashar trying to teach me how to be funny. Might as well have a stone teach a sponge how to be absorbent." Opening a door, he pulled out a tattered old ream of paper. Hobbling over to the tables, he put pens and paper down in front of Jacques, Raph, and Stanley. "Today is chess day, and we will see if you can avoid embarrassing yourselves. But first, questions!"

Stanley stared at the paper in front of him, trying to work out what was going on. The classroom had taken on a different hue in the last minute; the colors had grown deeper somehow, and more welcoming. The walls felt a little closer, four people more than enough to fill the room. But even as the conversations were going on around him, he could feel himself fade.

"Who was the thirty-second chancellor of the exchequer, which king did he serve under, and when did he die?"

"Thomas Thwaites," Raph said, without touching his paper. "Edward IV, 1503."

Stanley fumbled at the paper and pen.

What was he doing here? Why had he even come?

"In 1587, a colony was set up by Governor John White on Roanoke Island in what is now the United States. What happened to it, and what word is associated with the event?"

"Oh, I know this one," Jacques said, but no more words left his mouth. He gritted his teeth and slapped himself in the head as if to knock his memory to the surface. "I *know* it."

"They all disappeared," Raph said, smiling. "Nobody knows where they went. Like someone just erased them from the face of the planet. The single word left behind, carved on a tree, was *CROATOAN*, but it explained nothing."

"Good! Very good! Watch out, Jacques. He's getting better than you. What is the seventy-eighth prime number?"

"Ugh, primes?" Raph complained. "Really?"

"Yes, *primes*. Primes, indeed! Don't be so impudent. You came to *me*, remember, Raphael? You said you wanted to learn everything there was to know. You do not get to be picky about what *everything* consists of."

Jacques was scribbling furiously on his paper. Raph looked up into the air, his brow furrowed in concentration.

"Quickly, boys," he goaded. "Quickly now."

"Three hundred and ninety-seven," Stanley said, the numbers leaving his mouth before he could stop them.

"Good!" Waldman shouted. "Very good!" He was pacing in front of the table now, back and forth. "What is the longest-reigning empire in the entirety of world history, and how long did it last?"

Stanley held his breath. He'd spoken out—made himself the center of the room—and nobody had reacted. Nobody had mocked him. Waldman had merely moved on, like Stanley had always been there, one of them, and his getting a maths question right was the most normal thing in the world. Letting out a deep exhale, he found that he was smiling.

"The Kushite Empire of Nubia," Jacques said. "One thousand five hundred and seventy years."

"Ha!" Waldman shouted. "Wrong! The Kingdom of Kush was defeated by the Axumite Empire in the year 350, putting its reign at one thousand four hundred and twenty years, a full *sixty years* shorter than the Imperial Roman Empire."

"Except"—Jacques lifted a finger and leaned forward—"a recent archaeological dig in Sudan indicates that there were Kushite kings in Napata a hundred and fifty years before the disintegration of the New Kingdom of Egypt. The overlap means we must count the Kushite Empire as early as 1220 BC."

"What?" Waldman demanded, spinning around to face them. "Where did you read that?"

"I didn't." Jacques grinned. "I made it up."

"Ha! Excellent," he said, nodding his head. "Yes, most excellent. You almost had me believing you. *Almost*, mind you. Almost. Now, stop smiling. I might be blind, but I can feel your self-congratulatory smirk from here."

"I'm not smirking," Jacques replied, a grin plastered across his face.

"Oh, come now, Jacques! Now you insult me in front of our new guest. I can smell the smirk on you. You might be getting good at deception, but you're not that good. Now—chess! Stanley, I assume you know how to play chess?"

Stanley nodded quietly, then realized that Waldman couldn't see him. Gulping, he said, "Yes, sir. I mean, I've read the rules, and some techniques, but I . . . I've never had anyone to play it with."

"A travesty! An absolute travesty! Come, we will show you the way."

With the speed of a well-oiled routine, chessboards and pieces were extracted from the cupboards and drawers. They were slotted out of the bookshelves and appeared from under the desks. Before Stanley could properly process it, there were seven boards set up—three each in front of Jacques and Raph, and one in front of him.

"Chess is played on the first and third Wednesdays of every month. When you manage to check me with one board, you may move up to two, and then three."

"What if I manage to beat you?"

"Ha!" he blurted. "Beat me? Nobody beats me."

And so they played, Jacques and Raph working three games simultaneously, studying the boards in between turns and jotting down thoughts and ideas on their papers. With each move, they called out what they were doing to Waldman—"Rook to king's rook five," "Pawn to queen six"—and Stanley did the same, quickly picking up on the notation. Waldman, blind as he was, needed no more than this to keep all seven games in his head. He did not study the board. He did not wait. The moment any of the three boys made their move, he immediately called his out a second later.

"Knight to queen's bishop three! Ha! Try stopping that!"

He won all seven. He beat Stanley in six moves.

Before he knew it, Stanley was there every day after school. The four of them would play everything—backgammon, the Checkered Game of Life, Go—but chess was always Waldman's favorite. Jacques would lie, push, and weasel his way out of difficult corners. Raph would fumble awkwardly at the pieces but occasionally make a move so brilliant that Stanley would just stop and stare. As for Waldman, he would delight in thrashing the boys, in pushing them, in challenging their every move. And throughout it all, they would talk: Waldman would recommend books that Stanley would read late into the night and bring back to discuss the next day over a game of carrom or Camelot. Waldman would question them, test them, and somehow make the whole process feel not like learning but like life.

Stanley remained in the background in his classes, but where before he felt like he was fading, slowly receding into the wallpaper, he now felt alight with new ideas and new concepts—from Bach to Braque, from Milton to Bakunin.

And for the first time in his entire life, Stanley understood what it meant to have a home: the safety, the warmth, the freedom. He wondered if this was what it felt like to have a father, and if it was, maybe that wasn't such a bad thing after all.

One evening in early December, when the snow had just started to fall and the light was dwindling, Stanley asked the question that had been on his mind since the very first time he stepped into Waldman's classroom.

"How do you do it?"

"Hmm?" Waldman asked, leaning over Raph's second chessboard while the boy pondered his next move. "Do what?"

"Remember the positions of every move and piece in every game we play. Remember all those different facts and ideas."

"Ha!" He straightened up. "That's nothing. There are people who can memorize seventy thousand digits of pi. There are people who can recite the entire works of Shakespeare, or the Bible, without breaking a sweat. It's my certain belief that the human memory possesses unlimited depths. Unlimited! Depths that most people barely learn to even scratch. You could memorize every single word ever written if you only knew *how to do it*."

Stanley looked up from his board, and for some reason, those words that had been carved into him months ago swam their way to the surface.

That's what happens when you come from cheap stock. . . . You're never going to make anything with any quality.

He gripped the table underneath him. "Will you teach me?"

"Oh, my boy." Waldman shook his head dramatically. "What do you think we've been doing all this time?"

3

TRANSCRIPT NO. 273: Margaret Webb
DATE STAMP: 11 AUG. 2021
10 Hours, 4 Minutes, and 53 Seconds Until Dissolution

We've left your house?

> Yes, we have. I notice you're not using *home* anymore. Good—you're picking up the local language.

Am I still with you?

> Hold on. I need to ask you something. You were there with me; you experienced this. Why do you need me to tell you about it again? Did you forget?

No. I remember everything. But your perspective is the one that matters. It's the only thing that matters. I'm not important.

> What does that mean?

It's complicated, and we don't have the time to go over it. Stanley still isn't safe, and there are only a few hours until reset. All that's important right now is that you tell me everything you can, every detail, every thought. You will have seen things I may have missed.

> Okay, okay. Have it your way, Matt Helm. Oh God, you probably don't even know what I'm talking about. The worst thing about getting old is that all the people who still get your references are either dead or crazy.

I know who Dean Martin is. Is it relevant to the moment?

> Probably not.

Where are we going?

> We're in your car, but I don't know where we're going. It occurs to me that I've been caught up in the moment: An unknown man has entered my house, told me strange stories of memory loss and conspiratorial care homes, and suddenly I am in his car and we are driving somewhere.

How do you feel?

> I'm afraid that the things you've told me are true. And I'm afraid of you as well. You're facing straight ahead, your hands on ten and two and your gaze unflinchingly focused on the road ahead of you. The sun glints off your cheeks, and for a moment I think they are almost too smooth—like marble, like alabaster.
>
> "It's been a while since a man took me on a date," I say. I don't know why I say it. Probably because I can't bring myself to utter the thoughts that lie underneath it. Because discussing what we're about to do feels ridiculous said out loud. "Where are we going?"
>
> "The receptionist on the desk today is Isabella. She's new, so she might not have seen you before, but you'll still be in the system."

"Wow." I shake my head. My fingers are squeezed tightly around the sides of the seat, and my knuckles have gone a little white. I attempt a laugh. "So much for foreplay—you really are all business."

Your hands spin the wheel smoothly, mechanically, as you turn left. Your head doesn't move an inch. "They'll have no reason to suspect anything, not at first. You'll have to say you're taking Stanley out for a walk around the grounds. They might not like this, but if you act emotional, they'll let it happen. They're just employees, remember. They don't know the big picture."

"What *is* the big picture?"

There is a long beat of silence between us, and I struggle to unravel its complexity.

"Would you like me to be honest with you, Maggie?" The words are spoken to the road ahead, and I'm overcome with the sensation that I'm not actually in the car. That you're alone in this car and I'm outside of it, watching you on a CCTV recording in a courtroom somewhere.

I open my mouth and close it, a little afraid of what will come out. Despite myself—despite the beating in my chest and the hot flush running down my body and my white-knuckled fingers still gripping the fabric of my seat—I say, "Yes, Hassan. I think I'd like you to be fucking honest with me."

You barely react, but there's a flicker. It's like catching a statue blinking.

"The employees at Sunrise have been given strict instructions to keep a close eye on Stanley. To make sure they know where he is at all times, but they don't know exactly why. That sort of information isn't disseminated, not to the day-to-day nurses and carers. As time goes on, they get complacent. He becomes just another patient. That laziness is your chance, along with the fact that nobody in that building knows quite how important Stanley really is. But you get one shot: If you make a mistake, they'll know, and it'll all be over."

I consciously force myself not to gape at you. At some point during your little speech, you've managed to light another cigarette and put it in your mouth. I'm not sure how I missed that. A part of me twitches on the inside. I gave up smoking over fifty years ago, but the craving never quite leaves, and it returns more forcefully than ever.

What I want to ask is this: *What do you mean it'll all be over? What the hell are you getting me into?*

Instead, I ask, "Why is Stanley important?"

"That's exactly what we're trying to find out," you reply. A long puff of smoke billows out of your mouth, snakelike, and I breathe it in second-hand.

The car pulls to a stop. I look to my left and see that we're just outside Sunrise, parked on the road right across the street.

"I will be waiting here, out of sight. It is crucial that the staff do not see me. When you're taking him for a walk through the grounds, there will be a diversion. It will be unpleasant, and regrettable, but we are dealing with dangerous people. Rest assured that Stanley will not be harmed. When the moment happens, don't hesitate. You'll know it when you see it. Wheel him right out the front gate and onto the street."

I'm already getting out of the car and opening the door. I can't tell if it's because I want to get this all over with or because I don't want to spend another second in the car with you. Just as my foot lands on the pavement, you say, "Maggie?"

I turn.

You flash me the most charismatic smile. "If anyone causes you trouble, give them hell."

And somehow, impossibly, a wave of relief rolls its way through me, as if we've done this before—you and I—as if we're old friends pulling a crazy stunt like we did when we were kids.

I'm standing outside Sunrise, a building that I feel like I've been in a hundred thousand times. It sits peaceably along the side of the road, neither looming nor brooding but simply *there*. Part of the landscape.

The sun glints off the pond in the lawn, the two trees on either side of it standing upright. The grass is still wet with dew; the breeze whispers. I notice, for a moment, the sound of my own heartbeat, and a deep, penetrating loneliness sets upon me.

"Shit," I mutter. A young man to my left looks over at me, frowns, and then walks on. Do you know what that means?

What does it mean?

That means I am a batty old woman talking to herself on the side of the road. That's who I am now. That's who I've become. And I can't figure out when the hell it happened.

Leah used to make fun of me for it, back when she'd visit, and that made it okay. She'd laugh at me for forgetting to turn the oven on for dinner or for putting the kettle in the fridge, and I'd think, *If this is what getting old is, I can deal with that.* But when no one is there to laugh with you, it doesn't seem so funny anymore.

The last time she actually picked up the phone, she was in Portugal— in Lisbon, I think, working in a bar, but she wouldn't tell me specifically. She'd not responded to my texts for over a week, and I just wanted to check that she was okay.

"What do you want?" she said when she picked up. That was it—no "Hi, Mum." No "How are you?"

"Are you okay, sweetie?" I replied. "I've not heard from you in a while."

"How dare you ask me that! Or have you called to apologize? Because I don't want to hear it."

I remember those words so clearly, because I've never been so baffled in my entire life. The last time I saw her, she came round for tea. We made scones in the afternoon, and she stayed the night. She gave me a hug in the morning before going to see Stanley on her way home.

"Apologize for what? Leah—what's going on?"

"Don't play the crazy old woman card with me," she bit back. Even hundreds of miles away, the vitriol in her voice stung my ears. "Not after what you said to me. What you did. You're lucky I even picked up. I won't be doing that again. You want me out of your life? Fine. Stop calling me."

Little did I know it at the time, but the beep that followed marked the last time we spoke. It's been two years, and I've all but given up trying to work out why. Is it because I put Stanley in a home? But she'd seen me since then. She'd supported me. She'd been there when I, along with Hugo—one of Stanley's oldest friends and Leah's godfather—settled him in.

Sometimes, in the middle of the night, I wake up and still expect her to come running into our bed like she did when she was a child, scared by some night terror. In my half-awake state, I push aside the duvet to let her in, but all I get is a freezing-cold gust of air and a confused half question on my lips.

Sometimes that's what I feel like I have in place of a daughter now—cold emptiness and unanswered questions.

I don't even know where she lives, if she has a boyfriend, if she's happy.

She could be married, for all I know.

So instead I do the only thing I can: I carry on.

When people depict loneliness, they tend to show the isolation, the claustrophobia of it—someone curled up in a dark room, stuck in bed, unable to move. But real loneliness is repetition: doing the same routines day in and day out with nothing new to reflect on or look forward to.

Ironic, really. For so much of my youth, I did *everything* to stave off loneliness. The drinking. The partying. Multiple very inadvisable dalliances that did nothing but leave me hollowed out and hazy, constantly desperate for something new. It wasn't until Stanley that I learned you can't beat loneliness by running away from it or by smothering it with something else. You have to meet it head-on or find someone who is willing to do that with you.

But now? For all the wonderful life we built together, visiting Stanley is always the loneliest part of my day.

Until you, of course. Until you walked in and threw everything into the air. I can't tell if I love you or hate you for that. I can't tell how I'm supposed to feel about you. There's something not quite right about you—of that much, I'm certain.

You're getting distracted, and that isn't helpful to us right now. I'm completely fine.

There's nothing *fine* about any of this. I'm hooked up to an IV in an abandoned swimming pool, for Christ's sake. I don't know how I got here or what on earth I'm doing. This all feels like a hellish dream, some kind of fierce nightmare. None of this feels like it's actually happening.

It's happening. I'm here, right in front of you. I'm recording you because everything you say is important. You're crossing the street—what next?

I—I walk across the lawn and step up to the front door. They've installed one of those fancy new facial-recognition cameras, and it flashes at me, letting me know I've been registered as a relative. The doors slide open. There's music on: the constant tinkling of a piano playing in the background. The room is wide, an open-plan living area with a small kitchen on one side—the kind with the electric coffee machines that none of us old terrors know how to use properly—and a collection of armchairs on the right. A smattering of residents are hunched over in them, eyes glazed over and glued to a television playing a rerun of some sitcom I recognize but can't name.

There's an actual piano, of course, at the bottom of the main staircase, but nobody ever touches it. The tinkling is coming from the speakers.

The whole place smells of fake lavender, that chemically synthesized stuff. It's a poor replica, but it just about manages to cover the undercurrent of piss and cleaning products, so I'm thankful that it exists, at least.

"Margaret," the attendant at the desk chirps, a giant smile plastered on her face. "So lovely to see you again."

I've never seen her before. It used to bother me that new attendants would pretend they knew me by name when really the camera at the door just fed it right onto their screens. But I realized that they weren't pretending at all; nobody bothers to remember anyone's name anymore. Why would you when the information is always right there? Genuine interaction has been replaced by easily simulated authenticity. There's nothing wrong with that, per se. Society moves on, and so do its practices. But it does make me feel very, very old.

"Hello. We've not met," I say deliberately. "I'm here to see my husband, Stanley Webb. He's up in the—"

"Memory ward, yes." She cuts me off. "He's one of my favorite residents."

You've never even bloody spoken to him, have you, you absolute bint?

That's what I would have said if I weren't about to break my husband out of a prison I didn't even know he was in. And if I weren't absolutely crapping myself over the mixture of fear and adrenaline that came with this breakout attempt.

"Thank you." I give her a smile and walk over to the lifts that take me up to the second floor.

An attendant I recognize lets me into the unit and takes me to Stanley's room. He's lying in bed, staring at the TV. It's one of those newfangled smart devices that's linked in with the whole building. I sigh.

"Can you turn that off, please?"

"Of course, ma'am." The attendant nods, then picks up the remote and presses a button.

"I thought I asked that he not spend so much time with that damn thing on. It's not good for his mind."

The attendant's smile tightens. "He did *ask* to have some TV time. It's a documentary. About the Iraq War. They're very educational."

"Stanley hates wars and hates talking about them," I snap. "Oh, whatever. Leave us alone, then, will you?"

I don't mean to be such a nightmare, but seeing him like that—as empty as a hollowed-out sculpture or a recycled bottle—it brings out the worst in me.

The attendant closes the door, and then it's just me and Stanley. It's a small room with a decent facade of homeyness—wallpaper and plants, some nice blankets, old pictures of Stanley on some holiday in Australia when he was younger—just enough to make a visitor think it could almost feel like someone's home.

As the TV flickers to black, Stanley looks over at me, his brows furrowed.

"What did you do that for?"

"It's me, Stan," I say, pointlessly. Either he recognizes me or he doesn't. "It's Maggie."

"Well, I can see that, can't I? What do you think I am, an idiot?"

"Of course not, Stan."

"You're always talking down to me, treating me like a stupid child."

I wince. If there's anything I like less than his not recognizing me, it's one of his angry moods. He was never like this in life, always calm and phlegmatic, always understanding.

"Well? What are you doing standing there? I told you to get me a glass of water."

"Sorry, Stan." I walk over to the sink and fill up a glass. The old pipes sputter like they've not been turned on in a long time. It makes me realize that for all the high-tech dressings Sunrise forces residents to pay for, the building itself is probably older than I am. I wonder how long he's been left plugged into the TV, how long they've been ignoring him.

"Stupid woman," he mutters, just loud enough that I can hear it.

I bring him the glass and put it in his hand, helping him sit up. He accepts it, grumpily. "I used to be very respected by people, you know? At universities, in the armed forces. The secretary of defense once personally gave me a medal."

"I know, Stan." I nod. Sometimes he has clear memories—usually of when he was younger, before we met. He often refers to a barbecue he had on Portobello Beach in Edinburgh. And there's that holiday in Australia he's always banging on about. But sometimes external things—like this war documentary—burrow their way into his brain, and his struggling neurons, desperate for connections, mistake bits of it for memory. There's nothing to do but play along. Disagreeing would just make him angrier.

The truth is, I don't know why age and memory loss have brought this callousness to Stanley. But since he's been in here, a stone wall has appeared between us that has only grown upward and become more forbidding. Sometimes I can still find nooks and crannies in it that we can appreciate together, spots where sunlight peeks through and flowers remain. But of late, for many a visit now, it offers nothing but ice and rock.

There was a time, even here in Sunrise a couple of years ago, when we would read to each other. He liked to recite Shakespeare, to exchange lines from *Romeo and Juliet* with me, and we would pretend we were both teenagers, falling in love again for the first time. All that feels so distant now.

Just three weeks ago, he told me for the first time that he hated me. He was furious, and while I tried to remain calm, I was unable to fight back the tears. "I hate you," he said. "That's okay, Stan," I replied. And he shook his head. "No, no—it's not okay. I'm dying. I'm going to die while you get to live." I remember walking over to the window and looking outside at the gulls, wheeling and crying in the sky, and thinking, *But I'm not living anymore, Stanley.*

What an awful joke this all is.

"Shall we go for a walk outside?" I ask. "The weather is really lovely, Stan."

He waves a noncommittal hand, which I take for a yes. His anger has subsided into a listlessness, a compliancy. He lets me help him into his wheelchair and sit him upright. I wipe a little of the spittle away from his mouth, and he flinches a bit, like I'm going to hit him. That started happening only recently, as if the Alzheimer's has unlocked an old fear from his distant past, one that he's never spoken about, even if on some level I have always been aware of it. In another life, I might have asked him about it. It all feels too late now. Gently as I can, I tuck a blanket around his legs and arms to keep him warm.

As I push him out the door, the tight-lipped attendant reappears.

"Where are you going?"

"Oh, we're just going for a walk around the grounds. Stanley asked for it." I decide to push a little further. "Says no one's bothered to take him out for days."

The attendant shakes his head. "This isn't the right time. He's just had dinner, and it'll be bath time soon. There's no one to accompany you. He needs to keep to his routines. It's very important here."

"Are you telling me that I—his wife, who is paying for him to be here—can't take him out for a quick five-minute walk? What kind of gestapo institution are you running here?"

His eyebrows come together in confusion.

"There are rules, Mrs. Webb. We have to—"

I take a step around Stanley, who is staring blankly at a wall, and toward the attendant. I summon the last eighty years of my very best hell-hath-no-fury and layer it into my voice.

"From what I've seen today, your supposed routines are being ditched in favor of shoving residents in front of the TV to shut them up. How long has Stanley been watching that thing, hmm? Would you like me to request to see the system and look that up?"

He blinks, surprised that an old bat like me knows how to take advantage of a smart network.

"I didn't bloody think so. I'd already been thinking about moving him to another care home, but given the way *you've* been ignoring him, I think my decision might have just been made. I'll be sure to drop your name when I explain it to your boss. Now, we're going to go for a quick walk to get some fresh air, like we've been doing together for longer than you've been alive. I'd be deeply grateful if you could get the hell out of our way."

The man stutters and makes a mumbling noise that sounds like the start of an apology, but I've already pushed Stanley around him and into the lift.

As the doors close behind me, I revel in how good that felt.

Does Stanley say anything to you in the lift?

No.

Nothing at all?

He's in one of those distant states, like a fugue. Honestly, he barely knows I'm there.

Does anyone stop you as you take Stanley outside?

No. There are a few looks, side-glances from other attendants as I walk past them, but I don't stop. I push him right through the double doors at the back and into the gardens. There's a chill in the wind that wasn't there before, like a cold fist has gripped it and squeezed a few degrees of warmth out. The air is crisp, almost sealike, though we are miles from the coast. A shudder runs down my spine, and I wonder how far you've weaseled into my head. Because if what you told me is true, if Stanley really was being held securely, then surely it wouldn't have been this easy to get him outside.

Maybe the attendant upstairs was just being difficult. Maybe there is no conspiracy at all, and I'm here, pulling my own husband out of his care home for you to do God knows what with.

Then I remember the gaps in my own memory, and another shudder runs through me—this one moving upward, into my shoulders and neck, pulling them tense together.

There's a shuffle behind me, and my head snaps around so fast it almost falls off.

Nothing's there. The lawns stretch out flatly toward a row of bushes—hardy evergreen shrubs that barely need any watering—and beyond that, nothing.

Except I'm certain there *is* someone behind those bushes. Or, if not, then behind the corner of the wall or looking out the window.

I'd been thinking that I would just meander until the diversion, but now there's someone watching me. Following. I can't tell you exactly how I know, but I've never felt so certain about anything in my entire life.

I push Stanley a little faster. He mumbles something, a whisper that I don't quite hear. I don't lean closer. There isn't time. I push him toward the gates.

The sensation of being followed increases with every step. There are eyes at the window now, but I can't tell if they're residents or attendants. I know you told me there would be a diversion, but it occurs to me that I have no idea when or what it is. You've sent me in blind, and for all my doubts, I am suddenly very afraid.

The wheels of Stanley's wheelchair rumble as they hit the tarmac on the far side of the lawn. I'm just pushing him into the car park now, and from there, the street. Where you are.

"Mrs. Webb?" The voice to my left is whip-hard. "Where are you going?"

"Oh." I grind to a halt. The lady from the front desk is standing there, her posture tight as lightning, and all pretense of familiarity has disappeared from her face. "I just wanted to show Stanley one of the new shops across the road. There was someone we used to know who worked—"

"I think you'd better come back inside." Her hand is on a strange device, like a small black pipe, and she clutches it at her side like a pistol. I am trying to remember where I've seen her before. *At the front desk,* a voice whispers in my mind.

But what front desk? What am I doing out here in the car park?

"I don't . . . I'm not sure what—"

"That's okay, Mrs. Webb," she says. "Just bring him inside, and we can work this all out."

That's when the sound hits me: a pained moan of distress that makes me look down at Stanley.

He's clutching his arm and trying to speak, but the words are a slurred, half-formed jumble of moans. Oh dear God, is he having a stroke?

"Mrs. Webb," the lady says. "Step toward me and—"

There are shouts coming from inside the building, getting louder and louder. Stanley lets out a sigh and closes his eyes, slumping back into his chair, unconscious.

"Isabella!" A scream comes from the front door. The woman confronting me turns, her hand gripping her strange black object tighter. A man is standing at the front door, his hand over his mouth. "Isabella—we need you inside right now. We need everyone inside."

There are screams emanating from the whole care home. The sound pours out of the closed windows and locked doors, out of the gaps and seams in the walls.

Isabella's face is a painting of fury. "What the *fuck* is going on?"

"They're . . ." he splutters, almost unable to believe his own words. "They're fainting, Isabella. All of them, at the same time, just . . . collapsing to the floor. Jesus Christ—*all of them*, Isabella!"

She stares at the man by the door, torn between storming back over there and not leaving Stanley and me alone. I blink, my mind still awash in a muddle of half memories and intentions, my panic at Stanley's state overwhelming.

Then I see you on the other side of the street, and the *where* and the *why* and the *what* of my actions all come crashing back into me like a tidal wave.

You're standing by your car, gesturing for me to cross the road. I glance back over at Isabella, who has turned expectantly back to us.

There will be a diversion, I hear you whisper in my mind.

"Oh God," I say, shaking my head and putting on the feeblest old-lady voice I can manage. "Oh dear God, we need to go inside and get him some help." The man by the door is shaking; he looks like he's about to explode. "You go on ahead—I'll be right behind you with Stanley. Those poor people need your help."

Isabella sighs, gives me a curt nod, and then stamps her way back toward the building, her whole body rippling with anger.

I make a weak attempt to turn Stanley's wheelchair around. As soon as she gets to the door, and inside, I make a run for it.

I push ahead, crossing the road toward you. I give no thought to vehicles or dangers.

You don't budge an inch, though you seem to be willing me across, and I wonder for a moment if you can't move, if the road between you and the care home is some kind of line you are physically unable to cross.

I'm not as fast as I want to be.

I want to dash—to sprint to safety—but I can't get up to any more than a brisk walk, especially not with a moaning, wheelchair-bound invalid as luggage.

I don't look back. I can't.

"Hey, stop!"

There are footsteps on the pavement behind.

I'm panting hard. I try to speed up, but I *can't*. My body won't let me.

Every second feels like an hour, every foot a mile.

When I finally hit the pavement on the other side, just yards away from you, a hand grips my shoulder and twists me around.

Isabella's face, bright red and contorted with rage, is inches away. Her grip is strong—far too strong for old bones like mine—and it feels like she's crushing my shoulder to dust. Stanley lets out another little moan.

And then you are there. Beside us both.

Isabella's eyes widen, like she's seen you before. Her mouth opens to speak, but you place a hand on her face, and she stops. Her voice falls short. Her arms go slack. She stares at me, and all fury, all emotion, all *anything*, is utterly gone from her face. It's inhuman, like a mannequin's, like a suit of skin that's had everything scooped right out of it in an instant.

I want to scream, but I can't.

You've already lifted Stanley up, and you're strapping him into the back seat.

"What did you do to him? To her? What did you do to them all?"

"They'll be fine," you say. "Get in. It's time for us to leave."

I do, and you just sit there. You just . . . act like nothing at all has happened. And I don't understand. I have no idea what I'm doing.

Where do we go?

What?

Next? Where do we go?

I don't . . . I'm sorry. These memories are all swirling through my head. They're so vivid. The horror of it. The sheer, absolute madness. What did you *do* to her?

That's not important.

Wait—no, stop. Where is Stanley now? Right now?

That is what we're trying to determine.

How do you not know? Why is it just you and me in this bloody pool? Oh God.

What is it?

Where is Leah? Have you done something to her? Does she know about any of this? Someone has to tell her.

She doesn't matter right now.

She matters to *me*.

That makes no difference.

You can't say that. I need to know what's going on here, or I'm not saying any more. I'm not telling you anything else.

Then I will abandon you here. If you stop, there's no reason for me to stay. You'll be completely alone. No one will come to help you. Is that what you want?

No—oh God, no.

So focus. What happens now? We're in the car now, driving?

I . . . Yes.

What happens next?

Please.

Maggie, listen to me. What happens next?

You're driving. I'm next to you, not really speaking. Stanley is still unconscious, and I panic for a moment, wondering if you've done the same thing to him that you did to that poor woman. But glancing at him, I can tell you haven't. Sleeping, he looks different; there's still a person inside.

After about twenty minutes of driving, I ask the only question that I feel like I can without putting Stanley and myself in any more danger.

"How did you get them all to collapse like that? Did you put something in their food at dinner? Oh God, Hassan—did you drug all those people?"

You don't speak, but I swear that the corners of your lips curl upward into a slight smile.

"You're insane. This is crazy. Why did we just do that to those poor . . . Why are we doing any of this?"

"I haven't been completely honest with you, Maggie," you say.

I sit upright, do my best to regain my composure, and respond with a clear and level "You don't say."

"There's something inside Stanley's head that is hugely important. Something that he did, a very long time ago, before he met you. A choice that he made. The fate of all our lives depends on finding out exactly what that was."

I blink. It's not often that you hear phrases like "the fate of all our lives" and take them seriously. But there's something about the way you say the words. It's like stone and mortar. It's like a mountain range. It's unshakable.

"But Stanley can't remember a thing anymore," I say. "He can't get to any of his memories."

"I know," you say. "That's why you're going to break into his head and get them for him."

4 | Stanley
1952

AS STANLEY CLIMBED THE STEPS TO WALDMAN'S CLASSROOM, IT SUR-prised him how much he enjoyed this wistful sense of familiarity. Just two years ago, all familiar things were dangerous. All routine was to be feared or, at the very least, worried about. Yes, it was true that Whelton was not the fantastical dreamland he had once imagined it to be. In fact, it was often quite the opposite. But in Waldman's club, he had found a safe place among the danger. Over the past two years, that safety had trumped almost everything else.

"Pawn to king four," Jacques said, challenging Stanley as soon as he walked into the room. Stanley raised an eyebrow. Jacques leaned back in his chair and threw his hands up. "I know, I know. The Sicilian Defense. A seemingly uncontroversial move. But is there a ploy behind it? A bluff? A double bluff?" He lurched forward, slamming his hands on the desk. "A *triple* bluff?"

"Pawn to queen's bishop four," Stanley replied. There were no boards, no pieces. This is how they played now, like Waldman, in the deep re-cesses of their own memories. In the corner, two more boys sat opposite each other, playing on a real board. Hugo and Archie, both first formers that Waldman had recently recruited, were a good four years younger than Stanley and mostly kept to themselves.

Jacques sighed. "The Najdorf Variation? What a boring move. You have absolutely no sense of drama, Stan."

"Your obsession with drama makes you lose." Stanley sidled into a seat next to him.

"Ah." Jacques raised a long finger. "But I lose with *flair*."

Stanley grinned. Jacques, the small boy he had stumbled upon in Waldman's room, had grown considerably in both size and personality. He towered over even Raph—the other member of their small party—and, despite his tendency for histrionics, had proven himself to be extremely clever, if susceptible to the arrogance that comes with such cleverness. None of this mattered to Stanley, of course. It never did when you were dealing with a friend.

"Knight to king's rook three."

"That's a ridiculous move," Hugo muttered from behind them, which made Stanley raise his eyebrows. Hugo rarely said a word.

Jacques grinned. "And yet it has been done. Have you seen Raph today? Honestly, it's hilarious."

"What are you on about?" Stanley asked.

He grinned. "Oh, you didn't know?"

"Didn't know—"

The door swung open. Waldman hobbled in, his cane clacking against the stone floor. "O that this too too solid flesh would melt, thaw, and re-solve itself into a dew," he muttered. "Or that the Everlasting had not fix'd his canon 'gainst self-slaughter! O God, God! How weary, stale, flat, and unprofitable seem to me all the uses of this world!"

When he reached the desk, he turned to face the two boys—or, rather, somewhat to the left of them—and said: "Finish it."

"Fie on't! Ah fie!" Jacques exploded the next lines. "'Tis an unweeded garden that grows to seed. Things rank and gross in nature possess it merely."

"That it should come to this," Stanley added. "But two months dead."

"Nay, not so much, not two," Waldman continued, putting his cane down and taking off his jacket. "So excellent a king, that was to this Hyperion to a satyr."

He stopped, and a silence fell over the room. His brows came together, his milky-white eyes searching. Both Hugo and Archie looked up, though they knew neither of them were quite yet expected to recite the works of Shakespeare on demand.

"Well? Raphael? Are you going to tell me how loving the dead king was to your mother? Or can you not remember this particular soliloquy?"

"Raph's not here," Stanley said.

"What?" Waldman sputtered. "Not *here*? In the last fifty years, not a single student has had the audacity to show up *late* to one of my meetings."

"You haven't been teaching fifty years," Jacques prodded.

"I *know*, Jacques. It's called *hyperbole*. Bah! Telling me how long I've been teaching! Might as well tell a fish how to swim!"

The door creaked open. Head down, Raph's thin figure plodded over to his seat and collapsed into it, a falling tower.

He placed his head on the table, sullenly, like a tired dog.

"You okay?" Stanley asked. Raph offered a noncommittal grunt.

"The pangs of dispriz'd love," Jacques said with a grin.

"Shut up," Raph replied. "You don't know what you're talking about."

"Stanley certainly doesn't know what I'm talking about, and I don't think Professor Waldman does either."

Raph straightened up, his fists tightening. "Just leave it alone, will you? Why don't you just leave it?"

"Because it's important, Raph. It's a defining moment. We should all share in it."

"What is?" Stanley asked. Archie let out a giggle, but Raph flashed him a stare that made him immediately refocus on his chess game with Hugo.

"Indeed"—Waldman took a few steps toward them—"what is it that has sent you into such dejection, my dear boy? I can smell the sadness on you. You stink of it."

Raph dropped his head back down to the table. "I said it's not important."

Jacques cocked his head to the side. "Raph asked that Raeburn girl to the Founder's Day Dance."

Raph let out a deep groan and buried his head deeper into his arms.

"The girl you've been tutoring?" Stanley asked. "How . . . how did it go?"

Waldman roared with laughter. "How did it go? Stupid boy. Might as well ask the sun how hot it is. Listen to him! The dragging feet, the deep and emotional sighs. Why, he is the very picture of unrequited love!"

"Can we not?" Raph asked into his desktop.

"Oh, I really think we should," Jacques pressed. "I want to hear exactly how—"

"Jacques." Stanley's voice wasn't often hard, but when it was, it was like steel. "Leave it."

"I was just—"

"*Jacques.*"

He threw his hands up in mock surrender. "Fine, fine. Whatever you say. I, of course, already have a date to the dance."

"I don't believe you," Raph said. "How did *you* get a date?"

Jacques shrugged his shoulders. "Persistence. It really is just a numbers game. If you're going to take every rejection so damn personally, no wonder you're—"

"It *is* personal," Raph insisted. "A girl rejects you because she doesn't like you. There's no other reason. It's literally the most personal thing there can be."

"All I'm saying is . . ."

As the two bickered over his head, Stanley winced. With the discussion of the world outside this classroom, his sense of peace evaporated. Neither of the boys had asked him if he had bothered to secure a date for the dance. They knew there was no point.

For despite this lone space that offered Stanley a semblance of belonging, Whelton had grown around him like an ill-fitting suit, tightening in all the wrong places. He sensed it in every titter and whispered comment about his clothing; he saw it in every half-hidden smirk.

But it was okay because at least he was safe.

He could weather anything so long as he was safe.

Waldman, who had been absentmindedly fiddling with bits and bobs on his desk, turned around to look at Stanley. Or, at least, it felt like that sometimes. For while he knew that those cloudy eyes saw nothing, there were moments—brief flashes—where it seemed they saw everything all at once.

"I think it's time," Waldman said, his voice cutting through the boys' words like ribbons, "for us to move on to more fruitful discussions. There are more important topics to be asked about, after all, and time waits for no man. Our new recruits, how many digits are we at?"

"I'm at fifty-three digits of pi, Professor," Hugo piped up. "And Archie did seventy-five last night. I checked it with him."

Stanley gave him an impressed nod. "Nice work."

Raph bolted up, keen to engage with the fresh conversation. "I broke my record on the weekend. I'm at four thousand and fifty-seven."

Hugo's mouth fell open. "Whoa."

"Ha! Excellent!" Waldman exclaimed. "Good to see nothing holds you back! And as for Mr. Bashar and Mr. Webb, where do you two gentlemen stand?"

Jacques took in a deep breath and puffed up his chest. "Three thousand eight hundred and ninety-four. I used the color imagery technique you showed me last month, and it's really paying dividends. I could probably push further with more individual tuition."

"Hmph. Yes, strong work," Waldman said. Jacques nodded, his eyes gleaming hungrily. "We shall see, Mr. Bashar. We shall see. And Stanley?"

Stanley shuffled in his seat. "Seven thousand and three."

Raph and Jacques both turned as one, slack-jawed, to look at him.

"What? There's no way."

Jacques recovered, then scoffed. "Bullshit."

Waldman cracked his cane hard against the desk, and all the boys jumped. "I will not have accusations of falsehood in this room. What we do is based on trust. Without trust, we are nothing. Nothing!" He set his cane down again, then turned, warmly, back to Stanley. "My dear boy, that is most impressive. I cannot wait to hear a recital. What technique did you use?"

"The traditional memory palace, but grouping numbers into three digits wasn't giving me enough efficiency. I couldn't imagine a landscape big enough. So I started grouping them into four, then five."

"*Five?*" Jacques said, incredulous.

"Yeah," Stanley said. "It wasn't easy, but once you get the hang of it, it's workable."

"I never even thought of doing five."

"And that," Waldman said, raising a long finger, "is what makes all the difference."

Jacques slumped back into his chair, annoyed.

"Well, very good. Very good indeed! Today, our questions are not practical but philosophical. Tell me—why do we work on our memories?"

Raph's hand shot up. Jacques looked sullenly at his desk.

"Archie?" Waldman asked.

The young boy frowned, a little uncomfortable at being put on the spot. "Memory helps us learn, and knowledge is power."

Waldman nodded. "A little trite, but the sentiment has dignity. Yes, Raphael?"

"Building on what Archie said, memory is the basis for expertise," Raph said. "Studies that have been done on experts in their fields, whether it's chess grandmasters, concert pianists, or military generals, show that one of the key differences is their working memory in that field. A grandmaster can recite back whole games perfectly. A concert pianist can remember hours and hours of pieces. Generals intuitively *know* the best tactic, the best strategy, but we all know intuition doesn't exist. Intuition is based on subconscious memory. The more you remember, the more you can understand."

"A good answer." Waldman nodded his head. "A noble answer. Stanley?"

"Because our identities are defined by our experiences, and our experiences are just a collection of our memories. In that sense, our memories—both conscious and subconscious—are what make us human. Without memory, we would be blank slates. We would be empty."

"Ha. Yes. Excellent," Waldman replied. "And I sense an oncoming *therefore?*"

"If memory is what makes us human, then surely being able to remember more makes us *more* human."

"What a wonderful concept! I adore it! Jacques?"

"What they said."

"Excuse me?"

"I was going to say a little of what Stanley said and a little of what Raph said. I don't have any more to add."

Waldman frowned but then shrugged and turned away. "Very well! Now—speed cards. The winner gets to buy me my lunch tomorrow!"

The boys spread out about the room, opening drawers and removing packs of cards. They moved with the certainty of a well-greased machine, carrying out a routine that had been followed more times than could be counted.

Together, they placed the cards on the table, along with little wooden hourglasses whose sands ran for two minutes, five minutes, ten minutes, and challenged one another. Speed cards was simple: How many cards in a randomly shuffled deck could you learn to recite in ten minutes, or in five, or even in two? Could you remember more than the other players?

And as they settled into this old routine, Raph's morose bearing lifted, along with Jacques's frustration. Hugo and Archie opened up, growing in confidence. Stanley too emerged from the shell he had felt closing around him. They cajoled one another, they challenged, and they laughed. All the while, Waldman stormed between them, now and then slamming his cane across the table as a disruption or pushing one of them to go a card further, a second shorter.

Before long, an hour had passed, then two. When they finally broke for air, they were exhausted, both mentally and physically, and filled with a deep sense of exhilaration. *This is what life is for,* Stanley thought as he looked over his fellow memory athletes. This was why he was here.

THE FOUNDER'S DAY DANCE WAS A TRADITION THAT DATED BACK MORE than two hundred years. Boys from Whelton would get dressed up and be accompanied, if lucky, by the girls from Raeburn College, just over the road.

The main hall was converted into a formal dance floor, where the students would spend the evening in a mess of awkwardness and puberty, of poorly designed flirting and barely self-aware mating rituals, overseen by the watchful eye of the staff.

The stone walls were decorated with banners and glitter, the tables draped in cloth and finery. Students attired themselves in their very best clothes: tuxedos and bow ties bought for them by their parents, cuff links and watches passed down from generation to generation.

Stanley had never felt so out of place in his entire life.

But he had come, pushed into it by Jacques and Raph. They were all three of them outsiders—Waldman's strange nerds who knew too much about odd things and gathered together after class. They were talked about, Stanley knew. Whispered about behind their backs. It comforted Stanley to know that whatever he would have to face this evening, he would not have to face it alone.

But Jacques and Raph had known each other for years before Stanley arrived at Whelton, and for all their spats, he knew that something deeper ran beneath their friendship, something that he hadn't quite plunged into yet. Though they were an indivisible trio in his head, Stanley wasn't sure the other two saw it quite the same way.

"Come on," Jacques said to them as he grabbed a cup of punch. "My date's over there, and her friends are right sorts. At the very least, Raph, you could give it another go."

"I don't want to—"

"Remember Professor Halk's class, in second form? When you screwed up the presentation so badly you thought you wanted to die? What happened?"

Raph huffed. "I know what happened, Jacques. I was there."

"Then *tell* me."

"You made me beg Halk for another go, and I nailed it."

"*Exactly.* So let's go."

Raph sighed, seemingly resigned to the ordeal, and followed. Stanley lingered behind a moment, standing oddly by the punch bowl. Jacques hadn't addressed him, of course. Jacques knew that none of the girls would want to talk to Stanley. But with each step they took away from him, the more he felt a rising panic. He had nowhere else to go, so he followed with dragging feet.

"Ladies!" Jacques announced. "You're all looking stunning tonight."

The girls turned, looking him up and down. A few rolled their eyes. The girl who was supposed to be Jacques's date cringed a little, turning her head away. Jacques didn't appear to care.

"Have you met my friend Raph?"

Jacques grabbed Raph's arm and tugged him forward, and Raph stumbled onto center stage, surrounded by a group of girls.

"Hello," he said. "I'm Raph." They giggled.

"Hi," one said. "Raph's not a very Asian name."

Raph rolled his eyes. "Please—my family's been here since the mid-1800s. I'm probably more English than the new queen." One girl whispered in another's ear. Raph looked down and gave a resigned sigh. "Does anyone want to dance?"

"Okay."

"What?" Raph's head snapped up, staring.

The girl, blushing a little, shrugged. "Yeah, okay. Sure."

"Oh." He shook his head, as if to clear it of cobwebs. "Okay, then."

And as hands were taken and the sweet magic that only dancing offers grew, they all swirled about Stanley like a flutter of moths—a chaotic flurry of dresses and shirts, of whispers and promises. When they were gone, he was left alone. Forgotten.

He stood there for some time, wondering if anyone would notice if he just lay down on the floor and stayed there for the rest of the evening. Wondering if anyone would notice if he screamed.

He trudged back to the punch table. He stood there for some time too.

The evening drifted past him. He caught glimpses of Jacques and Raph as they swung by to check on him before returning to their dances and their companions. Each time, he told them he was fine, not to worry about him, that he was exactly where he wanted to be.

But that wasn't quite right. Because he didn't really want to be at Whelton. Truth be told, he hated it here. But he was safe. And after coming here to escape his father's house, going anywhere else had never really seemed like an option.

He was just about to leave when Jacques clapped him on the back. "You look like somebody's died, Stan. Aren't you having fun?"

Stanley was on the verge of replying, of saying good night, when Raph appeared as well. Soon the group of girls pooled around him like water over a shell, and he stayed where he was, silent, invisible.

Raph smiled at him, but while equally silent, he was still part of the conversation. He nodded at the right times. He spoke up occasionally. Jacques dominated: he joked; he flirted; he laughed uproariously, and despite themselves, the girls laughed with him. For a brief moment, Stanley considered saying something funny too. He pictured the girls laughing and maybe one of them taking his hand.

When he thought about what it might be like to dance with one of those girls, a warmth spread across his cheeks and through his chest.

But as others flocked toward the group, ballooning outward with Stanley stuck at its center, his anxiety bubbled up and over him. This wasn't Waldman's room, and these were not all his friends. He did not feel safe here. *But no one will notice me*, he told himself. *I am nothing. I cannot be seen.*

"Hey!" Stanley's heart dropped at the shout. "Look at that! Little Oliver Twist pretending he's got friends!"

He turned to see one of the older boys from upper sixth—he didn't

know who, as all the faces at Whelton blended into one—pointing at him.
A couple of people laughed. The girls turned their heads back to listen.

"Standing there expectantly, like a spare dick at an orgy. Does he think
one of them is actually going to be interested in him?"

More titters. Everyone was smirking now, even Jacques. He might as
well have been laughing too. Stanley could feel them all in his head—
mocking him, patting each other on the back. Stanley still hadn't said anything. He was struggling to process his thoughts.

"Are you girls actually talking to him?"

"Ew," the one holding Jacques's arm replied. "I didn't even notice he
was here."

Then Jacques *did* laugh, and it sliced open a wound that had never really healed. Stanley could feel his blood spilling right out of it.

"Just leave it," Raph muttered to him, leaning inward. "It doesn't mean
anything."

But it did. It meant everything.

Pushing past the group, Stanley stormed his way out of the hall and
into the corridor. His breathing was heavy, but he wasn't angry. Not at
Raph or even at Jacques, really. They were who they were. This should not
have come as a surprise. *They* belonged here.

He looked back into the room. Staring out at the faceless mass of bodies, all pressed together like so many crops, so many weeds, he felt an intense awareness of his own otherness.

He was not from the right family. He was from bad stock. As far as the
other students at Whelton were concerned, he might as well have come
from no family at all. And, therefore, by the very logic of the stone walls
and turrets, he wasn't supposed to succeed. Life wasn't set up that way.

Games with Waldman had taught him a truth that nobody ever seemed
willing to say out loud: It doesn't matter how well you play the game if the
other player gets to set up the board. If he wanted to find success or
happiness—if he wanted to find *anything* other than the safe mediocrity
he had let himself settle into—he would need to go elsewhere.

———

THE SUN HAD SET OVER THE FIELDS JUST OUTSIDE WHELTON. IN BETWEEN the main teaching quadrangle and the stately stone blocks where the dormitories sat, the graveyard glistened with an almost supernatural moonlight. The dance had ended, and there was a softness to the air—autumnal, not quite touched with the frost of winter. And between the crumbling hundreds-of-years-old shrines and the cobbled paths that now stood empty after all the students had returned to their rooms, there was laughter.

"I'm just saying"—Raph put his hands on his back, crooking it forward—"that he's stooping lower. I just didn't think it was possible. Before long, his nose will be scraping the floor."

Stanley shook his head, undoing his tie. "You're ridiculous. But your Waldman impression is great."

"Ha!" Raph shouted, spinning around to face the opposite direction, his back to Stanley. "Might as well call a frog a toad!"

Stanley chuckled. "That one doesn't make any sense."

"Oh, and Waldman *does*?"

Raph hobbled over to him, grinning, and sat down on the grass. They nestled there, side by side, backs against an old gravestone, and looked out at the fields before them.

Raph reached into his pocket and pulled out a packet of cigarettes, slipping one into his mouth and lighting it. Leaning over to Stanley, he shook another one out of the pack.

"Want a smoke?"

Stanley shook his head. "The last time Jacques gave me one of those things, I almost threw up."

"Yeah. He's the one who got me hooked, the arsehole." Raph took a long drag and let the smoke billow up into the air around him. There was a moment of silence between them. A moment of thought. "He really is a dick, you know?"

Stanley nodded, then gave a little shrug. "Yep, I know. But he's a mate, so . . . what can you do? He's not all that bad."

Raph snorted. "He's jealous. And he gets ugly when he's jealous."

Stanley frowned. "Jealous of who?"

"Isn't it obvious?"

He shook his head, trying to work it out. Waldman, maybe? Or the way Raph . . .

"It's you, Stan."

Stanley blinked, trying to resolve the words in his head. "Why . . . why would *anyone* be jealous of me?"

Raph snorted, shaking his head and letting a drag of smoke expel from his nose. "You're such an idiot that you don't realize how clever you are. Jacques was always Waldman's favorite, particularly after James graduated. After what his parents did to him, that meant a lot."

"His parents?"

Raph put his hand up. "Not my place to say. I wouldn't do that to him. It's not that he doesn't like you, Stan. He does. It's just . . ."

"But Waldman doesn't *have* favorites," Stanley insisted. "We're all in it together."

Raph just laughed. "And I love that you see it that way." He tilted his head back, his voice quieting. "It wasn't cool what happened tonight, at the dance. And him laughing, just because the girls were. I didn't like that."

You didn't stand up for me, though, did you? Stanley thought. *You told me to be quiet. To stay in my place.*

Stanley glanced at Raph, then back at the fields. He didn't say anything.

"You wanna talk about what happened?" Raph asked.

"Not really."

"Fair."

The wind rose a little. As the night took over, the air grew colder. Both boys shivered and, almost unconsciously, shuffled closer to each other.

"I'm going to leave Whelton," Stanley said. "At the end of the term."

"Seriously? And go where?"

Stanley shrugged. "I'm sixteen soon. There are colleges. Other places that will accept me. Other routes to go down. I think it's probably time."

"Have you told Jacques?" Raph asked. "Or Waldman?"

"I'd never hear the end of it. Jacques *especially* wouldn't shut up about it."

"That's true."

"I just . . . This isn't the place for me. I don't belong. I never have."

Raph shook his head. "That's bullshit. You deserve to be here as much as anyone. More, I'd say."

"But life doesn't work on what people deserve, Raph. It works on what they *are*. I figure it's like numbers—two plus two doesn't equal four because it deserves to. It just does. Sometimes you've got to accept that, because, well, what else can you do?"

"I still don't get it." Raph stubbed out his smoke on the stone of the grave behind him. For a moment, he looked skeptically at the pack before sighing and taking out another.

"You wouldn't." Stanley shrugged his shoulders. He didn't turn his head. He spoke the words to the wind. Raph just raised his eyebrows. "Not your fault. You've never been an outsider."

"*I've* never been an outsider? I'm, like, the most awkward person you know."

Stanley shook his head. "It's not the same. Not really. I've tried for a long time to fit in with this whole Whelton crowd. To pretend that I'm not from where I'm from, and that where I'm from doesn't matter, you know? You guys helped—you and Jacques and Waldman—you really did. But . . ."

Raph took a long drag. "But what?"

"But . . ." Stanley wanted to tell Raph everything right then. He wanted to tell him about his father and his mother and the fear that still struck him when he woke up in the morning, the way he still flinched when people got too close. About the deep and terrible shame he felt over being from a broken home, being made from poor stock, being faulty. But he never had, and so he couldn't now. The last thing he wanted was for Raph or

Jacques to see him in the same light those other Whelton boys did. And he feared that if he exposed too much of himself, if he told too much of the truth, that just might happen.

"Look," Raph cut in, "if you want to tell yourself you can't change anything, that's your right. But at least know it's a choice. Nobody's forcing you to leave Whelton, Stan. You're choosing to go."

Stanley blinked, letting the weight of the words settle over him. "I'm glad you had fun at the dance tonight, Raph. I'm glad you danced with someone. I really am."

Raph smiled, looking up into the sky. "I really like her. But I don't know what to do now. Do I . . . Ugh. I don't want to talk about it."

"Then let's not talk about it," Stanley said. "If you want to just sit here for a while longer, I'm cool with that. We don't have to talk about anything at all."

Raph sighed, squinting through slightly wet eyes. "I'm really going to miss you."

"I know," Stanley whispered, staring off into the distance. "I'm going to miss you too."

IT WAS LATE. RAPH DECIDED TO TAKE A LONG WALK, AND STANLEY TRUDGED back toward the main campus building. As he turned into the entrance gates, he bumped—quite literally—into Hugo.

"Oh," the boy muttered, flustered. "Sorry, I was . . . I—"

Stanley frowned. "What are you doing out of your dorm?"

"I . . . I didn't . . ."

"It's okay." Stanley put a hand on Hugo's shoulder. "You're not in trouble. You can do what you want as far as I'm concerned. I was just surprised. You okay?"

Hugo nodded slowly. He moved to walk past Stanley but then stopped.

"Did . . . did you really memorize seven thousand digits of pi?"

Stanley laughed. "Yes, I did."

"Whoa," he whispered, his mouth slightly open. It was then that Stanley realized this boy wasn't just impressed; he was awestruck. It was a deeply uncomfortable feeling.

"It's not that hard," Stanley said quickly. "I bet you could do it. I could help you."

Hugo blinked. "No. I mean, I wouldn't want you to . . . I mean. Would you, actually?"

"Of course. We'll take ten minutes after Waldman's classes; I'll show you some tricks." Hugo nodded so enthusiastically that Stanley worried his head might come off. "Right, now off to bed with you. It's late."

Hugo scurried away, leaving Stanley with a strange feeling that might have been nice if it weren't so utterly bizarre. Not wanting to return to his dorm, he took solace in a nightly routine. Passing into the main quadrangle and up the first set of spiral stairs, he crossed over into the part of the building that held the old staff quarters.

The walls were warmer here, the heating left on all night for those staff who lived permanently on-site. Stanley trudged up one of the spires to a big wooden door at the top and pushed it open.

"Close the door, Stanley," Waldman shouted hoarsely from across the room. "You're letting all the warmth out!"

"It might not have been me, you know."

"'It might not have been me,'" he repeated condescendingly, hobbling over to Stanley. "You smell. I have told you this before. I can smell you from a mile away."

Stanley grinned, shutting the door behind him. "Are you sure it's not just because I'm the only one who ever comes to see you?"

"Oh, very good," he muttered to himself. "Excellent. The great Stanley Webb saunters all the way up here just to make fun of an old man. Just to prove how clever he is. Might as well ask a fish to prove it can fly."

Limping over to his bookcase, he pulled out a tattered old tome, its edges frayed and its cover warped, and ran a finger down its spine. Waldman's living space was large, but its excess of items made it feel cluttered and busy. His quarters consisted of two adjoining rooms: the main office and living area connected by a doorway to a bedroom and, presumably, a bathroom on the other side. The central room was lined with bookshelves, each one containing a melting pot of literature and other curiosities: or- namental knives, statuettes, writing implements. Hints of a time before Whelton, before blindness. A time Waldman never spoke about. Shuffling back to Stanley, Waldman held the book out toward him. "Good timing, you coming now, Stanley. Very clever of you. Tonight, it's time for *King Lear*."

Stanley settled himself into one of the large leather armchairs by Waldman's fireplace and lifted the hefty book onto his lap. "Shakespeare again?"

Waldman knew all the works by heart but had always said that there was an immeasurable difference—all the difference—between knowing and *hearing* the drama of the words.

"It's particularly fitting," he replied with a grin. "The tale of an old man going mad."

"You're not going mad, Professor."

"Ha!" Waldman exclaimed. "And who are you to know that? Might as well tell a tree it's not growing!"

Stanley sighed, scooching back into his seat and breathing in the smells of the room—citrus and a hint of ginger. Waldman had changed it since last time. Or maybe Stanley was just sitting in a different armchair; he wasn't quite sure. Nestling into a comfortable position, he turned to the first page.

"I'm only reading the first act, mind you. You're not getting any more than that."

Waldman let out an almighty humph but did not argue. And as Stanley recited, Waldman paced back and forth, nodding as he let the words enter him and percolate down.

Stanley didn't mind *King Lear*, but it wasn't close to being his favorite. That was *Romeo and Juliet*. It wasn't the love story, necessarily; there was just something about the beauty of the imagery and the sumptuousness of the language that set his heart aflame. It was the first complete work he'd committed entirely to memory.

But as he read *Lear*, Stanley's mind drifted. He pictured himself, his younger self, only thirteen years old and leaving home for the first time to get a taste of freedom. That younger Stanley peered into the future and saw him at this moment, sitting on the armchair reading out loud to an old man. Two years older. He tried to imagine that he would be impressed, that his younger self would look up and see his older self as a success, but somehow it wasn't convincing.

The longer he sat and read, the more a deep and indefinable sadness fell over him, as though he had lost something precious that he never really knew was there.

When he finished, Waldman sat down, his milky-white eyes staring off into the distance.

"Beautiful," he said. "Thank you, my dear boy. Tell me, have you ever heard of the concept of apeiron?"

"I don't think so. Or, wait—is it Greek?"

"Greek indeed," he replied. "Fundamental to Anaximander's cosmological theory. Apeiron is the idea that before us, before people and things and gods and humans, there existed something else. A boundless reality, eternal and infinite, out of which all is generated and all is destroyed."

Stanley cocked his head in interest. "Kind of like whatever existed before the big bang?"

"Ha! Very much so. In the end, science and mythology end up returning to the same places. It's a concept that exists almost universally across cultures—in Chinese Taoism, it's wuji, or the 'primordial universe'; in Hebraism, it's Ein Sof."

"Okay, sure."

"'Okay, sure,'" Waldman echoed playfully. "These connections are *key*, Stanley. They are fundamental. There is a mistaken belief that only the empirical sciences, only mathematics and logic, are the languages of the universe, but this is narrow-minded. If we ignore our shared mythology, our gods, our *stories*, we neglect the very thing that makes us human. It is crucial that you understand this."

Stanley looked up at him. "Why?"

"You tell me. Why am I telling you this?"

"I . . ." Stanley hesitated. "I'm not sure."

The professor smiled. "Good. Think of it like a riddle, then. If you can work out why I'm telling you, maybe I'll give you the next clue." Stanley frowned, not sure what to say in response, but Waldman couldn't see it. "Now! On to the payment for your reading. As usual, you may borrow any book off my shelf. Which would you like?"

"I kind of want to read something dark," Stanley said eventually. "Something . . . sad."

"Ha! I know exactly what you want. Take *The Count of Monte Cristo* by Dumas. If you're not crying at the end, you're a heartless beast. It's on the top shelf, scented with pine and mint."

"I don't need to know what it smells like, Professor. I can read the spines."

"Fine!" He threw his hands in the air. "But don't come back to me when you're lost and searching among the dried figs!"

He got up and flicked through the books, laying his hands upon the work after a brief search.

"Have you been outside this week, Professor?" he asked.

"Hmm?" Waldman's back was turned to him.

"Have you been outside the building, or just outside your room and this classroom? Have you left this week?"

"Yes, yes," he said, brushing Stanley off. "Of course. Don't be silly." Moving over to the other side of the room, he put on an excellent pretense of looking for something important.

"And where did you go?"

"Hmm?"

"When you went out," Stanley pressed, "where did you go?"

"Oh, nowhere, really," he replied. "You know, here and there."

"Did you smell that beautiful lavender in the courtyard?"

"Oh, yes, yes," he said quickly, continuing to search fruitlessly for whatever it was he seemed to have lost. "Wonderful. Lovely time of year."

Stanley sighed. "It's October, Professor. You haven't been out in weeks, have you?"

"Bah! What does it matter? I don't know why you're always bothering me about it. I don't see what—"

"It's not good for you," Stanley told him. "Locked up in this building for weeks on end—months, even. It's not good for your body or your mind. You don't even know what season it is."

"Easy for you to say," he muttered, looking a little ashamed. "Young little thing. Good set of legs. Eyes. Can go anywhere. Can do anything. No, no. I'm better off here. Got you to keep me company, after all."

"And what happens if I stop coming?" Stanley said, approaching him. "What happens to you then?"

Waldman looked up at him with those colorless whites, and a deep frown fell across his face.

"Why would you stop coming?"

"I'm not saying I'm going to, Professor," he replied quickly. "I just . . . I worry about you."

"Ha!" he blurted, turning away. "Worry about me? Might as well worry about a lake! Or a mountain!"

Waldman shuffled back to his desk, his back to Stanley, and sat down. Stanley wondered if he should perhaps push the point further or talk to Jacques or Raph about it, but that might just make Jacques more upset. He considered, briefly, mentioning it to the faculty, but deep down he knew there was no use in bringing it to their attention. Nobody in this place really cared about Waldman. He was just a doddering old fool. Another outsider.

"Did you *really* get to seven thousand and three digits?" Waldman said eventually.

Stanley grinned despite himself. "I did."

Waldman's head tracked down toward his feet, then back up. "You are a very impressive young man, Stanley Webb. I think, perhaps, the time has come that I show you something."

"What is it?"

He fidgeted, seeming a little uncomfortable. "There is a problem that I have been working on, and I think I have got to the stage where I need some help. I will not lie to you, boy. It has consumed me these past years, but I have told no one else. If I tell you, I need a promise from you."

"What promise?" Stanley asked, leaning forward.

"That you will not tell the other boys. That you will work with me until it is done, until we have solved it."

Stanley blinked. He couldn't make such a promise. His mind was made up. He was leaving. But he looked at this old man, this outsider, this friend. And as Waldman stood before him, expectant and vulnerable, about to divulge his greatest secret, Stanley felt all his other plans and anxieties crumble away.

"I promise."

"Excellent!" He hobbled to the back of the room and, fumbling for a key, unlocked a large wooden chest. Out of it, he lifted a glass case, aswish with liquid. "There's no time to lose. We will begin tonight."

"Jesus Christ, Professor," Stanley said, staring at the gray blob floating inside the case. "Is that a human brain?"

5

TRANSCRIPT NO. 273: Margaret Webb

DATE STAMP: 11 AUG. 2021

8 Hours, 54 Minutes, and 52 Seconds Until Dissolution

When Stanley wakes up, I realize he's soiled himself. It takes me a long time to get him cleaned up. I make you stop so I can move into the back of the car and sort him out, counting myself lucky that I have plenty of wipes in my handbag. It's an awful job in an awkward space, but that's what I'm here for, after all. I've got to take care of him.

By the time we arrive at the location—an office building of some kind—he's lapsed into one of his sundowning states. He knows who I am, which is a blessing, but he can't get his head around anything else.

Me too, Stan, I think to myself. *Me too.*

"What's going on, Maggie?" he asks as I roll him in. "Where are we?"

The lobby of the building is conspicuously empty. I know it's the end of the day, and the sun is just setting, but office workers barely abide by the cycle of night and day in the city these days. The building is at least fifty stories high; there should be some kind of movement in and out of the big glass doors.

But there isn't. There's a single security camera with a blinking red light by the lifts and, off in the corner, a caretaker mopping the floor. I remember Stanley telling me that there would be no more caretakers when the automation boom happened, that all the menial jobs would be replaced by technology. Turns out, it's the other way around: technology is slowly replacing our lawyers, our teachers, our doctors. All the professionals who can afford to outsource their work to expensive software and then put their feet up. Sure, you can probably get some kind of machine these days to clean the floors in half the time, but that's the thing about capitalism: it doesn't work if you don't have a working class. There'll always be menial jobs for the people who need to be reminded of their place.

The sound of Stanley's wheelchair rattling fills the room. The setting sun glints off the glass and casts dancing shadows across the floor.

"Maggie," he says weakly, and I can feel the shame in his voice. "Maggie, I think I've messed myself again."

"It's okay." I try to keep my voice warm and comforting. I try to be what he needs. But when I look down, I can see the tears trickling down his face.

"I'm so sorry," he whispers. "I'm so sorry you have to see this."

It's all I can do to stop my heart from breaking. I turn to you. "Where's the bathroom?"

You point a long finger toward a small door on the right, past the lifts. There's a WET FLOOR sign outside it. The caretaker has gone round the corner and disappeared.

I clean him as best I can without fresh clothes on hand. I have to throw away his pants and leave him commando, but he seems chirpier. He's put the incident behind him, it seems, or forgotten it took place entirely. He's looking around. He's asking a lot of questions.

"Do you work here?"

"No, Stan," I say.

"Where *do* you work?"

I smile at him, wondering whether to be honest—tell him we're both ancient and retired—or comfort him. The truth is, I never thought I could hold down a job. Before Stanley, I bounced from part-time retail work to cleaning houses just to cover what I was busy assuring myself wasn't a growing drug habit. It was a lifestyle, that was all. I was partying, not running from whatever was making me feel empty inside. It's not like my parents would have supported me.

After we got married, I didn't need to work. Not financially. As Stanley's career progressed from researcher to program manager at various organizations and think tanks, I finally got what I thought I'd always wanted: the freedom and cash to let loose. But that's the beauty of marrying someone, isn't it? You don't do it because you want to stay the same. You do it because you want to be better, because having an ego against which to check your id makes all the difference in the world.

"I work at a charity," I tell him, hoping to spark an old memory. "For the homeless."

"One of the many things I love about you, my darling," he says, nodding sagely, and I can't keep myself from grinning like an idiot. "So why are we in this place?"

"We're just here for a little checkup."

"Oh? Is something wrong?"

"There's nothing to be worried about." I wheel him out of the bathroom, put the brakes on, and lean down to wipe some spittle off his lip. It's then that he looks at you. He sees you.

He sees me?

It's strange. He looks right at you, and there's an intensely serious look on his face. I've seen something like it before, when he's trying to decipher who I am but can't. For a moment, I think I see a flash of . . . I'm not sure.

You can't remember?

Oh no. I remember it. I can picture it clear as day. There's disappointment, maybe? Regret? It's a sad look, layered with more complexity than

I can decipher in the split second it's there. Then it's gone, and he's smiling again.

"Who's this?" he asks. "A friend of yours?"

"Yes," you reply. "A friend."

You've stopped. What is it?

How do you know Stanley?

Is that important to the current moment in the story?

It's just that I remember thinking: *Hassan's just said three words. Only three. And yet that's the most genuine emotion I've heard from him since the second he walked through my door.*

You were probably projecting your own heightened emotions onto the moment.

Hmm. Maybe.

Where do we go next?

That's exactly what I ask you. We get into one of the lifts, and I notice it doesn't have any buttons. There's just a keyhole—it's the only thing on the panel, right in the middle. You extract a key from your pocket. An actual key, not even a key card, as if we've just gone back in time fifty years. You stick it in the hole and turn.

The lift shudders like we're in a shitty council flat in the mid-'60s, completely incongruous with the sleekness of the building outside. Jerkily, the lift descends.

"How on earth do you get to the upper floors?" I ask.

You raise your eyebrows at me.

"I mean, if there's only one key and all it seems to do is take you downward, I'm wondering what you have to do to get up."

You shrug your shoulders. "You walk."

"Obviously," Stanley chips in happily.

Though I've been wanting to ask where we are for the last twenty minutes, I haven't wanted to worry Stanley. As the lift descends farther, farther—how far down does it *go*?—the question overrides me. I can't help myself.

"What is this place?"

"The skin is the human body's largest organ," you reply, "composed of layers upon layers of different cells. But the top layer of it—the stratum corneum—is made up of flattened cells that are almost entirely dead."

The lift shudders once again as it slowly lurches to a stop.

"Our outermost layer is a corpse. A cadaver. It falls away from us constantly—bits of ourselves, decaying matter. You shed anywhere between thirty and forty thousand dead cells every single hour. It's the great tragedy of humanity that we cannot escape entropy and decay. It is built into our very being." You raise your hands as if to grasp the very air. "Silently and remorselessly, we turn to dust."

The doors open, and we are greeted by an extensive laboratory. It sprawls outward, farther than my eye can see. There must be almost a hundred people in lab coats, bustling back and forth with documents and test tubes, pushing carts of fluids and syringes.

"Welcome to the Lazarus Institute," you say, "where we turn the dust back."

I take you inside the Institute?

I   You sound surprised for someone who was there.

What do you see?

I don't even begin to understand most of it. Machines, robotic arms, people. The main hall is well lit and expansive—it goes on and on—but off to the side, there are other rooms. Most of the doors are closed; some are not. Inside, there are surgical tables and giant mechanical tools. The whir and rumble of engineering is everywhere. I reach forward and touch Stanley's shoulder protectively.

He glances up at me and smiles like he's at Disneyland. He puts a hand on mine, squeezing gently. I look into his face and see genuine affection there, real love, and despite all the madness going on around me, my heart swells. It has been so long.

But I wonder how he's involved in all of this. Throughout our time together, he worked in all sorts of places—big corporations like Unilever, medical labs, think tanks. He never told me *what* he was working on, but he wasn't allowed to, so I learned not to ask. I tell myself that whatever secrets he had, he must have kept them from me for a reason. That there is nothing malicious in them. I make myself certain of this.

Why?

Because there is no alternative. I cannot imagine living in a world where Stanley is not the loving, caring husband I know him to be. I refuse to.

You lead the way across the lab floor. Others nod to you deferentially, making space for you to pass. This is clearly your kingdom. Of that, I have no doubt.

As we move deeper into the facility, I catch glimpses of wonder everywhere: A piece of fabric, thinner than silk, hangs from a hook. A lab-coated man passes a metal rod through it, and it shimmers, flowing around the rod like a stream of water before solidifying again. Farther on, an orb so black that it doesn't look real—a hole in the world, a tear in the fabric of reality—hangs suspended several feet in the air.

I am reminded of an Arthur C. Clarke quote: "Any sufficiently advanced technology is indistinguishable from magic." I think about what you did at the care home, and what you did to that woman, and as I look around this laboratory, it all makes sense. A trickle of worry runs down the back of my neck. What have I got myself into? Where have I brought my husband?

You lead me into a room with a conference table and a few chairs. Stanley lets out a little protest.

"Can I see more?" he asks, like a child. "There's so much more to see."

"I can arrange a tour for him," you reply. "A quick one."

My fists tighten around the handles of his wheelchair, not wanting to let him go. But there are many more questions I need to ask you that I don't want to bring up in front of Stanley. Too much will bring confusion, then anger. I can't have that right now. I want to cling to his being happy as long as I possibly can.

"Okay," I say reluctantly. I push my worries down, figuring I've put enough of my trust in you already. If we are in any danger, there's not much I can do about it now anyway. "But not far."

He nods, and without even a gesture, a man appears at the doorway. "Mr. al-Haytham?"

"Give our visitor a tour of our more interesting developments."

The man steps over to take the wheelchair from me. I pry my hands away. Leaning down, I try to give Stanley a kiss, but he's not looking at me. He's just staring out the door and into the lab with joyous expectation.

The moment he's rolled out the door, I explode.

"What the *hell* is going on?"

You take a seat at the head of the table. "You're angry."

"You're *very* perceptive."

"What do you want?"

"I've done exactly what you want," I say. "I've followed your instructions to the letter, and I've had to watch some pretty awful things take place. I think it's about time for you to actually tell me what's happening."

You ash your cigarette into a tray on the table in front of you. "Ask."

I pause, grasping at the ends of a hundred questions, all of them struggling to work their way through my brain and out of my mouth.

"Why are we here? You said I needed to break into Stanley's mind—what does that mean?"

"This laboratory is dedicated to a singular cause: the preservation of human life. The continuation of the species. The world is not what it once was, Maggie. You've heard it on the news. Global wildfires, mass extinction, sea levels rising—the past twenty years have gone swiftly downhill, but the dominoes were falling long before then, even before you were born. If we do not change something drastic, discover a new paradigm, then humanity is not long for this world. That is not conjecture. It is fact. The Lazarus Institute exists to fight this collapse. To do what needs to be done to save us all. I am told Stanley worked here once, for a brief time."

I blink, then look pointlessly around the room. "Here?"

"Not this room, necessarily. But for the Institute. Before you knew him, before you were married."

I take a seat, processing the information. "He never mentioned it. He . . . he doesn't like to talk about his younger days much."

"I don't think he remembers."

I look up at you. "Earlier, at my house, you said that you didn't think his memory loss was Alzheimer's. You thought it was being done to him. Why?"

"There are many projects here, Maggie, not all of them strictly legal. Governments and legal frameworks move too slowly to make a difference. In order to save humanity, we must act outside their confines. Many great minds have contributed to this mission in some form or another: the likes of Horiuchi Sachiko, Theodore Relkt, Isabel Thoreaux. Most who work here are given relatively free rein to pursue what it is they need to, so long as it is devoted to the common goal. My project is Stanley. I believe that he made a breakthrough, many years ago. That he discovered, or *uncovered*, something. A powerful technology—something significant enough to change this path our species is on. But when that happened, a separate organization of people discovered what he was doing, and they chose to bury it—to hide it so thoroughly that not even Stanley could recover it if he wanted to. That organization calls itself Sunrise, and it still works toward that aim."

"The care home?"

You nod. "I believe they erased whole swaths of Stanley's memory so that whatever he found would never see the light of day."

"But what about all the other residents? Surely, it can't all be there just for him."

"Even with the resources of the Lazarus Institute, I can't say what Sunrise is doing with all of them. Test subjects for different experiments? Merely a profit-making arm? The organization and its intentions remain, for the most part, behind an impenetrable iron curtain. Getting Stanley out took more planning than you are likely to comprehend."

As you tell me this, you don't break eye contact, not even for a second. I feel like I'm melting under the intensity of your gaze. I look down at my hands, at the table, but I still feel your eyes upon me.

"But . . . why? If Sunrise—whoever they are—is working so hard to make sure that what's in Stanley's head stays hidden, surely there's a good reason."

Your hands grip the table, and your fingers splay out across the glass. I can almost feel the pressure as your skin pushes down against it. It's silly, but I shuffle back slightly, just in case the glass smashes under your grip.

"There is never a good reason to suppress knowledge, Maggie. Throughout history, humanity has tried, from religions and censorship to inquisitions and dictators. People who benefit from the status quo. People who are scared of change. *That* is what Sunrise represents. But it never works. It never helps. Stanley was working for *this* institute, which means he was working toward one goal. Whatever his breakthrough, we must uncover it. This is clear to me."

I merely look at you. This all feels too outlandish to comment on.

"It's my hope," you say, "that if we can bring back those memories, then maybe we can bring back some others too. Maybe we can return your husband to you for good, and if I'm right, maybe you can both still have the rest of your lives ahead of you. Together."

I take a deep breath and let out a little chuckle. You know what's funny?

What?

I know I'm being manipulated. I *know* you're not telling the truth. Not the whole truth, at least. I know it in my bones. And yet you've got me. What you're offering me—how can I possibly refuse? It's the only thing I ever think about. It's the only thing I have left.

"What do you need me to do?" I ask.

You smile, and I suddenly understand exactly how Eve felt when she was offered the apple. You reach out to the panel in the center of the table and press a button. The lights dim and flicker off your dark, perfectly unblemished skin. I frown, thinking about dust, and skin decay, and how you get my aging references. Then it occurs to me: you are far, far older than you appear to be.

"Our search has resulted in a range of useful side products—technologies developed tangentially in pursuit of other goals." The table is lowering to the floor, and a contraption is taking its place.

What exactly is happening? This is important.

This is important?

Yes—very important. This is why we are here. Where is Stanley?

Still in the lab.

He doesn't see this moment?

Not right now, no.

And what do you see?

> A panel in the floor opens. Out of it, a contraption rises. It's like a dentist's chair but with straps and wires and drips. Above, a headset descends from the ceiling; it has spiderlike metal arms that spread out like a crown above the chair. There is a large monitor on the ceiling beside it. It's white and gray—clinical. It smells of disinfectant. Next to the chair, there is an empty basin sunken into the floor—a bath—with taps at one end and at the other another headset, this one like an astronaut's helmet.

Has Stanley ever spoken about anything like this before?

> I've never heard about anything like this contraption in my entire life.

What do I tell you about it?

> "This is a memory spade—a tool for digging into the memories of others. The subject sits here"—you gesture toward the chair—"and is connected to another, who delves inside their head." With your other hand, you indicate the bath. "You will experience the memories just as he did, a full re-creation of all the senses, without the mistakes of recall. The brain is surprisingly good at retaining this information when correctly prompted. The more memories the two subjects share, the easier the link and the greater the likelihood of being able to uncover the memories that are missing."
>
> "That's why you need me?"
>
> You nod. "You spent over fifty years together. Your shared memories will act like anchor points, allowing you to navigate other areas of his mind."
>
> The thought of sharing Stanley's memories fills me with a strange thrill. I crave the taste of our life together, of watching Leah grow up, of our first few years of marriage, of our very first kiss. There are butter-

flies in my stomach, like I'm a teenager with a crush. *What have you done to me, Hassan?* I think. *I am overcome.*

The door is pushed open, and Stanley is wheeled back into the room. He is despondent now; his eyes have that glazed look that comes with too much information. He mumbles something, but I don't quite catch it.

Together, you and I help him into the chair. The other man has already gone.

"What's going on?" Stanley whispers.

"It's okay," I say, my instinct for reassurance taking over. "It won't hurt you."

I flash a look up to you to check that I'm not lying, and you give me a reassuring nod. Stanley isn't convinced. He recoils from me a little, shaking his head.

"Who are you? Get away from me."

"I'm sorry, Stan." I push him back into the chair a little, and he gives way. He's so weak these days. So frail.

"No." He shakes his head. You're strapping his arms to the chair. "I don't want this. Get it off me! Who are you people? What do you want from me?"

I try to hold his hand, but he snatches it away from me. "I just want you back, Stan. That's all I want. I want you to come back to me."

The machine turns on, and Stanley shudders as he is injected with something. He sighs and settles back into the chair. His eyes close. The headset descends and clasps itself around his head.

"What do I do?" I ask, my voice shaking.

You run the taps, filling the basin with a clear liquid. It is thicker than water—more viscous.

"I would remove any clothes you would like to keep dry." You open a cupboard built into the wall, revealing a line of white gowns. "You may wear one of these."

You turn away from me as I change, my hands struggling to keep steady. I keep casting glances at Stanley, and he looks peaceful in that chair. But I can't shake the fear I saw in his eyes just moments ago. The panic.

It's just a mood swing, I tell myself. *He has them all the time.*

I dip a toe into the liquid, expecting it to be cold, but the temperature is so close to that of my own body that it barely feels like I'm stepping into anything at all.

"We have to make the link first," you say as I slide in. "Pick a memory. One that you share together. Focus on it as hard as you can."

Before I can reply, the helmet is placed over my head, obscuring my vision. There is a whir and the smell of something burning. My chest is beating hard, too hard for an old lady like me. The last thing I think is: *What the hell am I doing? This is all happening too quickly. This is a terrible idea.*

Then everything goes black.

6 | Stanley
1955

THE MORNING HUMMED WITH THE SICKLY-SWEET REMNANTS OF LAST night's cider mixed with the settling haze of an oncoming hangover. Stanley's eyes tried to open, sticky with sleep and railing against an unnecessarily bright sunrise. He was in a field, his side damp from morning dew, his sleeping bag half-draped across him.

Rolling over, Raph let out a deep groan next to him. His face clunked into an empty bottle of beer.

"Ow. Fuck."

"But soft, what light through yonder window breaks?" Jacques exclaimed. Stanley forced his eyes open. Jacques was sitting on the foldaway picnic table, eyeing a leftover sausage roll. "It's the two idiots. Finally awake."

Stanley lifted himself onto his elbows, wincing. "How long have you been up?"

"Me?" Jacques cocked his head a little to the right. "I never sleep."

Walking over to Raph, he kicked him in the gut.

"Ow," Raph repeated. "What the fuck?"

"Get up. I'm hungry, and I want to get some fish and chips before the awful lunch starts. Then we've got the leavers' ceremony to face."

Raph covered his head with his hands. "I think I'm still drunk."

He rose to his feet, towering. The last two years had been generous to Raph—he had been spending more and more time working out and now bulked outward like a house. He'd grown a beard: a thick black one that ran down his cheeks and across his face. Given his stature and his almost constantly sullen expression, he had become the sort of person old women crossed the street to avoid. Stanley smiled at the irony: He had never met anyone so gentle in his entire life.

Raph stumbled, putting his hand on the table as he lurched forward. "Oh God. Can we at least wait until the nausea passes?"

Jacques rolled his eyes. "Fine, but we're taking your car when we do. I'm not having you throw up in mine."

"I don't remember anything about last night," Stanley said, looking around at the empty bottles. "Did we drink everything?"

"Are you telling me you don't remember walking around High Street at two in the morning trying to find cheap gin because we ran out of booze?"

"Seriously?"

"You and those cans," Raph muttered, sitting down. "Shit—you were obsessed."

Stanley laughed, and his head pounded a little with each chuckle. He fell back, his body nestling into the cold grass. "Good night, then?"

"Solid night," Raph said, nodding.

Jacques smiled. "Couldn't have imagined a better way to say goodbye."

Stanley winced, partly at the aching in his legs and partly at the sound of that word: *goodbye*. It had been easy not to think about it last night, when they had been drinking, but today was their last day together at Whelton. Stanley's last day with Jacques and Raph.

He wasn't sure if he was ready to face the world alone, or if the world even wanted him to. Up until now, it had been easier to construct his own world—one that consisted almost entirely of his two friends and his mad professor. Everything else was just window dressing that he could push aside before it reminded him how out of place he really felt.

Stanley rubbed his eyes and looked around. "Why didn't we put up the tent?"

Jacques burst into a cackle of laughter. Raph shook his head, leaning forward. "You tried," he said, nodding toward the fabric strewn across the ground, the metal poles abandoned. "Honestly, it was the funniest thing I've ever seen."

ABOUT TWO HOURS LATER, THE THREE SAT UNDER A BIG TREE IN THE NEW Regency Park, just far enough away from the school to be neutral ground. They had brought back breakfast: large, crisply battered cod with chips heavy on the salt and lashings of malt vinegar. The only punctuation in the collective silence was the occasional chomp or slurp of a drink. Jacques ate the fastest, as he always did—*ravenous* being an adjective that described him in layers—and when he was finished, he leaned back against the tree and lit a cigarette.

After a couple of deep puffs, he let out a loud and satisfied sigh, closing his eyes for just a moment. How rare it was, Stanley thought, to see his friend quiet and completely at peace.

It didn't last.

Jerking up, Jacques started pacing back and forth in front of Stanley and Raph, both still eating. "I still can't believe this is it. The last day. It feels like I should feel something more, you know? Something bigger." He frowned, screwing his lips up into a tight ball. "Anyone want to play a game?"

Stanley groaned. "I don't have the mental capacity for chess right now."

Jacques shrugged, then started pacing again. He lit another cigarette. "Well, I want to do *something*. I can't just stand here and watch the two of you eat. It's painfully slow. God—you're like cattle."

Raph looked up from his chips. "What's your favorite piece of literature?"

Jacques stopped in his tracks, looking from Raph to Stanley. His face broke into a gleaming smile. "Oh, good question," Jacques said. "Easy, but good. 'Ozymandias' by Percy Shelley. No need to think about it. The whole concept of transience, that whatever we achieve, whatever statues we build or empires we make—they will all eventually turn to dust. Time is the great leveler. *Nothing beside remains.*"

Stanley gave him a curious look. "You think that's comforting?"

"Oh no." Jacques flicked his cigarette butt onto the floor and stamped on it. His eyes glimmered. "I think it's a *challenge.*"

"Stan?" Raph asked.

"Why the question?"

"Well," Raph replied, "originally I just wanted to ask something that would make Jacques talk for a while, so he could stop bothering us." Jacques shot him a dirty look. Stanley barely suppressed a giggle. "But now I'm just into it. I'm actually interested."

Jacques gave him a pointed stare, as if to say, *See?* But Raph ignored it.

"What's yours?" Stanley asked Raph.

"Huh," he said. "I'm actually not sure. There are some gorgeous moments in the Ramayana that I think—"

"A religious text? Really?" Jacques rolled his eyes. "I thought you were cleverer than that."

"Yeah," Raph said. "Sorry."

Stanley frowned. "What's wrong with religious texts?"

"Pfft. Thousands of years of human progress and people are still obsessed with myths some folk wrote down in the dark ages. It's bullshit. It's so *backward.*"

"I don't think so," Stanley replied. "It's a . . . different perspective, that's all. It's another way of looking at information. Empiricism is all well and good, but if we refuse to acknowledge more indigenous knowledge systems, we're just cutting out a whole—"

"Stan." Raph shook his head. Jacques had already turned away from him.

Stanley's mouth fell shut as he realized that he was poking a bear who should be left alone. After depositing Jacques in the junior school at Whelton and covering fees for his entire education, both of his parents had left the country, abandoning him to join a religious cult in the US. When Stanley finally heard about this from Raph, he wasn't exactly shocked that Jacques's parents were out of the picture—Jacques *never* spoke about them, after all, and Stanley could certainly empathize with that—but the suddenness with which they had severed themselves from Jacques's life had an impact that Stanley had never quite been able to understand.

"Mine is the myth of Thamus and Theuth," Stanley said, trying to bring an already prickly Jacques back into the conversation. "From Plato's *Phaedrus*."

"I don't know it," Jacques said, turning around.

"Waldman introduced it to me." Both of the boys rolled their eyes, as if to say, *Of course he did,* and Stanley cursed himself for another blunder. It was the source of more than the occasional jab that Stanley had spent much of his past two years cloistered away in Professor Waldman's office, just the two of them alone. "It's about the old god Theuth, who invented writing and presented it to the Egyptian people," Stanley said quickly, trying to shift the conversation intellectually. "He thinks it's a wonderful thing, that it will help people remember history and the past, but Thamus—the king—disagrees with him. He argues that it's a lazy cop-out. He says, 'For this discovery of yours will create forgetfulness in the learners' souls, because they will not use their memories. . . . You give your disciples not truth, but only the semblance of truth . . . having the show of wisdom without the reality.'"

"Wait," Jacques said, "so the argument is that the invention of writing is a *bad thing*?"

"It's a thought experiment," Stanley replied. "But it hints at something deeper. That there is something special about the human mind—something immutable—and that any attempts we make to externalize that, whether through writing or even art, is a dilution. It's a . . ." He shook his head. "I find the idea quite romantic."

"So is that what you're doing with the old man?" Jacques pointed his cigarette at Stanley. "Getting romantic while learning Plato?"

"No," Stanley said quickly, shaking his head. "No, I . . . We're just doing the usual. Playing chess. I read books to him. He likes the company."

"But without us?"

Stanley felt his face grow quite hot, a response not helped by the growing headache that was taking root in his skull. He had to be careful—there *were* things he could not say. Promises he'd made and lines he could not cross. He didn't want to lie to these boys, his friends, but sometimes loyalty was more important than honesty.

"It's not—"

Jacques shook his head. "Yeah, sure, whatever. I don't know where you get off lying to—"

"Leave it," Raph said.

"I'll leave it when I know what there is to leave," Jacques retorted. Stanley pressed his back against the tree behind him. "I'm just saying that—"

Raph stood up, and though Jacques was taller, Raph loomed over him. He stretched his thick arms out wide, like a bird showing off its wingspan, and then brought them in tightly. Watching him, Jacques fell quiet.

"Can I have a smoke?" Raph asked.

"I thought you quit."

"Yeah. So did I."

They stared at each other, Jacques's head tilted downward. The space between them became a vacuum. No words passed their lips. A decade of unspoken understanding—a closeness Stanley would often glimpse but never be able to touch—flowed between them. A bitter look flickered across Jacques's face, just for a moment. Then he sighed and reached into his pocket.

The breath Stanley had been holding eased out of him in one long exhale.

They stood for a while, the three of them, looking out at the fields that rolled back and back to the horizon. The tension dissipated, even if Stanley could still feel its aftereffects lingering in the cool air. Raph gave a small nod to Stanley, as if to say, *Don't worry about it.* This had increasingly been the way between the two of them over the past couple of years: close and thoughtful but recognizant that certain words should be left unspoken. Certain questions were not to be asked.

Jacques hated it.

The cold, clear morning and the biting air were doing a lot to ease the haze in his mind and bring some clarity. He'd never really liked Whelton and all the things that it represented. It felt ironic that of the three of them, he was the one staying here. Waldman had pulled some strings, wangling him a place as a teaching assistant for a year or two before he would ostensibly start applying to universities. In truth, it was a cover, an excuse for the two of them to keep working until the problem was solved.

You won't need a degree when you've won the Nobel, Waldman had joked to him once. Or, at least, he thought it was a joke. With the professor, you could never quite tell.

"Where do you see yourself in ten years?" Stanley asked, his mind now firmly fixed on the future. "What do you think you'll be doing?"

"Can I answer for Jacques?" Raph said with a smile. "Because you *know* he's going to say, 'Ruling the world,' or some other bullshit."

"Is that really such a bad thing?" Jacques asked, turning to them. "Honestly, though, I want to do something that makes a difference. Something that's remembered, you know? There's an old Jewish saying that you die twice: once when your body dies and the second time when your name is spoken for the very last time. If I can't prevent the first, I'm going to make damn sure I prevent the second. Maybe something in maths. My favorite idols are all mathematicians or physicists. People don't forget mathematicians. Their work doesn't become irrelevant. It's eternal."

"Raph?" Stanley asked.

"God, I have no idea. When I turn twenty-one, I inherit the family trust. If I didn't want to work, I wouldn't have to work a day in my entire life, you know that? It turns out my parents were pretty coy about their money. After they died, the lawyer told me that it's several *million*. In the face of that, I dunno. I could do anything. It's a little overwhelming."

"I can't imagine it." Jacques shook his head. "Raphael Lazarus, millionaire bachelor. Maybe I'll come live with you."

"God, I hope not. After twelve years, I can't believe I'm not going to have to see your smug face every day. Honestly, some people get less for manslaughter."

Stanley laughed, and soon Jacques and Raph were laughing too. Stanley knew he would miss this. He didn't know when he would ever see the two of them again. For they were going out into the wide world in search of further education, jobs, and full, bustling lives, while he was staying behind with an old man in an office.

But there was a strange protectiveness he felt when he thought about his time with Waldman. It was his, and nothing had ever really been his before. So, yes, he would stay, for they were getting close, so close to a breakthrough, and he knew that he couldn't afford to be anywhere else.

AFTER THEIR HUNGOVER BREAKFAST, THEY WANDERED BACK INTO THE archway of Whelton together for the last time, crossing the courtyard and climbing up the spiral staircase to Waldman's room. Second and third formers bustled around them, a new generation they didn't recognize and hadn't spoken to. They walked in silence—partly because their heads still hurt and partly because they all, in their own way, recognized the somber significance of this moment.

This little club had defined them, formed them over so many years. It would continue on without them, of course. Waldman continued to recruit from the younger years, if only in dribs and drabs, and Stanley knew he'd be helping them train their memories and practice their skills. But today was special. Today, it was just the three of them. And after today, that would be gone.

Jacques opened the door to find Waldman sitting on the desk, cane in hand, looking grumpy.

"What time do you call this?"

"A reasonable time, Professor," Jacques replied. "Just because you wake up at four in the morning doesn't make it normal."

"Ha!" He whacked his cane on the table. "I didn't think you were so boring as to strive for normality, Mr. Bashar. How disappointing."

"The only disappointment you're going to experience today is when I win at Risk, *again*."

"I don't want to play Risk," Raph said.

"Because I always win?"

"Because you *gloat*. It's tiring. I don't want my last memory of this room to be of you gloating."

"Chess," Stanley said quietly, closing the door. "It's the only thing that makes sense."

"The young Mr. Webb is indeed correct." Waldman slid off the desk and landed, with surprising nimbleness, on the floor. "Get the boards out. It is the only possible choice."

They fell into their routines with the comfortable ease of long years. Sometimes, when he couldn't find his way around a problem or his mind became stuck, Stanley would sit in his room and set up a chessboard: placing the pawns, turning the bishops and knights the right way, positioning the queen last—always last. It was an intimate experience. It soothed him.

Waldman played all three boards. The boys no longer used physical pieces when playing one another, but when playing Waldman, they took every advantage they could get. If that meant seeing something a blind man could not, so be it. Still, sometimes Raph and Stanley would forget to move the pieces for six or seven moves, then quickly realize and catch them all up. Never Jacques, though. Jacques kept a tight and watchful eye on every piece, every move.

Each game was thrilling. So much so that Stanley struggled to focus on his own, his eyes drifting to the fierce battles taking place on the other boards. Jacques drew black, employing a Robatsch Defense, looking to gain control of the middle game, where he knew he was strongest. Raph stayed traditional, fianchettoing his bishop into the Dragon Variation. A relatively safe move, but Stanley could already see Waldman shifting into the Yugoslav Attack, castling the wings and pushing the game into a level of complexity that Raph would struggle to manage.

Waldman paced back and forth, his cane tapping the floor. The room became punctuated with exclamations, with oohs and aahs, with the slamming down of pieces. Ground was gained, then lost; pieces were offered up, some as traps, others as bulwarks—brief moments of respite in an otherwise steady war.

"Check," Jacques said. "I think . . . yes. Check."

Waldman stopped. Everyone stopped. He put his hand to his chin, making a dramatic pretense at deep thought. "Pawn to king's bishop five."

"Bishop to king two. I have your queen."

Waldman blinked. He froze, the other two games gone from his mind. "Pawn to king's bishop six," he said.

"What?"

"You heard me."

Jacques shook his head, smiling. "You're giving up. You can see I've won."

"Pawn to king's bishop six."

"Knight to queen's knight three," Jacques replied. "I have both your rooks. You have nothing left."

"Pawn to queen four. Mate in three moves."

"What?"

Waldman put his hands on the table, leaning forward. "Check. Mate."

All three boys stared at the board, at Waldman's dwindling pieces, mostly pawns now. They saw how they were arranged: neatly, specifically, put in place with great care, while Jacques ignored their importance and pushed to gain ground. Silence dominated.

Eventually, Jacques said, "Oh, for fuck's sake."

He shook his head, stood up, and walked sullenly to the other side of the room with his hands in his pockets. It was no surprise—it shouldn't have shocked anyone. Jacques would sometimes win at other games: Risk or carrom, if he was lucky. But no one beat Waldman at chess. Ever. Sometimes you got close, but you never won.

Raph's endgame was turning into a long one—a war of attrition that neither side seemed willing to take any chances with. Occasionally, a pawn or rook would dart out of cover for a moment, briefly, before disappearing back behind friendly lines. A little ground was gained here and there, but not much. Slowly but surely, Waldman worked his advantage and pressed his way across the board.

Stanley had barely been paying attention to his own game. Moves slid off his tongue before he'd even had the chance to think about them. What had started as an Open Sicilian Defense had quickly shifted into a Taimanov Variation and then a Maróczy Bind. The middle game had become ludicrously complex, with every piece covered at least twice and a multitude of possible transpositions. Stanley wasn't thinking—not really. Some instinct, built upon hundreds of thousands of previous games stacked upon one another in his memory, had taken over. He found himself looking at the shape of the pieces, thinking about the gleam of light on the board. It's quite possible that he was the most surprised in the room when he eventually said, "Check. Mate in four moves."

Waldman froze. His cloudy whites squinted, replaying the last few moves in his head.

"Excuse me?"

"I . . ." Stanley blinked. "I think you're stuck. I think it's checkmate."

Raph jerked upward, his eyes greedily taking in their board. From the other side of the room, Jacques didn't move, didn't look, but his body became stiff, every single muscle constricted.

The silence as Waldman thought over the moves in his head was deafening.

"Yes," he said eventually, his face breaking into a huge grin. "So it is. Checkmate. Well, congratulations, young Mr. Webb. You're the first person to beat me in seventeen long years."

"Bullshit," Jacques said, looking out the window at the opposite side of the room. "You let him win."

"Let him win?" Waldman repeated incredulously. "*Let* him win? How dare you? Might as well say that I let the sun rise this morning, or let the tides go out!"

Jacques shrugged. "Sure, whatever. Say whatever you want. Don't pretend you don't play favorites."

Raph spun round. "Seriously, Jacques? Just because you didn't win? Can't you be a little bit gracious?"

"This isn't about me not winning, Raph. This is about the little secret best-friend pact that those two"—he pointed at Stanley and Waldman—"have seen fit to keep us out of for the past couple of years. What, am I not good enough for you, Professor? What was it that I did wrong? Am I not *clever* enough to sit up in your office talking about Plato and Thamus and fucking Theuth?"

Waldman's face twisted into an expression none of them had ever seen before: fury. Raph glanced from Jacques to Waldman and back again, his eyes panicked, but it wasn't Jacques that Waldman spoke to.

"You *told* them?" he whispered at Stanley, his voice barely containing the rumble of anger underneath. "You promised me."

Stanley balked. "I didn't tell them anything. We were just talking about literature, that's all. I . . ."

"Tell us what?" Jacques demanded, storming across the room. "What is it? What are you two hiding that's so secretive you can't tell the rest of us? You can't tell *me*?"

"This is none of your concern, boy!" Waldman slammed his cane on the table, the crack whipping through the room. Everyone fell silent. Raph stared down at his lap. Jacques glowered at the professor, his fists clenched. Stanley opened his mouth to speak, to do something to claw back the peace, but no words formed.

Waldman turned and walked toward the door. When he got there, he stopped. "Today is the day you leave school, when you cease to be children and become men. Act like it."

And he left.

The boys did not speak. A strange awkwardness hung over each of them like a heavy blanket. This was supposed to be a wistful goodbye: touching and emotional. It wasn't supposed to be an argument. None of this was right at all.

Jacques picked up his bag and walked out without another word. Stanley glanced over at Raph, who looked sheepish and, for some reason, a little ashamed.

"You should go check on him in a bit," Raph said.

Stanley stood up. "You mean Jacques?"

"You know who I mean."

He nodded. Raph was right—as always. He couldn't let their last meeting end this way, not after everything they'd been through. He'd go see the professor and make it right. He'd get him to reorganize the meeting, Raph would talk Jacques down, and they'd try again.

But a deeper worry had now settled into Stanley's conscious: He'd never seen Waldman angry like that before. Not at him, not at anyone, even though the professor had become more erratic as they got closer to a breakthrough in their experiment. Stanley wasn't an idiot. He knew there were some things Waldman wasn't telling him. But he hoped that whenever he found out what they were, it wouldn't be too late.

WHILE HE WAITED FOR THE PROFESSOR TO CALM DOWN, HE WENT TO FIND Hugo. The young lad hadn't grown much in the last couple of years, but he'd developed an intensity about him that almost scared the teachers, not to mention the student body. As such, he'd become a loner—even more so than the rest of Waldman's club members—and could often be found just walking the grounds, muttering to himself.

When he clocked Stanley, he gave a rare smile. "Not at the ceremony?"

"You're so observant. It's a real skill."

Hugo rolled his eyes, affectionately dismissive in the way only a fourteen-year-old can really manage.

"Hey," Stanley said. "I just wanted to say, it's a last day, but—"

"Don't do it."

"What?"

Hugo shook his head. "I don't do goodbyes. Not interested. If that's what you're here for, don't."

"Actually, I was here to tell you I'll be sticking around."

Hugo's eyes brightened up. "Really?"

"Yeah, helping the professor out with some bits and pieces. So you'll still see me around."

"Oh," he said, suddenly awkward. "Right. Well. That's nice, then."

He looked down at the ground and walked off without another word.

Never change, Stanley thought with a smile. *At least there's still someone as odd as me around here.*

PUSHING BACK THE DOOR TO WALDMAN'S OFFICE, STANLEY POKED HIS head through. The old man was pacing back and forth, mumbling.

"You smell different." His nose twitched.

"Were you talking to yourself again?"

"Was I talking to myself?" he repeated. "Does it look like anyone else is in here? Of course I was talking to myself! Keeps the mind fresh. Keeps the brain whirring."

"You're ridiculous."

Waldman approached Stanley slowly, sniffing at him like an old rat. "And *you* stink of alcohol. I knew I could sense something in that room, but I assumed it was Jacques. Are you drunk?"

"I'm *hungover,* Professor. It's ten in the morning."

For a fraction of a second, Waldman's eyes widened in surprise. Stanley wouldn't have caught it if he didn't know him so well.

"Well, of course it is!" he blurted. "Don't need to tell me that. Might as well tell the sun how hot it is!"

The professor turned his back and began fiddling with pieces of paper. About a year ago, after saving up his measly scholarship money, Stanley had bought the professor a braille slate and stylus so that he could jot down his thoughts.

Waldman rarely used it. He almost never wrote anything down. When he'd lost his sight, he'd refused to learn braille, claiming that he had no need for it. That everything he needed to remember would remain neatly in his head. Only after Stanley pressed him about needing some way to record things did he later pick it up. They learned it together.

Stanley smiled as he walked over to the desk and settled down. "I'm sorry about earlier. I . . . I really haven't told them anything about what we've been doing. We were just—"

Waldman waved his hand in the air. "No matter. We must stop anyway. The experiment is going nowhere. Foolish to even try."

A jolt went through Stanley's heart and down into his stomach. "What?"

"There's just no point."

"But we were getting close." Stanley stood up. "The discovery you made about the neural network in particular was—"

"I have already said it's over," Waldman cut in, his whole body tensing, his hands clenching the desk. "This is *my* life's work. I say we are done, we are done!"

"I don't understand," Stanley whispered, but he struggled to hear himself over the roar of his thoughts. He'd bet everything on this. Without it, there was no future for him. Nowhere for him to go.

Waldman had his back to him, frowning. Stanley didn't need to see his face; his whole body frowned.

"Oh, come on, Professor," Stanley attempted. "You really expect me to believe you're just giving up? Might as well ask a—"

"Enough!" he snapped. Stanley took an involuntary step back. "There is no more discussion. It is over. Forget it. Forget everything we have discussed. It is pointless. Go live your life. Get a job, a family."

Stanley reached forward to put a hand on his shoulder. "Why are you acting like this? What's happened?"

Waldman brushed him away. "You have a ceremony to get to. I shall see you there."

Muttering to himself, he pottered off toward the door to his room, sniffing as he went. With a clear sweep, he shut it behind him, leaving Stanley standing confused in his office, the window shutters clattering gently in the wind.

———

STANLEY SKIPPED THE LEAVERS' CEREMONY. IT WAS AN ABSURD AFFAIR: AN overly formal attempt to pretend that the last five years of Stanley's life had been collegiate, bustling with life and friendship. He'd not even told his parents it was happening, and they hadn't cared to ask. Jacques and Raph had pressed him into attending at first, so he was wearing a suit and tie he had borrowed, feeling too hot and a little stupid. But after his argument with Waldman, the last thing he wanted to do was subject himself to the circus of students shaking hands and giving trite speeches, cheering one another and mocking him with their silence.

He'd apologize to Jacques and Raph later.

Instead, he sat in the cemetery outside the main school building—the one where he and Raph would go when they needed a break from the drudgery of the school day. He looked over the crumbling, dotted stones and wondered what the hell was going on. He and Waldman had made breakthroughs recently, unlocked new plateaus that they'd previously thought unachievable. He couldn't fathom why they would give up now. Was this it? Was this actually the end of the road? Would he have to leave Whelton and go on to . . . what? University programs filled with more of the same. A job. A house. A world that had already rejected him.

He stood up, sighing, trying to keep the tears from his eyes, and wandered through the gravestones.

He'd done something wrong, whatever it was, but more than that, he felt like a disappointment. This wasn't a new feeling. He'd grown used to it from the other adults in his life, but never from the old man. Never from Waldman.

A hand grabbed his shoulder.

Spinning around, he was confronted by an old woman. Her hand gripped him as if it were holding on for survival.

"Stanley," she said.

He stared at her. She was strangely familiar, but he couldn't tell how.

Like seeing a minor celebrity from a movie that you can't quite put a name to. Though he couldn't think of when or where, he had the intense feeling that he had seen her before.

"Y-Yes?" He glanced left and right. The cemetery was empty—nobody else was there. "Who are you?"

"How do we stop it? You have to know. How does it stop?"

"I . . ." He tried to take a step back, but her hand held him in place. "I don't know what you're talking about."

She frowned. "What year is it?"

"Erm . . . 1955."

"Too early. Damn it." She released his shoulder, leaving a painful twinge, and shook her head. "I . . . I'm sorry."

Turning on the spot, she walked off, leaving Stanley standing alone and baffled, like the subject of some horrid prank. He stared at her as she walked around the chapel. He raised his hand, filled with a sudden desperation to shout *No, wait!*, to find out who the hell this strange woman was and what she meant, but no words left his mouth.

She cut round the corner and disappeared.

Gone.

She had said his name. How had she known his name?

Stanley burst into motion—a frantic dash to grasp this mystery. He sprinted up the path, but when he turned the corner himself, she was nowhere to be seen.

He slowed to a stop, spinning on the spot, breathing hard.

She was completely gone, as though she had never been there.

He screamed. A furious, pointless expulsion of rage. He shouted at the gravestones, at the chapel, at the hills. He kicked a rock, sending it clattering across the cobbles and onto the grass. And when he finally stopped, he felt deeply and immeasurably alone.

Somehow, this disappearing woman had become a distillation of all his failures—with Whelton, with Waldman, with the world.

No.

He would not accept this. He would not simply lie back and take it. Not anymore. Whatever nonsense Waldman was playing at, he would go back up to that office and demand the truth of it once and for all.

STANLEY MARCHED UP THE SPIRAL STAIRCASE TO WALDMAN'S OFFICE, each step ringing through the building around him. When he got to the door, he took a deep breath. He didn't want to shout at the old man, frustrated though he was. He loved him. He just wanted to know what was going on. He just wanted some answers.

He opened the door to darkness. The shutters on the windows had all been closed.

"Professor?"

Stanley saw very little at first as his eyes became accustomed to the dimmer light. There was a large form in the center of the room—like a pillar, or a rug that had been hung up to dry. He took a few steps closer, and his breath caught in his throat.

It was a person dangling there. Hanging by the neck. A man.

Waldman.

Stanley stared at him, not able or willing to believe. He took a few steps forward and touched his skin. His flesh was cold—pale and hard. In a daze, Stanley circled the body, unable to look at his face directly, just at the smaller features: his hands, gray and swollen; his shoes. His shirt was partially untucked, sticking out of his belt. The rope on his neck had tugged it upward. *He wouldn't like that—Waldman hated untucked shirts*, Stanley thought. *He hated them.*

The rope looped around a hook in the ceiling and was tied fast to the window. And the body just hung there, dangling, inanimate. Without thinking, Stanley untied it, and the body fell stiffly, as if it would break apart like a mannequin when it hit the floor, limbs tumbling away.

Stanley closed his eyes, choking back tears.

He sat next to the body and looked into its milky-white eyes. Reaching forward, he tried to close them, but rigor mortis had made the lids rigid and unmoving. He fumbled at them until they eventually stayed shut.

For a time, he sat there with it—no, with *him*—and cried.

He put his arms around Waldman, the man who had taught him everything, the man who had given him new life, and he felt the rough scratch of the rope still around his neck. The stool Waldman had used to lift himself up had been roughly kicked to one side.

Slowly, and then more frantically, Stanley pulled to untie the rope. He didn't want it there. He didn't want to see it on the neck of the man who had become his mentor, his friend, his father.

He threw it into the corner of the room, into the shadows. And as he sat there and stared at it, he was struck with a certainty.

The professor wouldn't have done this. There was no way. He wouldn't have chosen to abandon Stanley like this. Not unless he absolutely felt that he had no other choice.

So why?

What had Stanley missed? What had he not seen?

In a desperate attempt for answers, he stumbled around the room, looking through boxes and cases. There was nothing there—all that they had been working on, everything they had put together, had been removed or destroyed. Endless pages of dictated notes written by Stanley's own hand—missing, burned in the fireplace, torn to shreds. In his final moments, he'd demolished years' worth of research and experimentation, a lifetime of his own work.

Corners and scraps of leftover paper that had escaped the flames had half sentences and bits of words he could almost read—*memory entanglement, CROATOAN, apeiron?*—but they meant nothing to him.

That's when he saw it on Waldman's desk: a single piece of paper, pressed out in braille with the slate and stylus. A final note, something Waldman had printed before taking his own life. He ran his fingers over the indentations. It just said:

"*Odyssey*. Murray trans. Book 12. Lines 118–119."

Stanley stared at it. He didn't need to look it up. The classics, in their various translations, had been permanently drilled into his memory over the years. The lines rose immediately into his mind—when Circe warns Odysseus of the Sirens and then of the monsters Scylla and Charybdis.

An immortal bane, dread, and dire, and fierce, and not to be fought with; there is no defence.

He shifted the page, and on another piece of paper underneath the reference, scrawled overlarge in red ink by a messy blind hand that had not written a word in decades, there were two clearly distinguishable words:

IT HUNGERS.

7

TRANSCRIPT NO. 273: Margaret Webb
DATE STAMP: 11 AUG. 2021
8 Hours, 22 Minutes, and 16 Seconds Until Dissolution

You're at the Institute, with me and Stanley, and you've entered the memory spade.

I Yes—I remember it clearly. I put on the headset and everything shifts.

Where does it take you?

At first it's black, but deeper than black. Emptier. Then features appear, like . . .

Like what?

You know when you wake up from a dream—a really vivid dream? Everything is still so tangible in your mind, almost like you can reach out and touch it. And even as you do, things start to disappear. You reach for a moment, for something someone said, or you try and picture the place you were in, and even as you do, it drifts from you. Where does it go? Into nowhere, nothingness. Into a void.

I'm in that void, and I'm forgetting a dream in reverse. The world is taking shape around me: not just physically but mentally. Cognitively—place, time, context, as if I'm recalling a core memory. In dribs and drabs, I understand where I am. A pub. Not just any pub but the Merchiston Arms in London.

You know it?

Of course I know it. I've been there many times. But that's not why I know it at this moment. I know it in the same way you know something in a dream. There's no rhyme or reason or explanation. You just do. And as soon as the realization hits me—why I'm here—it sends shivers up my spine.

You asked me to pick a memory that Stanley and I share, a link between us, and even though I didn't really think about it, it makes complete sense. The only obvious place. I'm at the Merchiston Arms, just off Vauxhall Bridge Road. It's the fifteenth of January, 1967, at 8:15 in the evening. It's cold.

Why are you there?

It's the first time Stanley and I met. It's the clearest memory I have—stronger than our wedding day, than anything that came after. Except maybe Leah's birth, but that wasn't about us, not in the same way. I remember it more clearly than I can picture my own face these days. In so many ways, it was the first day of my life.

I'm standing in the corner of this pub, and it's so real. This memory—it's like I'm there. But I look down at my hands and I'm me: wrinkly old me, in the flesh, just standing there.

Your brain constructs an image for yourself in the memory. You are an observer, nothing more.

> There's the warmth of the fire in the corner, crackling away, mixed in with the subtler, more intimate warmth of people bustling in and out. Each time the door creaks open, a blast of winter air rushes into the room and quickly dies. There's life here: the thrill of conversation. I realize how much I've missed conversation—God, how much I've missed people.
>
> And I realize I'm looking around the room—at the bar where servers are pulling pints and pouring wine, at the people seated with menus, ordering plates of chips—but I am definitively and specifically not looking at the corner to my left.

Why not?

> Because that's where Stanley is. I know that's where he is. I remember it perfectly. But if I turn around and see him, young and able and fit again, I don't know if my heart will be able to take it.
>
> I walk forward to the bar, taking it all in, marveling at the technology you have made. Everything feels *real*—every sound, the touch of every surface, the beautiful pub-food smells from the kitchen. I put my hand on the hard wood of an empty barstool and sit down.
>
> "What can I get you?" the barman asks.
>
> My mouth falls open in shock. I'm in a memory, I think. One of Stanley's memories. How is he talking to me? I'm not here.

Because it's not real. Because it's a memory. The human brain is very good at contextualizing, at explaining things that don't make sense. You've inserted yourself, a foreign consciousness, into Stanley's memories. His subconscious is doing the only thing It can: It's remembering you getting a drink. Otherwise, why would you be there?

Yes—you explain this to me afterward as well. When I ask you. I'm starting to remember that now. Why can I remember some things and not
others? Almost all of this is only coming back to me as I'm retelling it,
but that's . . . that's not how memory works. Why can't I remember what
happens next?

That's not important right now. This is important. This moment—here. Focus
on it, or you might lose it.

But I—

You don't want to lose this memory, do you, Maggie? You don't want it to go
forever.

No. Never.

Focus, then. The barman asks you if you want a drink.

I eventually ask for a gin and tonic. I don't know how long I gape at him,
but he takes it in his stride. Once my drink comes, I put it to my lips. It's
delicious—cool and crisp, with a hint of cucumber. For all his amnesia,
Stanley can remember a pretty good G&T.
   Only then do I turn.
   And I see him.

What does he look like?

He doesn't look like any man I've ever seen before.

What do you mean?

He's beautiful. But he's more than just a man. He's—let me try to explain:
When I was sixteen, I went to a late-night party in my friend Ella's back

garden. She had one of those huge gardens that sprawl out into the woods, and you could barely tell where it started or ended. She called it a party, but it was really just a whole group of us getting as drunk as possible around a roaring fire.

There was such a sense of destruction in us back then, the kind that only exists when you're a teenager, I think. Some of us liked wrecking other things, but mostly it was self-destruction. We had friends who could get cocaine under the table from junky doctors and cannabis from the backs of jazz bars. The goal was to get as drunk or high as possible before the night was over. Make sure you were as wrecked as you could possibly be.

But we built this fire. We all pitched in, and it was huge—logs that had been cut from the surrounding woods—and over the night, we just kept chucking stuff on it. And it burned and burned. At some point, maybe three or four in the morning, I just stared into it. I was hammered and more than a little high. Everyone around me was in the process of collapsing, their limbs failing and their minds disintegrating until they just became a bundle of sleeping bodies that would have to be reconstituted in the morning. And in the midst of all this destruction and decay, the fire just kept going, brighter than ever, like some kind of Egyptian sun god, come to brighten up the darkest moments in our lives.

I passed out eventually, after enough drinking and dancing and night-dark fumbling—that was the point. The end goal. And when I woke up in the morning, just another piece of the human detritus that we had created, I felt so empty. That's what it's like having a hangover and being on a comedown. Like all the enjoyment had been scooped out of me.

But the fire was still burning. And I pulled up toward it, and felt its warmth, this beacon of light, and suddenly, almost religiously, I saw the self-destruction inside of me, and I rejected it. I wanted to create, to grow, to live, if only not to disappoint that fire.

That fire changed the way I looked at my whole day.

And that—sitting there in his corner seat, quietly reading a book—that's what Stanley looks like to me.

Oh my, Hassan. I think my heart just skipped a beat. I'm not ready for this.

What happens next?

I get up from my seat and move a little closer to him—to a table a couple of seats away. I'll be coming through the door any moment, and it'll happen: our first encounter. It feels like I'm approaching wildlife in the jungle—I want to be as close as possible, but not so close as to disturb a single thing. I know it's just a memory, but I've already seen how memories can change.

But do you know what I'm not looking forward to?

What?

Seeing myself. You've got to understand, I was a mess back then. I'd peaked at school, and to call *that* a peak is a good indication of how pitiful my life had been. When I walked into that pub, it was off the back of a decade of ditching dead-end jobs, facing failures, being unmarried—a fact my parents constantly reminded me of—and using drugs, a habit that I'd spent the better part of the previous five years convincing myself wasn't an addiction. God, I wasn't just a wreck; I was the *Titanic*. Scraggly hair, sunken eyes, borderline anorexia. Urgh. I have no desire to see that side of myself again.

Each time the door opens, I cringe. But Stanley is just sitting there, quietly reading, illuminating the whole room with his peaceful focus. And I know that without those dark, empty years, I wouldn't have met him, and I wouldn't have everything that followed.

The door swings open again—another burst of cold air whooshing through. Half-wanting to look away, I glance at it and see myself, *me*, at the age of twenty-nine, walking right in.

I almost fall out of my chair.

Is it really that bad?

No! It's ... I'm ... I'm beautiful. My skin is clear—glowing, even. My hair has still got that wave in it from when I was a teenager, all thick and glossy. I have a confidence—one that I definitely didn't come close to having until long after. I don't get it. I'm stunning. It doesn't make any sense.

These aren't your memories. They're his.

But he's not even looking at me. He's glued to his book as I walk into the pub.

The brain contextualizes, and when it doesn't know the answer, it creates one. This may not be how you remember yourself, but it's how he envisions you in his memories. Whoever you are or were, this is how he sees you.

Oh Jesus, Hassan, now I'm crying. I'm an old lady stuck in a fucking swimming pool, and I'm crying.

She comes right in—*I* come in—and she looks around the room. She's just after a drink: something to while away the evening before she has to go home and face the sheer misery of her living situation again. Of *my* living situation, I should say. Except the girl in front of me, from fifty years ago, is so damn distant from everything I am now that I'm struggling to think of her as *me*. Christ—why do you make this so difficult?

Using "she" is fine. I follow you.

As she looks around the room—and I remember this myself, so damn clearly—she sees that the only place to sit is next to the quiet man reading a book in the corner. All the other seats are taken, and she doesn't want to sit at the bar. Bartenders have a tendency to make conversation, and conversation has a tendency to devolve into lechery.

So she walks over to the . . . Wait.

What is it?

I'm sitting at a high table near Stanley—me, current old batty me who's dived into his memories—and that's why there are no other seats. I took the last one. Except, *I* also remember there being no other seats. So who was sitting at this table? Why aren't they here?

You're focusing on the wrong details. Stay on Stanley.

You told me to focus on all the details.

That was a generalization. There are times when you must focus on specific things. This is one of them. If you don't tell me now, it will get away from you. You'll miss it. What are you doing now?

I'm watching her stare at Stanley. She's sat down opposite him, a pint of lager in her hand because it'll last longer, and she's just gazing right at him. He doesn't look up from his book, but surely he notices. Why doesn't she *say* something? There's something about him—something in his posture, his look—that she's utterly entrapped by, and yet all she can do is stare. God, I'm getting jitters just looking at this. I want to jump over the table and slap her across the face.

And then he looks up. He notices her.

And he doesn't say anything.

He just stares back.

And for a moment that feels like a lifetime, the entire pub falls away, and a space opens up between them: a vacuum that is closed off from the rest of time and space. It throbs and it swells, as though both of their faces are black holes, tugging at one another, pulling and tearing. And I worry for a second that we will all be sucked into the sheer intensity of it.

But then he smiles.

Oh dear God, that smile. I have butterflies, even now. I have butter-flies thrice over: staring at him, watching myself stare at him, and telling you about it now. Each one compounds on the last.

He opens his mouth, and even though I'm not close enough, I know exactly what he says, because those words were burned into my skin from that day onward.

"Do I know you?"

She shakes her head, still caught in those eyes.

"I . . ." he starts, then stumbles. He lets out an awkward little laugh, which does nothing but endear him to me more. As I watch his lips move, I mouth the next words with him. "I feel like I've known you my entire life."

She blushes. She reaches for her hair—her impossibly thick, wavy hair—and pulls it behind her ear. She gives him a little smile, and I read it like a book. It says: *I am completely and utterly besotted by you. Take me. I am yours.*

They talk—slowly at first, in false starts and caesuras, but soon with more rhythm. They talk and talk and forget about their drinks. The book has long been dropped to one side. They discuss everything and nothing: life, art, history, pubs. They barely talk about each other, but it doesn't matter. They know all they need to know.

I can't quite hear them, but I remember the conversation clearly, the way it made me feel. They're talking about books she hasn't read since she was a teenager, reigniting a love for words she had almost forgotten existed. She looks down after half an hour, and her beer is untouched. She can't remember the last time that happened.

Once or twice, by accident or self-sabotage, she lets slip something she is sure will ruin it. I see it all over her face. Something about where we lived at the time, a filthy squatter's commune barely two steps up from sleeping on the streets, or what we did with our days, a mixture of recovering from the previous night and scrounging up enough money to fund the next. For an instant, she bends her head in shame, expecting the same judgment that drove her from her parents, but when she looks up, she is shocked to find that he doesn't care. He's not interested in where she lives. He wants to know who she is.

I am sitting here watching them, seeing the quiet glances and long looks, the animated eyes and passionate fervor with which they talk, and I am falling in love with him all over again. I look down at my hands to check that they are still there, and they are old, wrinkly things. This is not the body he fell in love with. These are not the hands. I want to chop them off. I want to burn them.

Then I hear your voice—quiet, tickling somewhere at the back of my consciousness.

It's time to come out, Maggie, you say. *That's enough for now.*

I look up at the two of them. At me and him. I don't want to leave this moment.

Maggie. Your voice is clearer this time, more imperative. *You need to leave.*

"No," I whisper. "I can't."

You must.

I feel a tug—like a lasso has been wrapped around my brain and pulled backward, like the split second when you fall backward in a chair and your breath catches in your throat. The room darkens, and I start to fade; Stanley starts to fade.

No, I think, and somehow—through some deep instinct I didn't know was there—I tug back. Hard. I launch myself in the other direction. So far that I am thrown right out of the moment, out of the Merchiston Arms, and I'm plunging through a kaleidoscope of moments and images, deeper and deeper into Stanley's mind. A vast expanse of desert. A torch in a cave, ancient symbols flickering on the walls. A laboratory of some kind, doing tests on rats. A man hanging from a rope in a dark room. It all moves too fast for me to focus on any one image.

I come to a halt with a jerk. I'm outside, and it's dark, freezing. There is none of the slow settling in of memory that I got before. My bones shake; my neck aches with the whiplash of its immediacy.

As my eyes adjust to the dim light, I see the snow underneath my feet. Flakes land on the bare skin of my arms, each one a tiny frozen bite. I am not dressed for this.

Pulling my arms tightly against my chest, I look around. I'm in a small garden; the only illumination comes from the streetlamps behind me and from the window ahead: that harsh yellow-white glow of artificial light. Taking a few steps forward, I peer inside and see, through the kitchen and past a door into the living room, a boy standing alone.

He must be about seven or eight years old, and he's standing bizarrely still, his head downward and his face staring intently at the floor. As I shift a little to the left to take in more of the scene, I see a man standing in front of him, waving his arms, shouting. The sound is muffled through the rooms and the glass, but I can just about hear the tone of it—the anger, the fury. The boy says nothing, makes no movement apart from an almost imperceptible shake of his head.

The man screams, and it's loud enough that I can make out the words.

"Fucking look at me when I'm talking to you!"

The boy looks up, and my heart drops because it's Stanley—oh, it's Stanley, and he's never looked so scared in his entire life. I want to run to him, to scoop him up in my arms and hold him, to shield him from this monstrous figure.

The man takes a step forward, swinging his arm wide, and smacks Stanley hard in the face.

He collapses to the floor. I *watch* him collapse to the floor, and my hand flies to my mouth.

But there's nothing I can do, because this is a memory. This already happened.

Oh, Stanley—he never told me, he never could, but I suspected.

He may not have kept any physical scars, but the internal ones never truly left: his refusal to ever talk about his parents, to discuss his childhood; the way he would recoil if you caught him off guard, the way he still does now when he's in a fog of lost memory. I remember the day we brought Leah home and Stan held her in his arms. He had the strangest look in his eyes, a mixture of fierce determination and fear—fear, I now realize, that he might make the same mistakes. I wish I could have told him it wasn't possible. I wish I could have held him and told him what a wonderful father he would turn out to be.

The man is on top of him now—he's not letting up. I can see by his posture, by his stumbling feet and clumsy swings, that he is blind drunk. But Stanley is so small, and as the blows rain down on him, he gets smaller and smaller, like he's going to disappear.

I stare through the window, helplessly. I don't want to see this. I want to get out. I want to get away from here.

"Take me out," I say, praying you're listening. "Pull me back out. Please."

There is another tug, and I am gone.

You're back with me?

No, not quite. I'm back in the Merchiston Arms—like I've been pulled back halfway but not completely out and into the present. I'm back on that seat, where I was before, except now I'm breathing heavily and tears are streaming down my face. A few people around me are looking concerned, glancing in my direction, like pieces of Stanley's consciousness trying to make sense of my presence.

But not the younger me, and not Stanley.

They only have eyes for each other.

I take deep breaths to calm myself. My heart pounds so hard that my head is hurting. I look at my younger self—still so damn young and beautiful—as she writes down an address for Stanley, a place and a time. They've agreed to meet again soon and made a promise that they'll both be there. I remember this happening. I remember being there. It helps me ground myself.

Stanley gives her a wide smile and a little salute that is honestly, to this day, the cutest thing I've ever seen, and she gets up and walks out the door.

She's gone. And when she goes, Stanley lets out a huge sigh, like something gigantic has been pent up inside him and he's only just now let himself release it. His smile drops away, and I don't know what's going to happen next. I wasn't there for this bit.

But he was. And you're in his mind.

I hear you again. *You have to come out, Maggie. There is a time limit for a reason.*

But even though I hear the warning in your voice, there's something about the way his face changed a moment ago, something that tells me I need to stay. I feel you tug on me again. Stanley is getting up himself now; he's leaving the pub.

You press into my brain, telling me once again that I must go.

And what do you do?

I resist you with everything I have. I don't dare push so hard as to fall deeper into his memories again, but I do push you to the back of my thoughts. You protest, you warn, and you even threaten me. But getting to my feet, ignoring you as best I can, I follow Stanley out the door of the pub and into the cold.

Well done.

Why are you smiling? I just told you I ignored you.

Sometimes I deserve to be ignored. Where does Stanley go?

We don't walk for too long, thankfully, as I feel frozen down to my old bones. I follow close behind him, keeping enough distance that I don't disturb anything or affect the memory in any way. He is purposeful, walking swiftly, and though I'm behind him and can't see his face, his whole posture exudes a silent determination. A desire to get something done.

After about five minutes of cutting through some side streets in Vauxhall, he takes the steps down to a basement flat that I've never seen before. When he lived in London, he lived in a three-bed flatshare on the third floor. What is this place?

He unlocks the door and enters, and I follow behind, seemingly able to open it myself. I don't know if he left it unlocked or if the memory doesn't care. The hallway is dark, and Stanley doesn't bother flipping on any lights until he gets to the main sitting room. He flicks a switch, and my mouth falls open.

Why?

The room is . . . strange. Downright creepy, actually. There are no sofas, chairs, or tables—those have all been cleared out. The windows have been covered with tarpaulin. Along the back wall, there is a row of antique computer units—long desks covered with wires and turning gears, as well as some technology I do not recognize. Off to the side, there's a medical-looking chair—like a dentist's chair—with a large headset covered in wires. Scattered across the room are vials of different liquids; some look like piss and blood, but the room is odorless, almost clinical.

What, exactly, is Stanley doing?

Is this it? Does this have to do with what we're looking for?

Yes.

He goes to a computer and starts tapping away at the keys, but he doesn't sit down. He seems too on edge, like he's full of electricity. I'm standing in the corner of the room, completely unnoticed. Not that he would notice me.

Does he use any of the technology?

That computer, yes—it's plugged into the headset, which whirs and flickers on.

He puts the headset on?

Not yet. He goes to the opposite corner of the room, where there's a large wooden chest. Opening it up, he pulls out the most bizarre collection of things, things I can't even begin to fathom.

Like what? Tell me exactly. Spare no details.

Wood—small planks and offcuts of wood, and some paper and cloth. There are bottles too, glass ones, filled with what look like different soils and some herbs and plants. There are pouches, but I don't know what's in them. And there's a knife: a big, ornate ceremonial knife of some kind.

He starts laying the bottles and cloth across the room, like he's performing a ritual, and right in the center, he strikes a match and uses the paper and wood to light a fire—a *fire*—in the middle of his own damn sitting room. As it starts crackling, he throws things on it. Herbs and leaves. The room is filled with the scent of lavender and something deeper, something earthier that smells like a whole field full of wet soil.

His face is so intense I can barely look at it. There is such focus there, such concentration, that the lines on his forehead seem like cuts. He works methodically—he is writing a letter now, stopping and thinking, occasionally going back to stoke the fire.

What is he writing?

I don't know. I don't think to look. Shit. I'm too focused on this crazy black magic that my husband has decided to perform just moments after meeting me for the first time. It isn't right. There's something very, very wrong happening here.

He puts on the headset, then walks over to the fire and sits in front of it with his legs crossed. He's taken off his shirt, and his skin shimmers in the light of the flames. He doesn't do anything for a moment—just closes his eyes and breathes. For some reason, I feel compelled to get close to him, to take a step or two closer and kneel down until my face is just a yard or so away from his. My back strains with the effort of getting down to his level.

The lights on the headset flicker again, and the contraption whirs.

His eyes flick open, and he's looking directly at me.

"I know," he says to me. But how can he be speaking to me? I'm not there. "Forgive me."

Lifting the knife to his chest, he slices a huge gash right across his skin; blood spurts out onto the floor, into the fire, onto me.

Everything goes black.

I jerk awake in the bath next to Stanley, in the present day, at the Institute. Frantically, I pull the helmet off my head and chuck it to one side. You are standing over me, your face severe. Tendrils of smoke are rising from your cigarette.

"What the fuck was that?" I say. Stanley is in the chair beside me, headset still on, his eyes closed. A little bit of dribble is coming out of his mouth. "What the hell just happened?"

"You should have come out when I told you to."

"That's not good enough," I snap, straightening up. I pull myself out of the bath, the liquid so viscous it barely leaves me wet. "I deserve an explanation as to what in the hell that—"

Stanley gives a small moan, and I turn to him, anxious. I lean forward to wipe the spittle from his cheek, and he opens his eyes. All I can see in them is that little boy, full of fear, and the smack of a fist as he topples to the floor. I throw my arms around my husband, clinging to him tightly.

"Oh, Stan," I say. "I love you. And I will always be here for you. I will never abandon you."

He looks up at me strangely, like he's remembered something but doesn't quite know what. He takes my hand into his and clutches it.

"Maggie," he says. "It's funny. Sometimes I feel like I've known you my entire life."

My breath catches in my throat, because he has *remembered*—some part of him has remembered me, and the pub, and the day we first met, and what he said. And I try something that I haven't tried in a very long time.

I say, "I have forgot why I did call thee back."

Why?

It's from *Romeo and Juliet*. It's his favorite exchange, from the balcony scene. We used to recite it to each other. Before he forgot it. Before he forgot me.

"Let me stand here till thou remember it," he says, and my heart almost leaps out of my chest. I take a deep breath.

"I shall forget," I say, looking into his eyes, "to have thee still stand there, remembering how I love thy company."

"And I'll still stay," he replies, "to have thee still forget, forgetting any other home but this."

I put my other hand around his and squeeze it as tightly as I can. Tears are streaming down my cheeks. And I become certain, absolutely certain, that if I can get him to remember that, then I can get him to remember everything.

I look up at you, and I ask, "What do we do next?"

8 | Stanley
1957

HOLDING A HALF-EMPTY BOTTLE OF GIN THAT HE HAD SWIPED FROM THE
back of his flatmate's cupboard, Stanley sat on the roof of an old terraced
house in Brixton and watched the fireworks off in the distance. The council had put them on over Brockwell Park to celebrate the turn of the year,
and from the top of their subdivided bedsit, you could just about see them.
People whooped and hollered in the streets below; a group of screaming
women danced in the road; a bottle of bubbly popped. All across the world,
people welcomed in the New Year as a time of new beginnings, of fresh
starts, just as they looked back on the year behind them and counted their
successes. Humanity as a whole was taking stock of where it was, where
it had been, and where it wanted to go.

Stanley took a swig of his gin and coughed.

He wanted to laugh, but it was difficult to. He knew that if he tried, it
would come out sounding harsh and grating, like metal cogs turning. But
what else could he do? If he couldn't laugh at what his life had become, he
might be forced to take it seriously.

He took another swig.

Coughing again, he spat the spirit out onto the ground. *Gin is fucking
disgusting neat*, he thought.

After a while, the fireworks started to annoy him. They went on and on, as if they were trying to make some kind of a point. He wondered if anyone else he knew was watching them, and where they were.

He hadn't been in touch with any Whelton boys for some time now. He'd exchanged a few letters with Hugo, who was still there, but before long, Hugo had started reminiscing about the old club and the professor and how different it was with him gone, and Stanley had not been able to reply.

He put his hands in his pockets and felt the crumpled-up piece of paper. Taking it out, he smoothed it and turned it over in his hands.

Another letter, from a different epistler.

Hey, mate. I know you don't really reply to letters anymore, but I'm thinking of you. Are you still in London? Would be nice to catch up if you are. R.

He stared at it for half a minute, then crumpled it back up and shoved it into his pocket.

Stanley hadn't seen Raph since Waldman's funeral a year and a half ago. Since the argument. Since he'd punched Jacques in the face during the service.

He clenched his fingers together and released them, trying to get the chill out. What he wouldn't do for a pair of gloves right now. He had been hoping the gin would do the trick.

Sighing, he leaned back, trying to remember what had set it all off. Something about not letting Jacques sully Waldman's memory. It seemed so long ago now. The reasons had all faded away, but the feeling was still there. The distance had grown with each successive month until it stood like an ocean between them: of unspoken bitterness, of self-justification. The longer time goes on, the more people remember what they want to remember—the version that helps confirm the feelings they still feel. Stanley knew this, but somehow it didn't help. He lifted the bottle to his mouth and let the gin burn its way down his throat.

After all, what had *he* done to honor Waldman's memory?

For a year and a half, he had toiled away, trying to recreate what Waldman had destroyed. For all Stanley had pushed to hone his own memory, he'd never felt that he needed to recall the exact numbers and processes, the minutiae of error margins and controls. He'd had Waldman for that, and they'd taken notes, all of which were lost. Recreating their breakthroughs on his own felt like trying to do it with both hands tied behind his back.

Still, he toiled. He worked dead-end jobs. He shined shoes at the railway station; he advertised in the streets for various companies; he cleaned toilets. He knew he could have gotten something more stable, more high-paying, but every time he tried to think about applying for something, a cloud settled over him. A voice whispering that he didn't deserve stability, that he wasn't cut out for success.

No—all his mental energy went into recreating Waldman's work. He procured old lab equipment, broken and dilapidated, from junk sales and stole the rest from schools. He bought cheap animals from pet stores: rats and mice to do tests on. When he found he couldn't stomach that anymore, he experimented on himself.

He took another swig. A final dribble of gin emptied itself onto his cracked lips. He lugged himself up, trudged down the fire escape stairs, climbed through the window to the main living area that he never spent any time in, and went over to the door to his room.

There were three locks on it; he opened each one methodically. His flatmate had never asked why he locked his door so judiciously, and this was part of what Stanley liked about him. He understood that Stanley wanted to be left alone.

The room was a mess of paper and tangled wires. His bed—a small single mattress in the corner—was covered with half-opened books, a mishmash of bookmarks and scrap paper sticking out of them. In the center of the room was a chair. It was a dentist's chair, originally, one that he'd picked up from an old skip. He'd stripped it down to just the metal, and wires ran through and around it. Near the headrest was a makeshift switching circuit connected to a power supply and a couple of vacuum tubes.

It no longer worked. It had broken yesterday. He'd only just managed to fix it a month before, with the very last of his money and some parts he'd stolen from a shop. He rubbed the old gash on his thigh, scarred over now, that he'd gotten while climbing a spiked fence in his frenzied flight from the shop owners.

There was nothing now. That was it—all his time, all his effort, all his *money*, had resulted in this: a stupid busted piece of junk.

None of it had worked. He couldn't remember the parameters, the data the professor and he had painstakingly calculated. He was exactly where he was after Waldman's funeral: alone, useless, and empty. He needed money, but more than that, he needed connections; he needed influence. He needed everything that a man of his background—a man of *cheap stock*—was not allowed.

He clenched his hand around the empty bottle. Through a gaze that was now swimming a little unpleasantly, he looked at the letter again.

Are you still in London?

Raph was the last shot—the final option to turn to, as much as he didn't want to do it. For four years, Stanley had held tight to the professor's secret mission, not told a soul. And though Waldman was dead now, sharing it with others felt like a betrayal of his memory. An abandonment.

Only, he wasn't the one doing the abandoning. The professor had chosen to take his own life, without any explanation beyond an ominous note. Waldman had chosen to leave Stanley behind with nothing. Was Stanley not the one who had been betrayed?

Most of all, he didn't want to admit that he had failed. He knew Raph would want to help him—would take pity on the poor working-class boy and use some part of his substantial fortune to make it right. It would be an easy sell: look sufficiently desperate and dismal, play into Raph's charity. But he loathed debasing himself like that—it was a confirmation of everything everyone had told him his entire life. That he was worthless. That because he was from the wrong background, there was something broken inside of him, something missing, and so he would never achieve anything on his own.

Stanley expelled a frustrated shout, smashing the empty gin bottle against the broken machinery's useless metal frame. Glass scattered across the floor. Gritting his teeth, he picked up a pen to write a letter back.

THE LAZARUS BUILDING LOOKED OUT OF PLACE. AFTER THE BLITZ AND THE firestorm of 1940, the work that went into rebuilding the city had been determined to look to the future. As the brick buildings were rebuilt, they were rebuilt taller and more imposing—symbols of the city's central power-house.

Nestled between all of this was a comparatively short building that defied the forward-looking tendencies of London's postwar architects. Built in 1903 in honor of Sir Athelney Lazarus, the building oozed the quiet sophistication of empire. Even when it was built, it felt anachronistic—designed to look more like the Georgian architecture of the eighteenth century than that of the modern age. Instead of looking forward, it looked back: to a time when hierarchy was explicit and unquestioned, and when the quality of your character was significantly less important than the class and circumstances of your birth.

When Henry Lazarus caused a stir in the '30s by marrying a woman who lived in Chinatown, that union meant Raph, and granted him every-thing it brought with it. Together, Raph's parents had been an intellectual power couple, and despite being lambasted as "Henry's Chinese bride" in the media, Athena Lazarus went on to solidify her legacy as one of the doyennes of 1930s industry, growing the family name into a truly interna-tional brand. Or at least that's how Raph always told it. The papers were never quite as kind. Still, after Henry and Athena died in a car crash when Raph was eleven, the entire empire was left to their only child.

Stanley didn't go into the building. Looking up at it from the street below, he wasn't sure that he would have been allowed in, even with his friend's name on the door. They were meeting in a pub nearby. Stanley had suggested going for a drink when they spoke on the phone, and Raph said something close to work would be easiest, particularly so early in the day.

Stanley's clothes had not been washed in two weeks, and his beard had grown increasingly straggly. He'd thought about shaving but decided that would run counter to the impression he was hoping to leave. He ran his fingers through his hair, trying not to feel a little sick. The heft of the documents and notes in his shoulder bag weighed heavy on him. He really didn't want to be doing this.

Pushing through the doors of the Red Lion, he felt a warm draft of air envelop him; with it came the comforting chatter of people and clinking of glasses. There was something eternally reassuring about a pub. When the project became too much and he needed an escape, he scrounged up just enough money to spend on a pint so that he could sit in the corner of a good pub and read a book.

"Stan!"

Raph waved at him from a table in the corner, a huge smile on his face. He was wearing a blue suit, perfectly tailored. As Stanley approached, he noticed the little things. Patek Philippe watch. Designer shoes. Hell, his tie probably cost more than everything Stanley owned put together.

Stanley placed a well-practiced smile on his face: just the right mix of cheery and downtrodden. This was, after all, why he was here.

Raph got up and threw his arms round Stanley in a big bear hug. Stanley felt the warmth of Raph's breath against his neck, and for a glimmer of a moment, Stanley flashed back: late evenings in the graveyard, huddled close for heat; sitting side by side in the library, ignoring classwork to memorize texts by Ovid and Seneca for Waldman.

A different life, blurry in his memories—refracted, like looking through a thick pane of glass.

Raph released him.

"How have you been?" Raph asked, by instinct more than anything.

Stanley caught Raph's eyes glance furtively down at him, then quickly back up to his face. His smile faltered for a moment, wondering if he had asked the wrong question. "I mean . . . it's been a long time, huh?"

"Yeah," Stanley said. "I've been better. Come on, let's sit."

They shuffled into their seats.

"Do you want a drink?" Raph said, eyeing up the bar. "Don't worry—it's on me."

"I wasn't worried."

"No, of course." He tilted his head downward, apologetically. "I didn't mean to say that you . . . It's just—"

Stanley laughed. For all his plan coming in, he'd forgotten just how awkward Raph could be. "It's fine, Raph. I'd love a drink. Whatever you're having. Stop being ridiculous."

Raph smiled. He seemed pleased his offer was being accepted. Stanley sat down and waited for him to bring back beers.

"So how have you been?" Stanley asked as Raph settled back in. "It seems like you've done pretty well for yourself."

Raph looked around the room a little sheepishly, as if embarrassed. He touched the watch on his wrist. "Well, not exactly *my* successes, you know. It's not exactly what I've dreamed of, but . . . well, I don't know. You know how it is."

Stanley took a sip of beer. "I really don't."

"Okay, okay." He put his hand up in concession. "Of course not. It's just—when I left school, they pretty much had this office job made out for me. With the trust fund coming through, I didn't really need the money, but I couldn't exactly say no. It's my parents' legacy. But it's all finances and loans and crunching numbers. Nightmare stuff."

"Sounds nice."

"Right? I've been trying to do some good, though. I've been using the little influence I have to refocus some of the company's trajectory—some charity work, homeless shelters and the like. Think Mum would have liked that."

"That's good, Raph." Stanley forced a smile onto his face. He didn't want to press the point too early, but Raph was doing all the work for him. "That's admirable."

"Thanks."

They fell silent. The unasked follow-up question lingered in the air: *And you, Stan, what have you been up to?* But Raph wouldn't want to seem like he was prying. Hearing about Stanley's life would be uncomfortable, depressing. He would avoid it if he could.

Stanley let the awkwardness hang for a few more seconds than was necessary so that any sentence—any request—would be a welcome reprieve. He took another sip of his beer.

"Look, Raph. I'm going to be honest with you. I need your help."

"Sure," he responded, a little too quickly. "You mentioned it on the phone. Anything for an old friend."

Stanley leaned forward. "Do you remember what I told you after the professor died? That we'd been working on something, on an idea—well, a problem, really."

Raph nodded. "You never spoke much about it. And after everything that happened at the funeral, we just never . . ." He trailed off, looking out the window.

Stanley took a deep breath. It felt surreal to be speaking it aloud. It felt wrong. "It's big. Or, potentially big. Before he died, the professor made a breakthrough. I've been trying to re-create it, but I . . . I need more resources. I need money, Raph. Lots of it if I'm going to make any headway. Probably more than even a good job would get me. You're the only one who can help. You're the only one who would understand."

"How much?"

"Honestly? I'll need to build a whole lab. I'm talking in the region of fifty to even a hundred thousand pounds."

Raph blinked. "Seriously?"

"I'm sorry, Raph, but . . . yes."

Raph nodded. He looked at his watch again.

Stanley caught the look in his eyes, the one that said: *He's crazy. He's obsessed with a man who died almost two years ago. He doesn't need money;*

he needs help. "Okay, fine. I'm willing to hear you out. I am. I want to hear about this problem, and I'm willing to . . . to look into this, but . . ."

"But what?"

"I have a condition—before you tell me all about this. I want Jacques to be involved too."

Stanley's face darkened. He leaned forward, placing his elbows on his knees. "Why?"

"Look—I know, okay? I get it. But if this goes all the way back to Waldman, then I think we both have a right to know. I want to know what you and Waldman were doing more than anything, but Jacques was there with us from the start, and . . . well, surely three minds will be better than two."

Stanley didn't speak. An awkward beat of silence passed between them.

"Look," Raph continued. "He's a friend—he's *our* friend—regardless of what has happened in the past. He deserves to be in on this. That's my offer. It's either me and Jacques or no one."

"I don't even know where he is."

"I do. He actually replies to my letters. He's working at some big research and development firm in the city—something to do with computers and medical research, I think. I can call him and—"

"No."

"Stan." Raph leaned in, looking him in the eyes. "The thing is, I've been worried about you. Thinking about how things were back in the day. I miss it, you know? I sit in my fancy office staring at my papers, and I . . . When you wrote to me saying you were still in London, I got excited. I wanted to get the old team back together."

Stanley's hand gripped his glass. "What did you do?"

"I told him to come twenty minutes late so I'd have a chance to talk to you first."

"You didn't."

Raph glanced up, over Stanley's shoulder and to the door. Stanley turned in time to see Jacques—dressed in American jeans and a turtleneck sweater, the ultimate in rich-casual wear—walk past the bar and slap him hard on the back. He jerked forward.

"Hello, losers. Long time, no see. How are my two favorite swots?" Falling onto the sofa next to Raph, Jacques pulled up a chair and put his feet on it, crossing his legs. "Whose round is it?"

Stanley stared at him, his mind whirring. This wasn't part of the plan. This wasn't meant to happen.

Raph stood up. "I'll get you a beer."

He left Stanley and Jacques alone at the table, and for a long moment, neither of them spoke.

"What are you doing here?" Stanley asked, his voice level.

Jacques shrugged. "Raph called me. I actually respond to his calls, you know?"

Stanley didn't reply. He looked downward and took a sip of his beer. For all their good times together, he couldn't get their last encounter out of his head.

"Look," Jacques said. "What happened *happened*, okay? I'm not proud of it. And I'm not going to sit here and pretend we're going to be best friends. But Raph is clearly desperate that we all come to some kind of peaceful reunion and bury the hatchet, so at the very least, let's put on a decent pretense, shall we?"

"Whatever you say."

"Good!" He pulled his legs in and sat up—always moving, always jittering, like he was filled with too much energy and it was bursting out the seams. "How about a game, then? I'll start. Pawn to queen's knight four."

"Knight four?" Stanley raised his eyebrows. "You've finally got more creative with your openings."

He grinned. "I've got better."

Stanley let out a little grunt. "We'll see. Pawn to king four."

"Okay, okay. Before we start getting all competitive"—Raph cut in, sitting down with Jacques's beer—"we've got some things to talk about."

He spoke with mock teacherlike sternness, but he had a big smile on his face.

"Yes," Jacques added. "Why *has* the old boy come out of hiding?"

"He's got a problem he needs some help on."

"Raph," Stanley said, "I said no."

"Yes, Stan. You came to me. I'm interested. But I'm not just going to throw money at you on a vague promise and tell you to go away. This . . . this is a great opportunity, don't you see? The three of us coming back together to work on Waldman's final problem. There's poetry in that. Symmetry."

It's not the professor's problem anymore, Stanley thought. *It's mine.*

He didn't say anything. The thought of revealing the secret to Raph was bad enough, but to Jacques as well?

"Whatever it is, it's important to you, and it was important to Waldman, so it's important to us. All *three* of us."

Jacques didn't say a word. He eyed Stanley carefully from the other side of the table.

Stanley looked down at his hands, which were still a little grubby from the roof. He didn't like to shower too often, because it would run up the heating bill. Even in the depths of winter, it was easier to just wrap himself in blankets and wait out the cold. Sighing, he shook his head.

He thought about everything that he had put into this. From the time when Waldman first showed Stanley the preserved brain—or, rather, *brains*—stowed in his office, all the way through their thought experiments and, later, real experiments. He thought about the work they had done together in the dead of night, when everyone else had gone to bed, about the secrets he had promised to keep.

He thought about his broken machinery. His dead ends. His failures.

He thought about Waldman's final message—the warning he had left behind.

IT HUNGERS.

This was it. The end of the road. Either he left here with Raph's money or he didn't.

"Fine. But it'll take some explaining."

Jacques grinned, leaning back and returning his feet to the chair. "We'll try to follow as best we can. Pawn to queen's bishop four."

Stanley nodded. "Bishop takes knight five. Right. Okay. Yes. This is . . . I feel like I need to give some background before we get to the main part, though. Bits and pieces of it you would have heard before from the professor, back in the day, but it's all linked: our memory exercises, our tests and competitions. It all comes together. You have to understand—we weren't just his pupils; we were his test subjects."

Raph frowned. "What do you mean?"

"Let's take a second to think about the history of memory. Memorizing huge amounts isn't a new thing. In fact, in classical times, it was basically the main indicator of intelligence. In a world with almost no books, memory was the benchmark by which to understand the world. People with huge memories were lauded, respected. Cyrus the Great could give the names of all the soldiers in his army. Lucius Scipio knew the name of every Roman citizen. Look even to Christianity: the single most common theme in the lives of the saints—besides their wondrous altruism—is often superhuman memory."

"Sure," Jacques said, waving his hand, "we've heard all this before. Great memories represented the internalization of a universe of external knowledge—the greatest possible expression of intelligence. What's the point?"

"The point is the *why*," Stanley said. His eyes were locked on Jacques now. "*Why* is this? Why was it deemed so important? Because memory is the key to creativity and therefore growth and progress, right?"

Raph frowned, sipping his beer. "What do you mean?"

"Okay"—Stanley was gesticulating, animated—"so creativity, whether in arts or sciences, can be defined as the ability to form connections between ideas and images—to create something *new* from the old, whether a building or a scientific hypothesis or a novel. If the core of creativity is linking disparate facts, then the more you have in your brain, the better you are at coming up with new ideas. This can't happen in the same way with externalized ideas, or at least not as intuitively. There is a reason why the classical goddess of memory—Mnemosyne—was the mother of the Muses. Having an expansive memory is the essence of creativity, and creativity is the cornerstone of all human progress."

"That seems hyperbolic," Raph replied. He smiled as he eased into the discussion. "You know—if I'm being honest."

"Not at all," Jacques said, leaning in. "Knight to queen's bishop three. Think about it: In terms of our physiology, we are the exact same humans as the cavemen who painted horse and bison in the Lascaux caves. Our brains are no bigger, no more complex than theirs were. If a kid were snapped out of their time at childbirth and given to adoptive parents in twentieth-century London, they'd grow up indistinguishable. Stan's got a point—all that differentiates us from them is our collective memories."

"And yet"—Stanley raised his finger up—"our culture now is built entirely on the false gods of externalized memory. People need to remember less and less with every passing day. But imagine if all the ink from all the books, and recorded pieces of data, suddenly disappeared tomorrow. Our entire culture would collapse. We would be plunged back into pictographs and myths told around fires. Where are the expansive memories of our statesmen and rhetoricians—people like Pliny and Lucius Scipio? *Gone.* But why?"

Jacques shrugged. "We've got TV now. Radio. New technologies. We just don't need them anymore. Don't forget your move."

"An easy answer," Stanley said. Jacques rolled his eyes. "And pawn to queen four. The real question is this: Did discovering these technologies cause us to be worse at remembering, or did our failing memories force us to create them out of necessity? Are our memories getting worse?"

Raph leaned back into his seat. "It's a quantity of information issue, isn't it? The amount of information, discoveries, knowledge, the sheer number of people during the classical eras was far less than now. There's just too much to keep in any one brain these days."

"That's the traditional thinking. Have you read *Hereditary Genius*?"

"By Galton?" Raph asked. "Years ago, I think."

"Galton argued that a person could only improve at physical and mental activities up until he reached a certain point, after which 'he cannot by any education or exertion overpass.' We all experienced it in Waldman's work with us—a plateau. A point beyond which, no matter how much we tried, it was difficult to remember anything more. But what if that isn't true?"

"What do you mean?" Raph asked, rapt.

"Okay, look. I want to conduct a brief experiment." Stanley rifled through his bag, pulling out an old folder filled to the brim with bundles of paper. "There will be a series of pictures on photographs, and I'm going to show them to you very quickly—less than a second each. I want you to try and remember as many of them as you can."

Jacques sighed. "We did enough of these with Waldman, Stan. What's your point—that you can remember more than us? I've not practiced these techniques in years."

"Exactly," Stanley replied. "Just bear with me. Don't bother with any of the classic techniques—the memory palace, the personification, the narratives. Just look and try to commit to memory."

Jacques put his feet on the floor, leaning in to look intently at the table where Stanley was about to lay the photos. Stanley smiled. If there was one thing that would draw Jacques in, it was his sense of competition. And Stanley was increasingly realizing that if he wanted Raph's money, he wouldn't just have to convince Raph; he'd have to convince them both.

He placed the photos down extremely quickly, barely leaving a second between: Marilyn Monroe pressing down her windswept skirt; a pair of red baby shoes; Winston Churchill giving a speech; a large chunk of blue cheese; the cover of Heidegger's *Being and Time*. Almost a hundred such random images were placed down, and both Raph and Jacques watched them closely. After the last image—a cat wearing glasses—Stanley bundled them up and put them back in the folder.

Even as they did this exercise, Jacques continued to trade moves, his eyes locked on the pictures. It was uncomfortable, and Stanley had to admit that Jacques had gotten more than a little bit better.

"Now," Stanley said, looking at the clock on the wall, "we wait. Not long.

Just enough for the curve of forgetting to set in. Thirty minutes should do it."

Jacques shook his head. "Of course. God—it feels like I'm back in Waldman's classroom again." Stanley glanced at Raph, who tried and failed to suppress a little smile. "I'm going outside for a smoke. I like the fresh air."

As they waited for Jacques, Stanley and Raph chatted. In fits and starts at first, then more smoothly, until soon they were reminiscing like they used to, telling old stories from the Whelton days and laughing. Initially, Stanley played along. He recognized that this was the sell for Raph: escaping the present and disappearing back into the past. This was how he would secure the money he needed. So he played into the role—he recalled old memories of them running through the graveyards, of them impersonating and mocking teachers, of them staying up late sharing books they'd read. But as time passed, he found that the smile on his face wasn't plastered there anymore. His laughter was genuine. It was the most human that Stanley had felt in a long time.

With this came a wave of guilt. Here he was, extorting his oldest friend, and for what? For a cause that the professor himself had given up on? Was it worth it?

Stanley expelled the thought from his mind. No—he was here for a reason. Continue the experiment. Find out what Waldman had hidden. Find out what he died for. If he let go of that, he'd have nothing left.

Jacques came in from the cold, stinking of stale cigarettes.

"All right, you two lovebirds? Having fun flirting without me?"

"Oh, for once in your life, don't be a dick, Jacques," Raph cut back.

Stanley grinned. "Don't think he knows how. Might as well tell a fish not to swim."

"Yeah, yeah, very funny," Jacques muttered as he plopped himself back down. "We've still got fifteen minutes, right? You going to play or what? Pawn to queen three."

Stanley took another sip of his beer. "Now *that* is a weird move. Okay—pawn to king's bishop four."

"Pawn takes pawn."

"Knight takes."

"Knight. Queen's bishop three."

The game continued, back and forth, with Raph commentating, re-marking on clever moves here and there. Stanley found Jacques's playing to be unpredictable, surprising. His middle game was phenomenal—entangling Stanley's pieces in elaborate complexities. Even so, Stanley remained calm, and by the time fifteen minutes had passed, they were down to a few final pieces, shifting into the endgame.

And then Stanley saw it: a clear line. The last few moves that would take his rook and surround Jacques's king. A clear path to victory while Jacques was too focused on promoting his pawns. The endgame had always been his weak point.

He hesitated. Just as he could see the next few moves of the game, he could see the moves after it ended. Jacques's sullen expression, his annoyance at having lost to Stanley again. He'd make a fuss, maybe even walk out. And that would be it. Without him, Raph wouldn't buy in. Not completely.

"That's enough," Stanley said. "That'll do for time."

"Oh, sure," Jacques said. "Just as I'm about to win. Not a coincidence at all."

Stanley smirked. "We'll come back to it after, I promise."

"No." Jacques's voice was hard, his eyes suddenly fierce. "We finish this now."

Stanley sighed. "Fine. Bishop to king's bishop four."

"Rook to queen five."

"Bishop takes rook."

"Ha!" Jacques almost leaped out of his seat. "Pawn to final rank and promote to queen. Immediate check. Mate in three."

Stanley forced a look of shock onto his face. "Oh, yes—you're right. Checkmate. Nice. I actually didn't see that one coming."

Jacques settled back down into his seat, his face a painting of smugness.

"Told you I got better. Right—let's see what this experiment is all about, then. The curve of forgetting will have set in properly by now. Let's get on with it."

Stanley nodded. The curve of forgetting was the classic graphical representation of how memories gradually decay. At the turn of the twentieth century, Hermann Ebbinghaus set out to quantify this inevitable process in time, demonstrating that for any detailed and rote-learned facts, if they were not revisited, approximately half would be forgotten within the first hour. After the first day, another 10 percent, and after the next month, another 14 percent. Once that span of time had passed, whatever was left would—more or less—remain in our memories for good. But it was those first few moments: They were the crucial minutes in which most of the memories disappeared.

Everything Waldman had taught them—the memory palace, the imagery techniques, the associations—had been designed to combat the curve.

"Have you ever wondered why?" Stanley asked, opening the folder back up. "Why does the brain remove these memories so quickly? What's the point?"

"It's a capacity thing. So your brain doesn't retain too much useless information that it doesn't need."

"Yes. That's what I once thought too. So, how many can you remember?"

Jacques and Raph both tried their best, but it had been years since they'd trained their memories in this way. Raph managed ten images. Jacques achieved an impressive seventeen but was still miles away from the full total.

Stanley shuffled the papers and opened another folder. "Now I'm going to show you two images. One of them was in the hundred I showed you; the other wasn't. I want you to tell me which is which."

The first slide showed Churchill on the left and a picture of a baby goat on the right. They both immediately identified the correct image. Then the next, and the next. Again and again, both Raph and Jacques could pick out with perfect accuracy which image had been in the selection.

"It's a little trick Waldman and I developed. The truth is, I could do this with ten thousand images and you'd get them right. The point is, it's not a capacity issue. Your brain hasn't forgotten which pictures it saw; it just isn't letting you access them. This is like a loophole—a little work-around to trick your brain into letting you remember them."

Raph shook his head. "I don't understand."

"What got us started was thinking about savants. There are reports of them throughout history—individuals with exceptional, almost infinite memories because their brains are wired differently. The professor believed that they weren't anomalies; rather, they were able to access parts of the brain that have been locked away."

Jacques stood up then. He paced around the table, his eyes intent on Stanley. He was still riding off his victory, energy surging through him. "What do you mean 'locked away'?"

"Why does the curve of forgetting exist, Jacques? Why do we forget things? Where do those memories go? In the context of this last experiment, or of savants, the capacity idea makes no sense at all. It only seems like it makes sense because we're naturally thinking about a brain like a filing cabinet, or like filling up a bucket. But it isn't. The metaphor constricts us. It was the professor's belief, and it's my belief, that there is no plateau. That there is no reason why we should not be able to remember everything we've ever encountered perfectly."

"So why can't we?"

"That's the big question. Maybe there's some part of our brains that is tucked away, under lock and key. Or maybe"—Stanley took a deep breath, letting a beat settle—"maybe it isn't that we are unable to remember; it's that something is *causing us to forget*. All of us. All people. If we can identify it, maybe we can fix it. The professor and I were working on something, the seed of an idea, and it was working. Our memories, they . . . We were *so* close before he . . ." Stanley trailed off. Jacques and Raph were silent. Waiting. Stanley put his hand to his temple, shaking his head. He hadn't mentioned the professor's mysterious final words, but they still rang clear in his head. *It hungers. An immortal bane, dread, and dire, and fierce.* He still had no idea what they meant.

"I believe he'd done it," Stanley said quietly. "*He* believed he had, or so he told me—broken through the plateau. Achieved *perfect* recall. But when he died, he took it all with him. All the details in his head. I've been trying to recapture it since then, but I . . . need more data. I'm not as clever as he was. I need equipment, and a lab, and money. I need help. But I *am* close. Just think about what we discussed earlier, what Waldman taught us— about creativity, about progress. If we can unlock perfect memory, we will unlock a whole new era of humanity. A new Renaissance but ten times larger. It will be the biggest discovery in the history of the human race."

"And we'll be at the forefront of it," Jacques whispered. "In charge of it all."

"Together," Raph said.

Stanley closed his eyes and nodded. "Yes. Together."

Jacques turned and walked back to his seat. He sat down, put his feet up on the table again, and gave Stanley a giant grin. "Well, when you put it like that, how can I say no?"

9

TRANSCRIPT NO. 273: Margaret Webb
DATE STAMP: 11 AUG. 2021
6 Hours, 52 Minutes, and 34 Seconds Until Dissolution

You tell me I need to get my brain scanned. You say it matter-of-factly, like it's the most normal thing in the world. Like we're getting tea.

"Why?" I ask.

"That was just a calibration test," you say. "To check that you were going to be compatible. It was a success, which is good. But if we want to go deeper, we need to get some clearer points of parity to ensure fidelity."

"I don't know what any of that means."

"You will," you say to me, and now I'm angry.

Why? Did something happen in the room?

I'm not angry in my memory, Hassan. I'm angry now, here, because I've experienced this conversation—this same back-and-forth—already today, except now I'm seeing it from the outside. It's a pattern: of you not telling me things, of you withholding information from me like I'm an idiot, of you promising me it'll become clear later. Except it's not clear, and I've had enough of being your puppet.

We need to make sure Stanley is safe.

So you keep saying, and saying, until it gets me scared enough to listen to you. But I don't know what it actually means. So how about this? Until you answer some of my questions, I'm not doing a fucking thing. It's not that I don't trust you. It's . . . Actually, no. It is. I don't trust you.

What can I do to alleviate your concerns?

Why am I only remembering these events chronologically? I'm trying to make myself remember what happened just before I got here, but I can't. I'm trying to picture what happened a day or two after diving into Stanley's mind, after the Institute, but I can't. It's not there. There's only the memory you *want* me to talk about, arriving in my mind in order as I remember it. That's not how memory works.

Memory is more complicated than it might first appear.

Don't be facetious. Answer the question.

You are experiencing what we call "horometrical memory." It's an induced state to help the consciousness focus on a specific memory without distractions. It forces the brain to consider memories sequentially from a specific starting point, like a narrative, and allows the individual to be fully immersed in that memory. It's immensely helpful for heightening focus and remembering specific details.

Why is it happening to me?

The pill I gave you a few hours ago.

> You told me that would help me focus. You didn't say that would rewire the way my brain worked!

We are in a hurry. I was unspecific about the details.

> Is it . . . is it like the memory spade?

It's based upon a similar concept, yes, but the outcome is different. It holds a different purpose. The Institute's work on memory has produced many different technologies, and they are used for different things. And it is not just us. There is also, for example, the technology that Sunrise developed to erase Stanley's memories, which you mistook for Alzheimer's.

> Oh God. And this pill—will it wear off?

Yes. It will stop working when all this comes to an end.

> And what about Stanley now? You keep saying he's in danger, that we need to find him. What does that mean? Where is he?

He's gone, Maggie. He has disappeared. He did something—we don't know quite what yet—and he disappeared. This is the moment we're searching for. What he did. All I know is that he is not safe. None of us are until we find him. We're trying to get him back, but only you can do that.

> When did he disappear?

That is a difficult question to answer. Let me level with you, Maggie. This is unusual. I am aware of that. Many things I have not explained to you, but that is because they won't make sense until some of your memories return. You will not have context for them. If you want answers, then keep telling me what happened in as much detail as you can. Your answers will come, I promise. Then you will be free to go. And, if we are lucky, you will be with Stanley again. But time is running out, and if we do not find the specific moment soon, all of this will be rendered pointless. All will be lost. We must continue.

Fine. Okay. I can accept that. But no more treating me like an idiot, please. This is difficult enough as it is.

I promise you, Maggie, that I do not think you are an idiot. Think back now. We are at the Institute. What comes next?

I'm holding Stanley's hand. I helped him out of the strange chair and into a row of more normal ones at the back of the room, like in a doctor's waiting room. He is out of it now: He seems confused about where he is and a little dazed. He gets these moments from time to time. I squeeze his hand a little and think about how frail it is in my own—the bones feel smaller, like those of a bird, like they would snap if you pressed too hard.

I don't like putting him through this. It's cruel.

"We have to move him to another part of the facility," you say. "For the scan. After that, we can give you more data about your next memory dive." You're standing over us like a monolith, quietly watching. It's strange, how you can have such a physical presence and yet sometimes I forget you are there.

"Give us a moment," I say.

You click impatiently. It's not a sound I've heard from you before, and it rankles me. "We really must—"

"Just give us a damn moment, will you!"

You take a step back. Not in shock. No—I can't imagine you've ever experienced shock in your life. It's a calculated move to give me space, to show me you're acquiescing.

"I'll be outside this door when you are ready."

I turn to Stanley, turning my back to you. I don't hear you leave the room, but when I look back over my shoulder, you're gone.

"How are you doing, Stan?" I ask. He's staring off into the middle distance. I'm not expecting a reply, but I know he likes to hear my voice. The shadow of a smile appears on his face. Not on his lips—not so bold as that—but on the sides, in the twitch of the muscles in his cheeks and in the slight curve of the lines around his eyes. I sigh and settle down next to him, pulling his hand close to my chest.

"This really is the strangest thing."

"Mmmm," he says, as if he's thinking long and hard about it, but his brain could be anywhere.

You know that classic question "If a genie gave you one wish, what would it be?" If you'd asked me six months ago, it would have been to peek inside his head, just for a minute. Just to see where he goes when he leaves me.

Now that I've done it, I find I want more. I need more. Despite the shock and horror, the thrill of the experience is still bubbling in my veins. I have not told you about the strange ritual yet, the one that I saw him perform.

Why not?

I figure it's better if I have some secrets too. It's clear that you don't know exactly what I saw in there—just some broad strokes, maybe, based on my heart rate and my emotional reactions. But I still need your help. It's clear that Stanley *remembered* after I last went in, that it helped bring back memories I had thought were long gone from his brain. They were there, hidden away. I search his face.

Why can't you access them, Stan? I think. *What's stopping you?*

I will do anything to find out. Put myself through anything.

He flinches a little, and I realize I'm squeezing his hand too tightly. I release, and as I do, I understand the danger in what I've just thought.

It was something my mother used to say to me when I was a young girl. *I would put myself through anything for you.* It was meant as an expression of care, but instead it always sounded like a burden, a cross to carry. Instead of love, I felt smothered—by her *need* to be there, to fight my battles, to make my choices for me. In those moments, I wanted to scream *But I don't want you to!* I couldn't, though. So I began hiding things from her instead. Began running away, even if just in my head.

So, yes, although I'd be willing to walk through fire to get my Stanley back, I have no right to expect the same from him.

I lean in close to him. "I'm not going to let anyone harm you, Stan," I whisper. "Including me. I want to promise that to you now. I want to say it out loud, not just in my head, because then it's real and I have to stick to it. However far this goes, whatever I am promised, I'm not going to let anyone harm you. Okay?"

He sniffs. "Yes, well, that all sounds all right to me. Sure."

I laugh. He has these bizarrely lucid moments, but they are just semantic. Just fragments of conversation. I don't for a second think he knows what he's agreeing to, but it offers me an odd kind of comfort. "Well, good," I say. "Wouldn't want you to be concerned."

"Oh, you know me," he replies with a grin. "Ready for anything."

I blink back the wetness in my eyes and stand up, dabbing them with a handkerchief. Leaning forward, I clean up some of the spit around the outside of his mouth and tidy up his hair a little.

"Do you think you can make it into your chair?"

"Well, I'll give it a bloody good go."

With his hand in mine, I help him get up and settle him down. I shake out his blanket and tuck it back around his legs. It's cold in here, and I'm overcome with a sudden urge to get moving. As I push him toward the door, it swings open for us. You are waiting there, standing passively like a statue.

"Follow me."

We trail through the Institute, and I pass by rooms upon rooms of things that I can't understand or explain. Many of them are empty; some of them have men in lab coats and test subjects inside. There are rooms with large human-size tanks, with gyroscopes, with headsets. There are operating theaters. I pass them all too quickly to get anything more than a glimpse.

A few people throw nervous glances at us, but they say nothing. It's clear they are afraid of you.

When we arrive at another set of lifts, it occurs to me that I have no idea how far down this place goes. It could descend into the very core of the earth for all I know.

Stanley looks around in wonder, boylike amazement on his face. This was a side of him I never understood. When he worked as a lab tech, he would never really talk about work. He would try, at the start, to explain what he was doing, but it was beyond me. Science and maths were never my areas, never how my brain worked. I'm an arts and literature gal— theaters, museums, novels. Always have been. Numbers and spreadsheets send me potty.

There are five lifts, all with different designations at the top of them. Greek lettering. Each of the first four is marked with a lowercase letter from alpha through delta: α, β, γ, δ. The last one is slightly separate, with a capitalized omega—Ω—above it.

You lead me left, to the alpha lift, and as we approach, it opens. I realize my phone hasn't made a single sound since we arrived here: no notifications, no messages, nothing. It's quiet—completely silent—for the first time in years. The absence makes me anxious.

The lift doors open just as we get to them. The platform inside is easily wide enough for all three of us, including Stanley's wheelchair. It looks as though it was designed for much larger industrial cargo. The walls are sleek metal, pristine, the gunmetal gray only interrupted by two thin black lines on either side. The floor shines.

"Where are we going?" I ask as I roll Stanley in.

"Deeper," you say. "Farther down." But I barely register you—my mind is too focused on the sign on the wall ahead of me. It looks official, with crisply printed letters and clear lines, but the wording is strange.

What does it say?

"You are in *a* lift. Caution: This is your FIRST time entering the Lower Deck. If anything you see feels familiar, alert a member of staff immediately. The Lazarus Institute values your safety and the safety of your timeline."

"What *is* that?" I ask. The lift doors slide closed behind us. You are looking not at the sign or at me but directly ahead at the cold metal wall.

"Déjà vu checkpoint."

"What the hell is that supposed to mean?"

You don't answer. Instead, without looking at me, you give that infuriating smirk. You know the one I mean—the one you've given me three times in the last hour while we've been having this interview. The one that says: *I'm not going to tell you, and there's nothing you can do about it.*

I don't realize the lift is moving until I see the lights change. The two black lines on either side of the lift reveal themselves to be window slits rather than paint. Floor after floor flashes past. We're moving very quickly indeed, and we were already underground.

How are we going even deeper? I wonder. This is followed by a second, more worrying thought: *What is so dangerous that it needs to be buried this deep?*

It takes me a moment to realize that the lift is stopping, so smooth is the movement. In this place, even my own body's inertia can be tricked.

The doors slide open again, and I am treated to a wholly different scene: Gone are the clinical white-and-gray walls, the lab-coated technicians, and the scary-looking metal implements. In their place is green-gray wallpaper and maroon carpeting, like something out of an old Georgian guesthouse. There's a sofa in the corner and a few chairs surrounding a dark wooden coffee table with a chessboard on it, its polish glimmering beneath the light of the many lamps. There's also a bookcase in the corner, stacked with a variety of tomes, but my eyesight is too far gone to really make out the titles.

There's a warm smell in the room—a mixture of lightly burning wood fire and hints of lavender.

To the left, there's a large ornate mirror and a closed door; to the right, another closed door.

"Welcome to the Lower Deck," you say, leading us into the room. "I suppose you would call this my office."

Stanley lets out a little sigh of pleasure, like he's been holding his breath the entire journey and can finally relax now that he's here. Like he's home. I can see why.

"Hassan, I've not seen wallpaper like this since the '70s. And even then, it was dated."

"It is admittedly a quite particular aesthetic." You cross to the coffee table, and there's something different about the way you walk. It's a little more relaxed, more—dare I say it—human. You sit down and do the last thing that I would ever imagine *you* doing. Like, honestly, if I were to create a list of actions that I would never expect to see you perform, this would be right at the top.

What do I do?

You put your feet up on the coffee table. You lean back into the sofa. I'm not going to say you look relaxed, because you don't. There's still an undercurrent of ferocity about you, even now, and I'd be a fool to forget it. But at the moment, it's *just* an undercurrent. Like an unboiled kettle. Like a lion sleeping.

It puts me at ease, and I'm immediately asking myself if that's a good thing. I look down at Stanley in his chair and realize he's fallen asleep. He lets out a little drool, and I stoop over to wipe it up.

You smile and throw a pointed glance at the closed door. "Time for your appointment, Mrs. Webb?"

"The scan."

"Indeed. It will be painless, I promise you. And once it's done, you can use my personal memory spade to complete another dive. We are getting closer to the root of Stanley's problem, of his forgetting."

I frown. "Why didn't we come down here in the first place?"

"I needed to be sure it would work. Not just anyone comes down here. I had to be sure you would be a compatible match for his brain chemistry. If not, all this would be for nothing."

Through the door is a similar room: It features the same carpets and wallpaper, but this one has a collection of screens along the back. There's an old corkboard on the wall with snippets of newspaper headlines stuck to it like it's some kind of murder board: a suicide at an independent school, a large fire in central London, a caving expedition in Greece. I have no idea what connects them.

In the middle, there is a chair. It's not a dentist's chair, like the one upstairs, but an extended armchair—softer and more comfortable. There is a similar headset at the top, but it looks much older. Wires extend out of it and attach to ports in the floor. You barely see wires on anything anymore. Beside it, the bath looks almost Victorian, freestanding with roll-top sides and brass taps. On a table sits what looks like a diver's helmet from the 1800s.

"It's an older model, but it works exactly the same."

"Why do you keep an older model?" I ask. I don't really care. I'm just trying to make conversation to ease the tension. I sit in the seat this time, rather than submerge myself in liquid. The wired headset is about to be put on my head, and then God knows what.

"Call it nostalgia."

The scan is over before I know it. I barely register it happening. The headset is on, and then it's off. Just a few seconds. I let out a big breath.

"That was easy," I say.

"I don't want to make this difficult for you, Maggie," you say. You touch my shoulder, and your hand is surprisingly warm. I don't know why, but I'd always imagined it would be cold. "I'm on your side here. I'm trying to help you both."

"Sorry. It's just . . . all this is so new. And with Stanley and . . . I'm scared, Hassan. I don't know who to trust."

You hold my eyes, and I can't look away. They draw me in.

"Trust me, Maggie."

And for half a second, I almost do. God, you're good at this.

Do you do another memory dive with Stanley?

Yes . . . not long after. I—

Go to that.

I thought you wanted all the details.

Not these details. I'm going to speed you up here. This moment isn't important. It's implied: I spend some time calibrating. You wake Stanley up. We put him in the chair, and you submerge in the bath. Correct?

Well, yes.

What instructions do I give you next?

You say, "Last time, we calibrated with your memories—a memory that you could recall extremely well. Now we need to establish fidelity between the brain waves. You need to find a memory that Stanley can still recall, one that he can remember with a lot of detail."

You're at the touch screens at the back, moving data and graphs around on a touch screen too quickly for me to follow. Stanley is awake but distant. He's barely in the room—his mind is off elsewhere. I'm eyeing the diver's helmet suspiciously because it looks so heavy; I worry my shoulders won't be able to hold it up.

"The barbecue at Portobello Beach."

You turn to me, raising your eyebrow.

"I wasn't there. It was before I met him, but he talks about it all the time. Some barbecue he had on a beach in Edinburgh with friends. Sometimes he thinks that I was there with him or that he's there right now, but it's definitely a clear memory. Sometimes . . ." I look at his face, his eyes glazed over. I squeeze his hand. "When I'm worried that he's really gone, that *everything* is gone, I ask him about that barbecue, and he'll start talking about it. He never forgets it."

Stanley blinks. "Barbecue? At Portobello? God, it was cold then."

"Yes, Stan." I kiss him on the forehead. "That's the one."

"Perfect," you say, identifying a brain wave on the screen and isolating it. "Focus on that idea. The idea of that memory. Both of you." You place the headset on him and then turn to put the helmet on me.

Even as it's descending over my eyes, Stanley becomes more alert. He looks at me curiously, blinking, and I swear there's a flash of fear in his eyes, of panic.

I open my mouth to tell you to stop. But as I do, the helmet descends, and the whole world dissolves before my eyes.

Pieces return, like falling into a dream. Feelings first. Cold and wind. The scent of the sea. The world takes shape but in disassociated segments: A beach hut appears on its own in the black. Then there are waves from the sea, on their own, not connected to sand or sky. Soon, the parts in between fill in.

I'm standing on a beach I've never been to before, but I feel like I recognize it. Like déjà vu. I'm in Stanley's memory but not one I have any experience of outside what he's told me.

I'm standing underneath a pier, just yards away from where the water is lapping up to the shore. It's cold—right at that turning point between autumn and winter. Late October or early November is my guess. The wind isn't up too much, which I'm thankful for, as I'm still in the clothes I was wearing at the Institute: just a light cardigan, a skirt, and a top. I'm glad I'm wearing thick tights.

The beach is almost empty. There are a few people walking dogs and ambling along the waterfront. Some couples holding hands. Some crazy thrill seekers actually swimming in the North Sea. I look behind me and see Stanley about fifty yards away.

He looks younger than he did when I met him—maybe twenty or twenty-one—but he's still got that same small frame and geeky charm. It emanates from him. There are two other people with him: a thin, bronze-skinned man in glasses, holding a beer, and a bulky Asian man standing beside them. They're hovering around a small barbecue that they've set up on the beach, trying to get it to light. I've not met either of them before, and I wonder why. In fact, the only person I ever met from Stanley's life before me was Hugo, his old schoolmate, and even then it felt like Stanley kept the two of us from ever getting to know each other. Like he was embarrassed, though I could never quite work out why.

I walk in their direction, cautiously, wanting to get a little closer to Stanley, wanting to hear his voice.

The thin man—my first guess is that he's Indian, or perhaps a Pacific Islander, maybe Samoan—glances toward me, then looks away. I'm just an insert into the memory, after all. The brain is explaining me away as a walker on the beach or a statue or something.

They're laughing. I can hear the warmth of it as I approach, see the smiles on their faces. But something is up with Stanley. He's not quite laughing like the other two. Their laughs are genuine—real joy, real happiness—but his is false. His eyes aren't creasing the way those of the others are. They look sad.

How do you know?

I've lived with the man for over forty years. I know what he looks like when he's sad.

"I'm just saying," the thin man says. "You guys have known him longer than me. Has he always been that *weird*?"

The bulky one shakes his head. "I dunno, Toby. Jacques has always been quirky, sure. I wouldn't say *weird* is the right term, though. And also"—he jokingly pokes the thin man in the ribs—"he's kinda your boss. You should be careful."

"Well, yeah, Raph, but you're like his boss." Toby turns to Stanley. "And Stanley's like your boss, right? Or is it the other way around? I can never tell."

"He has changed," Stanley says quietly. The other two look at him. "Jacques—he's not the same anymore."

I walk right past them now, just a couple of yards behind. As I pass them, I look over my shoulder, not wanting to let Stanley out of my sight. And he sees me.

He sees you?

He looks right at me, and he recognizes me. No doubt. This strange mixture of consternation and worry appears on his face. It lasts only a few seconds, but it's such an intense, strange, wild look that it almost feels like an accusation, like his face is screaming *What are you doing here?*

I have to look away. I pick up my pace, just to get away from it.

In the background, I hear the thin man—Toby—say, "I need to take a piss. Hold on."

My whole body is shaking. I try to rationalize it to myself: *That was just Stanley's brain trying to make sense of what I'm doing in that memory. He's just getting confused, trying to push me out of it.* But something doesn't feel right.

There was something in Stanley's look that makes me doubt you. Makes me doubt what you've told me.

Toby walks past me to my right, power walking his way to a public toilet up on the other side of the beach. I decide to do something drastic.

"Excuse me?" I say. He stops. He turns.

"Yes?"

"Can you see me?"

He frowns. "What kind of a weird question is that? Sorry, lady, I'm *desperate* for a piss." He turns away, then stops and sighs before turning back. "Are you all right? Have you got someone out here with you?"

"Oh, don't worry." I wave my hand. "I'm not crazy or anything. I just . . . Your name—it's Toby, right?"

"How do you know that?"

"I overheard you."

"Oh." He looks confused. "Right. Erm, yes." He nods his head forward awkwardly. "Toby Hauata, at your service. But, honestly, I really do need a piss. Are you sure you're okay?"

"Fine," I lie. "I'll be fine."

He gives me a last little smile and then dashes off.

And I think: *Tobias Hauata. I know that name.* It *is* Samoan. I've seen it before in one of Stanley's address books, the ones I uploaded to my laptop and our shared drive before he went into Sunrise. The number and the address will be on my phone, even without a network signal. It's in the local storage.

I turn back to see if Stanley is still looking at me.

And he isn't there.

There's nothing there.

No Stanley, no Raph, no barbecue. There isn't even a pier.

There's a hole where those things should be.

And it's *so empty.*

I'm gripped with a piercing fear that cuts straight into my heart. It's not a rational fear or one I can explain; it's deeper than that, more instinctual, like the fear of being suddenly plunged into darkness or looking over a cliff.

My heart is pounding in my chest. I want to scream, but I'm panting too fast. I can't catch my breath.

The void stretches outward, the edges of it starting to spread into the sea, across the sand, toward me.

I stumble backward, away from it. I turn around and see Toby from behind, still walking to the toilet, and I shout his name.

It comes out garbled, in a splutter and a strangled scream.

He turns back to me, and his face *isn't there.*

It's gone. It's . . . empty.

"Pull me out," I manage, breathlessly. Then louder: "PULL ME OUT, PULL ME OUT, PULL ME THE FUCK OUT OF HERE."

And the world goes black, but I breathe.

Because it's not the emptiness that I saw before. That was different. That was the worst thing I've ever seen.

The helmet is lifted off my head. I'm back in your office, with you peering over me. You look worried.

"What happened?" you ask.

"Is he still in there?" I demand, pulling myself out of the bath and shaking Stanley. His eyes are still closed. "Is he out?"

"The machine is off. He is no longer diving."

I shake him, softly at first, then harder. "Stan. STAN!"

His eyes open, and his lips curl up in anger. "What? What do you want, woman?!"

And I melt into him, my arms thrown around him. "Oh God. Oh God, Stanley, you're okay. You're here."

He bristles at my embrace. "Well, yes, stupid woman. Why wouldn't I be?"

"I don't know." I'm crying. I'm crying into his neck and chest. "I don't know. I was just so scared. I just . . . We were on Portobello Beach, at your barbecue, and suddenly—"

"Where?" His voice is harsh and throaty.

"Portobello. In your memory. In Edinburgh."

"Nonsense. I've never been to Edinburgh."

I sit straight up. "What did you say? Say that again."

He looks at me strangely, like he doesn't understand what I'm saying. "I've never been to Edinburgh."

I spin round and grab your wrist, tugging you toward me. "What have you done to him? He can't remember the beach. He *always* remembers the beach, and you put me in there, and *that happened*, and now it's gone. What did you do? Oh God—what the hell did you make *me* do?"

You do not pull back against my grip. You hold my gaze. "What do you mean 'that happened'?"

"They were there. Stanley was there, and then he just wasn't. There was a . . . an emptiness. A void. Like he'd been swallowed up."

You stare right into my eyes, boring down into me for seconds, minutes, hours. I don't know. It's the most intense expression I've ever seen on your face. It's not quite anger, or ferocity. It's . . . absolute certainty. It's obsession. It's . . . it's hard to describe, but it's a look of sheer force of will.

You pluck my hand from your wrist like it's a feather and walk right out of the office. You cross the main front room to the other door on the right-hand side, and you walk through it, closing it behind you.

I just walk out—without a word?

Yes. And I have no idea what to do, because I made a promise.

A promise?

That I wasn't going to let anyone harm him, but you have harmed him. Or I have. Something that *we've* done has harmed him. He's losing more memories, and I don't know why. But after seeing that look on your face, one thing becomes clear to me. You'll force us to continue if you have to. You're not going to let this end, even if I beg you to.

Stanley's muttering something to himself now, a little too quiet for me to hear, and as I look down at him, I realize I need help. I need someone—someone who isn't you—to help me understand all of this.

I take out my phone and check my address book. It's there—an entry for the thin Samoan man, Tobias. I pull up his address. If he's still alive, then he might have been involved with this somehow, with Stanley, before I met him. As I look around the office—at the corners and the windows and the buttons and the doors of a place that feels increasingly like a prison—it's then that I make a decision.

What decision?

I'm going to have to break him out. Again. And this time, I'll have to do it all by myself.

10 | Stanley
1959

THE RAT SCAMPERED THROUGH THE TUNNEL, SNIFFING AS IT WENT. EACH time it reached an intersection, it stopped for just a moment—a half second of indecision—before cutting left or right. Even if you weren't watching the rat, you'd be able to tell when this happened by the reactions of the three spectators. Their fists clenched a little; the tendons of their necks tightened.

"He's actually going to do it," Raph muttered to himself. He leaned forward a little, without noticing, and now crowed over the maze like the Tower of Pisa.

"I'll believe it when I see it," Toby said. His arms were crossed in mock disbelief, but his muscles were no less tense.

Stanley did not say a word.

The rat scampered farther, its tiny headset attached by a thin wire to the sprawling computers on the wall. To call it a maze was a disservice; it was more like a labyrinth. Spread across almost twenty yards of the laboratory floor, it was undoubtedly the most complex rat run ever built. The architecture of it had become a bit of a game to the members of the Lazarus Team—each one trying to outdo the others with false doors, dead ends, traps, and mirrors. Stanley was almost certain that if he were the size of the rat, he would be completely unable to find his way out.

"The neural circuits are on fire, Stan." Raph read from the printout that chugged out in front of him. The lab they were in was one of many in this building, hired out and paid for by Raph's excessively large trust fund. The walls were high, and the room was covered with equipment—whirring computers and hard drives that took up entire walls, the very latest in midcentury technology. "Maria—take a note. We're seeing activity in the CA1 region of the hippocampus, the dentate gyrus, and the parahippocampal and entorhinal cortices."

Stanley heard the scratch of Maria's pencil behind them, jotting down the readings on her clipboard. Raph's personal assistant was a small lady with mousy-brown hair only ever kept in a ponytail. Apart from the movement of her pencil, she kept silent at the back of the room.

Stanley didn't look up. He couldn't tear his eyes off this little rat.

You can do it, he willed. *Do it and you'll have enough cheese to eat like a king for the rest of your life.*

The creature stumbled to a halt again. The three inhaled a simultaneous breath.

Jacques's hall of mirrors—two doors that led to false exits, four false doors that were actually mirrors, false scents behind each one. There was no working this out on the spot. There was no solving this room by instinct. The rat had to *remember*—clearly, after only a single pass—exactly which route it had to take.

It sniffed at one of the mirror doors.

"Don't sniff at it, you idiot," Toby said. "That's not going to help you."

"Don't call him an idiot." Raph's eyes were flicking back and forth between the neural readouts and the maze. "Poor thing."

No rat had gotten through the hall of mirrors yet. The rats saw this part of the maze just a single time at least four weeks before they ran, long enough that the curve of forgetting would have fully set in. Long enough that they would need to rely on long-term episodic memory.

The rat took a few steps back, turning around, confused.

Come on.

Its head popped up into the air, and Stanley could almost swear he saw a tiny light bulb appear. The rat ran—wonderfully, gloriously—through the right door.

"Yes!" Raph punched the air. "You little genius!"

"We're not through yet," Stanley whispered. There was still the coded gate.

It was a small number pad that changed its eight-digit code depending on the color of the room—designed to change randomly. The rat would have to learn the corresponding code for each color and input it correctly. One wrong number and the entire maze shut down. It was an absurd expectation to place on a rat's brain, completely ludicrous.

But, then, *everything* they were doing here was ludicrous.

The rat didn't stop this time; it powered through the last few tunnels and toward the coded gate, highlighted in bright green, using its whiskered nose to press against the panel: 6 . . . 4 . . . 3 . . . 1.

It stopped.

They all knew what the green code was, and the first four digits were correct. The rat scrunched up its little face—such an oddly human expression for an animal—before continuing: 8 . . . 3—

The maze buzzed red. The door stayed locked. The rat tried pressing the buttons again, but no luck. It only got one try, and it had messed up.

Stanley released a long breath that snaked out of him, leaving him feeling a touch emptier inside. Toby put a hand on his arm. It felt a little sweaty, but Toby was always a little sweaty. He was a weedy Samoan man—as thin as a rake—and despite the fact that he only ever wore a T-shirt and lab coat, he sweated more than anyone Stanley had ever met. He was a top-rate biochemist, though, and he was slowly and quietly becoming a friend.

"You can't be disappointed at that, my man." Toby shook his head in disbelief. "That was amazing. I've never seen memory recall like it."

"He's right, Stan," Raph added. "If anything, this is proof. The stimulant drugs in the hippocampus weren't doing nearly enough. The shunt surgery has resulted in a *much* higher response. Maria, log the results into the system, please."

She nodded curtly, turning to walk out of the room without a word.

When she was gone, Stanley said, "It's not good enough."

Toby shook his head. "Seriously? Is anything ever good enough for you? That was . . . that was *groundbreaking*. I've never—"

"Stan's right." The three of them turned to the new voice. Jacques stood differently; only a year ago, he would have swaggered into the room or, at the very least, leaned casually against the doorframe, as if he were ordering a drink. He stood straighter these days. It was only when he stopped slouching that Stanley really noticed how tall he was. "Failure is still failure. Simple memory recall is not enough. If it isn't perfect, it isn't working."

Toby coughed, turning away and putting his head down to flick through some files. Raph took a few steps forward, frowning. "Where have you been? Nobody's seen you in days. Elias couldn't even tell us where you were."

He smiled. "Busy."

Jacques brushed past him and started pressing the buttons on the computers, analyzing the data from the printed readouts. The rat squeaked a little from the maze, and Raph bent down to pick it up, stroking it quietly in his hands.

"You went for the endocrine drugs again, I presume?" Jacques asked, not looking away from the readouts.

Stanley had to bite back a curt reply. These days, Jacques barely bothered to keep up with the course of experiments. "Surgery," he replied. "Shunt in the neural connections between the parietal and occipital lobes and the medial temporal lobe."

"Er, guys?" Toby took a few steps back, edging toward the door. "I'm going to check on the other staff, see how the drug trial groups are getting on?"

"Sure," Raph said. "Go ahead."

There was something about Jacques, Stanley noticed, that made Toby uncomfortable. He never said anything about it, never brought it up, but every time Jacques was in the room, Toby found an excuse to leave. Stanley didn't quite understand it, but it had made him recognize that something about Jacques had changed, and he couldn't quite put his finger on what it was.

Jacques turned back to the maze. "Mm. This one got through the hall of mirrors."

"It did."

"So you're onto something, at least. Knight to queen five."

Stanley blinked. Jacques had a habit of doing this now—they would play a match in their heads over several days, and he would wait until the most unexpected moment to surprise Stanley with a move. It never worked. "Bishop to king's knight two," he replied, shaking his head. "And, *yes*, we are making progress, but not enough."

"No." He nodded. "Not enough."

Raph walked over to the corner of the room, letting the rat scamper back into its cage before turning around. "Jacques—where *have* you been?"

Jacques turned around and looked at the both of them, properly *looked* at them for the first time. An intensity had grown behind those eyes. One that had always been there, Stanley thought, hidden beneath the cocksure arrogance and the tomfoolery. But, somehow, while Jacques was working in these labs and on this problem, it shone through.

"Elias and I have something to show you," Jacques said, and he walked out of the room. Raph and Stanley followed.

As they passed through the main atrium, Stanley marveled at how far they had come in just over a year. A few staff nodded their heads deferentially as he passed them, sharing readouts from their clipboards. Various doors opened and closed, leading to large examination rooms, small operation theaters for rodents, and sterile cleanrooms where new drugs were being synthesized and tested. Raph had hired three more staff last month, bringing the total up to thirteen. Stanley finally had a lab—a full, working lab—and the freedom to do anything he wanted. It was a miracle what money could do.

But when the day ended, he still returned to his dingy room in his cheap flatshare in Brixton. He was getting paid a salary but continued to sleep in all his clothes out of habit, because he didn't want to pay for the heating. It was a difficult habit to shake. He felt as if he had his foot in two different worlds, and it was becoming harder and harder to tell which one of them was real.

Now and then, he still had to fight the sensation of being caught out of place. A lab tech would come to him—someone who worked *for* him—and he would be filled with a sudden need to explain himself, to offer up some kind of justification for what he was doing here. He'd learned to bury it over time, but it still bubbled deep inside.

Jacques swept across the atrium and over to his section of the lab, separated off into another part of the building behind coded doors. When they first started up, Stanley thought the separation was ridiculous. They had been organizing what equipment they needed to purchase and what hypotheses would be tested first, and Jacques outright demanded that he have a section of the facility—at least three rooms—entirely to himself.

I don't want to have to double-check with you if I get a great idea, he had said. *I want my own space to test it*. At the time, they acquiesced. There were bigger things to worry about.

But the separation had grown over the past year, and Stanley had barely noticed. He was so focused on his own experiments—on reestablishing the baselines and assumptions that Waldman had set up, then building upon them—that he paid almost no attention to the other parts of the lab.

A few months ago, he'd overheard something in bits and pieces from members of staff: Jacques had changed the codes for the locks to his section, allowing only certain personnel to enter. Jacques was creating a private kingdom for himself. *Fine*, Stanley had thought. *Let him*. They should all have the freedom to pursue their own lines of inquiry. Jacques and Stanley used to share results, if and when they had any. Increasingly, however, they just kept to themselves.

But Raph had not done his own thing, really. Scientifically, he had just been in tandem with Stanley, which surprised him. At Whelton, Stanley had often felt like a third wheel in the long-running friendship between Jacques and Raph. But the more Jacques distanced himself from them and the world, the more Raph gravitated to Stanley's side.

What Raph *did* have was an almost wizardly gift for the financials. Over the past three years, Raph had used his position in the Lazarus firm to purchase an oil rig off the southern coast of Brazil, an East Asian manufacturing company that produced flame-retardant gear for oil spillages, *and* a controlling stake in a gold mine in Algeria. Stanley couldn't follow the full details of the scheme, but through about eight shell companies, three obscenely well-paid stockbrokers, and a transport firm, Raph was able to siphon an almost bottomless well of money into this project.

They followed Jacques through the atrium and up to a locked door, where Jacques pressed a quick code into the keypad, which flicked green.

They passed into Jacques's main lab, the walls lined with servers and whirring drives—from spewing printers came readouts that Stanley glanced at but didn't immediately understand how to read. Jacques had taken to developing his own form of shorthand, code that worked for him and him alone.

Elias passed them from the other direction, bowing his head slightly. Jacques worked exclusively with Elias, a lab tech he had hired personally— a bulky German man with a flat, serious face. Stanley didn't think he'd ever seen any emotion on it other than fierce industriousness or utter focus. He'd tried to engage with him multiple times and had been met with nothing but a blank practicality that verged on obstruction.

But they didn't exactly have the luxury of being picky. What they were doing here wasn't strictly by the book, wasn't strictly *legal*, and so discretion had become the most valuable asset among workers in this lab. That meant being far more liberal about background checks than Raph would have liked. The only way to find scientists who were not only of the caliber they needed but also willing to accept the legal risk was to find ones who couldn't get work elsewhere: the disbarred, the discredited, the previously convicted. This was as true for Maria and Toby as it was for Elias, so Stanley figured it was best not to probe too deeply.

Stanley passed into the next room, stopping in his tracks. In the center of the room was his old machine—the converted dentist's chair with a headset attached, wires running out of it—beeping and whirring.

"What is that doing there? I put it in storage."

"Elias got it out. I'm using it," Jacques said.

Stanley shook his head. "It doesn't work. It never worked."

"I disagree."

"What do you mean you disagree? I invented it. It doesn't work."

Jacques shrugged. "Maybe you give up too easily."

A fire sparked inside Stanley's chest, a little burst of anger. The muscles all along his back clenched. Before he could speak, Raph took a step forward.

"What is it you wanted to show us?"

Jacques turned to face both of them. "If a tree falls in a forest and no one is around to hear it, does it make a sound?"

Stanley shook his head in frustration, unable to take his eyes off the old machine. "Get to the point."

"While you two have been so focused on the neurobiology side of things, I've decided to branch out a little. Look at the bigger picture. Biology is a subset of chemistry, after all, and chemistry is a subset of physics."

"What physics?"

"Superposition and entanglement. The disparity between classical and quantum physics is, at its heart, all about observation. Reality only exists—is only *created*—as it's observed. If no one hears the tree fall in the forest, there wasn't a tree at all."

"I know the basics of quantum mechanics, Jacques."

A grin appeared on Jacques's face. "Of course you do. Pawn to queen's rook six."

"Rook to king four," Stanley shot back. "Check."

Jacques scoffed. "That's a nonsense check. Bishop takes rook. You're barely trying, Stan. I can tell."

"If you two have finished," Raph cut in. "What's the point you're making about observation?"

"If the present only exists when it's observed, what if the past only exists because it's remembered?"

Stanley frowned. "What do you mean?"

"I think there's a closer link between memory and the past than we originally thought. I know your memory machine was designed to access lost memories, to get inside people's subconsciouses and uncover what they've forgotten."

"Yes, and it doesn't work. When you access a memory, it changes. It isn't the same as it was when you first remembered it."

"So you thought—but you only ever tried it on yourself. Interviews with subjects suggest that something different is happening. What if each time we access a memory, we are literally accessing a sliver of the past?"

Stanley blinked, staring at him. "What?"

"What if—"

"Wait a second," Raph interrupted, taking a step forward. "What do you mean 'interviews with subjects'?"

Jacques waved his hand. "A slip of the tongue. I was speaking hypothetically."

"Jacques." Raph's voice was stern. "Have you been testing on human subjects?"

"Of course not."

"We agreed. Not until we're absolutely certain. We can't just start playing around in other people's heads. The legalities alone, not to mention the moral—"

"I promise, Raph. It was a thought experiment."

Raph fell quiet. He took a step back and started pacing around the room. He opened a few drawers, glanced at some files. Jacques paid him no mind—his focus was entirely on Stanley.

"You're suggesting that by accessing memories, we can literally access the past." Stanley spoke in a slow, calm voice, but as the realization of what Jacques was saying settled in, he laughed. "What, like *time travel*?"

The idea was ludicrous, but Jacques didn't blink.

"How does that line up with people having different memories of things?" Stanley asked.

"There is nothing in physics that precludes the idea of different multiple dimensions—multiple timelines, if you will—affected by the way the past is being observed. In fact, the multiverse concept is increasingly well accepted."

Stanley's face was serious again—focused. "Go on."

"What if by accessing these memories and changing them, we could literally change the past?"

Raph reached a door to one of the storage rooms off the back of Jacques's lab. There was a keypad on it, and he pressed the buttons. It flickered red and buzzed at him.

"That's private," Jacques said.

Raph sighed. "Which is exactly why I got security to install an override on all of them." He pressed the buttons again, in a different order, and they flashed green.

Swinging the door open, Raph revealed not a storage cupboard but what looked like a hospital room. A man lay on the bed: eyes closed, bone-thin, his topless chest pale and gaunt. Wires and IV tubes snaked in and out of his arms, but he didn't move an inch. He looked dead.

Raph spun around, his finger pointing furiously. "Who the fuck is that?"

"Ah," Jacques replied, "that would be one of the subjects I was talking about."

"You said that—" Raph rushed over to the man, putting his hands to the test subject's neck, feeling for a pulse. "Jesus Christ, Jacques. You *just* promised."

Jacques shrugged his shoulders. "Whoops."

"I knew it. I fucking knew it. You're *always* like this. You have absolutely no respect for anyone else's—"

"Is he alive?" Stanley interrupted.

Jacques put his hand to his head dramatically. "Of course he's alive, you idiot. What do you take me for? And he volunteered, for a fair sum of money. He's just in a medically induced coma; it was necessary for—"

"You put him in a *fucking coma*?" Raph shouted, spinning back to face Jacques. "He's not the only one, is he? This whole time, you've been experimenting on people. I should have known. After all these years, I should have known."

Jacques sighed in exasperation, as if Raph were a child who wouldn't stop talking. "Well, obviously. You really think you're going to solve this by looking at rodents? How pedestrian."

"Everything starts somewhere. The progress we made with the maze today alone—"

Jacques let out a burst of laughter. "Raph, I got a rat to clear that maze weeks ago."

"*What?!*" Stanley's head jerked up. He took a few steps toward Jacques. "How?"

"By actually trialing your drugs on more complex brains, on people I could talk to and take data from so that I could tweak as appropriate. You ask me how I did it? I did it with people like him." Jacques pointed to the comatose man. "I'm steps ahead of you because I'm willing to take the steps that are needed. You aren't, Stan. That's always been your problem."

"What are you talking about?"

"You think Waldman picked you because you were . . . what? The cleverest? Please! You're like a lost puppy. He *used* you, Stan, because you were like a pawn—content with being directed, with being told what to do rather than making your own strides. And here we are starting from scratch because you had only the slightest inkling of what he was *actually* working on."

"That's not true. He trusted me."

Jacques leaned forward, a good head taller than Stanley, his face perfectly calm. They locked eyes, mere inches from each other.

"Stan—the only reason we're having to do all this work now is because he clearly *didn't* trust you. Not enough to let you in on his real work. This isn't just about perfect memory; that was a smoke screen. There's more going on here; there always was. You were just a tool. Don't make the mistake of thinking your partnership with him was more than it was."

The air between them crackled. There was no sound. There was no space around Stanley and Jacques, no dentist's chair, floor, or ceiling. Just the intensity of their gaze, drowning out everything else.

He wanted to punch Jacques in the face again. His fingers itched for it, but even so, he heard the man's words echoing through his brain: *Maybe you give up too easily.* Is that what he had done? Had they made so little progress because he'd set himself up to fail from the start? There was a time when he would have done *anything* to get to the bottom of this, but here Jacques was, willing to do things that he wouldn't. Maybe Jacques was right. Maybe everything he'd done so far—with the project, with Waldman, with *himself*—just hadn't been good enough.

"Why did you call us in here?" Stanley asked eventually, his voice trembling with control.

"A tree falling in a forest, Stan. I wanted to do this alone, to prove that I could, but everything's changed. I can't any longer." He pointed at the man in the bed. "The last time that man—"

"What's his name?" Raph interrupted. "The *man* you put into a coma. What's his name?"

Jacques frowned, momentarily annoyed. He walked over to the desk behind him and picked up a file.

"Seriously?" Raph asked, dismayed. "You don't know?"

"It's Bill," Jacques replied, closing the file and turning back to them. "The last time Bill dived into his memories, I asked him to change something—something concrete. To take an object and hide it or bury it somewhere."

Stanley barely noticed that he was holding his breath. "And?"

"This is ridiculous," Raph muttered. "We can't just go about experimenting on human subjects. This is my lab. This has to stop."

Jacques pulled a photograph out of his pocket, then laid it on the desk.

Stanley walked up to look at it over Jacques's shoulder. As he peered at the photo, he felt a cog in his brain turn and latch into place. This was it: a new path, a new opportunity. This must have been what Waldman saw. This was the golden ticket they had been chasing.

"I'm sorry, Raph," Stanley said, "but you're wrong. We're going to have to keep experimenting on people. In fact, I think we're going to have to experiment on lots and lots of people before we're done."

11

TRANSCRIPT NO. 273: Margaret Webb
DATE STAMP: 11 AUG. 2021
5 Hours, 46 Minutes, and 1 Second Until Dissolution

You've still not emerged from the other room, the one I haven't seen into. I've rolled Stanley back into your main office—the anachronistic sitting room—and pushed him up next to the sofa. I try sitting down on the sofa, but I'm filled with such nervous energy that it lasts all of three seconds. I'm up again, pacing. Breathing. Trying to keep my shaking under control.

My first instinct is to call Leah. How sad is that? It's been two years since she cut me off, and I actually take my phone out of my pocket and get halfway to finding her in my contacts before I remember, and the fierce pain of that separation stabs into my chest all over again.

Stanley's asleep again, and he's snoring.

God, I hate that sound. I hate the way it drones arrhythmically, not even letting me settle into a steady repetition as I try to sleep; I hate the way it gets suddenly and unnecessarily loud at times for no apparent reason, like he's struggling to breathe; I hate how much I miss it when

I'm in bed at night on my own. I hate how lonely it has made silence become.

You're still planning on "breaking out"? On taking Stanley away from the Institute?

You're damn right I am. What you did to him, or what we did to him—or, more accurately, what you made me do to him in that chair—it scared the shit out of me.

You agreed to do this. At no point did I force you, by your own telling of it. It was your choice to come with me.

See, you say it's my choice, but I didn't really have a choice, did I? You show up and throw me headfirst into the deep end of the pool—excuse the pun—and you're the only one who has any answers. I realize this as I pace back and forth in your office: I realize that the only reason I've been going along is because you control all the information. I *have* to trust you, because without you, I'm a tiny little fish swimming in the middle of a giant empty ocean. If I leave you, I drown, and worse, I take Stanley with me.

But no more. Not after that memory dive. I've got a lead—Toby Hauata— and an address. Someone to give me another side to this whole story. I'm quite the detective. Now I just have to work out how to get Stanley away from you.

It does not occur to you to just ask me?

Ah, yes. The thought crosses my mind. I'll ask kindly and you'll just let me and Stanley go, let us walk off into the sunset and never worry about us again. Come on—let's not pretend either of us ever believed that.

I triple-check that I have the address, part of me worried that it'll just disappear. It's not something I would have expected to happen, previously, but recently I'm having to revise my list of things that don't happen.

It's 262 Gosforth Way, Kingsbury.

Kingsbury isn't close—it's a couple of counties over, but England isn't all that big. I wonder if I could order an Uber that would take me there, if there'd be someone willing to drive three or four hours. My guess is yes. It'd be a lot of money. But I haven't had a signal since we entered that first lift. It worries me how lost I feel without it.

When you eventually come out of the adjoining room, there is a smile plastered on your face, and I can tell you've forced it there.

Why is that?

It's kind. There's no mystery to it, no smirk of hidden knowledge or mischievous grin. There's no subtext to it. That's how I know: It's not a real smile. Something's wrong, but you're putting on a show for me.

I smile back, pretending to accept it. "Hassan, Stan really needs some air. While you were in there, he had a little wheezing fit." You take a concerned step forward. "Oh, it's nothing to be worried about. He's had it since he became middle-aged—old body falling apart on him. Doctors say the best thing to do is get him outside. Recycled air really messes with his lungs after too long. Shouldn't take long—twenty minutes or so."

I look down at Stanley, arranging my face into pity. I don't like using him as a prop like this, but I can't see any other way.

"Of course," you say. Before I can object, you're behind Stanley's chair, guiding him forward. Your grip is tight on his seat, almost possessive, as I follow behind.

You roll him into a different lift than the one we came down in. This one has a gamma—γ—above the door, but the inside looks exactly the same. The only difference is the letter.

You are in γ lift. This lift goes UP and OUT. If you end up anywhere other than the ground floor, alert a member of staff immediately. The Lazarus Institute values your safety and the integrity of its constructs.

We say nothing in the lift. We don't speak. And while we've endured periods of silence before—in the car, for example—this one is filled to the brim with things unsaid, questions unasked. I know you are hiding things from me, just as I know that asking about them is pointless. But at the same time, I'm certain you know I'm hiding things from you. Maybe I'm just paranoid, but I worry that if we spend too long in this confined space, the sheer amount of suspicion will cause it to burst.

The lift doors open, and we're on the surface again. Sunlight—real sunlight—streaks in through the windows, and it calms me immediately. Even though I've watched for my entire life as the natural world has slowly been cut down and replaced by man-made constructions, at least no one has been able to touch sunlight. No attempt to replicate it comes close.

You push Stanley a couple of yards out of the lift and stop.

"Will the parking garage do?"

I pick at my fingers. "Somewhere by the road, ideally. He likes to watch the cars. They soothe him."

"He's asleep."

"Your powers of observation are unparalleled, Mr. Blake," I say. "But he also does wake up now and again."

I briefly hope for a laugh from you, just to ease the tension, but you don't. You give me that infuriatingly empty smile and push him to the right. It occurs to me that you probably don't even know who Sexton Blake is.

I know who Sexton Blake is.

Ah, right. So you're just being a grump. I've been on this planet eighty-three years, Hassan. The least you can do is humor an old lady.

Where do I push Stanley?

We go out a set of glass doors to a small garden by the side of the building. It's fenced but near the main road. I give a pretense of stretching my legs as I walk around it, looking for an exit. There's a gate at the back end, but I need to get closer to see if there's a lock on it. I've got images of Stanley and me on the run—like Bonnie and Clyde—foiled by a garden fence.

I take in a few breaths, the scent of freshly cut grass in my nose.

As I pass by the gate, I see that it's ajar. There's no lock. It'd open with one push, and we'd be out into the street.

Circling back around, I see Stanley resting in the sun, his eyes still closed. You are behind him with your hands still tightly clasped around the handles of his chair.

"Hassan," I say, "I need to find the ladies' room."

"We'll pass one on our way back inside."

I give you a weak smile. "I don't think you understand. Sorry, this is a little embarrassing, but at my age . . . let's just say I don't have the luxury of patience anymore."

You turn a little to look back inside the building.

"If you cross back through the corridor we just came through, past the lifts, and take a left, there's a—"

"Oh, I'm not going to remember all that! Are you really going to let an old woman wander about in there on her own and get lost?"

You frown. "Very well. We can come back out when—"

And perfectly on cue, as if he knows exactly what I'm doing, Stanley lets out one of those god-awful snores. There used to be two or three a night, and they'd shock me right out of my sleep: a mighty rattling, as if his lungs were about to collapse. He is, of course, completely fine.

I rush forward to him. "Oh, Stan!" I say, bringing my hands to his face. "Hassan, he can't go inside; he's having one of his wheezes again. He needs the fresh air, at least for another twenty minutes or so."

"You said you couldn't wait."

"I really can't. This is a nightmare for you, I know, caught between the geriatric failings of two old farts. Look, I deal with this all the time. Leave Stan here in the garden; he'll be fine. Just let him bask in the sun a bit. Take me inside to the loo, then bring me back, and we'll wheel him in."

You pause, thinking, but I don't want to give you time to do that.

"Christ in heaven, Hassan, don't make me piss myself!"

"Fine! Fine!" You throw your hands in the air. Lifting your foot, you clip Stanley's brakes into place. "Let's do this quickly."

As you stride forward, I potter behind you, giving my best impression of a desperate toddler. It actually takes me some effort to keep up with your long legs. I wonder if you were a giraffe in another life.

I clock the direction we take exactly: two lefts and back around a similar distance. When we get to the bathroom, I realize it must be along the same side of the building as the garden. You open the door for me and let me in with a gracious smile, but I can see that you want me to hurry up. You've just realized how little you like leaving Stanley out there on his own, but it's too late. You've committed now.

I'm sure you think you're extremely clever.

Oh, I do, Hassan. I do. Because even though you think you've got everything under control, even though you're waiting for me right outside the only door, there's one piece of information that I know for a fact. Something you haven't considered.

What's that?

No one ever expects the frail old biddy with bladder issues to climb out the window.

It's a large window, thankfully, but a little high, and the hinge has one of those lock mechanisms that doesn't let it open the entire way. Quietly as I can, I pass the stalls to my right and grab the large bin by the sinks. Turning it over, I climb up on top of it.

My legs shake. I have to cling on to the blinds like a newborn child to stop myself from falling, knowing full well that if I do, I'll probably break my hip. When was the last time I climbed on something? Twenty years ago? I glance down, and it looks like a mile. My eyes go a little dizzy. This seemed like a *much* better idea in my head.

Taking a couple of deep breaths, I poke my head out the window and look to my left—there's a glimpse of the garden where we left Stanley. This is it. This is going to work. If I can get out, I can get to him.

I grip the ledge and steady myself, taking out my phone. It connects to a signal, and I have to hold back a loud cheer. I open the Uber app and request a pickup on the nearest street outside, pressing the button for a wheelchair-accessible vehicle. The map loads and loads for what feels like a decade, but eventually a driver pops up on the screen.

Youssef. BD51 SMR. He'll be there in four minutes.

The bottom of the window is about the height of my chest. Grabbing the ledge, I pull myself upward. Or I try to. I exert as much effort as I possibly can, and I move about three inches before I feel like I actually *am* going to piss myself. Letting go, I fall back down on the bin, and it clatters, wavering a little.

Fuck, I think as I throw a furtive glance at the door. *Did he hear that?*

And then: *How the hell am I meant to get up here?*

I haven't got a choice, though, and I know it. Rather than rely on my arms, I lean to the side—panting—like an incompetent gymnast and try to lift my leg as high as it will go. It clicks about three times as it rises past my hip, and a sharp dart of pain snakes up my back.

I bite down on my lip to stop myself from screaming.

My foot hooks on to the ledge; I'm hugging it with my whole body now, flat against the wall, my other foot tiptoeing on the top of the bin. I have no idea how I got it up that high—thank fuck for "Seniors Yoga with Morganne" on YouTube.

I take in the biggest breath I can manage, and on the expulsion, I pull myself up, using everything: my spindly arms, my creaking legs, my cracking hips. Sweat drips down my forehead. I'm painfully slow, moving inches at a time, and I swear I'm going to drop.

I'm going to fall onto the floor and break my back. You're going to rush in and see me, curled up next to an upside-down bin, sobbing.

But I don't. I *make* it. I'm lying face down on the window ledge, gasping like a whale.

Before I have a second to think about how the hell I'm going to get down on the other side, I lose my balance. As I teeter, my hands dart out to try and grab the blinds, but they miss, and I tumble.

Outside.

Right into a bush.

I hear the crack a half second before I feel it. I have just enough time to register a quick *That's not good* before the pain slices through my shoulder. Then I do scream.

There's not a thing I can do to help it. It bursts out of me like a feral banshee for a good couple of seconds before I can clamp my mouth shut.

And there's no way you didn't hear that. In my head, I'm picturing you storming into the room, seeing the overturned bin and the open window and looking out to find me here: starfished in a bush like an idiot.

My phone gives a little chime that lets me know my Uber has arrived and is waiting for me.

Christ, I think. *Did that actually take four whole minutes?*

I heave myself to my feet, cradling my left shoulder. It's probably broken, but there's nothing I can do about it now. I'm shocked that the rest of me is in such good shape.

I'm running along the path to the garden—well, limping, because I've done something to my left foot as well, and my ankle is refusing to bend. Each time I step on it, I hear a crunch, like the bone has been stuffed with dry leaves.

I don't look back. I don't want to see you, your face staring at me as I hobble. I don't want to even think about you. All I want is to get Stanley out of here.

He's awake when I get into the garden, just looking around him like there's nothing wrong. He smiles when he notices me hobbling toward him, but then he sees me clutching my arm, and his face drops.

"Are you okay?"

"We have to move," I try to say, but I'm totally out of breath. "We have to get out of here."

"What happened?" His head is darting around, his eyes looking pan-icked. "Who are you? You look hurt."

Great, I think. I click off the brakes and roll him toward the gate with one hand—my other one is useless, the whole arm sagging at my shoul-der. I'm trying so hard not to let the pain take over, but it's consuming me. I can barely think.

When we get to the gate, I make the mistake of looking back.

You're there.

Not close but at the other end of the garden, where the doors are. You are standing absolutely straight and solemn. You remind me of one of those statues from Easter Island—you look like you were designed to last centuries. I cringe, cowing involuntarily, as I expect to see fury on your face, anger at my betrayal, but there isn't. There's only . . . disap-pointment.

And you know what the strange thing is?

What?

I actually feel bad. Some inexplicable part of me wants to turn Stanley round, to go right over to you and apologize, to beg for your forgiveness. That scares me more than anything else.

You walk toward me.

Not run, not even a brisk walk. You take your time. As if you know I'm not getting away. As if you think I'm pathetic.

I get Stanley out the gate, and we're onto the path up to the road. I can see it ahead of me—the Uber I ordered, parked and waiting. We're so close, just twenty or thirty yards away.

Every bone, muscle, and tendon in my body is screaming at me: *You're falling apart; you can't do this.*

I push him forward.

"Where are you taking me?" Stanley shouts, suddenly angry. "I don't know who you are! What are you doing?" He shifts in his chair, throwing his weight around, and my single arm can't hold him straight. I try to bring my other arm up, but it won't work. It's useless.

The wheelchair veers left, hitting the wayside of the path and toppling, sending us sprawling to the ground. I land on my hands and knees, but Stanley—oh God—he's fallen onto his side with a sickening crunch. He lets out a yelp and falls silent, too silent.

You step out of the gate, still walking—slowly, indomitably—toward me.

I tug helplessly on Stanley's leg, on his trousers, with my one working arm, but it's pointless. He's a deadweight, and I can barely lift a book right now, let alone a person.

As you approach, I picture the woman who tried to stop us when we left Sunrise and what you did to her—the way the life drained out of her in an instant. You're going to do that to me. You're going to kill me.

And I realize what I have to do.

Oh God, I'm sorry, Stanley. I'm so sorry.

"I will come back," I say to him. "Once I find out what's going on, I will come back and save you. I promise you."

Tugging against every instinct I have, like I'm ripping off one of my own limbs, I let Stanley go. I back away, hobbling to the Uber as fast as I can. The door opens as I approach—one of those automatic sliding ones.

As I tumble into the back seat, I see you kneeling by Stanley, and I swear there's a smile—there's a real fucking smile—on your face.

"You okay, ma'am?" the driver asks. "You look hurt."

"I'm fine," I pant. "Just, please—drive!"

The door slides shut.

And I fall apart.

Curling myself inward, I cradle my broken shoulder, try to pull my God-knows-what ankle up onto the seat. And for the first time since you showed up on my doorstep, I let myself cry. It gushes out of me: wave upon wave of guilt and regret and anger, each one hitting harder than the last. I *left* him. I ran.

I think the driver is talking to me, but I can't hear him.

I close my eyes, playing the events of the last day over and over in my brain, trying to work out if I've made the right choice, if I did the right thing, and I can't. I don't have enough information. I suppose that's why I'm going to see Toby.

When I eventually open my eyes, we're almost there.

"Good morning," the driver says. "You fell asleep. I ... thought I'd just let you."

"Where are we?" I whisper.

He points at the map on his phone. "Almost there. Six minutes."

I take a deep breath. I realize I hadn't slept since you picked me up yesterday afternoon, and we'd been working at the Institute all through the night. The four hours of sleep hardly makes me feel any better—worse, in fact—but there's not much I can do.

The Uber rolls to a stop outside a large country house. I step out, thanking the driver and adding as big a tip as I can to an already extremely high bill, then peer left and right. There's nothing else here. It's deserted.

Thirty years ago, this probably would have been a beautiful countryside spot—rolling hills and farmlands, cows and sheep in the fields, and animals frolicking in the woods. Most of the land is repurposed now, used for mass farming.

There are just roads and wheat fields as far as the eye can see.

And this house.

It's three stories and looks like it has about six bedrooms. There's a garage that juts out to the back and a sprawling garden with a shed and a greenhouse. Whoever Tobias Hauata is, he must be loaded.

I limp to the front door, wincing in pain, and ring the doorbell. He's got one of those doorbell cameras that's trained on my face. I can see the blinking red light recording.

After a minute, the door cracks open.

"Yes?"

I lean forward to see through the crack, but it's dark. There's the outline of a face, scanning me suspiciously. When he sees I'm just an old woman—a limping one at that—he pulls it all the way open.

It's him. It's the man from Stanley's memory, there's no doubt about it, even if he is a good fifty years older. He's thinner than ever—gaunt, even—his skin looking like it's been stuck to his bones with glue.

"Can I help you?"

"I need to talk to you," I say, realizing that I'm still out of breath from just holding on to the pain. "About Stanley Webb."

He frowns. "I've never heard of him. Who did you say you were again?"

"I'm his wife. Margaret Webb. And that's not true. I know you know him."

"I'm afraid you're mistaken. I do not know that name. I'm sorry you have wasted your time. . . ." He moves to close the front door, and I take a step forward.

"You had a barbecue together, on the beach in Portobello, years ago. And you were acting like good friends there. Stanley Webb. Don't pretend you don't know who I'm talking about."

"I really don't have any idea what you . . ." he starts, then falls short. His mouth falls open, gaping. He takes a step back from the door and looks me up and down, like he's appraising a wardrobe he's about to buy. He blinks a few times, in shock, and I grasp what's going on.

He *recognizes* me. He has seen me before.

"Dear God," he whispers. "They did it. They actually did it."

A few seconds of silence pass between us.

"Toby," I say, "*what* did they do?"

He ushers me inside, looking left and right to make sure nobody else is around. "How did you get here? Are you alone?"

"Yes, I'm alone. I got the address from Stan, but it's just me."

"Is Stanley alive?"

A pang hits my chest, and I can't tell if it's physical or not. "Yes. He is."

Toby directs me down a corridor and into a stylish sitting room: comfy-looking armchairs, a fire crackling warmly in the fireplace, and more books than I could possibly read in a lifetime stacked against the walls.

"You're hurt," he says, seeing me hobble and wince my way forward, clutching my shoulder.

"Yes, I . . . I fell. Tripped on my way here."

He shakes his head. "And you haven't seen anyone about it? Here—let me get you something for that. I've got some painkillers in the kitchen." He smiles, shaking his head. "Honestly, I've got a whole bloody pharmacy in there. Simvastatin for the cholesterol, lisinopril for the blood pressure. You know what it's like at our age. Take a seat, please."

I oblige, realizing how nice it is to talk to somebody normal. Up until recently, the only people I ever spoke to were Sunrise workers, all much younger than me; Stanley, who barely knows who he is half the time; and you. And let's be honest, you're hardly *normal* company.

By the time I actually manage to settle my body down and rest my aching arm on the side of the armchair, he's back in the room with a glass of water and a couple of pills. I take them, thanking him, and knock them back.

"They're the industrial-strength ones," he says. "None of that paracetamol shit you buy at Boots. They'll take the pain away. Then we really should get you to a doctor."

"Toby—you know me. How? Have you been in touch with Stan and—"

"The beach," he says, sitting down opposite me. "Portobello. You were there."

I blink. "You remember me from the beach? I was *there*?"

"Yes, yes," he replies. "And you haven't aged a single day from the looks of it. Amazing. I take it you went back recently."

"Went back?" I struggle to follow him. "You mean, I . . . I time-traveled?"

"In a sense, yes. You used the memories as an observational tool to affect the reality of the past. That was always the theory, anyway." He leans forward, intent. "Why did you go to that moment, though? You must understand—I've tried very hard to leave all of that behind. There are very dangerous people who think I know too much, who think I've seen too much. They want to control who knows about this, and I'm a loose end, you see. Where did you hear about me?"

"I didn't go there to find you. I went back to find Stanley, to access some of his memories. I was—"

He shakes his head. "No. Stan wasn't there."

"What?"

"It was just me going for a walk on the beach, and then you approached me. I think I was going for a piss, no? It was so strange—you just came up to me, and then when I looked back, you'd disappeared and . . ." He frowned. "Can't really remember what happened after that."

"No," I say, confused. "You were there having a barbecue with Stanley and another man—Raph, I think his name was? They were with you, and then you—"

"I think I would remember if Raph and Stan were there."

"Well, what were you doing before you bumped into me, then? Where were you?"

"I was . . ." His eyebrows furrow together. "I was just out for a walk. I don't remember *exactly* what I was doing. It's been almost fifty years."

I lean back, feeling a little strange. This doesn't make any sense. He remembers *me* but not Stanley or that other man? Then I think about that yawning hole where they were, that emptiness that swallowed them up, and my whole body goes cold.

He leans forward, his voice insistent. "I *really* need to know how you found me."

"There was an address," I say again. My head is feeling a little fuzzy, presumably from the painkillers. "In Stan's old address book. In my phone."

He gets up and starts pacing, getting frustrated with me, though I'm not sure why. I'm suddenly quite thirsty. I reach forward to pick up the glass of water, but my arm doesn't move. Neither of them do.

Toby plucks my phone up from the side of the chair and looks at it.

"I trusted Stan. He was one of the good ones. But . . ." Toby shakes his head. "So they're using the memory spade again, after all this time. And it works. It actually *works*." He turns to me, and there's a wobble in his voice. It drops to a whisper, as if he's afraid someone might be listening, and he says, "What did you do about Omega?"

"I don't know," I say. "I don't know what that is."

He tuts. "Of course not. You're just a pawn. I can see that now. Just like we all were."

"I can't . . . ," I mutter. "Toby, I can't move my body."

"Well, yes. That would be the drugs I gave you kicking in. Can't risk you getting out now, telling people where I am, even if you are old and injured. Can you imagine what a chase that would be with the two of us?"

My breathing feels thick in my throat, heavy like tar. "Getting out?"

"The tools you're playing with. The powers you're—" He shakes his head and throws my phone into the fire. It crackles and spits. "No. There's no other way around it. Can't risk them finding me again. And I'm too old to go on the run. I'll bury your body in the wheat fields, though. I won't just leave you out to rot. That wouldn't be right."

Bury me? I try to say, but my lips have stopped working too.

My whole body is frozen in paralysis. I can't feel a thing. *Well, at least you're not in pain anymore*, a sarcastic voice inside my head japes, trying to lighten the mood.

It doesn't work.

He's going to kill me. I'm going to die, and Stanley is going to be left all alone to suffer whatever experimentation you have planned for him. And I promised him I would come back for him. I promised.

"You shouldn't have gone back." Toby stands in front of me, shaking his head. "Whoever you're working with, they shouldn't have touched this. Some things are buried for a reason, and they need to *stay* buried."

As he talks, the strangest thing happens. If my whole body weren't paralyzed, I probably would have screamed. A tall shadow appears in the hallway behind him, and as it grows, it slowly reveals the shape of a man.

Who is it?

It's you.

You're standing behind him, just a few yards back, shrouded in darkness. You don't make a single sound, not even a breath.

"I thought we all knew it was too dangerous." Toby is still talking. He hasn't noticed you. "I spoke to Stan. I thought we *agreed*."

You take three swift steps—covering the distance between you and Toby in an instant—and lay your hands on his neck.

He jerks around to face you. You're a good head taller than him.

I can't see the expression on his face, but his voice shakes with panic. "Y-You?!" he stammers. "How?!"

You purse your lips and go, "Shhhhhhhhh," like you're admonishing a child.

Then you give his head an almighty twist. The crack of his neck snapping rings through the room, followed by the thump of his body hitting the floor.

You step over his body. Toward me.

I still can't move. I can just gaze at you out of frozen eyes, like I'm watching a film play out and there's nothing I can change. The ending's already written.

"Thank you for leading me to Tobias, Maggie," you say. Your voice is soft, almost tender. "He was more dangerous than you know. I understand why you tried to get away from me. You must understand that I have never tried to hurt you or Stanley. I am only trying to protect you. That is why I kept things from you, to protect you from men like him. I can see now that this was the wrong decision. I can see you're too strong for that."

You lean over and pick me up, like I'm a feather. You barely even exhale. I'm cradled in your arms like a child, like a lover, as you walk me out of the house and into the street, where a large army-style truck is waiting.

"I will take you back to your husband. He is safe and happy. You need to rest. When we get there, I will explain everything as best as I can."

12 | Stanley
1960

THE SUN WAS JUST BEGINNING TO SET OVER THE CITY. IT WAS EARLY STILL, just after four, and the streets were not yet full of commuters bustling their way home. A tranquility—like the calm before a storm—settled over the cobblestone pathways and twisting alleys.

The bottle of champagne popped, and a thick flow of white oozed into the coffee mugs. They were the only drinking ware that could be found in the lab on short notice.

"This feels like tempting fate," Stanley said, chinking his mug against Raph's. They were sitting on one of the balconies of the Lazarus Building, outside Raph's office. "We haven't done anything yet."

"This is going to be the one," Raph replied, taking a swig of champagne. "I can feel it. Also, it's not like I bought this bottle specifically to celebrate. My dad used to get sent, like, five million of them over Christmas, and they just ended up accumulating in his office and in storage, so now I just dive in whenever I want. You looked like you needed to clear your nerves. I mean, when's the last time you had champagne this good?"

Stanley chuckled, shaking his head. He couldn't remember the last time he'd had a drink that didn't taste like paint stripper. If he was honest, he'd been so focused over the past few months that he hadn't had a sip of any booze at all.

"Is it worth it, do you think?" he asked.

Raph shifted uncomfortably. "What do you mean?"

"I'm not blind, Raph. I know how uncomfortable these experiments have made you, particularly in the last four months."

He waved his hand, as if to swat the thought away. "It might not be *legal*, but I've done everything I can to ensure this is as ethically sound as possible. They're all consenting adults."

"But you still don't want to do it. We bullied you into it. I hate that we did that."

Raph shrugged. "You'd have done it without me either way. You're more like Jacques than you realize, you know."

Stanley didn't reply. He stood, then walked up to the edge of the balcony. He leaned over the railings and stared out at the city.

"It's the drive," Raph continued. "I've never had it in the same way you do. Both of you. You set your sights on something and you become . . . an unstoppable force. Like a storm, or a tidal wave, or something. Everything else just gets swept up in your wake."

Stanley took a sip of his champagne. It *was* very good champagne. "Is that what's happening here, Raph? You're getting swept up? Because I . . . I don't know. All this work, all these years of focus, everything I did with Waldman. I . . . I know I lack self-awareness sometimes."

Raph leaned forward in his seat. "What are you saying?"

"I don't think I'm capable of looking at this objectively anymore."

Raph didn't reply. They looked at each other, and Stanley's thoughts filled the silence.

"You remember my evolution hypothesis?" he said, eventually.

"Yeah—that maybe we evolved away from perfect memories, that we evolved to forget things."

"Yeah, okay, so, if that's true, I've been thinking: Why does evolution happen, like on a basic Darwinian level? Survival of the fittest, right?"

Raph nodded. "Sure."

"We evolve into characteristics that make us more likely to survive from predators. More likely to survive as a species. And if forgetting things is one of those characteristics . . ." He trailed off.

"I know the basics of evolutionary theory, Stan. You know I do. What's your point?"

"I don't know!" He threw his hands in the air, turning to face the city. "I don't know. I've been working this problem for so long that I feel like I can't see the woods for the trees. But sometimes I lie awake in my bed, and I think, *What the hell are we doing? Are we making a mistake?*"

He didn't say the words that plagued him, that ran through his head over and over again: *An immortal bane, dread, and dire, and fierce.*

He'd not told another soul about them, had tried to bury them deep in his mind, along with the image of Waldman swinging from the rope. But no matter how hard he tried, they would return unbidden: in the middle of the night, when he was in the shower or out for a walk. He couldn't get rid of them.

And Waldman's last two words, the most ominous of them all: *IT HUNGERS.*

He turned back around to face Raph. "If you tell me not to go through with this, I won't. It stops now. Just say the word."

"Seriously?"

"Seriously. I trust you, Raph. Implicitly. When I came to you a couple of years ago, it was just as a means to an end. But you helped me, because you've always been a better person than me. I trust you more than I trust myself these days. So it's up to you. You've never been comfortable with what we're doing here. You tell me to stop, and I'll stop."

Raph leaned back, his expression one of bewilderment. "I don't know what to say. I don't think it matters. Jacques would never let us stop. Not now."

"I can deal with Jacques, if I have to."

A throaty chuckle burst out of Raph's mouth. He got up and joined Stanley by the balcony's edge. "The thing is, I've never been anything without you two. I don't know. But I look at you some days and I think about . . . Do you know what Lorca said about being an artist? About what makes people create art?"

Stanley shook his head.

"I read it about a year ago. He said that the heart of that drive to create something strange and passionate and wonderful lies in 'trying to heal the wound that never heals.' And as soon as I read it, I thought of you. All your life, you've been trying to heal this wound, and I don't know what it is— maybe you don't even know what it is. But I'm hoping that if we actually pull this off, if we do this, then maybe your wound might heal. It might close up. That . . . that's worth it for me."

Stanley paused, shuffling uncomfortably. "Despite all your moral reservations? Despite all your objections last year?"

Raph sighed. "Yes. You're my best friend, Stan, and I love you. I'll see you through this."

Stanley edged in toward him a little bit until they were shoulder to shoulder. He wondered how he had ever doubted this man and the honesty of his friendship. He'd had other friends drop in and out of his life— Hugo, Toby, even Jacques, during better times—but none of them trusted *him* so completely. That kind of trust was priceless.

On the streets below, some workers were leaving their office buildings: getting out early, trying to beat the crowd and make it home to their families before dinnertime. Not many, though. This city could give you a strange sense of priorities, he thought. This world could leave you out in the cold if you didn't have someone to give you a little warmth now and again.

"Do you think we can actually do it?" Raph asked, breaking the silence. "I mean, actual *time travel*, capable of changing the past, of affecting the present in some meaningful way? Is this what Waldman was after? It's so . . . science fiction. So magical."

Stanley turned around, leaning back on the railings. "I don't think I ever knew what Waldman was really after. I thought I did, but he was more of a closed book than I realized. Did he see the thread—perfect memory leading to perfect observation of the past leading to actually *manifesting* in the past? I don't know. If he taught me anything, though, it's to believe that anything is possible."

Stanley checked his watch. It was time. He poured the last dregs of his champagne onto the balcony floor, and the liquid snaked its way down the drain. It was a nice gesture, but he wanted to be as focused as possible for what they were about to do.

THE WHOLE LABORATORY HAD ONLY SIX PEOPLE IN IT, INCLUDING RAPH, Stanley, and Jacques. They needed some staff to help run the machinery, but they had been picky. Only Toby, Maria, and Elias had been allowed to participate. There was too much at stake, too much to lose if someone they didn't trust decided to take their research to someone else, or to the police.

Stanley had vouched for Toby himself. They'd worked closely for almost two years, and he'd found himself impressed with the man's keen intellect and his determination. If you had a job that needed doing, you could give it to Toby and it would be done within the week without question or complaint.

Jacques had insisted on Elias, and no one had questioned whether or not Maria would be there. She had increasingly become Raph's right-hand woman: unobtrusive but always present when needed.

Maria walked past Stanley and gave him a curt, professional smile, placing a pile of folders on Raph's desk. He smiled back.

Stanley settled into a chair as Maria made her way out of the room. They had set up one of the offices as a makeshift observation deck, with a glass panel looking directly out into the central hall. It was Jacques's idea: He wanted the subject to have as little stimulus from the present as possible. The three of them would be in the next room over and would only talk to the subject through a radio intercom, watching from a distance.

He looked through the glass at Jacques and Elias, setting up the wiring on the chair. There was an understanding between the two of them—a sort of pact—that made Stanley a little uncomfortable.

"Stan?" He turned to find Toby standing behind him. "Can we talk?"

Stanley nodded. "Sure. What's up?"

Toby glanced outside the door and then pulled it closed so that it was just the two of them. "I know now is not exactly the time—what with the big experiment and all—but, well . . . you know when you've been meaning to tell someone something for a while but don't know how to say it? And then you just get to a point where you know that if you don't tell them now, you might never tell them?"

Stanley wheeled his chair forward. "What is it?"

"So I was looking at some of the drug trials for the fourth iteration a couple of weeks ago, and I needed to get some data from Jacques's section of the lab. Usually, I'd just get it from Elias, but he wasn't around, and . . ." He trailed off, glancing back at the door.

Stanley stood up. "Toby—what?"

"Whatever Jacques is working on, it isn't this. Or, at least, it isn't *just* this, the memory stuff. I think—I mean, it looks like—he's funneling money and resources into about six different side projects and writing them off as failed memory experiments so they don't look suspicious." Toby was talking very quickly, like he was trying to get it all out. "Raph's getting so much money from the oil rig thing that I think he barely notices the dips. Some of the projects, I couldn't make heads or tails of. Don't know if it was encrypted or in a different language, but it was gibberish to me. Others, well . . . there's stuff about computing in there, and biology— pictures of animal vivisections, reports about human organ regrowth. I don't know. I know it's not my place to judge, but the bits and pieces I saw looked a little disturbing, you know?"

Stanley put his hand to his brow, feeling an oncoming headache. This was the last thing he needed today. "How long have you known this?"

"Like, maybe a week and a half. I don't know how long it's been going on for." He bit his lip nervously and waited for half a second. "Look—if you talk to Jacques about this, just please don't mention my name, okay? I just . . . I thought you should know."

Then he slipped out the door, closing it behind him.

Stanley took a deep breath, an undercurrent of nervousness running through him. He couldn't think about this—not today. He'd address it later, bring it up with Raph, but today he had to focus completely and utterly on the task at hand. The honest truth was, they needed Jacques if they were going to get this done. He couldn't afford to antagonize him right now.

Reaching into a drawer, he pulled out the photograph that Jacques had shown him four months ago: Bill—the test subject—in the back garden of the house where he grew up, in the present day. He's taking a photo of himself, kneeling next to a hole he's dug. In his hand, still covered in mud, is a small school trophy like the ones you get for winning football matches in primary school. It's Bill's face that says it all—the look of wonder and bewilderment, the complete disbelief. It couldn't be clearer what he had done—gone back into his childhood memories and buried the trophy, only to dig it up now in the present.

It was proof. Proof that they could effect change in the past. That they could travel in time.

Except the trophy didn't exist anymore. It disappeared shortly after the photo was taken, and nobody ever saw it in person. When Raph went with Bill to investigate, they eventually found the trophy in the attic, years of dust on it, as though it had never been touched.

Whatever Bill had changed, it had reverted as soon as he tried to show it to someone else.

That's when it clicked for Stanley, when all the disparate parts of his work fell together neatly, like pieces of a machine.

The barrier was perfect memory, just like it had always been. Bill's memory of his past was flawed—it had changed and adapted over the years, as memories only do. When he went back into his memories, he was seeing a version of the past that only he had experienced. His brain had adapted his memories, thereby creating a purely individual timeline, and any changes he made existed only in that local timeline. As soon as he showed it to someone else, it reverted. Only the photo remained.

But if they could overcome the memory plateau *first*, if they could ensure that their test subject had access to what Stanley had been trying to unlock from the start—perfect, flawless objective memory of the past—then the observation of the memory should entangle with the collective past. The changes would exist for everyone, everywhere. They would *stay*.

Was this what you were after, Professor? Stanley thought as he fingered the edges of the picture. *Was this always the end goal?*

The door opened. Raph and Jacques came in, sitting down on either side of him. Toby followed behind but wavered a little, waiting at the door.

"It's time," Jacques said.

Stanley took a deep breath, trying to push what Toby had just told him to the back of his mind. He looked over at Raph, who gave him a warm, reassuring smile.

Looking through the thick glass partition, he could see their test subject—a young man named Kier, as Raph was sure to keep reminding Jacques—settling into the chair underneath the memory spade. They'd started calling it that after the seminal picture of Bill digging in the garden.

"This is it," Raph said. "We've tested all the parts of this separately. They all work. We're ready. Kier's ready."

Stanley nodded. Pressing a button in front of him, he turned on the intercom that connected the two rooms.

"Maria," he said, "please begin the procedure."

Maria administered the first set of drugs to Kier intravenously. He'd already undergone surgery earlier in the week, and the drugs were designed to work in tandem with the changes they had made to his neural connections.

Elias stood waiting impassively at the door, watching on in case any support was needed.

"Are you okay?" Maria asked. "Comfortable?"

Kier nodded. "Fine."

"It will take a few minutes for the drugs to take effect, and then we will administer the second dose."

The process was strict—every step laid out, every member or participant fully briefed beforehand. Stanley could feel his hands sweating.

After the second round of drugs, he felt that Kier's eyes looked a little wider, a little more alert.

"How are you now?" Maria asked, her voice playing over the speakers in the observation room.

"I can..." Kier muttered. "I think... I think it's working. Everything's so clear, like it just happened ten minutes ago. It's all coming back. I can see the lake I learned to swim in when I was three. It's... this is amazing. It's like I was *just there.*"

"Did you hear that?" Raph said excitedly. "Did you?"

Stanley put his hand up. It wasn't time for celebration yet.

"Maria," he said into the mic, "the questions, please."

She nodded, picking up her clipboard with the prepared questions. Questions they had assembled after months of delving into Kier's life. He did not know what any of them were going to be.

"In 1943, you visited your cousin's house in Kent once. What was the address?"

"Sixty-Eight North Farm Road, Tunbridge," he responded immediately, and then his mouth fell open in amazement. "Wow. I mean... wow."

She gave him a brief, professional smile. "You had a female teacher—Mrs. Tilscher—in year two of primary school. She occasionally mentioned her husband in passing, maybe once or twice. What was his name?"

"Harry," Kier said. "It was Harry Tilscher. Oh God—it's *all* there. All of that information. All those memories."

The back-and-forth continued through all twenty questions, testing him to the furthest reaches of his recall. He got every single one of them right.

Stanley's heart was pounding in his chest. His fingers gripped the intercom mic so hard that his knuckles were white.

"We did it," Raph whispered, staring through the glass. He got up. "Stan—we actually did it! Perfect, flawless memory. I can't believe it."

Stanley felt a wave of emotion wash over him—excitement, relief, bewilderment. He could barely pick them apart. He let out an involuntary laugh, and a huge smile grew on his face.

"We did it," he echoed, turning to Raph. They grinned stupidly at one another, and Stanley tried to keep his hands from shaking. He felt like he was about to cry. "Who would've thought?"

Jacques took the intercom mic.

"Thank you, Maria." His voice was cold and flat. "Please proceed to phase two."

She nodded.

Phase two—the memory dive.

Lifting the headset, she placed it on Kier, clipping the strap underneath his chin. The wires rolled out of the top and ran down the back of his head like a ponytail, attaching to the machinery underneath.

"We're going to ask you to return to a specific memory," Maria said. "From 1952—just like we practiced before, except this time you are going to bury an object in the garden outside the front of your house."

They had secured the plot of land there, untouched in the eight-year interim, and could access it after the experiment.

Kier nodded. Maria clicked on the machine, and he closed his eyes, his breathing quickening.

"Can you hear me?"

"Yes," Kier said. "I'm there. I'm actually there. I can see the house. God—I can see *myself*. What if I just . . . ?" He trailed off.

Kier's face, with all its fascination and excitement, had fallen flat. His arms went slack by his sides, his expression completely blank.

"Kier?" Maria asked. "Are you okay?"

He didn't reply. He just stared out into the space ahead of him.

Maria shook Kier, trying to get a response out of him. She took off the headset, putting her hands on his face. Elias started forward but hesitated, unsure—he didn't know what to do.

Raph turned his head to Stanley. "What's happening? What's happened to him?"

"I don't know," Stanley said. "I don't know. He was fine a moment ago. If we—"

"Hello?" Maria's voice came over the monitor. It was scared, panicked. "What's going on? Where . . . where am I?"

Stanley's head snapped back to look at the room. "What did she say?"

"I don't know where I am. I . . ." She was backing away from Kier, staring at both him and Elias. "Who are you? Who is *this*?"

Jacques spoke into the mic. "You are okay, Maria. You're having a brief episode. Neither of those men intends you harm. The one to your left is called Elias, and the man in the chair is . . ." He trailed off, frowning.

"Oh, fucking seriously?" Raph shouted. "His name is . . . it's . . . Stan, why can't I remember his name?"

"What?!" Stanley's heart dropped into his stomach. "I . . . Oh God." He couldn't remember it either. He raked for the knowledge in his own brain, but it wasn't there. "How do I not know? He's a test subject for the experiment, I know that. I *know* it! But . . . everything else is gone. It's just gone."

In the middle of the room, the subject remained completely still. He was breathing, alive, but his eyes stared listlessly ahead.

"Oh, fuck this," Toby muttered, halfway out the door. "No, no, no. I didn't sign up for this shit." And before anyone could say anything, he was gone.

"I don't know who I am," the woman said, growing increasingly frantic. Stanley couldn't remember her either—what the hell was going on? "How do I not know my own name?" She grabbed the files off the table and threw them to the floor. "How do I not know my own name?!"

Elias took hold of her, trying to keep her from doing any further damage. She sobbed, struggling to break free from his grasp. "Calm down," he said. "Your name is . . . Your name . . ." He stopped, letting her go.

His head turned toward the glass, looking directly at Stanley, at Raph, at Jacques.

His eyes were pure panic.

"Wo bin ich?" he said. "Was ist los?"

Jacques shot up from his seat, crossing the room and walking out the door.

"Where the hell are you going?" Raph demanded. Jacques ignored him.

Stanley's whole body shook. What the hell was going on? Why couldn't he remember who any of them were? And when he tried to think about the other two scientists—the woman and the man in that room—his mind came up blank. There was no memory of them. Nothing.

There was a loud beep. Stanley looked up, through the glass and into the experiment room, to see the light above the door turn red. Locked.

The man turned to look at it, frowning. He stormed over and futilely tried to get the door open.

Jacques reappeared next to Stanley.

"You locked them in?"

"Do you remember who I am?"

He hesitated. "Yes, of course I do."

"And do you remember who you are?"

"I . . . yes. What are you saying?"

"Whatever happened to the woman, it happened after she touched the subject in the chair. Whatever happened to that man, it happened after he touched the woman. We need to treat this like an outbreak."

"An outbreak of *what*?" Raph said. He was pacing back and forth, shaking his head.

"But you don't remember *their* names either?" Stanley asked Jacques, pointing into the room. "Or who they are?"

"No."

The man banged on the door, shouting, throwing his full weight against it. The woman pressed herself into a corner, shaking, shivering.

"Jesus, you locked them in," Raph repeated, spinning round. "Jacques . . . you *locked them in*. They're people. They—Oh God. What are we going to do?"

"Let me out!" the woman screamed, tearing at her hair. "*Please*. Whoever you are—let me out!"

Stanley pressed the intercom button. "Please try to remain calm. You are safe. We are attempting to fix this—"

"Ich kann dich nicht verstehen!" the man shouted. Whoever he was, it was clear he didn't speak English. "Was hast du mir angetan?"

The woman was still screaming, her words dissolving into incomprehensible panic—just a shrieking wail punctuated by staccato breaths.

The man shouted at her in German, but she didn't reply. She barely noticed he was there. Reaching under his lab coat, the man pulled a gun from the back of his belt.

Everyone froze.

"What the fuck?" Raph whispered. "Why does that man have a gun? Jacques! Why does that man have a gun?!"

Jacques waved him away. "I don't know! I'm not responsible for what other people carry on them."

"Bullshit!" Raph snapped back. "That's bullshit!"

The man waved his gun, shouting at the woman, bellowing at her.

Stanley's hand was tight on the mic, but he didn't say a word. He had no idea what to do. The same phrase just kept running through his head, over and over: *An immortal bane, dread, and dire, and fierce.*

The woman's wailing grew louder. It felt as if it could pierce through flesh and penetrate bone. Stanley winced, putting his hands over his ears.

"Halte die Klappe!" the German man yelled at her, brandishing his weapon. "Halte!"

But she wouldn't stop—she just kept screaming. Grimacing, he closed his eyes, and two gunshots rang out through the room. She convulsed, jolting with each bullet, and fell silent.

The man stumbled backward, one step, then two, bumping into the locked door.

"Was habe ich gemacht?" he said, staring at his hands in horror. "Was hast du mir angetan?"

He lifted the gun to his mouth and fired.

The three of them just stared in shocked, powerless silence at the bodies, at the blood, at the carnage.

And in the middle of it all, the test subject—eyes empty as a mannequin's—stared lifelessly back.

13

TRANSCRIPT NO. 273: Margaret Webb

DATE STAMP: 11 AUG. 2021

4 Hours, 48 Minutes, and 42 Seconds Until Dissolution

When I wake up, I'm in bed. It's comfortable—a soft duvet with that recently washed hotel feel and a mattress with just the right amount of give. The room is sparse, decorated in that minimalist style that dominates interiors these days, as if people are ashamed to have possessions or show them off.

I feel well rested, almost spry, in fact. I sit up in bed, and apart from the usual creaks and twists of an eighty-year-old body, I don't feel any pain. And then it floods back to me: the falling out of the window, the breaking of my shoulder and wrecking of my ankle. The paralysis. Either I have recovered exceptionally quickly or I have been asleep for a very long time.

I don't know which I find scarier.

As I ease out of bed, I realize I'm still in the same clothes I was wearing when I passed out. This brings me comfort. I can't bear the thought of someone—of you—undressing me and putting me in pajamas like I'm a child.

Then I think about Stanley. I don't know where he is. I need to find him.

I head straight for the door but have to stop.

Why?

My head feels woozy, like I've had too much to drink. The room spins, and I have to hold on to the wall and take a few breaths to orient myself.

That's when the door opens.

You're on the other side, smiling. This time it's genuine. I can tell—I've seen enough nature documentaries. It's the smile a wolf gives before it bites you.

"Maggie," you say, your voice warm, "I'm glad you're feeling better."

"Where's Stanley?"

You step to the side and put your arm out as an invite, as if you're expecting me to take it. "When we get to the—"

"No, Hassan." I steady my voice. I keep it utterly under control. "Enough of the 'When we just . . .' and 'If you'll let me . . .' Enough of the prevaricating and the gaslighting and the bullshit. Yesterday, I watched you kill a man. A man who was about to kill me. So I only have two questions, and I'm not going anywhere with you—I'm not *doing* anything for you—until you answer them: What is going on, and where the fuck is my husband?"

Your arm drops, but your smile doesn't.

"Decades ago, before you met him, your husband and some others discovered a method by which to access and effect change in the past. You might call it time travel, if you wish. It was the single greatest invention in human history. In an effort to bury this discovery and destroy this research, another group of people—people like the man you met yesterday, those who trade under the name Sunrise—did terrible damage to both Stanley's mind and the world as we know it. I am trying to reverse that. I am trying to help your husband regain both his memories and the recognition he deserves. Your husband is currently inside the Institute, and I am here to lead you to him. Perhaps you would like to ask any further questions on the way?"

I blink at you, a little overwhelmed by the frankness of your response. I expected you to wave my question away with a vague statement or a hint of a threat. Something has changed.

I follow you down a corridor that feels halfway between a hotel and a hospital—there are many doors to what I assume must be other rooms. I wonder who is being kept in them. I wonder if they are allowed to leave.

"And these people—Toby, Sunrise, the ones who have done this to Stanley—why do they want to bury his discovery?" I ask.

You start walking again, forcing me to follow. "Shortsightedness. Idiocy. A lack of historical perspective."

I look up at you, raising my eyebrows.

"They are scared of it," you add, with a hint of a sigh. "And they believe that knowledge can be contained, despite the entirety of human history proving otherwise. It's not that we here at the Institute do not realize there are dangers inherent in such a discovery; we merely acknowledge that these things cannot simply be buried. That if they are to be dealt with, they must be dealt with head-on."

We arrive in a lift lobby—these lifts thankfully devoid of the bizarre Greek lettering and unsettling warnings—and you press a button.

"Why are you so intent on finding it?"

You turn to look at me. "Have you seen the world we live in, Maggie? Have you seen what we have done to it? Whole ecosystems are dying. Seas are rising. Wildfires rage across continents. We are on a one-track path to destruction, and nothing is being done to reverse it."

The lift doors slide open, you beckon me inside. "The powers that your husband tapped into are incomparable in scale to anything that we have discovered before. Like the splitting of the atom, they usher in a new era of scientific thought. A new paradigm. If we can gain control over the past, does this not give us control over the future? With Stanley's discovery, with *your* help, we can take the reins of this planet in our hands. We can push back the tide."

"And Stanley?"

"Think what we can do if we can change the past, Maggie. Think what progress we can make. Modern medicine has come a long way in the past hundred years, further than many realize." You give me a meaningful look, and I think about my shoulder and how it was broken just yesterday. "Unlocking the past will do more than just allow us to travel. The knowledge will spark a new scientific and technological revolution. It's my absolute belief that with these new perspectives, the first man to ever live to be a thousand, or a hundred thousand years old, is already alive today. Perhaps we will even be able to give you and Stanley decades more time together. There's a happy extended life ahead of you. All you need to do is work with me."

I'm making a conscious effort to keep my breathing regular, to stay calm and rational, but it's difficult. I'm standing opposite a genie who has looked into my heart, found my deepest and most burning wish, and offered to grant it for me.

But I know my fairy tales: Genies are not to be trusted. Wishes are not what they appear to be.

Still, I say, "What do you need me to do?"

The lift doors open.

We are back at the Institute, in the main laboratory, where you brought me when I first arrived. I stop, staring around me, trying to reconcile the sudden shift. The rooms were in the towering building above, I realize, on-site accommodations for people working here. You step outside, and I follow in your wake.

"Sunrise has done a better job than I initially imagined. I had hoped all his memories would be recoverable by you on a few approaches, but that seems not to be the case. I have, with some success, mapped out the points in Stanley's memory that we can access. This is largely due to the scans I was able to make of your brains while you were diving. In theory, these will act like anchors so that you can travel to other parts of his memory, moments he cannot access alone. I need you to go back into his head with the spade, into these moments in his past, and find out what happened there."

"Into the past?"

"Yes—through his memories. That is how the machine works."

"Why can't you do it?"

"Sunrise has removed much. If the memories are there, they are deeply buried. It needs to be someone with a close connection to the subject, with enough shared memories that the link is established with clear fidelity. You shared decades together—you are by far the best candidate."

The lab seems to be working as normal. Nothing has changed: Men and women with lab coats and clipboards bustle from room to room, dealing with strange technology that I do not recognize. They throw us quick, furtive glances. They put on forced smiles as we pass. Seeing it a second time makes it all the more clear—everyone in this building is terrified of you.

You lead me into a β lift, and it descends back down into your strange anachronistic office.

Stanley is sitting in his wheelchair in the middle of the room, watching an old nature documentary on one of the screens. When I see him, I let out a little sound of relief, somewhere between a sigh and a squeal, and I rush over to him, taking his hand.

He doesn't react. He briefly glances over at me, like one might at a bird flying past the window, and he grunts before turning back to his screen. He recognizes me today—I can see that in his eyes—but he simply doesn't care. He is aware but distant, like his mind is on another planet.

"Morning, Stan," I say, stroking his arm. "So glad to see you're all right."

He tuts, as if my talking is bothering him, but I don't care. It's so good to see him. Because though I try not to, when I look at him now, I don't just see *him*; I see possibility. I see not being tied to visiting a care home every day just to see his face. I see the potential of a real future together again, with real conversations and date-night meals and Leah visiting over Christmas, perhaps having a glass of wine and opening presents with us. Because maybe if he came back to me, Leah would too, and everything could be okay again.

Maybe I could live again.

Standing straight, I step away from him before I become overwhelmed. I must be strong, because I still have questions.

"The last time I went into his mind," I say, "on that beach, what happened?"

You are already at the monitors, tapping in data. "Stanley forgot. That is what Sunrise did to him. They made him forget things. You were unfortunate enough to see one of the holes in his memory—one of the pieces that has been expunged."

"But why couldn't Toby remember him being there?"

You look momentarily confused, then shrug. "He's an old man, I suppose. It was an inconsequential moment decades ago. He wasn't superhuman. He forgot things too."

I frown, because that doesn't feel right.

Why not?

There was more to it than that, I'm sure of it, but I can't quite explain why.

"What is Omega?" I ask.

You stop tapping at the screen. You turn to me, slowly, like a marionette, and some deep instinctual part of me screams: *You shouldn't have said that.*

"Why do you ask?"

I take an involuntary step back. "Toby mentioned it. He asked what we had done about Omega. I . . . I didn't know what he was talking about."

You shake your head, annoyed. "It isn't relevant. It's not something you need to know about."

"But . . . ," I say, suddenly unsure, "he seemed worried; he seemed—"

You take two steps toward me, until you are close enough to touch, and my words fall short. You take my hand. A little jolt of electricity runs up my arm when your skin touches mine. It's so soft, so smooth and un-blemished, like you've been crafted from silk. Like you've been grown in a vat.

You lean down toward me, face close to mine.

"Maggie, I understand that you are scared, but this will only work if you learn to trust me. You act as though I am out to get you or hurt you somehow. I do not deserve this. Think: Since the moment we met, I have helped you break your husband out of a prison you didn't even know he was in. I have helped you reconnect with his memories. When you ran from here, even though you were always free to leave, I saved your life. I healed your broken body. Throughout all of this, I have not harmed you or your husband; I have not restricted you; I have not lied to you. Per-haps, after all I have done, you can do me the courtesy of showing me a little good faith?"

And I don't know what to say.

Do you believe me?

Yes. I mean, I don't debate the truth of anything you've just said. It is true, and when you lay it out like that, it's obvious. It's just . . .

Just what?

It doesn't *feel* like the whole truth. There's some part of me, some non-logical gut instinct, that tells me this isn't the full story. You are leaving out some very important parts.

What do you do about it?

I look over at Stanley and then over to the room with the chair and the bath in it: the memory spade. The door is open, and the spade sits there, waiting for us. I think about the possibilities you offer, and I take that gut instinct and crush it. I bury it deep down inside of me. You're right, I think. You've done nothing but help me. It's time for me to return the favor.

With my help, you move Stanley into the room and settle him into the chair. He seems less worried than before. Perhaps he is simply more vacant.

"Where do you need me to go?"

"There is a specific moment we need to see. It's a blip, hidden from my scans—as though it has been deliberately buried—and I need you to access it directly. It is here." You tap the screen, and a date shows up: May 17, 1969.

I stare at it. "Are you serious? Why *that* day?"

Your face hardens. "You recognize it?"

"There is no way I could ever forget it. It's the day Stanley and I got married."

"That," you say carefully, "is very interesting."

"Why?"

"I don't know yet. When you go in, make sure you observe everything you can, particularly everything to do with Stanley, but do not interact. Do not talk to yourself, or Stanley, or anyone. If you keep yourself distant, the brain will just resolve you out of the memory, like fighting off an infection."

"I don't understand. I thought I was going into the past."

You shake your head. "Not quite. Like before, you are entering the liminal space between memory and the past. Think of it this way: The past, like memory, *wants* to remain as it is. It does not like intrusions. If you remain a feature of the background, a mere observer, it will ignore you. In order to effect change, you need to consciously disrupt the narrative of events. I would ask that you not do that."

"Why not?"

You raise your eyebrows. "It's your wedding day. I wouldn't want you to ruin it."

I can barely focus as you strap Stanley into the machine and I prepare myself for the bath. All I can think is: *Our wedding.* It was a wonderful day—a beautiful memory—and the thought of being able to see that in the flesh after all these years makes me buzz with excitement. I'm so consumed by the idea as I place the helmet over my head that I barely notice you turn the machine on until my whole world disappears.

And then it returns—piece by piece—but it's less disorienting each time.

I know what to expect, and my mind is ready for it. I'm growing used to the travel.

Squinting, I raise my hand to block out the bright sunlight shining down from above. I take a deep breath of air—really fresh air—and it fills my lungs like honey.

I am there: Capheaton Hall in Northumberland. I still remember the first time I set eyes on the centuries-old English country house. When I was a teenager, I never thought I'd get married at all, let alone in such a grand place. But Stanley had a lot of money squirreled away from a bunch of different research jobs he did in his twenties. I never asked that much about it back then, because when I did, he would clam up, but I'm starting to realize what some of that research must have entailed.

We're up in Northumberland because that's where my family's from. They weren't rich—or, at least, they didn't come from money—but they'd managed to climb up a class rung or two in their lives and had the giant chips on their shoulders to prove it. It always felt like the wedding was, for them, more an opportunity to show off to friends and family how well they'd done than it was anything to do with me. Sums up my upbringing, though, I suppose. How you appeared to others trumped every other concern. They all but disowned me when I started showing up drunk and wearing clothes they felt would be judged by others, but now, a *wedding*, an opportunity to show me off, and it was like we'd never been on anything but the best of terms.

Stan didn't talk about his family—only his mum got an invite to the wedding, and she didn't show up. My parents found this baffling but just about managed not to comment.

I can see the guests in the distance, starting to arrive. Taxis are pulling up the long front drive, framed by trees on either side. All around is nothing but miles and miles of country.

I'm about a hundred yards away from the hall, out in a field. God knows why the memory dropped me here. I'm sure I look out of place—an old woman standing in a field—but I remember what you said, about me not being seen if I just observed, so I walk toward the hall.

As I slip inside, it all comes back to me: the table decorations, the cake, the damn guest list. All the arguments with my mother over who she said *must* be there, despite the fact that Stanley and I both wanted a small wedding, despite the fact that Stanley's side of the guest list consisted of about four people and my mother's side had over forty. God, it's been fifty years, and I'm *still* angry about it.

Though it's not like I had many friends to invite anyway—all of them were people I'd met after Stanley, through the charity job or local community events. Everyone I considered a friend in my early twenties was lost to the fog of time within a few years. It's not like we had mobile numbers back then, and it was almost impossible to track someone down if they didn't have a steady address.

The clock on the wall says it's 1:13, and the ceremony is at 2:00. I must be upstairs, getting ready. My maid of honor, Linda, is trying to get a whole bottle of champagne down me to calm my nerves. The thought of her brings a pang to my heart. She died seven years ago. Breast cancer.

Despite my overwhelming urge to go and see her, still alive and laughing, I remember why I'm here. To find Stanley.

He would be in the adjoining suite with his best man, Hugo, at the moment. Leaving the downstairs preparations behind, I start to climb the stairs when I gasp.

My mother, in all her matriarchal glory, is swooping down toward me. My mind cycles through a million emotions: how much I can't stand her, how infuriating she is, how much I miss her, how much I just want to stop her and tell her that I love her before she's dead and gone.

I'm almost thirty years older than my mother is at this moment, and the mere sight of her makes me feel like a child again.

But she doesn't even register me.

She's in full project-manager mode, and I'm just another old lady—probably a cleaner or a florist—whom she doesn't have time to talk to. Bustling past me, she calls out for my father in a shrill voice and storms into the next room.

I take a deep breath. Focus. *That's not why you're here.*

When I reach the top of the stairs and the long corridor that connects all the upstairs rooms, I see Stanley step out into it. He's got his back to me, turning just as he exits the room, and I resist the urge to run over to him, to grab him from behind in a giant embrace.

He starts walking away, and I follow, quietly, until he reaches the set of stairs on the west-facing side of the house. He's all dressed for the occasion, suited and booted, but he's alone. I wonder where Hugo is.

At the top of the steps, he pauses. He waits for about five seconds, maybe more, rubbing his hands together. He seems jittery, even worried, but that makes sense. I remember how nervous he was on our wedding day. I remember how cute it was, and how he eased up after the main meal. He really hates speeches.

I follow, keeping a healthy distance, but with each step, an unease grows inside me, a sense that something is not right.

Why?

He's not going down to the ceremony room or the main reception area. He walks straight out of the building and across the driveway, heading for the field. Our wedding is in just over half an hour. He was there. He wasn't late. Where is he going?

You're still following him?

Yes—how could I possibly not? He's quickened his pace, but it seems more out of gnawing anxiety than urgency. We've cut into the forested area and have been trekking across the undergrowth for a good minute or two now: he all dressed up in his three-piece suit, ready to get married, and me twenty or thirty yards behind, struggling to keep up. He's walking so determinedly that he never even looks around him.

A few steps later, I see where he's headed. At the front of the long drive, near where the grounds of the property begin, there's a gatehouse. The owners told us that it was abandoned, having fallen out of use in the 1920s. It's more of a relic now, wallowing in an ever-increasing decay.

It looms into view as we exit the copse of trees—the stones are broken and muddy; the windows are without glass, just open holes for vines and tendrils to creep in. As I approach, the scent of lavender drifts through the air.

He enters the gatehouse, pushing back the decrepit wooden door, only just barely hanging on its hinges. It creaks so loudly I jump. I hadn't realized how quiet it was out here.

I approach slowly, unsure how much distance I should keep. I remember your warning, but I *need* to know what he's doing in there. This happened just half an hour before we got married. How did I not know? What else has he been hiding from me all these years?

For a moment, I think I smell something pungent, like petrol. But the scent of lavender rises over it as I near the door, overpowering almost everything else, and a sudden memory hits me like a train: of Stanley demanding that we order loads of lavender bouquets for the reception; of me baffled but happily acquiescing; of the florists telling us on our wedding day that they must have made a mistake, that all the flowers we ordered had gone missing.

Are they here? Did Stanley hide them?

Why?

I push open the door.

The first thing I see is Stanley lighting a match and dropping it. A pile of wood underneath explodes into flames. Propelled by gasoline, the fire shoots all around the room—across the floor, up the walls and ceiling. There are symbols on the walls, painted in what I'm desperately hoping is red paint and not blood. They look old, like Egyptian hieroglyphics or Babylonian cuneiform scripts.

All around the room are flowers and herbs: mostly lavender, but I see a mixture of jasmine and wisteria too. They're wedding florals, with ribbons and filler greenery. They look so utterly out of place. After the initial burst of flame, the bonfire in the center now burns and crackles happily, lighting the dark interior.

Stanley is standing in front of it. He turns, but his face is masked in silhouette.

"We have eight minutes," he says. "Any longer and the sanctuary loses integrity."

He steps forward, and the light reveals him. He has a huge smile on his face.

"Maggie. It's really you. I wasn't sure I'd ever see you again."

I stare, unable to fully process that Stanley, the thirty-two-year-old man I married, looking even more handsome and charming now than the day I met him, is looking at me. Talking to *me*, like he expected me to be here.

"I wanted to believe," he says, "but it's been years. I . . . I didn't think you'd come."

"I'm not meant to talk to you," I say. It's the only thing I can think to say.

He takes a few more steps forward, then takes my hand in his. "And since when have you ever done what you're meant to, my dear?"

And I melt. I just collapse into him. He catches me in his arms and holds me tightly, pulling me into him. I look up at him, and he kisses my forehead, then my lips, and my whole body shivers. I don't know how long it's been since I've been kissed.

I flinch then, realizing where I am, *who* I am, and I pull away from him. "Stan," I mutter, trying to keep the tears out of my eyes. "I can't . . . I'm not . . . I'm *so old*."

He doesn't let me go—not fully. He holds my hand as I straighten up, and his eyes are filled with emotion. "You're beautiful. You have always been beautiful."

Then the tears come. They trickle down my face. "I've missed you so much," I manage. "I've tried so hard, but . . . but I—"

"It's okay," he says. "I know. I wish we had more time, but we don't. This was the best I could manage. There are far more powerful forces at work."

His shift in tone pulls me back into reality. *Pull yourself together, Maggie*, I think as I straighten up. *Whatever this is, it's important.*

"What's going on?"

"I have so much to tell you." He bites his lip. "So much that you need to know, but I need to do this right. I only get one shot. What date is it where you're from?"

"August 10, 2021."

He nods. "You were right. It's barely been a day."

"What do you mean?"

"This is not the first time we talk to one another across the decades." He looks down at the floor, at his feet. His voice breaks. "In fact, I think this is the last time I ever do, and that's already running out."

I pull him closer. "What can I do? You led me here to talk to me— why?"

"Because you told me to, before. In my past. In *your* future, I think. You told me to be here at this exact time and to set up the protections so we can talk. You told me it was necessary. It was the turning point."

I grip his hand in mine, relishing his touch as I try to take it all in. "And what did I tell you to say?"

"That I am going to need you soon, the next time you go back. I'm going to need you to be patient with me, to be there for me when I'm at my lowest. You need to find me on two dates: November 9, 1961, and October 7, 1963. Be there. I am counting on you."

I take a deep breath, closing my eyes and repeating the dates to myself three or four times. Then I look up at him. "How many times have you seen me before—I mean, me like this, *old* me?"

His face breaks into a glorious smile. "Oh, Maggie, you have no idea."

I want to throw myself back into him. I want to be kissed again, to lose myself in his embrace, to forget everything around us. But I can't.

"There's more," I say, "isn't there?"

He nods solemnly. "There is a man with you in your present—Hassan. Whatever he says, he can't be trusted."

I almost laugh. "I actually don't think I needed you to tell me that."

"Oh," he said, "and when you see me, you might want to suggest a trip to Australia."

"Australia? You mean that holiday you were always on about? And what does Hassan want? And—" I fall short. There is no end to my questions.

He opens his mouth, but nothing comes out. His face scrunches up in frustration. "I'm sorry, Maggie. I can't. There's too much at play. Bootstrap paradoxes. Events that *must* happen in a certain order. I wish I could, but—"

"It's okay," I say, seeing his guilt, wanting to do anything I can to soothe it. "Tell me what you can."

"There is a larger game at work here than you are aware of. Some of us are pawns, and some of us are players. Your best protection right now is to keep Hassan thinking you're a pawn. Keep him thinking you can be played. And when it matters, when the time comes, go to Thamus and Theuth. Remember that. Tell no one."

"Thamus and Theuth," I repeat back, followed by a mention of the two dates and Australia. "This is a lot to remember."

"You'll remember. I promise. You already have." He looks at his watch and lets out a sigh. "Time's almost up."

"No," I say, pulling on his hand, drawing him near to me. I want to feel his body around mine. I need to feel his shape. He acquiesces, enveloping me whole as I press my face into him.

"I've got a wedding to get to," he says, and I let out a little burst that is somewhere between a sob and a laugh. I'm curled into his chest, crying into it.

Oh God—he showed up at the ceremony with a wet patch on his shirt. I remember it so clearly. He told me he spilled water on it, and I teased him for being so clumsy on our wedding day. But it wasn't water. It was never water.

"Don't let me go," I whisper. "Never let me go. I want to stay here with you."

"It will all be okay," he replies, his voice soft. "Remember that I love you. I'm going to go into that house right now and prove it. I have always loved you, even before you met me. I love you here, and I love you out there, now, always, forever. Whatever else is taken, they can't take that from us."

He releases me, and I feel like I've been dropped into the middle of an ocean—alone, cold, drowning. He checks his watch as he steps past me and walks out of the gatehouse, back across the field, and toward the house.

I stand in that room and cry for a while. Not for long—just long enough to gather myself together.

I can't stay here forever. There's a wedding about to happen, and I wouldn't miss it for all the world.

By the time I make it back to the house, the ceremony is just about to begin. Stanley is already standing at the front of the aisle with Hugo. Everybody is in their seats, waiting expectantly, and someone is playing Schubert on the piano.

I come in through the back door, sidling my way to the back of the room and staying out of sight. And I don't know if it's coincidence or some subconscious knowledge that's drawn me to this spot, but I realize exactly where I am.

I'm where I waited before I walked down the aisle.

I turn, and there I am.

There *she* is.

More beautiful than I have ever pictured myself being—the dress, the hair, the smile. She is an angel. She is perfect.

And I think: *This can't be the past, the objective truth of what I looked like. Nobody looks that good. These are Stan's memories, but then, how am I affecting things?*

That's not relevant.

Except it is. I have a sudden urge to know, to understand. I approach her and stand in her way, directly in her way so that she has to notice I'm there.

That's not a good idea. I told you to just observe.

She blinks. "Can I help you?"

This is a mistake.

"The bananas are flying to Montenegro," I say. It's nonsense, but I want her to remember it. I think, *There's no way that I'll forget a batty old woman telling me about bananas in Montenegro just before I walk down the aisle. No possible way.*

And what happens?

I don't remember it. In *my* memory, there's no one there. There's just the aisle and the wedding and the beautiful reception that follows.

It doesn't make sense.

It's happening.

Oh God. What's happening?

You shouldn't have spoken to her. You should have walked away.

I can't choose what I do in the past, Hassan! It's already done. She steps around me, looking understandably confused but probably assuming I'm a crazy aunt. There's no time for her to worry about me. The music has changed.

It's showtime.

You're not going to leave?

No, Hassan. I'm going to stay, and I'm going to watch like an idiot. Because I can't help it. It's my wedding. I need to see it happen.

She's in perfect form. She's alone, the relationship with Dad too strained for his walking her down the aisle to be anything other than awkward, but that doesn't matter. She walks down with the grace of a hundred practiced hours, pacing back and forth in her bedroom, dreaming about this moment. She basks in it.

Stanley throws back a glance at her—he can't help himself—and I can see the wonder on his face, like he's looking upon one of the ancient wonders of the world or the birth of a new sun.

She arrives at the front, and they stand side by side, ready for the registrar to perform the ceremony, to pronounce the words they have been so waiting for.

But the registrar isn't there.

My heart drops into my stomach.

In her place, there is a twisting, empty, sickening *nothingness*. Like a tear in the fabric of the universe. It yawns outward and consumes the podium that was in front of her, the tables and books to the side.

Screams rise from the seats—they can see it too. People stumble over one another, backing away.

But the emptiness grows, stretching outward like it's *hungry* for more. It takes and it takes and it takes. The flowers, the decorations, the ceiling.

Stanley stumbles backward, trying to pull Maggie—young Maggie—with him, but all she can do is stare. He trips, falling to the floor as the emptiness spreads and envelops her and swallows her whole.

"NO!" Stanley screams, but I can barely hear it over all the others. I'm locked in place, unable to move, as I watch this *thing* spread and swallow more and more guests, chairs, the building itself.

People are pushing at each other, shrieking, tripping over decorations.

Stanley rushes toward me and grabs me by the shoulders, the emptiness hot behind him. His eyes are wide. They are distilled panic.

"This is wrong," he says. "This isn't meant to happen."

With a shove, he pushes me away from him.

"RUN!"

I stumble into a run, or as close to a run as I can manage these days. My heart is pounding in my chest, my whole body shaking.

I make it out the back door and into the driveway. I turn to see the entire house encircled by emptiness and everyone in it consumed: Stanley, the guests, myself.

Gone.

There are others running, spreading into the field, but as I watch it, I realize it's futile.

There is no running from this thing. There is no power that can fight it.

I take the only way out I can: Feeling for that pull in the back of my mind, the one I held on to the last time I dove, I tug backward. I rip myself up and out of the memory just as the surrounding emptiness is about to touch me—

And I'm awake.

I'm in the bath, at the Institute.

And the wedding is gone. It's *gone*.

Yes.

I . . . I can't remember it. I can't remember getting married. Not just then, at the Institute, but now, here, in this godforsaken swimming pool. I can remember everything up to that moment, but I can't remember my own wedding anymore. Why can't I remember it?

Because it's gone.

What do you mean it's gone? I thought this pill was supposed to help me remember everything. How can I have possibly—

It is, unfortunately, not a question of memory. No one will ever remember it. It was taken. It is gone. Forever. It no longer happened.

What?! But I know that I'm married; I know that it took place. I just can't access the . . . the . . .

No. It has been wiped from the past. It no longer took place, for anyone. The day never happened. You merely have a memory of the memory of your wedding. Of the times you have thought about the concept, afterward, but not of the actual event. It has been wiped from the past.

Jesus Christ, Hassan, what have you done?

I have done nothing. You chose to deviate from the path, to affect events. You have encountered Omega—the final word. The end of all things. I had hoped it would not come to this.

So what you told me before, about the beach disappearing, when you said that was just Stanley and Toby being forgetful—

I lied. They were not forgetful. That moment has also been taken from the past.

That's it? That's all you have to say? You *lied*?

It was a mistake, Maggie. As we have just seen, we all make mistakes. In the face of such forces, do not be so quick to judge mine.

I   Such *forces*? This is crazy. This is insane.

Why do you think I have been so focused, Maggie? Why do you think we are here, kept in this pool? It keeps us safe, much like a Faraday cage blocks electromagnetic fields. There are protections upon protections here.

I   Protections from Omega?

Many years ago, Stanley performed an experiment, and he unleashed something that had been dormant for countless millennia—a primordial force beyond our understanding. It hunts, Maggie. It hunts him and everyone who was in that room. It's hungry, and it will never be sated. That is also why he loses his memories—bits of his past are being consumed by it. And soon, once it's done, it will spread to all of us as well.

I   Oh God.

I am trying to stop it. That is why I press you so urgently. We have had systems in place—layers upon layers to keep it contained—but it's lashing out. We can only just keep it at bay, but we need the full picture. In order to get that, we need Stanley. Only he knows how to stop it completely. Only he discovered the solution, and in your memory somewhere—this memory you are recounting to me—is the key to where it's hidden.

I   Hassan, I . . . I don't know.

Not yet, no. But you have already been more helpful than you realize. Sunrise has kept me out for so long. Without you, I would have achieved none of this. We must continue. Everything depends on it. There is not much time left. You are back at the Institute—are there any other details you can remember?

I'm breathing hard and fast, hyperventilating. I can't get air into my lungs quick enough. The horror of what I've just seen, that vast impossible emptiness, is lodged in my mind. You're asking me questions, but I can't focus on anything beyond the panic. I'm struggling to breathe, struggling to sit upright or lie down.

You inject something into my arm, and my breathing slows. I manage to lie back, letting my mind decompress. A weariness trickles through me like molasses, like tar, pressing me back against the rim of the bath.

I look to my right and see Stanley next to me now, peacefully asleep. I wonder if you gave him the same thing.

"What did you see?" you ask me, leaning over me. "What happened?"

"What did you give me?"

"A sedative," you say. "To calm your nerves. Nothing more. You must tell me what you saw in that dive."

I try to tell you as best I can. My head is a little woozy from the drug you just gave me, and I think some of it comes out garbled. I tell you about the wedding, and about Stanley.

"He was waiting there for you?"

My breath catches in my throat. I don't want to tell you. I shouldn't, because I know you can't be trusted. But you are standing over me so expectantly, and Stanley's words echo in my head.

Your best protection right now is to keep Hassan thinking you're a pawn.

"Yes," I say, slowly, weighing up what to tell and what not to. "Yes, he set it up for us."

"Set what up? Describe it to me."

And so I tell you: about the fire, about the flowers, about the symbols on the walls. You press me for further details as I talk—what flowers, exactly? what did the symbols look like? what did he say to you?—and I try to explain as best I can, all the while leaving some little details out. You press further, bowing over me like a vulture. It's the most passionate I have ever seen you.

"He just said that he needed me to be there for him, in my future," I say, cutting the rest of our conversation out completely. "He said he needed me to keep going back. That was it. Then everything got . . ." I shake my head. Everything after that moment is gone. A blank. It never took place.

And yet you are telling me everything now, even the things you chose to hide from me then.

Yes.

Why?

Because I'm tired, Hassan. Because I want this all to be over. And because I clearly tried lying to you in the past and look where that got me: drugged and interrogated in a fucking swimming pool. Obviously, whatever I was trying to do didn't work. It didn't save Stanley.

Indeed. And how do I react to your revelations?

You nod your head, smiling. You seem pleased with your discoveries. You step away from the bath to check on Stanley, and I feel the sedative take full effect. I close my eyes, letting out a long, deep breath.

But as the silence settles over me, I crack one eye open. You are bent over Stanley, examining his sleeping face. You pull out a cigarette and light it, taking a long drag as the wisps of smoke dance in the air above your head.

I assume you must think that I am asleep, and that you are alone in the room, because as I watch you lean into him, I hear you mutter the strangest thing.

"Knight to king five, old friend," you whisper. "Check."

14 | Stanley
1960

STANLEY DIDN'T QUITE KNOW WHAT HAD HAPPENED. HE REMEMBERED what their plan was. He remembered his balcony chat with Raph over a glass of champagne. He remembered the excitement that had come with breaking the memory barrier. And then—

There were three people in the experiment room before them. Two were dead, their blood slowly seeping out of their bodies and across the white laminate floor, oozing like spilled honey. The third looked back at Stanley—face blank, eyes drooping—as though his very soul had been scooped out.

He didn't know who any of them were. He had never seen them before in his life.

Nobody said anything. Stanley's brain was in panic, like a thousand voices were screaming all at once and he was unable to properly concentrate on what was being said. Every time he looked at the bodies in the other room, he thought of finding Waldman's corpse, dangling from that rope.

"What are we going to do?" Raph whispered eventually, staring out at the strangers. They were all staring. "What the hell do we do?"

Stanley glanced at Jacques and Raph. Jacques stood impassively, like a robot. Like a machine running through calculations. Raph's face had gone pale, his hands shaking.

"We need to find out who they are," Stanley said, turning to something that might give him some power over the situation, some semblance of control.

"We've all gone mad," Raph muttered. "Some kind of mass hysteria. Or memory loss. It doesn't make any sense."

"No," Stanley replied. "No, I won't believe that. There's an explanation here, somewhere. I remember . . . I remember *why* they were here. We were doing a memory experiment, a dive."

"Yes," Jacques said, his voice like steel. "I remember remembering them, but not the people themselves—you know what I mean?"

"The . . . the concept of them is . . . ," Stanley whispered. "I remember that we *had* staff, but when I try to actually picture them . . ."

"They're not there," Jacques said. "Removed. I know nothing about them."

Raph was wordless. He held his head in his hands, staring off into space.

Stanley flicked through the files in front of him in an attempt to get more information, but as he turned the pages, his eyes widened in horror. They were written in his own hand. They *should* have outlined who the test subject was, who was going to be involved in the procedure, and the plan for each stage.

Whole swaths of them were blank.

There were small sections that remained: notes about the drugs they were administering, references to Jacques, Raph, and Stanley himself. But as soon as the notes touched upon anything having to do with the three people in that room, the page was just empty. It was as if nothing had ever been written there at all.

A sickening bubble grew in Stanley's stomach. "I don't think this is just a memory issue."

Jacques turned to him, his whole body shifting like an obelisk. "What do you mean?"

"What if we haven't forgotten them? What if . . . I think maybe they don't exist anymore. I think they never existed."

"What the hell are you talking about?" Raph demanded, his fists clenched on the table in front of him. "I can see their bodies. I can *see* them. Are you going to tell me they aren't there?"

He shook his head. "I don't know. But I . . . I think they're just bodies. Like empty receptacles. Like suits of skin. I don't think there's anything else there."

Raph pointed at the man. "Tell that to the guy who's still alive."

"Raph, look at him," Stanley said, the bubble of horror ballooning inside of him, pushing at the walls of his body. "I mean, *really look*. He's breathing, but I don't think you could describe him as alive."

Raph collapsed into a chair. "What have we done? Oh God—we need to call an ambulance. We need to call the police. Get someone in here to—"

"Don't be ridiculous," Jacques snapped, slicing Raph's sentence in two. "We need to deal with damage control while we still can."

Stanley nodded. "He's right, Raph. We don't know what's in there."

"It spread," Jacques said, walking over to the observation window and staring out. Stanley could almost hear the cogs in his brain cranking. "Didn't you see it? It started with him before spreading to her and then to the German-speaking one with the gun, like an infection. And I haven't forgotten about anything outside of that room, have you?"

"No," Stanley replied. He looked over at Raph, who gave a small shake of his head.

"Then it appears to have been contained when I locked the door," Jacques continued. "When I kept them inside. We all seem to remember who *we* are. So now—we have to deal with them."

Raph looked up at him in dismay. "And what does 'deal with' mean to you?"

Jacques turned around. The lines on his face were very hard, like stone. "We burn them."

"What?!" Raph's eyes went wide. "Are you fucking kidding me? They're people. They . . . they have families. We need to—"

"Somehow," Jacques interrupted, "I do not think that their families will remember them."

"But you can't just . . ." He stood up, storming to the window. "One of them is still breathing!"

They turned to the man in the chair, who hadn't moved an inch since everything went wrong. He hadn't blinked. He hadn't done anything but stare back at them, expressionless.

"If it would make you more comfortable," Jacques said, "I could make him stop first."

Raph froze.

"You're insane," he said. "You're officially insane. We need to get him medical help. Stan? Stan?!"

Stanley tried to speak but found he was struggling to breathe. His stomach threatened to empty itself onto the floor of the lab. The horror inside of him had expanded to the size of his whole body now, and he felt it pressing further against the inside of his skin, as if he might burst at the seams.

Without a supporting voice, Raph frantically turned back to Jacques. "How the hell would you even burn them anyway? What, you want to set this lab, this whole building, on fire?"

"I have an incinerator," Jacques said. "I bought it a few months ago."

Raph gaped at him. "Why the *fuck* did you buy an incinerator?"

"I don't see that it matters," he said, waving the question away. "What's important now is that it's useful. It's not large enough for a whole body, but if we cut them up and do it in stages, it should work."

"I can't do this," Raph muttered, shaking his head. He got up, walking toward the door. "I can't do this. I'm going to the police. Two people are already dead because of *me*, and because of my funding, and I can't even remember who they are. I can't sit here and just talk about—"

"Raph, wait." Stanley put a hand on his shoulder. He couldn't let him leave. He couldn't be left alone with Jacques, with these bodies. "Please. We need to . . . to think about this together. We're all in this together. Don't walk out on me. I need you."

"There really isn't any discussion," Jacques continued, splaying his hands out as if he were explaining a concept to a student. "Whatever has been unleashed here must be stopped before it can spread. This is ground zero. Can you imagine the havoc this would wreak if it spread out into the world? Whether he is alive or not, we have to assume he is a threat. Whatever erased them from our memories could spread to us, then to anyone. If we can stop this here, now, we need to. We *must*. That or one man's life—and I think Stanley's right in saying he's not really alive anymore—is hardly a choice. We kill him. We burn the bodies. We work out what caused it and how we can stop it from ever happening again. Agreed?"

"No." Raph's whole body straightened up, stiff as a metal post. "Not fucking agreed. I don't care what your arguments are. I'm not going to agree to kill someone, whatever state he's in."

"Raph," Stanley said weakly, "I agree with you in principle, I do. But . . ."

"But?" Raph blinked at him. "Seriously?"

"I don't know, Raph!" he shouted. He had been warned about this. He had been warned to leave it alone, but he had pressed on anyway. This was his fault, and if this got out into the world, it would be his doing. "I don't know, but Jacques makes a damn good point."

They were standing together, facing one another in silence. Jacques watched them quietly, waiting.

"I think we have to do something," Stanley said, barely able to bring his voice above a whisper. "Here. Now. I think Jacques is right. We have to stop this before it spreads."

"You can't just—"

"You don't have to be a part of it if you can't handle it," Jacques added with a shrug. "I can do this for you. For you both. Just give me *time*."

Raph fell silent, looking at Jacques in shock, then back to Stanley, his mouth half-open. Stanley gave him a shrug, as if to say, *What choice do we have?* Raph stared at him for a few seconds, then sagged, his shoulders dropping and his chest deflating. When he got to the door, he stopped, as though he were about to say something, but he didn't.

The door closed behind him, leaving Stanley and Jacques all alone.

Jacques turned back to his desk, and Stanley wondered if he was hiding a smile.

JACQUES WENT FIRST TO THE CLEANROOM—THE ONE WHERE THE DRUGS were synthesized and where Raph kept the protective suits in a cupboard. They had mocked him when he bought them, teasing his overcautiousness and his worry. But Jacques donned one now, sealing himself from head to toe, and handed another to Stanley.

"I don't want to . . ."

"You don't have to *do* anything," Jacques said. "But if you're coming in with me, then you need to be protected. We don't know how this thing spread, but we can't take any chances."

As Stanley pulled the suit over his clothes, Jacques disappeared into his section of the lab and reappeared with a bone saw. Stanley didn't ask why he had it.

Jacques opened the door to the experiment room and had to step over the German man's body. Following behind, Stanley tried not to look but couldn't help it. His head was split open, an empty slab of meat whose contents were splattered all over the wall. Blood dripped from the instruments and spread in a thin sheen across the floor. After a couple of seconds, Stanley forced his eyes upward, staring intently at the ceiling to stop himself from throwing up.

Jacques leaned down cautiously, keeping a distance from the man. Slowly, inching his hand out, he tried to pluck the gun from the man's clutched grasp without touching his skin.

The dead fingers clung to it, and Jacques had to pull hard, lugging the body sideways by its arm.

Stanley went to look at the test subject. He lowered himself opposite the man, facing him eye to eye. The subject was sitting up, breathing, his heart beating, but there was no reaction.

You're not there, Stanley told himself. *You're brain-dead. There's nothing left.*

Just as he was working himself into believing that, Jacques walked up to the man and shot him in the temple.

Blood exploded out the other side of his head, brains and tissue spraying Stanley's face shield. He stumbled backward, gagging, as the ricochet of the bullet dinged around the room.

"Shit!" Jacques yelled, ducking low to the floor.

Stanley fell on his back, hands over his face and bile rising up his throat, into his mouth. He swallowed it back, grimacing in disgust. "What the fuck?" he managed, frantically trying to wipe bloody brain matter off his suit.

Jacques straightened up, breathing hard. "Sorry. I've never fired a gun before. When we were in the other room, it looked . . . neater."

Stanley tried to get up but slipped in the blood beneath him, tumbling back to the ground. He lay there, feeling faint, taking deep breaths to keep himself from passing out.

Jacques took a few steps toward the body of the woman. Cautiously, he took her by the arms and dragged her to the center of the room.

So there would be space to dismember her, Stanley realized grimly.

He got up slowly, on his hands and knees first.

"You still remember who you are?" Jacques asked him. He nodded. "Okay. Time to get to work."

It was a long, exhausting, gruesome business. Stanley kept having to look away as Jacques pressed the saw into the flesh, slicing open the skin and cutting deep into the muscles and sinews. Their hearts had stopped, but while the blood no longer spurted out of them, it still came—oozing and spreading across every surface.

There was a sickening clunk when the metal of the saw hit bone. Jacques had to cling to the dead leg, leaning his whole weight into the saw. It was drawn-out work, and with each scratch of metal against bone, Stanley felt his stomach turn again.

At times, he sat down and pressed his eyes shut just to get through it. But although Jacques told him he was welcome to leave the room if he wanted, this was his mess. Even if he was secretly grateful to Jacques for having the decisiveness and strength to do something about it, that gratefulness came layered with guilt: that he was pleased another man was dealing with his bodies for him, that he was relieved about any of this at all. So while his conscience wouldn't allow him to actually help Jacques with the dismemberment, it also wouldn't allow him to leave Jacques alone.

Jacques wasn't completely impervious to the horror. Even he had to put a bag over the poor woman's head in order to saw through her neck. But in two hours, he had broken apart her whole body into four limbs, a head, and a torso, then piled the pieces into hazardous-waste bags.

Wordlessly, Jacques walked over and sat down against the wall next to Stanley, clearly needing to give himself a few minutes to recover before he started on the other two.

The hours pushed on late into the night. After a while, Stanley helped to clean up the blood with soap and bleach, scrubbing the floors. He kept hoping that with each new body, with each new limb to be sawed, it would get a little easier. He would get more used to the horrific act he was witnessing. He didn't. If anything, each one was worse than the last.

Once it was done, they carried the bags out into the atrium and over to Jacques's section, through to an inner portion of the lab. Stanley had not been here in some time, and he noticed how much it had changed. There was new equipment: the incinerator at the back, yes, but also a range of more extensive surgical tools. There were saws and clamps. Animal organs in jars. Vats of different types of fluids: blood, bile, acid. Toby's warnings echoed in Stanley's head.

Whatever Jacques is working on, it isn't this.

Silently, they cleaned their suits and sprayed themselves down, putting the remnants into the bags. Raph appeared at the door as they were loading the remains into the incinerator. Wherever he had been, he'd seen them carrying the bags through and followed. His face was gaunt, and he was shivering.

"Are you okay?" Stanley asked, looking up at him. They were kneeling down by the incinerator, turning it on.

Raph shook his head. "No. I mean . . . fuck. I should be asking *you* that. Of course I'm not okay. I've been thinking about it. Whatever happens, we're going to need to make some kind of statement. We're going to need to let the authorities know that—"

"Don't be an idiot," Jacques spat.

Raph recoiled like he'd been slapped. "It's the right thing to do."

"Right and wrong don't enter into it," he said, taking off his now sterilized suit. "I doubt the police would even have any record of them. Not after what we've seen. The discussion alone would get this place shut down."

"Good," Raph replied. "It should be shut down. This is over, Jacques. This has to be over."

"We can keep this secret," Jacques insisted. "It is by definition already secret. We can—"

"Jesus Christ, Jacques, we're just kids! I'm twenty-three years old. I'm scared as shit. I have no idea what I'm doing. This has gone way too far. We . . . we should never have done anything like this."

Stanley watched on, Raph's words about their youth sparking off a terrible thought. Waldman had sacrificed himself for this: to keep this buried, whatever it was. Stanley was sure of it. He thought of the slip of paper he'd saved from Waldman's fireplace, brailled with the word CROATOAN— a reference to the lost Roanoke colony that had been erased from history. He had died to keep this horror hidden. He had died for a purpose, and the culmination of all of Stanley's work had done nothing but render his sacrifice meaningless. Make his death pointless.

There is no defense.

And Stanley hadn't been able to let it go. He'd been obsessed, forcing not just himself but also his friends down a path they never should have taken. He should have left it alone. That's what Waldman had wanted. That was his dying wish.

"An immortal bane," Stanley whispered.

"What did you say?" Jacques turned to him, eyebrow raised.

"I . . ." Both of them were looking at Stanley, frowning at him. "It was the last message Waldman left me when he died. I never told anyone about it. He wrote out a reference to the *Odyssey*: 'An immortal bane, dread, and dire, and fierce, and not to be fought with; there is no defence.'"

He gulped. He couldn't bring himself to say Waldman's final two words out loud.

Raph's eyes were so wide it looked like his eyeballs might pop out. "And you didn't tell us?"

Stanley's voice was very quiet. "I didn't want to scare you away from it."

"Oh, great," he replied, his voice dripping with fury. "That's perfect. Well, I'm sure glad you didn't *scare us*, Stan. You intentionally misled us both! But I'm glad you knew what you were doing. That there was nothing to worry about."

"No, no. You're looking at this all wrong, Raph," Jacques cut in, excited. "It confirms exactly what we've been discussing. That this *is* some kind of phenomenon that's more universal, something Waldman encountered too. We can't give up now. This is our first big breakthrough."

"You call that a *breakthrough*?" Raph screamed, his anger bubbling over. "Three people are dead!"

Jacques took a slow step toward Raph. "Three people. *Three*. In the grand scale of our discoveries, that's nothing. A rounding error."

"A *what*?"

"Don't you understand?" Stanley shouted, grabbing Jacques's shoulder and turning him round. "What if this is it? What if this is why we forget? It's not a mistake or an evolutionary offshoot. It's *survival*. Whatever this sickness, this phenomenon, this *thing* is . . . the more we push these boundaries, the more we risk setting it loose again. They were removed from the past, Jacques. *Erased*. This power is beyond us. We've uncovered something that should have been left alone. There's only one thing to do now: Run from it, forget it, leave it behind."

"Cowardice," Jacques sneered, looming over him. "If you want to change the world, you can't make decisions based on fear. When Oppenheimer looked upon the first atomic bomb explosion, he recognized its power, its immensity. 'Now I am become death, the destroyer of worlds,' he said. Yes—he recognized the potential damage that it would cause, the chaos and the havoc, and yet he still continued. Do you know why?"

Stanley didn't reply. Raph took a step back, his eyes now properly taking in Jacques's inner lab.

"Because you can't close Pandora's box. It doesn't matter what you do. Whatever we have discovered here, someone else will stumble upon it in time. There is no question of that. All we do by trying to bury it is pass the buck. We ignore our responsibility in it. That is not the action of a pioneer. That is the action of a coward."

Stanley stared at him dumbfoundedly.

"There's so much more for us to do here." Jacques's voice fell quieter, more insistent. "We must proceed carefully, but we cannot stop. We must not."

Raph paced around the room, ignoring him. He examined the strange specimens—the bubbling vats of liquid, the suspended organs, the stretched lengths of what looked like skin. He took the whole macabre scene in.

"Jacques," Raph said, his voice low, "what have you been doing in here?"

"He's been using your money for other projects," Stanley said, waving his arm at the room. "He's been experimenting on God knows what under our noses, funneling cash away to buy new equipment while we've been so focused on our *breakthrough*."

Raph picked up a glass jar of liquid with a heart suspended in it. "What experiments? Whose is *this*?"

Jacques shook his head in disdain. "I've been doing what you all should have been doing from the start. You have access to an almost endless well of resources. We've made some of the most significant leaps in research in the last fifty years, and you content yourselves with *one* project?"

Raph put down the jar and picked up another, examining it slowly.

There was something not quite right—he was too calm, like the tide pulling out before the tsunami. Like the winds before a hurricane.

"With my lab, with my funding," Raph muttered, as if to himself. He was no longer looking at Jacques. At either of them. "What was the cost?"

"As if my expenses matter to you," Jacques jeered. "You were so engrossed in your own world, you barely even noticed."

Raph's eyes could have slit throats. "I'm not talking about money, you idiot."

"Don't be so shortsighted, Raph. I am on the verge of *so much*." A hungry grin grew on Jacques's face, a pride swelling in his voice. "Do you know what I've achieved? Spontaneous human cell regrowth. Artificial tissue transplantation. There are possibilities here for curing aging, maybe even reversing death. Now, if we can harness the memory spade *as well*, just think! To have power over not just mortality but time itself!"

"You're a monster. This is over. All of it—done."

"You can't mean that, Raph. Come on. When we're so close to uncovering so much—the shortsightedness is pathetic!"

Raph slammed a jar onto the floor. It smashed, glass scattering. Yellow liquid splattered across the ground. "Pathetic?!" he shouted. Stanley took an involuntary step back, his shoulder blades pressing against the wall. "How's this for pathetic? All of this research is mine. The laboratory is mine. I own all of it, and I say it's done! We will bury it, we will bury this whole place, and we will never fucking talk about it again!"

"You're a loser," Jacques hissed, stepping closer to him. "You've always been a loser. You think you have power over me? What are you going to do—take this to the courts? All of this would get you locked up faster than you can cry to Mummy and Daddy. Oh, wait, they're dead."

With a bellow of anger, Raph threw himself at Jacques. He plunged through the air, tackling Jacques into the wall. They crashed into another set of jars. Glass shattered into Jacques's back, and he roared in pain.

"Stop it!" Stanley shouted.

Jacques shoved Raph backward and lurched forward with a heavy right hook, his fist colliding hard with Raph's nose.

"Agh!" Raph stumbled backward, hands rising to his face. "Fucker!"

Stanley stepped forward to grab Jacques but missed. Jacques lunged toward Raph again, fist raised for another punch. But Raph ducked and came up hard, slamming his shoulder into Jacques's chest and sending them both sprawling to the floor, tumbling into a table of surgical tools.

"Enough!" Stanley screamed, grabbing Jacques's body and pulling him away, pushing him back against the wall.

"All you've ever done is hold me back," Jacques taunted over Stanley's shoulder. "All you ever *do* is hold everyone else back."

Raph roared, rising to his feet. Jacques wrested free of Stanley's grip and shoved him away. Too late, stumbling back, Stanley glimpsed the long scalpel Raph had picked up off the floor.

Swinging wildly, Raph approached again, screaming "I hate you! I hate you!"

Jacques collided into him. Wrestling over the blade, they fell to the floor, rolling on top of each other.

"Stop!" Stanley shouted, unable to see where the scalpel had gone.

Jacques threw his hands upward, lashing out protectively, kicking at Raph's legs until they slipped and Raph's whole body fell forward.

As he collapsed into Jacques, Raph jerked. A gargling sound escaped his lips.

"No," Jacques said, eyes wide. "Raph, no."

Raph fell on top of Jacques, rolling to one side and onto the floor, the scalpel lodged halfway into his windpipe.

"Stan, help me," Jacques said, pushing Raph over onto his back. "Fucking help me."

Stanley scrambled over, blood spurting out of Raph's neck like a fountain. Jacques put his hands over it, but a jet shot into his open mouth. He fell back, spluttering and coughing, Raph's blood spilling out of him, dribbling down his lips.

Stanley put his hand over the wound, not sure if he should dislodge the scalpel. The blood flowed around it, warm against his skin. Raph's eyes widened as his throat gurgled loudly, and then it stopped.

Everything stopped.

Stanley opened his mouth, staring, impotent. He looked in his friend's face, eyes glazing over, and he had this overwhelming sensation that everything in his life was destined to turn out this way. This was it. This was what people got for working with him. No matter what he did, no matter how hard he tried, he would always end up in the same position—looking at a corpse. Waldman first, now Raph.

Jacques pushed back, shuffling away from the body. "I didn't mean to," he whispered. "I . . . I didn't think he would . . . Oh, fuck."

Getting to his feet, he started scrambling around the room. "There must be something I can do. I can fix this. There's a way to reverse this, to *control* this, I just need to—"

"He's dead, Jacques," Stanley said solemnly.

"But if I could just—"

"He's *dead*."

Jacques stopped moving.

"Oh, fuck. I don't . . . It . . . it wasn't my fault. He came at me. I was just trying to—"

"I know."

Stanley stood up. He wasn't shaking or crying or panicking. He wasn't in shock, he didn't think, though he couldn't really tell. There was nothing inside him at all.

"What are we going to do?" Jacques asked. Stanley didn't answer. The room felt cold, and a little empty.

Jacques walked up to him and grabbed his shoulders. "Stan—we can't just leave him here."

"He won't be forgotten like the others," Stanley said quietly. "His name is on this building. Police will want to know what happened. They will search this place; they will find your prints all over him. Our names are all over the record sheets. They will work out what happened here. Or enough of it, at least."

"We . . . we could say he was working here alone today," Jacques said. "That an accident happened."

"Jacques—when they find this body, they're going to know someone else was involved. He's got a stab wound in his throat."

Jacques's eyes flickered to the other side of the lab. "Not if we incinerate the evidence."

A sudden fury exploded in Stanley. His hand darted up and grabbed Jacques by the throat, pushing him against the wall. "Are you actually fucking suggesting that we chop up our best friend?!"

"No," he said. He was shaking. "No. It's just I . . . What do I do?"

Stanley took a deep breath and let go of him, stepping away. The body on the floor didn't even really look like Raph anymore—just another corpse. Just another mistake Stanley had made. Another failure.

Part of him thought about turning them both in. Maybe if they were locked up, they wouldn't be a danger to anyone. But as he looked in Jacques's stricken face, he knew he couldn't. For all he had changed, he was the last one left—the last link to that warm classroom, sun glinting off the chessboards, the last connection to the only years in his life when he'd actually had a home.

They sat in silence for a long time, wordless. Stanley floated outside his own body, watching quietly from a distance as shock washed through him, turning first to worry, then to grief, and finally dwindling into nothing—absolutely nothing at all.

"I will tell the police that just you and Raph were here today, nobody else," Stanley said eventually. "They're going to need a suspect, and that's going to have to be you. I'll get Toby to say the same—we can be each other's alibis. I'll incinerate anything that suggests otherwise. It's the middle of the night; there's nobody else here. Then I'm going to burn this place to the ground. The only way you get out of this is if they think you died in the fire too. Without a body, it won't be conclusive, but it'll confuse them long enough for you to—"

"Wait," Jacques said, glancing about his lab. "What if I had some human tissue? Some of my own, with my own DNA."

"What do you mean 'human tissue'?"

"A foot? Maybe as much as an arm? Enough to convince a forensic team I died here."

Stanley blinked, staring at him. "Why do you have a . . . ?" He fell short, putting his hand to his head. "You know what? I don't care. Sure. Fine. Leave it out. Leave your clothes with it too."

"Okay." Jacques nodded. "Fuck, okay. And then what?"

"It's over, Jacques."

He shook his head. "It can't be. It can't just be *over*. There needs to be—"

"Jacques, it's done. What are you going to do? Stay here? You'll be tied up in the investigation for the rest of your life. You need to run. We both do."

"Run?"

"Go into hiding, at least," Stanley said. "That's what I'll do. Use what you have left of Raph's money to get out of the country. Probably change your name. Just start a new life, away from all this. It's the only way."

Jacques looked down at his hands, still covered in blood. "I can't just give up. I'm not a failure, Stan. I'm not. I can do more. I can *be* more."

Stanley sighed. *We're all failures,* he thought. *We always have been. That's what attracted us to Waldman in the first place.* But he didn't say a word. He just stared at the floor.

Jacques looked around the room one last time—at the wreckage, at the broken glass and upturned tables, at the body on the floor. "I . . . I'm sorry, Stan. It was never meant to turn out this way."

Stanley picked up the bloody suit and carried it over to the incinerator. "It never is."

An hour later, Jacques was gone. Stanley had found a barrel of highly flammable hydrocarbons and doused the entire place in it—every room, every surface, every piece of godforsaken paper.

This was his life. This was the culmination of everything he had ever done from the moment he met Waldman up until now.

He lit a match and threw it. There was a whoosh as the fire caught, rushing across the floor. He closed the door behind him as the flames licked up the walls.

It was a cold night. Wrapping himself in his coat, he decided he would walk home.

15

TRANSCRIPT NO. 273: Margaret Webb

DATE STAMP: 11 AUG. 2021

3 Hours, 40 Minutes, and 44 Seconds Until Dissolution

I'm sitting in the main room of your office, on the sofa next to the chessboard. Stanley is in his chair to my right, eyeing up the chessboard as if he wants a game, and I chuckle to myself at the idea. I can picture him making two moves and then forgetting which side he is playing on, distracted by the thought of a horse ride he went on when he was a child.

"Do you remember that old playground by the canal?" he asks me. I smile and nod. I have no idea what he's talking about. He's lost again in one of his old memories, from before he knew me. Something from childhood.

Where am I?

You've gone into the other room again, the one I haven't been in. I'm sorely tempted to get up and follow you—to crack the door open and find out what's going on in there—but within moments, you reappear. You have made coffee.

I laugh. I can't help it. Of all the macabre, impossible things I imagined you having behind that door, a coffee machine wasn't one of them. Somehow, I'm a little surprised you drink coffee. I'm a little surprised you eat and drink anything at all.

"I'd like to have a longer discussion with you about your last dive," you say obsequiously, as if I have a choice. "It will help us make a plan for what we do next."

"Very well."

You sit opposite me, the board between us. The pieces have moved since I was last here. You've been playing with someone. Maybe yourself.

"Mum would push me on the swings for hours," Stanley says, staring off into space. "Could never get me to leave."

You hand me a cup of coffee, and I smile at you.

It's actually entertaining—this little make-believe—like we're partners in crime, working toward the same goal. I know you don't believe it, but I wonder if you think I believe it. I wonder whether you think that I think *you* believe it. I could just ask you these things, of course, but where would be the fun in that?

"Before we can go any further," I say, "I need to understand how your machine in there works. I can affect the past but only some of the time?"

You lean back in your seat, taking a sip of your coffee. "Time is not what you think it is. Reality exists because it's observed. The past exists as a collective group of observations, or memories, that coalesce and form something real. Something tangible. The memory spade allows you to enter that tangible creation and interact with it directly."

"And the allotments with the boat," Stanley interjects, following his own personal train of thought. "I loved those little seats."

"Yes, dear," I say, patting his hand before I turn back to you. "So that allows you to change the past?"

"When it was first created, no. The issue is that memory is fallible;

it's not a perfect observation of the past. When the subject's memory of the past diverges from the collective objectivity, any changes made do not hold. The universe, it seems, is capable of self-correcting." You put your coffee down on the table. "The version of the spade we use today does two things: It sends you back to interact with the past memory, and it simultaneously stimulates areas of your brain to unlock objective memory. As it sends you back, it also makes certain that memory is completely accurate. The new model ensures that all changes are held true. They do not revert."

"All changes?"

"Well," you say with a shrug, "within reason. If you stay out of events, if you merely observe, as I have guided you to, then the past is not changed. Imagine it like a river. Simply placing a finger in the water is not enough to change the current—it merely flows around your finger and returns back to where it was. But if you place a large enough rock, or a log, it forms a dam, and the direction of the river is changed. Your passive observation is like a finger. Talking to someone, interacting with someone—you build a dam."

I nod, quietly taking it all in.

But something occurs to me now, talking to you. The pill you gave me that is making me experience all of this again—you said it's based on the same technology.

In concept, yes, but the pill itself is not enough. It sharpens your memory, but it's not the memory spade. It is not sending you back. Without that technology, your memories are merely your memories.

I   Why?

We would run out of time before you even began to understand the science of it.

I   Okay, fine. I can accept that.

Go back to your memory. What are you thinking?

I'm thinking about being in Stanley's memory, before the wedding was erased, and interacting with myself. If you are right, this should have caused a change. I should remember it. But I don't. I remember everything right up until being at the front of the aisle, which is followed by a blank, but I don't remember being confronted by an old woman.

I decide not to tell you this. It's another piece of information I tuck away, hoping to use later.

I take a deep breath. "Tell me about Omega."

Stanley frowns. "Oh no. No, we don't want to think about that."

"It's okay, Stan," I say. "It's important."

He huffs but then shrugs and leans back in his chair. After a moment, a little smile appears on his face, and I can tell he's lost himself in another memory.

You sit forward in your seat. "It's the trade-off for the power we wield. Each time we access perfect objective memory, we weaken the walls and give Omega access to our past. Once it establishes a physical link, it can shift in its present from person to person, erasing as it goes. And, no, I do not know what its purpose is. Maybe it has no purpose. Maybe it is just a force of nature. It is, perhaps, beyond our comprehension."

I glance furtively at Stanley. "But if it's devouring Stanley's past, then surely we—"

"Until recently, we have been able to keep it at bay. In fact, it has not made an appearance in many years, and this is hardly our first time experimenting with the spade. There are methods—far too complicated for me to go into now—that have kept us safe from it."

My mind goes to the lifts, to the one at the end of the row, separate from the others and labeled with an Ω. "You've trapped it somehow?"

"Hardly," you say, lighting a cigarette. "Such powers cannot simply be trapped. Rather, we have encouraged it to stay dormant. Sated. For want of another term, it sleeps. This allows us to use the spade, now and again, without repercussion."

"I'd hardly call what happened to my wedding 'without repercussion.'"

You nod gravely, tapping your ash into your empty coffee cup. "Indeed. That was unfortunate. It's curious that Stanley was able to protect your meeting in the past but not the wedding itself. He was surprised by it, unprepared. Did you interact with the memory in any other way? Did you attempt to change anything?"

I don't say anything. I shake my head, looking down at the floor, mainly because of the guilt. Because it hits me: Trying to confront myself before I walked down the aisle is probably what drew Omega to us. It was my fault. I erased our wedding.

You give me a solemn look. "Normally, it wouldn't matter. We have been using the memory spade for years, with Omega remaining contained. But for whatever reason, it grows . . . restless. It stretches against the bonds we have put on it, and I'm afraid we will not be able to hold it much longer. Once it is loose, it will consume everything. All of our memories. All of the past. It may not stop until there is nothing left for it to take."

I gulp, trying to get my head around what that means, around the implications of it. Then I think again of the lifts, of the bizarre warnings about déjà vu and timelines, and I see it. My guilt blossoms inside of me, my cheeks burning as it transforms into an almost uncontrollable anger. I realize why we're here, what you've done. You've gone too far.

What do you mean?

You couldn't help yourself, could you? Stanley wanted to bury it for exactly this reason, but playing with time and the past was just too damn enticing, and you couldn't leave it alone, so it noticed. It started reaching out again, *hunting*, first with Stanley, then with Toby, and then—I'm guessing—with you. That's why you came to me. You're forgetting things too, aren't you? You're losing bits of your past when you go back. After whatever Stanley did, whatever experiment in the past, someone actually managed to put the lid back on Pandora's box. But *you*, and the others like you in this place, just couldn't stop prodding the bear.

Hindsight is always twenty-twenty, Maggie.

Why don't you just *stop*? Why don't you just leave it alone?

Look around you. I think we both know it's far too late for that now. We have crossed over the event horizon. There's no closing the box now; there's no sending it back.

And you expect me to *help* you? This is all your fault.

I have made my share of mistakes. I can admit to that. But assigning blame is pointless now. It doesn't matter who did what. All that matters is that if we don't stop it, it will consume everything. Only Stanley has the key. He's the only one who can stop this now.

You tell me that at the Institute too, and I'm not sure I believe you. You say, "Stanley found a way to stop Omega for good, completely and utterly, and he hid it somewhere deep in his memories. That is why his memories are being taken from him. There are those who do not want this solution to be found."

"I know," I say. "Sunrise. I remember. But *why* don't they want it to be found? And if Stanley discovered a way to end this horror, why did *he* hide it in the first place? That doesn't make sense. If this thing could be stopped, why didn't he do it?"

For half a second, I swear I see your eyes flicker down to the chessboard.

"I don't know," you say. "That's something we need to find out. Perhaps he did not have time. Perhaps he hid it somewhere so that Omega itself would not remove his discovery of it from the past. Perhaps he knew Sunrise was trying to get to him and it was his only way of protecting himself. I don't know. All I know is that Sunrise is both devious and forceful, and Stanley would have done anything he could to shield himself from those behind it."

I look to my right, at my husband, still lost in his own little world. Every word you just said is a lie. I am certain of it. It takes every ounce of my willpower not to leap over the table and scratch your eyes out.

Instead, I give you a warm, understanding smile that says, *I believe you. I buy the bullshit you are selling me right now.* And then I take another sip of my coffee.

"When I saw Stanley during the last dive, before Omega at our wedding, he gave me two dates. He told me to go to both of them because he would need me there. I imagine those would be a good place to start."

"I would agree."

"But how can I be sure that Omega won't find me when I go back in? How can I make sure that I don't accidentally allow more of Stan's past to be wiped away?"

"I've recalibrated the machine," you reply. "I wasn't expecting you to interact so fully with the past. I have been in touch with those who are responsible for keeping Omega dormant. We have increased the protections. It is safe to use the spade now for brief periods of time, and to interact if need be. If we approach a point where that is no longer true, I will pull you out before anything happens. You have my word."

My look must tell you how much your word means to me, because you add, "I don't want him losing any more of his past than you do. That's where my answers are."

I'm not convinced, exactly, but I can see that we want the same thing for now, and that reassures me.

"The rabbit was called Spud," Stanley mutters, his lips pulling up into a smile. I take his hand in mine.

"Let's get on with it, then," I say.

Before long, Stanley is being strapped in again, and I'm descending into the bath. I think about how familiar this is becoming, and the idea disconcerts me. Nobody should be familiar with such things.

"What was the first date?" you ask.

"November 9, 1961."

You input some lines of code into your screen. "Do you know it?"

I shake my head. "No—nothing but the date."

"Then it will be difficult to triangulate. With the beach memory, you at least knew where he was and what he was doing. You could focus on that. This will be much more difficult."

"I can do it," I reply, and I know that I can. I've been getting more used to how it feels to be in his memories. It's oddly intuitive—and becoming more so with each dive—like relearning to drive a car after you haven't been in one for twenty years.

You nod, and as you press a button on the screen, I lower the helmet over my head and disappear into the past.

There's a strange sort of limbo that takes place in the moments between dissolving into nothingness and waking up—as though the machine is asking your subconscious where it wants to go, where you want to be.

Nineteen sixty-one, I think. A very long time ago. A time before he knew me.

I will myself there, to the exact date Stanley gave me, hoping that the combination of my brain and the spade will work out the navigation.

Around me, the world wakes up. Gravestones pop into my consciousness: first one, then five, then too many to count. A large chapel looms over me, and a cool summer breeze whistles past my face.

I'm in an empty cemetery.

No, not empty. As I turn around, I see a man standing about ten paces ahead of me. His back is to me, and he's staring silently up at the clouds. It's Stanley—I'm sure of it, and he's upset about something. I can tell by the way he's standing, the shape of his back. From just the contours of his shoulders, I could trace you a perfect map of his thoughts.

My heart beats a little faster as I walk toward him, recalling how overwhelming it was the last time we met. I need to stay focused on what's important here, on Omega, on the solution.

I place my hand on his shoulder, and he jerks around.

"Stanley," I say.

He stares at me wide-eyed, like I'm a ghost. "Y-Yes? Who are you?"

"How do we stop it?" I ask. "You have to know. How does it stop?"

"I . . ." He squirms underneath my hand on his shoulder, and I realize this isn't right. He's young—too young. "I don't know what you're talking about."

I've gone to the wrong point. He should be in his twenties, but he looks barely eighteen. "What year is it?"

"Erm," he says, "1955."

"Too early. Damn it." I'm about to say something else—a warning, perhaps—but the confusion on his face is too much for me to bear. I shouldn't be here. I need to leave. "I . . . I'm sorry."

As quickly as I can, I move away from him. I want to get behind the chapel before I tug myself out. I don't know what my disappearing into thin air would look like for him, but I can't imagine it would be something he'd forget. I'm trying to be a finger in the stream, not a log.

Fortunately, he stands in place, dumbfounded. I get round the side of the building, and with a thought, I lurch myself back into the void for another try.

I focus harder this time, and it's easier because I have context. In my head, I can see a line between where I just was—1955—and the present. It lets me visualize the distance I need to travel. Though I use these words—*line, visualize, distance*—the experience is, in fact, nothing like that at all. I lack the language to express it. You know when you're in a dream and you just *know* something? Like you know you have to be somewhere or go somewhere? That's how this feels. The knowledge appears as an unconnected certainty in my head, fully formed and ready to go.

When the world reconstitutes this time, it's easier. It is more fluid with each dive.

I'm in an alleyway in London, just off a main road. I know this intuitively. There's the hum of cars and buses, the occasional punctuation of beeping and revving from around the corner, but there's less of it in this decade than in my present. It's quieter. It's dingy—the ground is a little wet from a broken pipe, and there's a huge collection of rubbish bags sprawled across the ground. We must be out back behind a restaurant, I think, or some café.

It's the middle of the day, but the light is mostly obscured by the buildings on either side. Apart from a few rays glinting off the windows, the alleyway is quite dark. It's also empty. I turn around a couple of times, trying to work out what's going on.

There's a shuffle, and I jump, taking a few steps backward. My body tenses up, instinctively readying itself to run.

Another shuffle, and this time I locate it among the bins. One of the bags rolls out of the way, and a man stands up. He's filthy—he's wearing layers of mismatched clothes, and a scraggly beard covers his face. He stumbles a little, walking with the sway of a drunk and holding some thrown-out leftovers he's discovered.

I back away, worrying that he might be dangerous, until he steps into a ray of light and I gasp.

It's Stanley.

Without a second thought, I rush forward to him, but the stench takes me by surprise, and I recoil involuntarily.

He looks up at me, frowning, as if he's trying to work out whether I'm really there, and then he stumbles sideways into the wall. He slides down it, his body giving out on him, and collapses onto the ground in a heap.

I kneel down, putting a hand to his chest to check that he's breathing. He's fine—just passed out. Too much to drink, I suspect, given the smell of booze that's wafting off him like fog.

Settling down next to him, I realize there's not much I can do. It's not exactly like I can pick him up and carry him somewhere—he's far too heavy for that.

So I wait.

It takes almost three hours.

In the interim, I leave him for little segments of time, praying that he won't go anywhere. I pop up to the main road and steal some water, a couple of sandwich rolls sitting in paper bags, and some chocolate bars from a small corner shop. Somehow, nobody gives me a second glance. Maybe nobody expects an eighty-three-year-old to be nicking a packed lunch.

I sit next to him, a hundred questions running through my mind, including the instructions he gave me on our wedding day. Something about Australia. And the names Thamus and Theuth.

His head turns to one side, and he lets out a sickly cough. What happened to him? Why is he like this?

I'm going to need you to be patient with me, Stanley had said. *To be there for me when I'm at my lowest.*

I can do that. There's a certain poetic justice to it, I think. When we first met, I was a wreck—no job, no future, barely any friends other than addicts and people who wanted money off me. But he was there for me. Somehow, through it all, he saw in me not the person I was but the person I *could* be.

There's a quote that's always stuck with me, one that I heard from a lecturer in my art history course, the one Stanley pushed me to take after we got married. It's often misattributed to Michelangelo, talking about his sculpting process, but the lecturer made it clear that was apocryphal. Either way, it's always stuck with me. Allegedly, he said, "The sculpture is already complete within the marble block, before I start my work. It's already there, I just have to chisel away the superfluous material."

When I heard it, I thought, *That's what Stanley did. He saw the woman I was going to be, underneath all the superfluity, and he helped me carve her out.*

I look at him now, passed out drunk in an alley, and I see a block of marble. I know what he really looks like inside.

When Stanley wakes up, he has a scowl on his face.

"Get away from me," he mumbles.

I smile, hand him a sandwich, and say, "No."

He frowns, confused by the combination. Without replying, he reaches up and takes the sandwich, pulling it out of the paper bag.

"Are you homeless?" I ask.

"What is it to you?"

I settle back against the wall next to him. "More than you can possibly know, Stan."

His eyes dart to my face, scanning it. There's anger there, and fear. "Who are you?"

"My name's Maggie," I say. "I'm here to help you. To get you back on track."

I take out the water and a chocolate bar, placing them on my lap.

He gives me a long, hard look, grabs the chocolate bar, and gets up.

"Fuck off," he says. And turning away from me, he walks toward the main road.

And even though I was not expecting this to be easy, his rejection pierces me right through the heart. It's so cold, so callous, so completely antithetical to the man I know.

Pull yourself together, Maggie, I think. *He needs you.*

Getting up, I follow him out into the street.

We're just off Brixton High Street, down the road that cuts off from the Academy. It's got that raw, electrifying feel that I've always loved, especially before they added a Tube line. We went to a gig here once, the two of us, in the late '60s. We smoked a joint out back with a couple of Jamaican bassists and drank cans of Red Stripe until two in the morning. That was before Leah, of course. I remember being a little scared that partying like that again would send me back down a dark path, but Stanley wasn't. It was like he knew that part of my life was over, and his faith was what carried me through.

Brixton these days is too commercial, too ugly—sanitized by gentrification and property developers. For a couple of blocks, he pretends not to notice me. It's not like I'm hiding or anything—I'm just a few yards behind him, sticking to him like a shadow. It's as though if he ignores me hard enough, I just might disappear. Now and then, he throws a glance back in my direction, and the frustration is evident on his face. He hates me. He wants me to leave.

I brush it off. I remind myself that after the last ten years of dealing with him in the present, this is nothing. Every hurtful comment Stanley has made, every time I've visited and he's forgotten who I am—they've hardened me. These days, I feel like I could walk through the fires of hell and back and barely flinch.

After about half an hour, we arrive at a block of flats. Stanley pushes open a door with a broken lock and climbs up a dim stairwell with a flickering lamp. Dogs bark in the street behind us. Rats scamper along the floor.

When he gets to a door about two flights up, he stops and turns around.

"Stop following me."

I put on the best smile I can possibly manage. "No. Can I come in?"

"What do you want?" he shouts, slamming his hand on the door-frame. "How do you know my name? How do you—in fact, forget about it. I don't care. Just leave me alone."

I shrug. "Can't do that, Stan. I'm here for a reason. You look hungry—you look like you haven't eaten in days. If you let me in, I'll cook you a meal."

"I don't have any food," he grumbles. "Or money."

"Nor do I," I reply, but I think of what you said about sticking your finger in the river, about how the past will just flow around me if I let it, and I think of my experience with the sandwiches. A big grin grows on my face. "But I think that I might just be an excellent shoplifter."

An hour later and I've gone to the butcher's and the greengrocer's. I've stolen a feast—there's a chicken in the oven, gravy on the hob, and about as much fresh veg as I could carry without looking ridiculous.

The kitchen is disgusting. I'm surprised it has any electricity. It's clear that Stanley's squatting here and the building's been abandoned. He must have stumbled on it recently, and the company hasn't had time to cut the power yet.

He's letting me cook, ignoring me. He's hiding in the remnants of a living room, pretending to read a book. I can tell he's pretending because I know exactly what he looks like when he reads: the way he puts his hand on his cheek, the way he curls his legs in. There's none of that now.

When I'm done, we both eat in silence. I do my best to scrub the grime off the crockery I find, but it's difficult without soap. Can I even get salmonella in the past?

He's acting like he doesn't enjoy it, a scowl plastered onto his face as he hoovers the food into his mouth, but I know differently. I'm not an arrogant lady, but sometimes you have to be honest with yourself. I'm a fucking great cook.

When he's done, he leans back and looks at me. He stares long and hard. I wait, letting him soak me all in—this strange old lady who's appeared out of nowhere and is now following him like a lost puppy.

Eventually, he says, "Tell me why you're here."

"I'm here to help you. I'm here to get you out of this mess. I'm here to put you back on track."

He flinches a little, almost imperceptibly. "There is no track."

"There's a future ahead of you, Stanley. You need to be ready for it."

"Bullshit," he says, snarling. "There's nothing for me."

"That's not true, and I think you know it."

He shoots up, throwing his plate to the side. "What the fuck do you know?"

I take a breath, remaining as calm as I can. "That this isn't you, Stan. You're better than this."

"Better?" he shouts. "Better?! Everyone I have ever loved is dead. Everything I have ever built has collapsed. Everything I touch, everything I have ever touched, I have ruined. Fuck you."

He storms into the other room. I clear the plates.

We live like this for three more days. I cook for him, I clean the place, and I even steal him some new clothes. He begrudgingly accepts me into his life, even if he won't admit it. I try not to push too hard. Whatever happened to him, it's going to take time to get it out. I wonder how long I have in this memory, how much time I have to work with, but you said you couldn't be sure. You just said you'd tell me before I went too far, and I haven't heard you yet.

At night, I hear him crying. He tries to stifle it, but apart from the barking of dogs and the creaking of walls, there's no other sound. He's on a ripped-up old couch in the living room. I sleep in the other room on the floor, inside a sleeping bag that I've nicked from a sports shop up the road. My back screams at me in the morning, and I have to stretch for half an hour just to feel like a human.

On the third day, I sit down opposite him with a cup of tea. He keeps asking me to steal him some booze, but I never do. It pisses him off immensely.

"Are you going to tell me what happened?" I ask.

He stares at me. "What do you mean?"

"You weren't always like this. You had hopes. You had dreams once."

He shakes his head in annoyance. "Dreams are pointless. Hope is worse. Life's just a bunch of traps set out to screw with you. You hope for anything else and it'll get taken away."

I lean in, pressing him harder. It's been long enough. "What got taken away?"

He flinches away from me. "Don't."

"Did you lose someone?"

"Stop it."

"It's not your fault."

He stands up, storming to the other side of the room, putting his back to me. But he doesn't leave.

"You don't know anything," he says.

"I know you're destined for greater things than this."

A humorless laugh that sounds more like a cough bursts out of him. "If the raw materials are subpar," he says bitterly, "you're never going to make anything with quality."

"What?"

"It doesn't matter," he mutters. "If there's any destiny for me, it's to destroy everyone I love."

"I know that's not true, Stan. I know it for a fact, because I love you, and you love me, and here I am."

He spins around in fury, as if he's about to shout something in my face, then stops dead. He stares at me, his brain whirring, his mouth open.

"I know you," he whispers.

"Yes."

"At graduation, in the cemetery. Before Waldman . . ." He shakes his head. "You haven't aged a day."

I smile. "Always the charmer."

"And before—I've . . . I've seen you before. As a kid. I'm sure of it. That time in the park, with my dad, and the . . . Oh God. Who are you?!"

I stand up, staying level with him even as he looks like he's about to keel over. "I'm from the future. Your future." I pause, wondering how far I should go. "I'm your wife."

His eyes go wide. "You're using the spade. You found out a way to make it work."

"You could say that."

"No." He starts pacing back and forth, and I worry that I'm going to lose him again. "No, no, no. I can't. It's over. I can't go back there again."

"It's okay, Stan."

"No, it's not. It's *not*."

His hands are shaking. He's freaking out, and I don't know what to do. All I can think is: *What would he do if we were swapped?* I remember him just before our wedding: the feel of his arms around my body, the touch of his skin.

I walk forward, old and frail as I am, and I take him into my arms. I pull him close. He resists for an instant, pulling away in shock, but then he curls into me.

"It's going to be okay, Stan. I know it is, because I know you come out of this. You get your life together. You marry me, and we have a daughter, and we live fifty gloriously happy years together. You make us feel so loved, and you don't ruin any of it. I promise you."

"I don't understand."

"You don't need to," I say, holding him like a child, like a baby. "Just know that I'm here for you, always."

He's sobbing. His whole body is shaking, and I guide him down onto the old sofa.

A voice reverberates at the back of my skull. *You have to come out now,* you say.

No, I think. *I'm not done here.*

We're reaching the edge of our protection. Your voice is hard. *If you stay longer, all will be lost. This will be pointless.*

I pull Stanley up and make him look at me. "I don't have much time," I say quickly. "Listen to me: I believe in you. There is a way to make things right, to make this all worth it, but you need to find a way to stop it. I'm meant to tell you to go to Australia."

He blinks tears out of his eyes, the confusion taking over. "Australia?"

"I don't know why. There's some kind of ritual, with fire and lavender. And there was wisteria too. And some . . . some symbols." I get up, scrambling for something to write with. A piece of paper. A pen. There's nothing.

"Symbols?" he asks.

Maggie, you insist.

I grab ketchup from the side and squeeze it onto my hand, painting one of those strange cuneiform-type symbols from the wedding on the wall. He looks at me as if I've gone insane.

"Something about Australia," I say.

He stares at me.

Now, Maggie. There is no more time.

I dash forward and grab his hand, squeezing it tight.

"Australia," I say one more time. "Lavender. Fire. I trust you. I love you. Always."

And then I pull, and he disintegrates in front of me, my senses melting away.

When I open my eyes, you're standing over me with a cigarette. My heart is pounding so hard I think it's going to explode.

"Well," you say, glancing at the monitors, "I think that went quite well."

16 | **Stanley**
1963

STEPPING OUT OF THE SMALL BIPLANE, STANLEY LIFTED HIS SCARF AGAINST the red dust. It was a reflex, one he now knew was pointless. After spending the last eight months in the outback, he'd realized there was no way to keep it out. The dust was a part of him now—he could feel it in his blood.

From his last expedition in South Australia, he'd flown over the Great Victoria Desert and the Gibson Desert, landing at this small airstrip in Western Australia, built primarily for the giant iron ore mine in Newman. The dry ground crunched underfoot, the makeshift runway barely distinguishable from the thousands of miles of empty land surrounding it. As far as the eye could see, the ground was lifeless: red and cratered like the surface of Mars. The bitter taste of earth coated the back of his throat.

A short woman scurried toward him from a dust-stained jeep, and Stanley readied himself for the onslaught of questions. This was the fourth archaeological dig he had visited, and it was beginning to feel a little repetitive.

"Mr. Webb." The woman held her hand out. Stanley guessed her shorts and shirt might have been khaki once, but they were now caked in red. She shook Stanley's hand vigorously. "Isabella Summers. Or just Ella is fine, if you want. So pleased to have you here, sir. So pleased you've taken such an interest in the dig."

Stanley nodded, smiling uncomfortably. He was still not used to the deference that money provided. He understood it: These archaeologists were mostly poor, struggling to get by on dwindling research grants. To have a mysterious benefactor suddenly appear and offer to fund your project was like something out of a myth, a fairy tale spoken around campfires at archaeological digs. And yet Stanley's status sat uneasily upon him, plaguing him with a sense of dishonesty, a sense that he was wearing borrowed robes.

The money was his, the lawyers had assured him. Raph's sizable fortune, one that had only grown over the Institute's years, had been left in its entirety to Stanley. When they had finally managed to track him down, the authorities had informed him that he'd become one of the richest people in the country overnight. He'd reached out to an old friend from Whelton, Hugo, who was now a lawyer. On his advice, Stanley invested most of it, placing the bulk of the money in Sunrise Holdings—a fund he created to maintain the wealth and pay him a consistent salary from the investment profits in perpetuity. Hugo managed the fund, more than happy to step into the easy role, and Stanley was set up for life. He'd never have to work another day if he didn't want to.

All because his best friend had died. All because Stanley had dragged him into something that he couldn't control.

He followed Ella to the jeep. That was why he was here—so he could understand what had happened, so he could make sure it never happened to anyone again.

More than anything, he couldn't stop thinking about Maggie. She haunted his every waking moment and most of his dreams too. He didn't know why. He didn't understand it: how this old woman had appeared out of nowhere and in the course of a few days saved him from descending into total oblivion.

But there was something about the way she'd looked at him, like she *knew* him in a way that no one before ever had. There was something about the way she spoke to him. Every time he stopped to think, he found himself replaying their conversation over and over in his head.

You marry me, and we have a daughter, and we live fifty gloriously happy years together. You make us feel so loved, and you don't ruin any of it. I promise you.

Could it be possible? Could it be true? And if so, did he deserve it?

"The dig is relatively recent," Ella said, her hands on the wheel as they trundled across the desert. "But we've come across some really exciting stuff that seems to corroborate what's been seen at the Mungo site. It sounds crazy, but we're genuinely being pushed to the limits of radiocarbon dating here."

"What do you mean?"

Ella smiled. "It's amazing how the dating of Aboriginal culture in Australia has shifted. Some people will tell you it's cultural bias, but much of it is just the lack of data. Think about it—in the '40s, everyone thought that the Aboriginal peoples had only been here a few thousand years. In the '50s, it was twenty-five thousand, then forty thousand, now maybe even sixty thousand years, but that's where we hit a roadblock."

Almost on cue, the jeep jerked as it bounded over a protruding rock. Stanley grabbed on to the door handle as his body shook.

"What roadblock?"

"Radiocarbon has a half-life of approximately five thousand seven hundred and thirty years," she continued, her voice taking on the excited buzz of a scientist explaining her work. "Because of this, you can't really date anything with carbon dating beyond around fifty thousand years. It just doesn't work—so much of what we're doing now is guesswork. Sure, there's been some progress with other methods of dating. There was John Boewel's expedition in the '50s, of course. And then, well, you've got the crazy Kimberley discovery just a few years ago."

"Kimberley discovery?"

Ella nodded enthusiastically, her eyes staying on the long red stretch in front of her. They'd been driving for some time, but to Stanley the landscape hadn't changed in the slightest.

"The researchers were calling it 'the outback Stonehenge,'" Ella said with a chuckle. "Woodford posited that it was as old as one hundred and seventy-six thousand years, almost tripling the amount of time we think humans have been occupying this land."

Stanley raised his eyebrows. "That's a long time."

"That's longer than a long time," Ella replied. "People talk about the earliest examples of human culture as being maybe twenty thousand years old. The Lascaux caves are what? Seventeen thousand years? I've heard some reports of things like tools found in South Africa forty-four thousand years ago. But in Australia? We've discovered rock engravings that we can date back seventy-five thousand years based on the rock formations themselves. That dramatically pushes back our conception of human art, of human culture and knowledge. It's like . . . well, it's almost like there was a whole era of lost human history that existed here before everything we know about today."

Stanley turned his head askance. "Almost?"

"I mean," Ella said, shrugging. She looked down at the steering wheel. It was clear that these theories had been challenged before. "It's a crazy idea. It's just a hypothesis, really. We're still . . . just gathering data."

Stanley nodded, settling back. Much of this was fitting into what he had been discovering over the past eight months. He didn't know why Maggie had sent him to Australia, but he could see the pieces fall into place.

A whole lost era of human history, as if it had been wiped out or forgotten about. Had this thing they'd unleashed—the plague that had infected their work—existed long enough ago to be responsible for such a loss? There was something hidden in the deep past here—in the distant recesses of time—and the more Stanley was learning about it, the more he felt he was getting closer to some kind of answer, even if he didn't really know what the question was.

The jeep pulled up to a collection of tents and shacks in the middle of the desert. There were a few trucks and vans, all covered in red dirt, and workers getting in and out of various dig sites. It was a small operation, but Stanley was here for a very specific reason.

"If you'd like, I could give you the tour?"

Stanley shook his head. "Maybe later, thank you. I'd really like to meet with one of your dig workers, actually. A man named Simon Yarramundi?"

Ella raised her eyebrows. "Yarramundi? He's just a local hire—Aboriginal fellow. A digger. Doesn't know that much about the project other than the digs he's contracted to work."

Stanley smiled. "I've got some personal business."

"Of course, of course," Ella said, opening the jeep door for Stanley to get out. "Anything you want, Mr. Webb. And if there are any issues with him, we can always—"

"No, no. No issues. Just want to chat about something."

Ella's ingratiating smile was tinged with confusion, but she nodded anyway. "Let's get you into one of the tents and get you a cup of coffee. I'll find him and bring him right over."

STANLEY STOOD WITH HIS COFFEE—A RIDICULOUSLY HOT DRINK FOR SUCH a hot climate, but he felt he couldn't refuse—and stared out at the landscape. Ever since he was a young boy, he'd felt an inescapable awe at how much he still didn't know about the world, how much there was left to discover. As he looked out at the sprawling red, he felt the concept literalized—as if our entire conception of the universe were just a scratch on the skin of something so much larger, an almost infinite underworld of possibility underneath. The longer he spent on this land, the more it became a certainty to him.

And perhaps if he could find it, it would explain the tragically failed experiment, it would explain Waldman's choice, and it would explain Raph's death. And then maybe, just maybe, if he got some answers, he might be able to move on.

He wondered what Jacques was doing right now. After they'd parted ways in London, he'd not seen him. He'd asked Hugo to use some of the Sunrise funds to put out feelers, and there were rumors of him—in Cairo, in Istanbul, and later in Iceland. Of a man called Hassan, matching Jacques's description, putting together teams, buying up property. Stanley had tried to keep closer tabs on him, but Jacques was slippery, never anywhere for very long.

He still woke at night with images of chopped-up bodies and organs in jars haunting his thoughts. It worried him that he didn't know what Jacques was capable of. Stanley had hoped Jacques would stop meddling and settle down somewhere quietly, but even as he thought it, he knew how naive it sounded. That was not Jacques. That had never been Jacques.

"You asked for me?" a deep voice rumbled from behind him. He turned to find a tall, dark-skinned man wearing a big hat. "What can I do for you?"

"Simon Yarramundi?"

The man nodded, his face impassive. "Yes."

"I was told to come and find you. I was told you could help me with something."

"Don't know who would've told you a thing like that."

Stanley pulled off his backpack and placed it at his feet, leaning over to unzip it. "Woman named Grace Baiyungu, down near Yellabinna. I showed her something, and she said, 'You'll need to see Simon about that.' Took me a long time to track you down."

Simon lifted his hand to his chin, rubbing it pensively. "Old Grace tell you that? And what did you show her?"

Stanley pulled a notebook out of his pack, flicking to the back page. On it, he had scrawled the symbol that Maggie had finger-painted with ketchup on the wall back in London, just before she'd disappeared—like a wisp of smoke in the air. He turned it round and showed it to Simon.

Simon didn't blink. His expression didn't change. He just stared at the symbol for a good thirty seconds in silence.

"So," he said eventually, face still hard as a rock, "you're looking for old times. Before."

"Yes," Stanley replied, his voice barely above a whisper. "Yes, I am."

Simon burst out laughing. He leaned over, putting his hand on his belly as the laughter rolled out of him. Stanley just stared. "What is it?"

Simon stood back up, wiping his eyes as the last few chuckles left him. "Ah, whitefella," he said, "just when I think I've seen all the dumb shit you do, you go and do more of it. Meet me at the edge of the dig at sunset. I'll take you where you want to go."

"Why sunset?" Stanley asked, ignoring the jab and instead feeling an urgent need to move. All these months, and finally he had something concrete. "Why not now?"

"Got a job to do, boss. Got a dig to work."

"I'll pay you for the day's work. Hell, I'll pay you for the year."

He shook his head. "Not about the money. That's what people like you never understand. Listen—this is some request Grace is sending you with. You sure you ready for this?"

Stanley straightened up, his voice hard. "I've spent the last year looking for anyone who can tell me anything about this. I've spent months trying to find you. I'm ready for anything."

"Your call," he said with a shrug. And he wandered off, shaking his head to himself and smiling, reliving whatever it was that he had found so very funny.

Stanley spent the rest of the day thinking about Maggie. Again.

Somehow, he knew, she had always been there, pressed into the pages of his life, even if he couldn't quite remember all the instances where she'd cropped up. At the time, they had been forgettable, each individual one like a faded photograph. But for a brief moment in that abandoned living room in London, they had all crashed together in his mind, like a convergence of planets and stars. And as Stanley had reeled from the shock, she'd held him tight, and Stanley had felt—impossibly—an overwhelming sense that everything was going to be all right.

He had never felt that before.

But he knew he would do anything, *anything*, to feel it again.

It was just after six o'clock when the sun kissed the horizon. Orange and yellow spilled out of it, piling upon the endless red dust; the sky and land merged into a deep rainbow of warmth. Stanley took a breath, taking it all in.

"It's beautiful," he said to Simon, who appeared beside him.

"Always has been," he replied. "You got water? You got a jacket for when the sun's fully down? We'll be walking for a little while."

Stanley nodded and put his pack on. Having it made him feel a little more safe—it held a torch, some medical equipment in case of emergencies. He pulled it tightly against his back. "Where are we going?"

Simon just smiled at him. "Always living in the future. Take it easy. You'll find out when the time is on us. Enjoy the present. It's happening right now."

And with that, Simon set off, walking into the distance. Stanley followed, confused. As far as he could see, the ground stretched out to the horizon without a single blemish—not a tree or a hut or even a large rock—but for a large mountain in the distance. It had taken the jeep a solid hour to get here from the airport, which was in the opposite direction. And yet here they were, just *walking* out into it.

It felt as if they had just dipped into the shore at one end of the Pacific Ocean and started swimming outward, hoping that eventually they'd find something before they drowned.

"Not many white folk come looking for the before-past," Simon said as they trod across the crusty ground. "Not many whitefellas interested in the deep time."

"The before-past? The deep time?"

"Whitefellas like you use the word *dreamtime*—but it's a reductive term. Covers everything from the Altjira of the Arrende people to the Jukurrpa of the Warlpiri, as if they're all the same thing. For me, I'm talking about the time before time. And the time after time. Thinking on a deep scale."

Stanley frowned. "What do you mean?"

"Deep time is the time that is far longer than any single human life, far longer than any single human civilization," Simon replied. He didn't stop or turn. He spoke the words ahead of him, out to the horizon. "It's impossible for you to understand. Your culture is based around shallow time. You see? Everything you do, everything you set out to achieve, it's based around a single lifetime. A few years. Even those who plan for future generations only think about fifty, maybe a hundred, years into the future. That's shallow time. Deep time humbles the human moment. What do the tens of thousands of years care for your plans?"

Stanley didn't reply. He just kept up pace, trying to take in what he was being told, trying to contextualize it.

"When the colonizers first came here, they wondered, *Why don't these people have towns? Why don't these people have cities?* They think we must be primitive, little more than animals. But does deep time care for your cities? They're a shallow thing, and in time they will all be dust."

"Why are you telling me this?"

Simon raised his eyebrows, giving Stanley a funny look. "You asked."

"I . . ." He shook his head. "You said I had come looking for the before-past. What is that?"

"The nothingness that predated the world. The limitlessness. It's how we all came to be here."

A flash surfaced in Stanley's mind.

Greek indeed, Waldman said from the recesses of his memory. *Apeiron is the idea that before us, before people and things and gods and humans, there existed something else. . . . It's a concept that exists almost universally across cultures—in Chinese Taoism, it's wuji, or the "primordial universe"; in Hebraism, it's Ein Sof.*

He looked at Simon, lines crisscrossing and connecting in his mind. "Like a creation myth? Something that happened long ago?"

Simon shook his head again. "No. It is now. It is always. It is the past and the present and the future. It is everywhen."

Why am I telling you this? Waldman prodded in Stanley's mind.

I . . . Young Stanley hesitated. *I'm not sure.*

The professor smiled, a smile he missed so much. *Good. Think of it like a riddle, then. If you can work out why I'm telling you, maybe I'll give you the next clue.*

"I don't understand," Stanley whispered aloud. "I still don't understand."

"I know," Simon said, nodding. "That's why you need to see it. See the before-past for yourself."

AFTER WHAT MUST HAVE BEEN A FEW HOURS OF WALKING, TIME STOPPED meaning what it had meant before. Stanley had put his watch in his bag, mostly to keep it from getting caked in dust, but he hadn't bothered to check it. Wherever Simon was taking him wasn't dependent on time—it made no difference how long they were walking, merely how far they had gone. He had no metric for that.

It felt like they had walked into eternity. The landscape had barely changed, except that the dig they'd been at had disappeared out of sight and faded into the horizon behind them. They were in an endless sea of red now, and there was no telling where the end might be.

It occurred to Stanley just how desperate he was, how little he had to lose, to have blindly followed this man. Simon seemed unfazed, like he'd been walking for just a couple of minutes. They had not talked in a long time, and the sun had fully set—the stars twinkled above, untouched by light pollution. The Milky Way stretched overhead, like a smear of glitter against the eternal black.

It was cold, and Stanley took his jacket out and put it on. The moon hung heavy in the sky—large and ominous. Stanley was surprised by how bright it was, how much light it gave off once his eyes had adjusted. He hadn't touched the torch in his bag. It felt pointless, and a little silly, to get it out.

"How do you know about that symbol?" Stanley asked, finally, unable to bear the continued silence. "The one I showed you."

"Everyone who knows the land knows that symbol."

"But . . . then why have I not been able to find any information? I've been to libraries all across the country, to universities. I've funded digs. It wasn't until your friend down south saw what I was showing people that I got anywhere with it."

"Because you're asking the wrong people," he said. "The people who don't listen."

"But if this is . . ." Stanley searched for the words to explain the thoughts that had been plaguing him. "If this is what I think it is, if you have information about what I'm searching for, this should be huge. This is world-changing."

Simon laughed at him, but it wasn't mean. It was a kind little admonishment of his naivety.

"What is it with you people and trying to change the world?" Simon stopped, then lightly pulled Stanley round by the shoulder to face him. His eyes were wrinkled and warm. "Stanley, it wasn't until very recently that the colonizers took any kind of interest in our cultures. Before then, the departments that dealt with us were the same ones that dealt with wildlife—flora and fauna. Two years ago, in '61, they established the first council for the Australian Institute of Aboriginal Studies. There wasn't a single one of our people on it—just whitefellas. It doesn't matter what knowledge our people may or may not have. We haven't been hiding it. The whitefella just isn't interested."

"But with something as big as this, that could all change."

Simon shrugged. "I doubt it. It's a structural matter—they view knowledge from a window that has been carefully placed to exclude the kinds of knowledge we have: old knowledge, Indigenous knowledge. What may have begun as an ignoring of our peoples turned into habit, a continued forgetting. Tell me why you have been in Australia for eight months—sent here, specifically *here*, to find out about this thing—and have only just this last month spoken to one of the people who actually come from this land. Why is this?"

"I . . ." Stanley blinked. "I'm not sure. It wasn't intentional. I wasn't—"

"It's a question of what you value. You've grown up thinking that your rigid Western approach to problems is the only one that exists. It's not that you ignore the knowledge we have; it's that you ignore the entire knowledge framework. Any knowledge that isn't come to by strict logic and empirical science is unimportant. If you have a question about the solar system, you don't go ask the frogs down by the lake, do you? You don't even think to do that. It would be crazy. That's how the whitefella sees us; that's how *you* see us, huh? As having nothing to share."

Stanley recoiled from the sting of the accusation, but he couldn't challenge it. It was true—he'd been in this country for almost a year, and Grace had been the only Aboriginal person he'd spoken to, and even then, only by accident. He thought about all the other Indigenous communities around the globe, and the ancient practices that he had previously dismissed as little more than cultural ritual. What did they have to teach him? What more could he learn? "So why bring me here, then? Why even bother with me?"

"You asked," Simon said with a shrug. "Makes the difference."

In time, shapes grew ahead of them: flickers of firelight and the silhouettes of tents. A campsite. How Simon had managed to lead them here, without a compass, Stanley had no idea. He had asked him earlier, but all he got was talk of songlines and dreamtracks—concepts he struggled to understand.

As they grew closer, he saw that there were many people here. Men, women, children. A whole community. But their campsite had clearly been set up recently and was not built to last. These were nomadic folk, ready to move on soon, when the time was right. It made Simon's act of finding them out here in the middle of the night even more impressive.

An old woman waited for them at the edge of the campsite, smiling. Though she wore just a thin dress, the light of the moon cast dark shadows across her face, making her seem shrouded. She took Simon's hand first, exchanging close conversation in a language Stanley could not understand.

"This is Killara," Simon told him.

"Simon says you've come to learn about the before-past," she said, her voice low and accented, her words dancing on her tongue. "About the time-beyond-time."

"Yes, I think so. I think I was . . ." He thought of Maggie and the message she left. "I was sent here. I've been searching for a long time."

Killara chuckled, like Simon, shaking her head. "We weren't hiding."

She turned, giving Simon a jovial slap on the back, and together they walked toward the fire at the center of the camp. He expected others to be watching him, an outsider here, with suspicion. But they did not. Some smiled and gave little waves. Most ignored him entirely.

Beckoning Stanley over, the old woman sat by the fire and put her hands out to warm them. Stanley sat beside her. Reaching into a cloth bag at her feet, she picked up some herbs and leaves. She threw them onto the flames, which crackled loudly and changed color—from red to purple, then deeper, until they seemed almost black.

"Tell me why you're here," she said as people milled around them, going about their business.

He took a deep breath, looking into the fire. The words didn't come quickly, or easily. He had kept too many secrets for too long, buried things so deep that he wasn't sure if he could dig them out anymore.

But this is it, he thought. *This might actually be it.*

If he held anything back now, like he'd hidden Waldman's warnings from Raph and Jacques, he'd just be making the same mistake. For the first time ever, he explained everything. He had never quite put it into words before—not the full story. But now he reached deep inside himself and he wrenched it out: Whelton and Waldman, the warnings and the experiments and the deaths, the memory loss and the time travel. Maggie. He went through each moment in detail, and as he did, he realized how crazy it all sounded. He had been worried that if he ever told anyone all of this, they would think he was insane, that he had lost his grip on reality.

But this woman did not. Nor did Simon. They nodded and accepted his story as if it were the most natural thing in the world.

When Stanley was finished, Killara repeated, "And why are you here?"

"What happened to us?" he asked. "In that lab—what did I unleash?"

"That is not an answer to my question. Those are simply more questions. Why are you here? Why did you come all this way?"

He bit his lip. Did he know the answer to that? Somewhere, unbidden, Raph's voice echoed at the back of his mind from beyond the grave: *All your life, you've been trying to heal this wound, and I don't know what it is—maybe you don't even know what it is.*

"I'm trying to heal a wound," he said.

Killara didn't reply. Not straightaway. She reached into her bag again, pulling out another bundle of leaves—purple and green, like lavender. When she threw these, the flames exploded upward with a whoosh, as if she'd poured petrol on the fire. Above, the smoke danced in the moonlight, and the wisps twisted themselves into shapes.

"Back in the beginning, at the start of all things, there was no time," she said. Her voice fell low, lower than Stanley's. It reverberated with a quiet thrum of energy. "Only chaos. Only Dreaming. It is all moments at once—it encompasses all things. People—*humans*—lived here across the world with the creatures of the Dream, the ancestral beings who made and remade the world as they saw fit. These were the spirits—of the rocks, of the lizards, of the bats. They shaped our world. And man lived in harmony with them."

Stanley nodded, thinking of Waldman's apeiron, of wuji, of all the cultures that shared this same idea and had their own name for it. She leaned forward, staring deep into the flames. "Until one day, some humans desired more."

The wisps of smoke twisted downward, curling in on themselves, pushing the fire back.

"Not content with simply living and being, they felt the urge to change and grow—to become *more*. To learn and to build and to create. Somehow, and out of somewhere, they made the one thing that they needed to progress—*time*. Without time, there is no change, and without change, there is no growth. There only *is*. And so time trundled into existence, stumbling at first like a child. But as it gained momentum, it moved forward, inexorably, into the future. Nothing could stop it. The ancestral beings were not able to live in time, so they were trapped in the rocks, and the land, and the dust. You can see their footprints on the earth today."

Killara opened her arms out to the land around them. "They are still here. They still live. They are everywhere, they are everywhen—they are our essence of being, our connection to the land."

"And what about the thing—the thing that . . . erases time?" Stanley asked, his eyes fixed on the flames.

She looked at him gravely. "That is a story that cannot be told. It needs to be seen."

He tore away from the fire to look at her. "What do you mean?"

"Do you know why Simon brought you here?"

Stanley blinked, glancing over to Simon on the other side of him, but Simon was already gone. They were alone. "To learn."

She nodded. "And to learn, you must walk. Some things cannot be taught. They must be experienced for themselves. You have seen a lot, Stanley Webb. If you want to understand it, you must go for a walk; you must find the ancestral now and feel it yourself."

He looked around him at the endless plains of dust. "A walk?"

"Simon has gone to prepare for you. There's no time like the present."

"What . . . what do I need to do?"

"You leave your things here, your backpack, your clothes. You take a big drink of water before you go." She turned and pointed out into the distant black. "You pick a direction—or, more likely, a direction picks *you*— and you walk. You keep walking until you're done."

Stanley stared at her. This was insane. "How will I know when I'm done?"

She smiled back at him. "You'll know."

"But—naked, with no food or water? I'll die."

"Maybe. Maybe not." She put a hand up to his face and cradled it. It was surprisingly intimate, and Stanley could feel his cheeks growing hot. "You're trapped in time, Stanley. What you seek has been forgotten. It can only be found outside of time."

He looked into her eyes—they seemed as deep as the sky above. "How will I find my way back? How will I survive?"

"Faith," she said. "You have to have faith."

"In the spirits?"

A low chuckle rolled out of her. "Don't be stupid. Faith isn't about them. It's about you. We can't all have faith in the same thing. The question is: What will you put your faith in, Stanley? What will you believe in?"

TWENTY MINUTES LATER, STANLEY STOOD NAKED AT THE EDGE OF THIS campsite where he had only just arrived, certain he had gone mad. There was no other explanation for it. The wind was freezing against his bare skin, the earth brittle against his soles. His heart pumped hard in his chest. This was suicide.

And yet here he was. What other choice did he have?

It was a leap of faith.

But he didn't believe in God, and he wasn't sure he quite believed in the spiritual mumbo jumbo he had just been told. He was a man of science, of learning, and his science told him that if he walked out alone into that barren landscape, he would end up dead from either dehydration, starvation, or injury.

And yet.

You marry me, and we have a daughter, and we live fifty gloriously happy years together. You make us feel so loved, and you don't ruin any of it. I promise you.

If she was right, if it was true, then he wouldn't die here.

Could he have faith in that? Could he have faith in *her*?

It was a strange feeling, an inexplicable one—he'd only spent three days with the woman, and most of the time, he'd been angry at her. But here he was, ready to place his life completely and utterly in her hands.

Oh, Maggie, he thought to himself, *what have you done to me?*

It was still the middle of the night. The moon still hung above, bathing the red dust in cold light, making it look like a lunar landscape, a reflection of the heavens above.

He took a big swig of water, then handed his bottle back to Simon, who stood behind him, and took his first few steps out into the black.

After about twenty feet, he could have sworn he heard Simon's distinctive chuckle.

"Whitefellas. All of them crazy."

Stanley kept walking.

THIS WAS RIDICULOUS. HIS FEET ACHED AND STUNG—THE SMALL ROCKS and stones underfoot had cut into his soles, leaving bloody footprints in his wake. It was still dark, but he didn't know if he'd been walking for one hour or nine. Time soon stopped meaning anything.

He kept walking.

His mind cycled through different thoughts—first, a scientific approach. How long could a man realistically walk out here in one direction before bumping into someone else? Maps of the Australian outback, ones he had memorized perfectly to keep him entertained on the flight over, told him it could be hundreds of miles, possibly a thousand or more. Days upon days of walking. Longer than he could go without food or water, especially with all this movement.

He didn't think about that for too long.

He found himself recounting his life—all the choices he had made to lead him here, all the things gone wrong. He played them out over and over again in his head, trying to work out if there was some common thread that tied them all together.

Flies and midges circled around him, and he swatted them away pointlessly. His legs ached now too, and his stomach rumbled in hunger.

He found it difficult to focus on any one particular thought, so instead he let himself sink into the rhythm of the walking. He walked. One step, then the next, toward the horizon. Toward nowhere at all.

He took a shit at sunrise. There was nothing to wipe himself with, so he just kept walking, leaving his waste to be swallowed by the dust, along with everything else.

It got worse when the sun came up. Sweat poured from his body and evaporated in seconds. As the sun grew overhead, each breath of hot air turned his mouth as parched as the land itself. Twice he thought he saw water, but it was just color refracted through the waves of heat. Mirages to trick him. His vision was becoming hazy. The last remnants of the food he'd eaten—some potatoes back at the dig site—seemed to suck the moisture from his very blood. He longed to reach the shore of a river or a lake and plunge his head in its cool waters.

In time, the rocks changed. The eternally flat landscape gave rise to hills and outcrops. In the distance, Stanley thought he saw a river, and excitement bubbled up inside him. A desperate plea. He pushed forward toward it, his legs barely capable of holding him up.

It was definitely a pool of water. He became certain of it. And as he got closer, his feet trod onto wetter and wetter soil, forming a crust above the dry, cracked land. He ran—hurriedly, frantically—until he reached it: a small pond connected to a river that had all but dried up, just a slow trickle keeping it going.

Stamping to its surface, he threw himself down and began scooping the water into his mouth. The taste was brackish and foul. A fire burned down his chest, and his stomach exploded. He rolled over and retched, and then his mind went blank.

He woke up shivering and cold. It was night again, but his body stung. His skin was bright red, having burned to a crisp in the summer sun. Every movement was agony.

Instinctively, he pushed himself away from the water. A briny taste rose from his stomach and stuck to the vomit on his tongue. He longed for a sip of water, *clean* water, to cleanse his mouth and throat. His mind was frazzled, but if he didn't leave here, he would die. He needed to keep walking.

He tried to crawl, but his hands gave way. He sunk into the mud, spluttering and cursing. Lifting himself up again, he lugged himself onward, ahead, to something, to nothing. He'd stopped questioning why he was doing this. He'd stopped thinking anything at all. Apart from the echo of his dragging footfalls, the desert was silent. The full moon rose once again in the night sky.

With it came strange things. The rocks around him shifted, no longer staying in place. They lifted up off the ground, and he swore he could see them following him, like animals stalking in the night. But there were no animals here, only him.

The ground itself moved now, and as the rocks glittered beneath him, they mirrored the starry sky above—eternal and infinite. He wondered how he was walking on them, walking on the sky as if everything had been turned upside down.

Wisps of smoke and color pushed their way to the corners of his vision. He saw people—the shapes of people—in the dust, twisting and dancing and shaking.

He couldn't feel the cold or the thirst any longer. He couldn't feel anything. He had been dropped into a dreamworld. He wondered, for a moment, if he was still awake. If he was still alive.

Keep walking, some voice in his head whispered. *Keep walking*.

He walked, and the visions took shape, threading themselves into a narrative he would not have been able to follow even if his mind were not so frazzled. But, somehow, he could put together the pieces: People shifting and jumping between memories, people darting through the smoke of time, traveling from present to past and back again.

Then he saw *it*.

Eating its way through mist, erasing those that shifted through time.

He recognized it not just as a vision but as a feeling, so clear because all other feelings were gone. It blazoned out—a panic and a forgetfulness and a certainty. But it was still so new, so fresh. It had not been around for long.

It had been *made*. He saw that, and he knew that, as clearly as he had ever known anything.

It wasn't a being or a malevolent, hungry force out to hunt anyone. It was a safeguard, put in place to keep the passage of time moving forward, to stop anyone's attempts to change it. It was not there to hurt anyone, just to correct.

People had made it, before history even remembered there *were* people. Humans had created it.

So there must be a way to stop it.

He tripped, falling to his knees, gasping.

He wasn't dead, but he was dying. He was certain of that. He was dying.

His body was giving up on him.

But there were answers here, if only he knew how to work them out.

It didn't matter. He was in the middle of the Australian outback, miles from any town, or person. He was naked and dirty, and his body was falling apart.

He lay on the ground, his back against the dust. He thought it would consume him. It would cover him, and he would become one with it, and that was how his life would end.

But he didn't want it to end.

For the first time in his life, he knew—furiously, undeniably—that he wanted to live. He wanted to have a real life, filled with love and happiness and everything that was promised to him. He wanted it so badly.

Maggie, he thought. He couldn't consider any thoughts longer than two syllables. They were beyond him. His brain was shutting down. Just *Maggie*.

He said it over and over again, staring up at the moon. *Maggie, Maggie, Maggie*.

And like a miracle, like an angel descended from heaven, she was there.

He didn't believe his eyes. He was hallucinating.

She was standing over him, bent forward with a frown on her face.

"Oh, bloody hell, Stan," she said. "This is even worse than last time."

17

TRANSCRIPT NO. 273: Margaret Webb

DATE STAMP: 11 AUG. 2021

2 Hours, 12 Minutes, and 0 Seconds Until Dissolution

He's naked.

Naked?

Not just naked but broken. Oh dear God, he looks like he's dead. I can barely distinguish between the blistered red of his skin and the color of the mud that coats it. If it weren't for the gasping breath and the haunted look in his eyes, I would have thought I was looking at a corpse.

"Maggie," he whispers, his voice barely above a breath.

I bend down, kneeling beside him, my old bones still creaking, despite whatever you did to me. There's a coolness in the air that makes me shiver. Putting my arms around him, I pull him up, cradling him on my lap. He is hot—feverish. His limbs are floppy.

"It's going to be okay," I say, more to myself than to him. "You'll be fine."

For the first time since I materialized, I take a good look at the world around me. The first light of morning is just starting to glow on the horizon, bathing the landscape in the soft brushes of a new day. There is nothing but rock and dust and cliff, endlessly.

Did Stanley give me this second date so that I could save his life? Or is there more I'm expected to do here?

I assume we must be in Australia. I have never been, but I've seen plenty images of it from Stanley's old documentaries, and I remember the message I gave him at our last meeting. There's a ruggedness to the terrain, a wildness that makes me stop and take in a few breaths, and then it hits me:

There are no humans here.

No signs of cars, or houses, or factories. I've not seen anything like it in decades.

Its beauty overwhelms me.

Stanley coughs, curling into my lap, his face burrowed into my stomach. I am snapped back into the urgency of the moment. My husband is dying.

"What do you need?" I ask.

He looks up, opening his mouth, but just a rasping sound comes out. I shake my head, blinking at him, and he tries again. This time, it has more shape to it, more color.

"Water," he says. "Water."

Of course. I almost slap myself in the face for being so stupid. I don't know how long he's gone without it or what madness brought him here; he won't last long without water. That much is obvious.

"But I don't have anything," I say desperately, feeling suddenly powerless. "I'm not prepared. Oh, Stan, why didn't you tell me? Why didn't you tell me what you would need?"

He looks up at me, lost. I don't know if he can hear me. I don't know if he's even aware I'm here.

There must be something I can do. He can't die here.

Then I remember how I got here.

I remember what I can do.

Seizing control of the technology that is becoming second nature to me now, I flicker out of his present. I dive back into his timeline, his memories, willing myself into a space and time where I can find what I need.

The universe materializes around me once more: the hard stone beneath my feet, the rising turrets, the bustling bodies. A loud buzz of conversation fills my ears as I turn, and I realize I am surrounded by people—by children. Students.

I am in a courtyard at a large school, a centuries-old building that oozes grandeur and privilege. Whelton College, I realize. Where Stanley went.

A group of students bustle past me, and I step out of their way, turning to see *him* sitting on a small bench, eating his lunch. He is young—around twelve or thirteen—and he is utterly alone.

Oh, Stan.

The world passes around him like ocean currents unfazed in their movements. Nobody casts him a second glance or look. He is invisible to everyone. But to me, he is a beacon. My heart aches for him, wanting to hold him tightly, to give him some comfort, but I know that it is not time. That is not why I'm here.

He has a large water bottle next to him, almost a liter, and it's full.

Of course he does, I think. I decided what I needed to find, and I came here. Increasingly, I have begun to feel like Stanley—my Stanley, in the present—is helping me. Perhaps he doesn't know it, but on some subconscious level, he is guiding me through his memories to where I need to be.

"Excuse me, young man," I say, approaching him. He glances up, surprised that anyone is speaking to him.

"Y-Yes?"

"I'm going to need that bottle of water."

He blinks, baffled. "My water bottle?"

I put five decades of maternal conviction into my voice. "Yes." I extend my hand. "Now."

Without hesitation, he hands it over. I give him the warmest smile I am capable of and then turn a corner before I disappear; he has noticed me now, and I do not think a twelve-year-old boy needs to see an old woman vanish into thin air.

In a blink of darkness, I am back in the desert. Stanley is so weak that he barely noticed my absence. Cradling him once more, I hold the bottle to his lips, and he sips at it. Gently at first, then greedily, leaning forward to get more into his mouth. I have to hold him back.

"Slowly," I say. "You'll make yourself throw up, and that would be a right waste. You don't know how far I went to get this."

He sags in my arms after he has drunk, and he falls asleep. I lay him down on the ground—the hard, rocky earth—and he is still naked. His body is blistered and burned and filthy. I cannot let him sleep like this.

So I dive again. And again and again.

I embrace the power that I have been given over time and space, flickering into small moments of his life to procure what I need. I keep to the shadows, and as long as I do not call attention to myself, I am out of mind. I slip between the cracks.

I steal clothes from Stanley's dad, back when Stanley still lived at home. I take a sleeping bag and find some aloe for his burns. I find tissue paper and plasters, along with disinfectant to clean up his wounds. Most of the time, Stanley doesn't even know I'm there. When he does notice me, it's just for a brief instant.

There is a park where Stanley goes to get away from his father, to be lost. I take a sandwich from him when he's not looking, and he sees me, catches me out of the corner of his eye, and there's a moment of confusion on his face, like he's seen me before but can't be sure where. Like he's fighting with his brain to stay focused.

"STAN!" his father shouts, barreling up the road in a swirl of clenched fists and red cheeks. Young Stanley snaps away from me, and I disappear again.

Gone.

I am a ghost. I am a specter between worlds.

In the outback, I tend to him. He drifts in and out of consciousness, muttering about dreams and the deep past and something to do with time. It means nothing to me. This is what I realize—all of this means nothing to me. All that's important is that he's okay, and that we are together.

The rest is noise.

When he wakes properly, the first thing he does is reach out to me and take my hand in his rough, callused own. I worry that he will treat me like he did the last time I went into his past—that he will hate me for having stormed into his life uninvited.

I have fed him in his brief moments of consciousness, and he has regained color in his face. His skin is healing, if slowly, the outer layers peeling away like plaster. He cocks his head to the side, trying to work me out.

"I have forgot why I did call thee back," he says, half in a daze. I can't help it—a huge grin breaks out on my face.

"Let me stand here till thou remember it," I recite in response, and his eyes go wide. His fingers tighten around mine.

"I shall forget, to have thee still stand there, remembering how I love thy company."

"And I'll still stay," I reply, "to have thee still forget, forgetting any other home but this."

"*Romeo and Juliet*," he whispers, staring into my eyes. "My favorite play."

"I know."

And in an instant, I see the man I married. Not the mistakes he made or the person he has been but the one I love—the one who gave me my daughter, who held me and fought with me and traveled with me and grew with me. He is here, finally, and he is mine.

He sits up and looks around him, surprised to find himself clothed, wrapped in a sleeping bag.

"How is this possible?"

I smile. "Have a little faith in your wife, dear. I can be resourceful when I need to be."

Something about that makes him laugh. He winces as it happens, his hand going to his chest. I hand him another bottle of water. "You're not out of the woods yet," I say. "Or out of the desert, rather. What happened here, Stan? Why are you even here?"

"I came . . ." He struggles to find the words. "I needed to find an answer. A way to make everything right."

"You're looking for a way to stop Omega," I say.

He frowns, sitting up and propping himself against a rock. His breathing is labored. "Omega? I . . . I don't know. I have not heard that name before."

"That's what it's called, in my present. There is a man who is helping me with the spade in the year 2021. That is what *he* calls it—the thing that eats the past."

Stanley leans forward, wincing. "Yes. I think. Or . . . I'm trying to find out what it is. Where it came from. *Why* it exists." He shakes his head. "I need to understand before I can do anything else."

I look around me at the endless dust. "And the answers are out here?"

A weak grin appears on his face. "Partly, but I think I need to look elsewhere too. If I am right, there will be clues across the whole world."

"Idiot," I chide. "You almost died out here. You would have died."

"Never." He takes my hand in his. It's hard and rough from the dirt. "I knew you would come for me. You think I don't remember, but I do. You're always there, aren't you? Tucked in between the pages of my life."

"I still have so many questions," I say. There is so much about his life I do not know.

He takes a deep breath. "Try me."

"How do we stop Omega? How do we preserve the past?"

He shakes his head. "I don't know. Not yet. I . . . I don't think it's as simple as that."

"Okay, let me tell you this. When you find the answer, the solution you are searching for right now, you hide it from the world—why?"

He furrows his brow. "I . . . I don't know."

Then I take a deep breath, preparing the question that has been sitting on me since this all began, feeling it weigh down on my chest. "Why didn't you tell me? All our years together—our marriage, our *life*. Why did you never tell me about any of this? You told me that you were a researcher, that you worked on government programs, at think tanks. All of this, I'm realizing now, was probably a lie. Where did you *go* during your days? Where were you working?"

"I'm sorry," he says. I can see that he truly is. His eyes glisten with the pain of having to tell me. "I really don't know. I fear you may have come too early for all that."

I grimace. "It certainly seems that way."

"I'm really not being very helpful, am I?"

"No."

A silence settles between us. It rests for a moment, for much more than a moment. It takes up quiet residence.

"I hate to think that I am putting you through all this," Stanley says quietly. "I don't know why I hid it from you, but because of my mistakes and my selfishness, you are having to go through such a terrible trial. I could . . . I could change course."

I frown at him. "What do you mean?"

"If . . . if you told me where we first met and I skipped our first meeting. If I never met you, you could live a life without me. You would never have to go through this pain."

My heart skips a beat, like someone has put their fist around it and squeezed. I kneel down next to him and take a deep breath. Then I look him in the eyes and utter as clearly as I possibly can: "Don't. You. Dare."

"But I—"

"No." I grab his hand and squeeze it in mine. "Our family is the best thing that has ever happened in my life. You do not get to take that away from me, no matter what the consequences are."

He looks back at me, and I think I see a hint of fear in his eyes.

"Back in London," Stanley says slowly, cautiously, "you said we had a daughter."

My stomach constricts, twisting inside me. "Yes. We . . . we had her late—really late. I'd had a few miscarriages, and I'd almost given up on the idea of children. I'd accepted it would just be you and me. But then, when I was forty-five, there she was. Our little miracle."

"What's she like?"

And I want to say: *She's wonderful. She's kind and loving and intelligent, and you love her so much.* I want to sing it with all the pride and joy and celebration of motherhood, but I can't. Because all I can think about is how she doesn't talk to me anymore, how utterly I must have failed her, and I don't know why. I can't even tell him why.

He notices me hesitate. He leans forward, just a little. "What is it?"

"She's . . ." I blink, trying to keep the tears from my eyes. "She's *so* stubborn."

Stanley's eyes widen, and then he lets out a little laugh. It washes over me, eases me. It makes everything feel like it might be okay.

"When she first went to university," I say, the words suddenly flowing out of me, "she would call us every week just to tell us all the exciting things she was doing. New clubs. New hobbies. She'd joined the student newspaper. One week, she told us she was thinking of skipping a couple weeks of uni to go to France, to practice French and meet new people and discover a different culture. We both—in our own ways—tried to talk her out of it. 'You can't just *go*,' we said. 'You have commitments now. Life doesn't work that way.' And"—I smile, thinking back on the memory—"the next time she called, she called from a hostel in Paris, and you burst out laughing, just like you did now. That's just who she is. Determined. Headstrong. She doesn't take shit from anyone, Stanley, and you *love* that about her."

He's got a broad grin on his face. He looks around him, at the endless red plains, and then at me, standing in the middle of them. "I wonder who she gets that from."

"Oh, stop it," I say. I tell him nothing about the inexplicable fracture between me and our daughter. I don't want to ruin the moment.

He's sitting up straighter, more awake and rejuvenated. "I know I've been pretty useless, but is there anything you think I *might* be able to answer?"

"At this point, who knows? Can you tell me what Thamus and Theuth are?"

He blinks at me. "Thamus and Theuth? From Plato's *Phaedrus*?"

"I'm guessing so."

He tries to stand up but wavers. I step forward to catch him, grabbing on to his arm. He leans into me, and I feel like I'm about to fall over too, sending both of us tumbling into the dirt. "It's a retelling of a myth by Socrates," he says, straightening up. "About the invention of writing and the decline of memory. It . . . it was one of my favorite pieces of writing, once."

"Once?"

He looks at the ground, his eyes darting away from me. "It's associated with some pretty bad memories," he mutters.

"You told me to go to it. You said, 'When the time comes, go to Thamus and Theuth.'"

Sighing, he kicks at a rock. It skips across the ground. "I don't know what that means either. I think, perhaps, that you need to find me at a better time."

"I can't leave you here."

"Yes," he says, his voice certain. "You can. Thank you for coming here. For saving me—in more ways than one. But you have done your part, I think. And it sounds like there are more places you need to go, but I can't come with you. There is more for me to do here, more to discover. I have only just scratched the surface. I think I may have to spend many more years here." He looks at me, and his eyes soften. "I'm sure you'll see me sooner than I'll see you. You seem to take shorter roads."

I take a few steps toward him and stop. We are inches away from each other. I want him to hold me, like he did at the wedding, when I needed him most. Or I want to hold him, like I did in that abandoned flat. Neither seems appropriate now. I am too old, from a distant world. This is not where I belong—not yet.

The air electrifies with the static of expectation.

"How do I know you'll be okay?" I ask.

He smiles and opens his arms. They fold into mine, and we are pulled close—symbiotic, two parts of a single body. "If I weren't," he whispers in my ear, "I think you'd already know about it by now."

But still, I feel like I can't simply *leave*. I want to drag out the moment; I want it to linger.

"Is there anything more you need before I go?"

He shrugs, stepping back. "Difficult to say. There was a compass in my backpack, but I left that behind at the camp a few days ago. Shame— would have been useful."

"How many days ago?" I ask.

And just as he tells me, I flicker away. I'm back before he can blink; I can tell by the look on his face. In between one breath and the next, I've slipped into his past, gone into the tent where that tall man placed his backpack, and brought him the compass. I'm getting very good at this.

"Thank you," he says, taking it from me.

"Be safe," I reply. "Come back to me."

And then I go.

You pull out of the dive?

Not quite. Not yet.

Why not?

Because jumping through time has shown me something: I have so much power. I can do so much, and I know so little. About Stanley's life, about my place in it. About what I mean to him.

There is a universe between us. An immeasurable distance of space and time.

More and more, I have felt like nothing but a fleck—a small pawn moved this way and that by decisions made long before I was aware of them, by ethereal hands moving pieces out of my control. And because I have been alone for too long, too scared, too paralyzed, I have let myself be moved. I have let this distance between us stretch into an infinity.

But as I step away from him this time, I decide that I've had enough.

I am done with the space between us.

I will have no more cowardice in my life, and I will be no one's pawn. Not anymore.

I want to stay in Stanley's life, to see more of it. I want to experience all the things that I have missed for so many years. And there's a part of him that's helping me. I can feel it—some symbiosis of Stanley's memories and my intentions that is giving me more control with every movement. For the first time in many years, I feel free.

You aren't concerned about Omega?

You assured me you would warn me when time was running out, just as you did last time. I have to believe that; otherwise, all of this is pointless. Some part of me recognizes that I *want* to believe that, because it gives me more time in the past.

Oh, don't give me that look. I'm not an idiot. I could feel it coming last time too, just before I pulled out. I could feel it creeping in at the edges of my consciousness. If that happens again, I tell myself, I'll leave.

Please continue. We are running out of time. Where do you go?

I go forward, into our life together. I want to be reminded of the beautiful times, the ones that have existed only in my head for so long.

When I materialize, the first thing I hear is my own screams. They pierce through the hospital ward, shifting between shrieks of pain and a low bellowing, like a mooing cow. I'm on all fours—*she* is. The nurses are stemming the excess blood with surgical swab upon surgical swab, and Stanley is hovering over her, hand rubbing her back.

He doesn't know what to do. I can see it in his face. He's read every book there is to read about labor—about breathing and water births and hypnobirthing and pain relief—but when he's in the moment, he's useless. I smile, feeling bad for him in a way that I didn't back then.

All he wants to do is make sure I'm okay, to ease the pain, but he can't.

I'm standing at the door, just to the side of the action, and I'm invisible. I don't intend for anyone to notice me, so they won't. I'm just here to watch.

She moos in pain again, and the midwife tells her to keep pushing—the head is almost through. As I watch on, my back twitches in response, some deep muscle memory rising to the surface. Stanley is almost jumping up and down in exhilaration and worry. After so many miscarriages, he is so scared that something will happen again. He tries to offer her some water from a bottle he brought, but she slaps it away. He apologizes pointlessly, but it's drowned out by more mooing.

And then she appears. Once her head is through, she slips out, like at the end of a bloody waterslide, right into the midwife's arms. Leah lets out a sob—just a small one to let us know she's alive—and she is deposited right on her mother's chest. On *my* chest.

I remember the feeling like it was yesterday. Her legs kick, and I recall thinking, *Those are the same kicks I felt inside me. Those are the same legs. This is real. This is all real. Our child, our little miracle.*

Leah puts her head down against her mother's chest, cuddling up against it, breathing in the warmth like a blanket against this loud, cold world. Stanley cuts the cord. Even though nobody ever did back then, he insisted. His hands are shaking. He can't look away from me, from her, from the whole scene. His eyes are so filled with love.

And I am crying. Me, here, now. They are tears of pure, unadulterated joy. Because despite everything that is happening in the present, these are the moments lives are made of. These are the moments that define us. *I can bear anything*, I think to myself, *anything at all, so long as my life has these moments in it.*

All the rest of it—the pain, the heartbreak, the loneliness—it's worth it. It was all worth it. Because I got to experience this.

And I almost want to come out of the memory and hug you for finding me, for introducing me to the memory spade, for showing me how to experience this again.

I wait in the corner of that room for another three hours, just watching the love pass between the three of them: the looks in their eyes, the lightness of their touches. It is heavenly.

When it comes to an end and Stanley has to leave the ward, I almost want to go back and see it all again. But I don't.

This was not the only beautiful moment in my life.

I have fifty years of beauty to choose from.

And I do: I dive forward again—to her first steps and her first words; to the night Stanley and I made love under the stars in Bologna after Leah had been put to bed; to the camping trip we took to Skye when she was eight.

I watch Leah grow up again—all her achievements and celebrations, all her failures, all the times she needed me to give her a hug.

I linger in a long moment where she has crawled into our bed, awakened by a night terror, and instinctively curled up with her head against my chest, only the rhythm of my steady heartbeat able to calm her frantic heart. I watch as she lies curled there until there is no other sound but our breathing in unison, the whole world still around us.

Now and then, I stop in on a small, nondescript moment with Stanley, and I take some time to watch closely. There are things I need to know.

You've got to understand: Stanley is a genius. I've always known this. He's smarter than me in a million different ways, and there were times over the years when my neurosis got the better of me, told me that he couldn't possibly be content with just me, that he must feel like he had settled. Surely, one day, he would grow bored of our little life together.

Recent discoveries have only compounded this feeling. What a life he has hidden from me. Secret labs and tangled mysteries and grand adventures. How could a quiet life with me ever compare?

I'm watching Stanley and Leah in our kitchen together, cooking dinner. My younger self must be in the other room, watching TV. It's a quiet evening, with no particularly special memory attached. She is four, and he is teaching her to be his little sous-chef: how to hold a knife properly, which herbs to use with which vegetables. She picks it up quickly—he is a very good teacher.

They are making some kind of Moroccan couscous dish, and I can smell the cinnamon and the paprika and the apricot. Every time Stanley turns his back, Leah sneaks a raisin into her mouth. She thinks he doesn't notice, but he does. He smiles, and it is unmistakable.

He loves her, and me, and he loves his life. He hasn't settled for a damn thing.

He is so happy.

And so am I.

Whatever happens next, I can live with it, because I have seen this.

And I want to see more. Oh, I want to see so much more.

But there is a creeping feeling at the back of my mind—it's like ice-cold water slowly trickling, draining the warmth bit by bit. You have not warned me, for some reason, but I know I am outstaying my welcome.

It has sensed me, despite your protections, and it's coming for me.

I reach for the thread I know so well, the one that pulls me back into the present, and I tug.

Nothing happens.

I tug again, harder this time.

But I don't move. I am still in the kitchen, the creeping water rising.

My heartbeat doubles in speed. Triples.

It's not working, I say in my head. *Hassan, if you can hear me, it's not working. You need to pull me out.*

No, you reply, your voice ringing clearly. *There is more to do.*

I've done everything I needed to do. I saved Stanley. I was just—

You are not there to save Stanley. You are there to find the solution to stopping Omega.

But I don't know!

You have not been looking. I have been tracking you, flitting across time. You dillydally. You use my machinery for your frivolity and foolishness.

I am getting tired of you ignoring what I have sent you here for, Maggie. I'm not letting you out until I have the solution.

The darkness presses in around me.

No, I beg. *Please. You can't. There's no time.*

You can still move through the memories. Shifting to another memory will give you more time. It has been slowed. If you keep moving, you can stay ahead of it.

Not for long, I say. *It knows where I am now.*

I have waited long enough, you say. *You will have to search quickly.*

Then I see it—the yawning void. It starts at the bottom of the kitchen table, slower now than before, but it works its way up, erasing, *eating,* eradicating the moment. This beautiful moment of happiness.

"No!" I shout. Stanley jerks up at the sound and looks at me. His face panics.

I run.

I shift into another memory, desperate to escape, to be anywhere but here, anywhere but our life together, so that it doesn't get taken.

I don't know where I am when I rematerialize. It's an old stone room, and there are rows of bookcases and shelves scattered with strange scents and oils. It's nighttime; the room glows with the dim flicker of candlelight and nothing else.

There's a sofa in the corner with a boy sleeping on it. I take a step closer and see that it's Stanley. He looks almost like an adult, around seventeen or eighteen.

"What are you doing here?" a voice demands, and I jerk around to find an old man staring at me from the other side of the room.

"You can see me?" I ask, because I haven't done anything to call attention to myself yet. "You know I'm here?"

"Pah!" he exclaims, waving his hand. "See you? *Smell you* more like. Of course I know you're here. Might as well ask a fish if it knows it can swim!"

He gets up, grabbing a cane to move, and I realize that he's blind.

"The question is," he continues, waving his stick in my direction, "how did you get here?"

The candlelight dims further, and a deep cold trickles through my whole body. I stumble back, looking around the room to check if it's all there.

"There's no time," I say frantically. "It's coming for me."

He frowns. "What's coming for you?"

"Oh God," I say, because it's already here. It has followed me all the way back in time. "It's here. It's slower than before, but it's *here*."

And I can see that he knows it, even though I can't see the emptiness yet. He has better senses than mine. He sniffs the air, feeling the edges of it creeping in. His face blanches in panic. "It's *real*? Roanoke? The lost cities? It's all *real*?"

"I'm so sorry," I say between panicked breaths. "I have to go. It's coming. It hungers, and it's after me. It's after us all." I take one last look at the young man on the sofa. "You have to warn him. Whatever it is he's working on, whatever it is he's trying to uncover, you have to stop him, or it will be the end of us all."

His voice has dropped to a low murmur, quivering with intensity. "What is it? What does he unleash?"

"I can't explain," I say, my mind clouded by the urgency of the moment. The darkness is almost at my feet now. "It's too fierce, too dreadful. There's no fighting it, no defending against it. All we can do is run."

And I'm gone.

I'm on the run again.

Hunted.

It's autumn, and the leaves are just turning red. The air is crisp. I'm in a park, and about twenty yards away, Stanley and I are pushing Leah on one of the swings. But I can already feel the rising cold—Oh God, it's already here.

Let me out, I beg, tears running down my cheeks. *Just let me out. I promise I'll do better next time.*

Not until you find the answer.

I don't know what to do! I don't know where to look!

Go further ahead in the timeline, you say, your voice indomitable. *Find a Stanley that knows.*

"There isn't time!" I shout aloud. People turn to look at me—a crazy old lady shouting in a park. Stanley looks at me, and Leah too, though she doesn't know what she's looking at. But for some reason, *I* don't look up. I don't notice. "It's going to take everything, you psycho. What do you want from me?"

I want you to stop fucking with me, Maggie. I have waited far too long for this. Do not think I am not tracking you through time. I'm bored of watching you play out your relationship again like a lovesick teenager. You are here for a reason. See to it.

"Okay," I say, taking deep breaths to steady myself. "Okay."

I pull myself forward, rematerializing decades into the future. The walls appear around me—beige and yellow, with pictures of flowers—and I am enclosed inside a building.

Sunrise: the care center where Stanley is.

I am in his room, and he is old again, looking out the window and staring listlessly at the sky. He has not noticed me here.

"Stan," I say, but he doesn't react. I walk over to him and shake his arm. *"Stan."*

But there is nothing. He continues to stare, lost in one of those distant phases where he barely recognizes anything around him. This is not going to be helpful.

His door opens, and a man walks in—one of the carers. He sees me by the bed and frowns, confused, as if he's trying to work out whether I'm really there. Behind him, behind the door, I see a creeping blackness starting to emerge, and all I can think is that it's coming for me.

If we stay in this room, it's going to take all of us, Stanley included.

I need to get out of here.

"Get back!" I shout.

"W-What?" He cocks his head at me, the blackness licking at his feet.

I rush forward, pushing him out the door and into the corridor. "You need to get away!"

He tumbles backward, startled by my push, and rolls onto the floor. I almost bend down to pick him up, but something stops me. Something about his face.

What is it?

It's completely blank. He looks like he's sleeping without his eyes closed—no emotion, no anything. Like he's in a coma.

"What the hell is going on?" I whisper.

It shifts. It is trying different tactics, you reply from behind my eyes. *Omega, it fights against its chains. You must hurry, Maggie. This is not the right moment either. You are too late.*

As I back away, another attendant notices us and rushes over, leaning down to check on the first carer. As she touches him, her face goes blank too. It's spreading. Oh God, it's like an infection, moving through this present, taking everything as it goes.

I dash into Stanley's room and find his key. Coming out again, I slam the door shut and lock it from the outside.

I cannot let it get in there, or risk the chance that he might come out. Not until this is over. I cannot let it get to him.

"It's going to erase them all," I say, moving away from the scene of the crime as quickly as I can. "You—you did this."

It will get some of them, yes, but not all. Sunrise is not oblivious to this threat and has some rudimentary procedures in place to contain it.

Not comforted in the slightest, I have a sudden urge to dash down the stairs and see how many people are in here, how many people we have doomed to erasure. As I get to the lobby, I hear a scream from upstairs. It has taken more people. It spreads.

Attendants and carers notice and rush to see what the source of the panic is, headed for their own demise. I open my mouth to warn them, to tell them to stay back, but my whole heart leaps into my throat.

I cannot speak.

Outside the front doors, just about to walk into this building—this place infected with an ancient and ravenous sickness—is my daughter.

I run as fast as my old legs can carry me, pushing open the double doors and confronting her on the porch.

"Mum?" She frowns in confusion. "I thought you were at home. I just left you."

"You need to get out of here, Leah. You need to leave right now."

She shakes her head. "Don't be ridiculous. I'm just popping in to see Dad before I head off. I won't be long."

"There's a fire!" I lie. "Inside. You can't go in."

She pauses, looks at me, and then looks at the building. "If there's a fire, why is there no alarm? And why are you out here when Dad's inside? What's going on?"

"It's . . ." I grasp for words. How can I explain everything in a way that makes sense? "You've just got to trust me. Please. You can't go in there."

She tuts at me, like she used to do when I was being old and crazy. "You're being silly, Mum. Come on, let's go inside." Stepping forward, she moves to take my arm and lead me in *there.*

"You *can't!*"

But she ignores me, now annoyed at my behavior. She lets go and pushes past me. She is so stubborn, so headstrong.

She'll go in there, and it'll infect her, and she'll be erased. My daughter will be erased from all time and history, and I will forget she has ever existed.

That cannot happen. At any cost.

"Dad doesn't want you there!" I shout.

She stops, turning back to me, her face a portrait of shock. "What?"

"I've just been speaking to him. He doesn't want to see you." I take a deep breath, loathing every last word that is coming out of my mouth. "He can't stand the sight of you."

She stares at me, baffled, taken aback, hurt. In a new voice—softer, more childlike—she whispers, "He said that? Did . . . did he know what he was saying?"

And then I realize that I must be a party to this as well, or she will never buy it. Not outright. Maybe if I were younger, quicker, smarter, I would think of something else. Anything besides this. But in this moment, with my heart racing and the screams from upstairs echoing through my head, it's all I can come up with.

She must leave. She must flee. There is no time for anything else.

I choke back the tears that are rising in my throat, because I realize that this is it. This is two years ago. This is the moment she stops talking to me.

This is how I lose my daughter.

"Yes," I snap. "Frankly, we've been talking about it for a while. He's disappointed in you. What have you done in the past twenty years since you left home? You've done nothing but piss about. We even paid for you to go back to uni to retrain three years ago, and what have you got to show for that? Dead-end jobs at bars and hostels. No career, no family, no nothing? You're an embarrassment to both of us."

With each word, I feel my heart rend in two, because she is shrinking in front of me. She is growing smaller and smaller by the second, retreating into herself at my onslaught. I know she will never forgive me for this, but I have no choice. If she goes in there, she is lost. If I have to sacrifice my daughter's love to keep her alive, then so be it.

"You visit us once every couple of months, if we're *lucky*," I continue, laying into her, feeling like I'm going to throw up. "Be honest, Leah. You've left us both to rot. Dad said so himself. Go back to your car and get back to whatever waste you're making of your life, because neither of us wants to have anything to do with you. Honestly, I'd be happy if we never saw you again."

She stares at me, shocked, backing away as tears run down her cheeks. All I want to do is reach my arms out and hold her, pull her close to my chest like I used to do when she got nightmares, breathing with her until she was okay. But I know that I can't. I know that I will never hold her again.

She doesn't even look at me as she barrels past me to her car. I stare, hopelessly, as she gets in and speeds away.

What have you done, Hassan? What have you made me do?

If you don't want to have to do something like that again, I suggest you get moving, you say.

"Fuck you," I spit back—at the air, at the building, at myself.

I pull myself forward, rematerializing a good few decades into the past. The first thing that hits me is the heat—the sweltering humidity slaps me in the face, and the air is thick in my throat. The sun above beats down on me with an unadulterated fury.

Spinning around, I see deck chairs and a tiki bar.

It's our holiday in Cambodia in 1993, our first trip without Leah. We're in Phnom Penh, at a small boutique hotel with two gorgeous swimming pools.

This trip was a gift from Stanley for my birthday. I didn't know quite how he afforded it, but I never really pressed the topic. Stan was always good with money, so I left the financials up to him.

I turn around and see myself. I'm eye to eye with my own face.

"Maggie," I whisper. "Please. Where's Stan?"

He must be nearby. This is *his* memory.

She looks confused, squinting her eyes like something's gone out of focus. It's like she can't see me.

"Where is Stan?" I repeat as forcefully as I can.

"H-He's . . ." she stammers. "He's right there." Her hand points vaguely behind her at the bar where he is sitting. I would have seen him immediately if not for myself.

I step aside, and she wanders off to the toilet, confused. I think for a short minute about how strange it is that I don't remember this encounter. I remember Cambodia, and I remember the hotel, but I *definitely* don't remember bumping into myself.

There's no time to consider it.

The darkness is closing in on me again. I can *feel* it. It's so hungry.

I have to get the answer and get out, or everything is lost.

Pushing past a young couple, I rush over to the bar. Stanley's sitting at a table, finishing his breakfast coffee, and I sit down directly opposite him.

He looks up at me, and realization washes over his face.

"What are you doing here?" he demands. There's shock in his voice but also anger.

"I need to know how to stop Omega. You know. You discovered it before I met you. You have to tell me. There is no time."

He leans back and puts his hand to his head. "You're not meant to be here. You're not meant to come here. Oh, Maggie, what have you done?"

"I had to," I insist. "It's following me, and there's nowhere to go but your memories. Hassan won't pull me out until I give him the way to stop it. Please—the things I've had to do. That I've *done*. We don't have any time."

He looks furious. For a moment, I think he's going to smash his cup on the ground or upend the table. "I worked so hard to protect these moments. This life of ours. You're not meant to be here. The wedding was supposed to be the last time I interacted with . . ." His fists clench. "Do you know how hard it was to isolate the wedding? Do you know how long that took?"

I open my mouth, but no words come out. I can see the truth of it on his face. Everything I have done—all the things I have said—it has been for nothing.

I have ruined everything.

"Please," I beg, desperate. "There must be a way. We can still stop this. You . . . you discovered how."

He shakes his head. "I . . . I can't give you the solution! I don't know it! It's gone. I got rid of it. I erased it from my mind."

"But . . . *why*?"

"Precisely in case something like this happened! The man in your present—Hassan—I know what he is after, and I know he will stop at nothing, *nothing*, until he gets it. I can't allow that to happen. He can never have it. Never."

I stare at him. "But we'll lose everything. Your entire life. Our life. It will be eaten. It will have never existed."

His face hardens. "So be it. This is bigger than us, Maggie. I came to this decision a long time ago. There are more important things at stake."

"I . . ." I look around me. "How can there possibly be anything more important than this?"

"I'm sorry," he says, biting his lip.

At the edges of the restaurant, I see that the walls are not there anymore. There is *nothing* there anymore.

It's here. It's closing in.

There's no more time.

18 | Stanley
1967

IT WAS STRANGE BEING BACK IN ENGLAND. AFTER TWO YEARS IN THE AUS-
tralian outback, a year and a half in the deserts of Egypt, and another nine
months in the cave networks of southern Greece, Stanley had become
used to heat. The cold January wind coursed around him, and he found
himself opening his jacket to let it in. He longed for the air to touch his
skin like a ghostly hug, to make the hairs on his arms and chest shiver.
Though he had never been that happy here, it still felt like he was being
welcomed home.

The years abroad had changed him, had taught him more about the
world than he'd ever expected to know. While tracking the phenomenon
and establishing patterns, he had gone from learning from the cultures of
Australia to finding the strange symbols scrawled on cave walls across
Europe and on old stones in North Africa. With time, he had learned to
survive on his own, moving alone through the desolate wilds of various
countries.

And with that isolation came knowledge: of a deep past lost to humanity, of a history long forgotten outside the old remnants of mythology and
ancient religions. Of Omega, as Maggie had called it. He learned where it
had come from, how it had come to be, the processes needed to stop it. In

the end, all he had to do was step away from the traditional frameworks of knowledge he had once relied upon and accept that a wider world existed beyond the confines of what he knew to be true.

He took a deep breath, looking across the road at the building in front of him. The Lazarus Building had mostly been repurposed—after the fire, after Raph's death. The company still lived on, of course. At a certain stage, corporations grow to be larger than their people; they become self-sustaining entities, taking on lives of their own. But the building was mostly for show now, the real operational headquarters having moved elsewhere.

The pub opposite, the Red Lion, had not changed at all. Stanley pushed through the front doors and walked over to a far table, feeling like he'd stepped back in time. There was the familiar clink of the glasses, the warmth of the seats. When he pictured the three of them—him, Raph, and Jacques—sitting in here, discussing memory and evolution, it seemed like many lifetimes ago. A lump formed in his throat, and he had to swallow to clear it.

Jacques, of course, was the reason he was here.

Not that he'd made contact directly. When Stanley had arrived at Heathrow last night and approached the immigration desk, the officer had given him a routine smile as he took Stanley's passport and checked it.

But something—some warning popping up in Stanley's file—had caused the officer to call his superior over. Stanley couldn't see what it was, but the look of poorly concealed confusion on the officer's face made it undeniably clear. There was an anomaly of some kind.

The officer hadn't addressed it. Instead, after a brief conversation with his boss, he'd placed a small note inside Stanley's passport and handed it back to him, wishing him a nice day.

The message just said: *The Red Lion, tomorrow, three o'clock.*

Stanley had to stop himself from laughing at the absurdity. Even if the location hadn't given it away, there was absolutely no question as to who had sent him this message. It was a chess move—a calculated posture to tell Stanley precisely one thing:

Look what I am capable of. Look what I can do.

It was drama, total showmanship, and it was just so utterly *Jacques*. If he wanted to meet, he could have just called.

But still, Stanley was here, because he needed to know. When he'd checked in with Hugo for updates on Sunrise's outposts in Hong Kong and Dubai, the news he'd gotten was concerning. Jacques—or Hassan, as he now called himself—had his fingers in too many pies to count, both legitimate and criminal. Huge amounts of money, coming from oil reserves throughout the Middle East and dealings in Afghanistan's heroin trade, were flowing toward what appeared to be R&D black sites set up across Europe and North Africa. Governments were being paid off with cash made from selling bleeding-edge technologies to less-than-reputable buyers. Jacques was building an empire.

But some part of Stanley knew that wasn't the goal. It was a means to an end, and after everything that had happened, he needed to know what the end was. More than ever, he felt that Jacques was his responsibility. He had let the man go. He had covered for him. If anything terrible transpired, he would be to blame.

The minute hand on Stanley's watch edged onto the hour. He was about to get up and get a drink when one of the staff approached him.

"Mr. Webb?"

Stanley looked up at him. "Yes?"

"If you'd be so kind, could you please follow me? Mr. al-Haytham thinks a more private setting would be preferable."

Stanley nodded, concealing a little smile. "Sure, whatever you say."

He got up and followed the man past the bar and into a back room. They went through two doors and up a metal stairwell that looked like it belonged in another building. After opening the last door for him, the man stood to one side, allowing Stanley to enter.

It was a large office—the long wooden desk at the back wall faced full-length glass windows that looked out over the streets of London below. There was a sofa and two armchairs in the center, as well as a bar in the corner.

The man closed the door behind him and left him in the empty room. In the absence of any other information, Stanley went to the bar to pour himself a drink.

He sniffed at the brown liquid in the glass decanter—whisky, and a fancy one by the smell of it. Filling up a small glass, he walked back over to the sofa and settled down. He took a sip: It *was* fancy.

The door clicked open.

"Stan," Jacques said, walking in. "So good to see you, old friend."

Except it wasn't Jacques, not quite. On the surface, he looked like Jacques—the features were the same, the general shape of his body and face—but for Stanley, who had known the man since he was a boy, the effect was fleeting.

There was something not quite right about him: the skin was too smooth, the movements too fluid. He had none of the flaws or imperfections that made a person look *human*.

Stanley sat up. "What have you done to yourself?"

"Oh, this?" he replied, looking down at his body. "It started as some adjustments here and there, some small replacements, some experimental surgery."

"The cloned tissue you were toying with at the Institute," Stanley said. "That we used to hide you."

"It's all a little complicated," Jacques said, sitting in the armchair opposite Stanley. He put his feet up on the table, but the gesture was not quite as relaxed, not quite as natural, as the one Stanley knew. "But let's just say the human body is like any other piece of technology. It can be experimented with. It can be improved."

Stanley stared at his old friend, a shiver running through him. "What have you done, Jacques?"

Jacques cocked his head like a snake eyeing up a mouse. "In time, people will be clamoring for what I have achieved. And the name is Hassan now—things have changed since we last saw each other."

"You're telling me," Stanley replied. He took a sip of his whisky. He was trying very hard to keep calm, but there was a tension in the air. He no longer felt completely safe here. Something was off, though he couldn't put his finger on it yet. "Why 'Hassan'?"

Jacques—no, *Hassan*—waved his hand in the air. "Styled after my favorite scientist, Ḥasan Ibn al-Haytham, one of the greatest polymaths to ever walk the earth. Theologian, philosopher, celestial physicist, and the father of modern optics."

A genius, Stanley thought. *Of course you named yourself after a genius.*

"Do you know what made him so special?" Hassan leaned forward. "His ability to see things from an entirely different perspective. He was the first to show that when we look at an object, we aren't seeing the object—not really. We're seeing the light reflected off the object. He understood that the whole concept of *vision* doesn't really exist, except for the electrical reactions that take place in the brain as we piece this light together. He understood that in order to understand the world, sometimes we need to throw out everything we think we know. Sometimes we need to shift the paradigm."

Stanley scooted further back on the sofa, Hassan's fervor putting him on edge. "Is that what you're doing, then? Shifting the paradigm?"

Hassan licked his lips. He inched further in toward Stanley, his voice dropping to almost a whisper. "I can't even *begin* to tell you what I have achieved in the last eight years—what is possible with the right resources, with the right perspective. There are technological leaps that even you would refuse to believe." His eyes swirled as he spoke, hungry, devouring the light between the two of them. "But there is one thing that I have never been able to get past. It's my white whale, Stan. It's my curse."

Stanley felt a lump lodge in his throat. "The memory spade."

"*Yes.* To travel through memory, to change the past. Can you imagine the possibility? But every time, the results are the same as the last."

Stanley blinked. "You . . . you've experimented with it again?"

"Of course I have. Haven't you?"

Stanley's breath felt short in his chest, blank faces and blood flickering through his mind. "What about the subjects?"

"All the same, I'm afraid. They are erased from the past. They are deleted, and everyone who has ever known them forgets they exist. We have nicknamed it Omega—the end of all things. But I think it does not *have* to be an end."

Stanley stood up, putting his hands to his head. "Are you *insane*?"

Hassan frowned, confused. "Not at all. The test rooms are always quarantined, as we did before. We do not allow it to spread. I have learned from my mistakes."

"That's . . . that's not what I'm talking about!" He tried to push images of chopped-up bodies and incineration from his head. All these years spent trying to understand it so that he could make sure it never happened again, and Hassan had never stopped. He'd continued right on as if nothing had happened. "Don't you remember what we did? Don't you remember what we did to *Raph*?"

Hassan waved his hand dismissively. "I haven't forgotten, but Raph is dead. He's not coming back. How long are you going to let that hold you back?"

"Longer than you, clearly," Stanley spat. He stormed across the room, unable to look at Hassan. Was there any of Jacques left in there? Or had there never been a Jacques as he knew him?

"How many other people have you put through this horror?" Stanley demanded, turning round. "How many people have you erased?"

Hassan stood up, shaking his head. "You're focusing on all the wrong things. People know what they're getting into. Their families were appropriately compensated."

"Their families don't even know they *existed*."

"Listen," he huffed. "The point is I've made progress by studying the subjects: their brains, their timelines. We can do so much. Do you know we have technology that can replicate that same kind of loss now, that can remove people's memories with a touch?"

"Oh, and that's meant to reassure me?"

"You're missing *the point*, Stan." His voice grew tense, tinged with an undercurrent of frustration. "If you help me, we can overcome this. I know where you've been. I know you've been watching me, but I've been watching you too. You found it, didn't you? How to stop this thing."

Stanley breathed hard, turning his back to Hassan, his mind whirring. This was worse than he feared. Hassan was insane. He was beyond insane. Stanley needed to get out of here, but as he glanced at the door, he wondered if leaving was even an option. If Hassan would let him.

Stanley felt a cold hand on his shoulder and jerked, jumping back.

He hadn't even heard Hassan's footsteps approaching.

"I am trying to help you," Hassan said, looming over him. "I am trying to help everyone. Already, I have begun to overcome the strictures of mortality, to overcome decay, to transcend into something greater. But my work has only just begun. If we can change the past, we control the present, and he who controls the present defines the future. Look at the direction the world is headed in: overpopulation, starvation, war. You know this as well as anyone. I need you, Stan. This is Waldman's legacy. With you by my side, helping me, we can move the world into a new paradigm. We can be the ones to guide humanity to the right path."

Of course—if Hassan was free to dive into anyone's past, to change the very fabric of time itself, the world would be his to control entirely. Who could stand up to power like that? Who could even try? No. For all Hassan's claims of noble motivations, Stanley didn't want to picture what a future defined by this man would look like. *Waldman's legacy.* Stanley's eyes pricked with tears. He couldn't have imagined anything the old man would have wanted less.

He looked Hassan straight in the eyes—eyes that glimmered with an inhuman sheen.

"I'm not going to help you," he said. "Omega was created precisely for people like you."

Hassan didn't move an inch. He didn't blink. "What do you mean?"

Stanley took a deep breath, steeling himself. "You're not the first person to believe he can control the universe. You're not the first megalomaniac. This has happened before—that's *why* Omega was created. Waldman thought it was some kind of malevolent entity out to hunt us all, and he was scared he might set it free, but he was wrong. It's not a predator or an evil thing; it's a *safeguard*. It exists to keep time flowing neatly on its track, just as *we* evolved away from perfect memory in response. Because people shouldn't be able to control time. Not me. Not you. Not anyone."

"If it was made," Hassan said, slowly, deliberately, "then there must be a way it can be unmade."

"No," Stanley said. "It can't be done. It's baked into the universe. A force of nature that can't be controlled."

Hassan raised his eyebrows, bemused. "Everything can be controlled. You're lying, Stan. I can tell when you bluff. I've always been able to tell. You *will* tell me, one way or another."

"No," he said. "I will never tell you." He would not let himself be bullied. Not anymore. He stood steadfast, unyielding. "You will never find out. I can promise you that."

Hassan stared at him for a few seconds, then turned and walked over to the desk. Leaning down in a surprisingly casual gesture, he flicked open a drawer and pulled out a small device—about the size of a tape recorder. "Are you sure, Stan? You'll never tell me? You seem awfully confident in yourself."

"What is that?"

"This is a recent invention of mine, one of the side projects from our work on timelines. The engineers who worked on it have nicknamed it the Dissolution Engine." He turned the device over in his hands. "Something about splitting timelines, I'm given to understand, but I do think the name has got a certain charm. The half-life is still quite short, a maximum of about thirty-five minutes for now, but I'm told they're improving on it."

Stanley felt a sudden worry—a pressing in of the walls. His confidence disintegrated. He didn't want to be in this office anymore. He didn't know what that thing was, but he didn't want to be anywhere near it.

"You know what your problem has always been, Stan? You play it too safe. Your middle game lacks drama. Oh, sure, that'll win you the match nine times out of ten. But play enough times . . ." He trailed off, fiddling with a dial on the device.

Stanley gulped. "Don't do this, Jacques."

For the first time, a smile—a *real* smile—appeared on Hassan's face. "My name is Ozymandias, King of Kings," he said, holding up the device. "Look on my Works, ye Mighty, and despair!"

There was a click.

Then static.

Then nothing.

Stanley sniffed at the brown liquid in the glass decanter—whisky, and a fancy one by the smell of it. Filling up a small glass, he walked back over to the sofa and settled down. He took a sip: It *was* fancy. Though he had the strangest sensation of déjà vu, as if he'd drunk it before at some point, maybe in another life.

The door swung open.

"Oh God, Stanley," Jacques said. "I'm so glad you're here. You can't imagine how much I've been hoping to see you."

Stanley turned. Before he knew it, Jacques had barreled into the room and was sitting down by his side, his face earnest and concerned. There was something not quite right with his face: the skin was too perfect, the eyes—

"I wanted to see you the moment you touched down in the UK," Jacques stammered. "Really, I did, but I've been dealing with a fuckup of monumental proportions, and I've only just managed to get away. It's really bad, Stan. It's really bad."

Stanley blinked, taken aback by Jacques's urgency. He put his drink down on the table and leaned into him. "What's happened?"

"Do you . . . ?" Jacques shook his head, looking at the floor. "Do you remember the experiment we performed with the memory spade? The one that went wrong?"

An old terror rose in Stanley's chest. "What did you do?"

"Nothing!" He put his hands up. "I promise. I would never go near that

again. I mean, seriously—after what happened to . . . Raph? After what I
did? How could you even suggest it?"

Stanley looked away, feeling a little ashamed.

"I didn't know until recently," Jacques continued, wringing his hands.
"An old employee of mine—very clever man—he took everything I had
from right under my nose, and he's been attempting to recreate the experiment, the memory dive."

Stanley's stomach tightened. "And has he?"

Jacques shook his head, looking out the window at the streets below.
"It's all gone wrong, Stan. It's all going wrong again. He . . . he encountered
the same thing we did. The sickness. Except he didn't quarantine it. It's
spreading from person to person to person. The reports I'm getting are
horrific—eighty, ninety, a hundred people all being erased from the past,
like they were never there. Soon it will be in the hundreds, maybe thousands. We're . . . Oh God, Stan, we're running out of time, and there's no
way to stop it. And I don't know what to do."

Jacques grabbed on to Stanley's arm. The feel of his skin was strange,
like silk, and Stanley sensed that there was something he was missing
here, that there was something off with this whole encounter.

Omega didn't work that way. It cleaned up everyone who attempted to
mess with time—everyone who was *involved*—and then it stopped. It
wasn't the cleanest of tools, and sometimes people got caught in the cross-
fire, but once the wound was cauterized, it would settle again. But maybe
Jacques didn't know that; maybe he still thought that—

"I'm at a loss here, Stan," he said, his eyes shuddering in panic. "I need
your help. You've always been the cleverer one among the two of us."

Stanley blinked.

What?

He stood up, shaking Jacques's hand off him. "Jacques—what the hell
is going on?"

"What do you mean?" Jacques said, looking up at him confused. "I just
told you that—"

"There isn't an incident, is there? You're lying to me. Why?"

Jacques sighed, and all at once, his body changed. The fear disappeared from his eyes. The panic was gone, as if it had never existed. He stood up tall and utterly calm.

"It was the 'clever' thing, wasn't it? I laid it on too strong." He shook his head. "There's always something."

Stanley stared at him, unsure what was going on. Jacques walked over to the desk and lifted a small device from one of the drawers; it was about the size of a tape recorder. "I thought the nightmare crisis scenario would have worked on your bleeding heart, but I forgot how self-flagellating you are sometimes."

"You . . . what?"

"No matter. We'll get there eventually, old friend." He turned a dial on the device. "You and me, we've got all the time in the world."

Click.

Static.

Stanley sniffed at the brown liquid in the glass decanter—whisky, and a fancy one by the smell of it. Filling up a small glass, he walked back over to the sofa and settled down. He took a sip: It *was* fancy. Though he had the strangest sensation of déjà vu, as if he'd drunk it before at some point, maybe in another life.

The door opened.

"Stan," Jacques said with a smile. "It's nice to see you again."

"It's been a while," Stanley replied, his eyes passing over Jacques's strange figure. There was something not quite right about his body. Something off.

"And yet," Jacques said, settling down on the seat beside him, "it feels like just moments ago. Funny how time does that."

Stanley nodded. For all the years since the incident, it *did* feel like just yesterday. The horrific images—of the gunshots, the bodies, Raph gurgling in a pool of blood—still haunted him. They'd defined every moment of his life since.

"You called me here," Stanley said carefully. Now more than ever, he felt that he needed to be careful around Jacques. There was something about the way his eyes looked, and the way his skin gleamed unnaturally in the light, that made Stanley feel strangely unsafe. "You left me a message."

Jacques waved his hand dismissively. "Nothing too important. Just wanted to catch up. You've been out of the country a long time. Been busy?"

Stanley sipped at his drink. "You could say that. You?"

Jacques's lips curled up into a predatory smile. "Don't be so coy, Stan. I know you've been checking up on me. I know what you've been doing with Raph's money. You're not as sneaky as you think you are. How much do you know?"

"I know you've been building a tech empire, though what you've been doing with it is secretive." Stanley leaned forward. "What are you working on?"

Jacques sighed. "Many things, Stan. Many things. Much would be beyond you now, I fear. What we discovered in that lab was just the starting point to so much more."

An old terror rose inside Stanley's chest. "The starting point? You mean you've still been experimenting with the memory spade?"

Jacques chuckled, getting to his feet. He walked over to the bar and poured himself a drink. "Oh yes. How could I stop? But we've moved on from there. There are bolder discoveries to be made. Time is not what it appears to be." He glanced down at himself, and his body almost seemed to glimmer. "Nor, indeed, is mortality."

Stanley blinked, trying to wrap his head around the implications of what Jacques was saying, but couldn't get past the fact that Jacques was still using the spade.

"What about the subjects?" he asked. "What happens to them?"

"Oh, we've made some mistakes here and there, but you know what they say about omelets and eggs. There was a recent outbreak in one of our facilities that we've only just managed to contain, but that will be dealt with soon enough."

Stanley stood up, his hands shaking a little. "Wait—what do you mean 'contain'? What do you mean 'dealt with'?"

"The thing—Omega—was let loose during further experimentation. Quarantines were not properly in place, and it spread among the staff. We've got all those infected locked down now, though, in individual rooms. None of them know who they are, and we don't know who they were." He chuckled. "It's quite funny, really."

A sick, nauseous bubble grew in Stanley's stomach—a sense of tragedy unfolding, of history repeating. "What are you going to do with them?"

"What else can we do?" Jacques shrugged, sipping his whisky. "We've got to kill them all. It's not like anyone will notice. Nobody else remembers that they even existed."

Stanley went very still, taking a breath before asking the question he wasn't sure he wanted the answer to. "How many of them are there?"

"Hmm?" Jacques raised his eyebrows, considering the question as if he'd never really thought about it. "Oh, it was one of our big facilities, and the spread was pretty bad before we could lock it down. Five, maybe six, hundred staff?"

Stanley felt his face go white, the blood draining out of it.

Six hundred.

And Jacques was just going to kill them all.

Like that man in the lab all those years ago.

Like Raph.

"You can't do that," he said.

Jacques laughed. "Well, all very well you saying that, but it's not like we have any other way of stopping the spread. You know that. I mean, come on. If there were any other solution, sure." He shook his head. "To be honest, I'm not even that bothered anymore. There are other breakthroughs we've made that are far more promising. Consciousness transferal, isolating timelines, quantum entanglement. After we've dealt with *this* situation, I'll probably just archive the memory spade and move on."

"What if . . . ?" he said, then fell short.

He didn't want to tell Jacques what he had learned. He didn't trust him. But he couldn't do nothing. If he just let Jacques do this, he would be no better a man than when he let Jacques murder that test subject all those years ago. Than when he let Jacques kill Raph.

He couldn't let that happen again.

Jacques was eyeing him casually, a bemused look on his face. "What if what, Stan?"

"What if I knew a way to stop it?"

Jacques waved his hand dismissively. "I've been over this a hundred times. There *is* no way."

Stanley took a step closer to him. "There is. It took me a very long time to find it, but there is. A way to stop it. We've been looking at it all wrong. It's not an infection—not really. Think of it more like a fail-safe, and there's a way to disable it. To turn it off."

Putting his drink down, Jacques turned to face Stanley. He loomed over him, his face impassive. "Well, if you knew a way, then I suppose we wouldn't have to kill them all. I'm not sure what kind of lives they would have now, forgotten by the world, but it would certainly save some time and money. I'd appreciate the help."

Stanley blinked, looking back into Jacques's shimmering eyes.

"If you take me to where it's happening, I can—"

Jacques shook his head. "No, no. There's no time for that. The lab is in Japan, just outside Tokyo. It's too far away, Stan. The spread needs to be dealt with today to be certain. The operation is set to happen"—he glanced at his watch—"in just under two hours."

"But—"

"Look, if you can give me something I can pass on, maybe," he said dismissively. "If I can make an international call, you can explain what to do. That might work. But that's the only way."

Stanley nodded. He didn't like it, but he didn't have a choice. He couldn't let those people die. He couldn't just let anyone die. Not again.

"Okay," Stanley said. "Sit down. I'll tell you what I know."

And he did. Jacques didn't need a notebook or a computer to take down any of the words. Stanley knew this. Waldman had trained them all well enough that his brain wouldn't forget a single detail.

He told Jacques what he'd discovered in Australia, from his walks and experiences with the people there, and what he'd seen on the journeys he'd then taken across the globe. He told Jacques about the right mixture of plants that needed to be used—a ritual collection of lavender and wisteria, jasmine and sage. He told him about the ancient symbols, designed to work against it and transcribed from languages that no longer existed. And he told him about the importance of fire and flame. Stanley didn't know quite *how* these worked, but that was no longer important. The ritual he was describing—it was like a command line plugged into the mainframe terminal of the universe. It would pause the process momentarily, long enough to stop the spread. Keep the fail-safe quiet and in stasis.

But these things would not stop it for good. They would not allow the spade to be used freely in the future.

Stanley made no mention of the blood rites. He did not talk about the final ritual of the knife, the command line that would disable the fail-safe for good, opening up time and space to manipulation once again. He kept these to himself, because he did not trust Jacques. The information he had provided would be enough to stop this spread and set the poor victims free. Then, if there were no more experiments, Stanley would be able to assess the situation himself, to watch over these people and where they went. He would contact Hugo at Sunrise, and they would set up procedures to do it together.

He didn't tell Jacques that, of course. He pretended that what he had given was all there was, the full solution. It was a calculated chess move— offer up the queen so that your opponent doesn't see what you're hiding behind it.

When Stanley finished talking, Jacques looked up at him.

"Thank you," he said. "That will be extremely helpful."

Jacques walked over to the desk, opened a drawer, and took out a small device—like a tape recorder. He flicked a switch on the device, pocketed it, and headed for the door.

"I've got to make some calls to sort all of this out," he said, smiling.

"But I'll be in touch soon. I'm glad to see you're doing so well. Honestly. I've been worried about you."

Stanley gave a weak smile, but Jacques barely registered it. The door clattered shut behind him.

LATER THAT EVENING, STANLEY SAT ON HIS OWN IN THE MERCHISTON ARMS. It was just after 8:00 p.m., and he had spent most of the afternoon pondering the strange encounter with Jacques. The more he had thought about it, the more bizarre it seemed.

Straight after the meeting, there had been no doubt in Stanley's mind that Jacques wasn't telling him the whole truth. As much as an hour or two later, he had been pacing the streets outside, waiting to hear from Jacques—to see if he had managed to stop the mass murder in Japan—but there had been no message. Nothing. He then contacted Hugo to see if Sunrise's contacts had heard anything, but no one knew what he was talking about.

He started to doubt that anything had happened at all.

It was a ploy, Stanley realized, to panic him, to get him to reveal how to stop Omega.

This didn't surprise Stanley entirely, but there was something else. Something in the words Jacques had used that bothered him, but he couldn't quite put his finger on what.

Stanley had brought a book with him to the pub so that no one would bother him. He needed a space to think but had found that if he just sat on his own, people would eventually talk to him. So he placed the book in front of him, pretending to scan the pages as his mind whirred. He sipped at his beer, which was slowly getting warm on the table in front of him.

Something Jacques had said was niggling at the back of his mind. A word or a phrase. He ran through the conversation again and again, but for the life of him, he couldn't identify exactly what.

Just as he was about to get up and leave, his heart leaped into his throat.

Maggie stepped through the door.

Except it wasn't the Maggie he knew, that astonishingly fierce old lady who had saved his life over and over again. No—this was a young woman. She looked barely thirty, and as she entered the room, she was without all the confidence and certainty that her older counterpart displayed. She seemed shy, nervous.

But there was absolutely no doubting it was the same woman.

She was beautiful.

Stanley tried not to stare at her. He tried to focus on his book, not knowing whether this was the time they were supposed to meet or if it was just coincidence. He didn't trust himself to not say the wrong thing.

But there was only one free seat in the pub, and it was directly opposite him.

She sat in it, drink in hand, and Stanley's heart felt like it was going to explode.

He stared at her. He just *stared*.

He had no idea what to say. Here she was, his wife-to-be, whom he had only met after fifty years of a marriage he had not yet experienced. Whom he had, despite himself, fallen in love with years ago.

She stared back, and he couldn't fathom what must be going through her mind. In the absence of words, he smiled; he smiled as though his life depended on it. Did she know? Did she understand the complexity of this moment?

"Do I know you?" he asked, the absurdity of that question layering every word.

She shook her head but didn't look away. The space between them tightened. This was her first time meeting him, he realized. He had to say the right thing. He had to give the moment meaning.

"I . . . I feel like I've known you my entire life," he said.

She blushed. She reached for her hair—her gorgeous hair—and brushed it behind her ear. She leaned toward him, as if drawn by gravity, and told him her name.

"I'm Maggie," she said.

I know, he thought. *Oh God, do I know.*

Before he knew it or could understand what was happening, they were talking. About little things at first: the pub, history, art galleries, music. Their drinks were forgotten, left to the side. They barely talked about themselves. Somehow, they knew all they needed to know.

As the evening drew to a close, she gave him an address and made him promise to meet her again soon. Stanley smiled, wondering just what that next time would look like.

As she got up, Stanley wanted to get up with her—to hold her and kiss her and tell her that he would always be hers, forever and ever. But he knew he couldn't do that, so he stayed in his seat, settling for a strange little salute.

The moment he did it, he blushed. A salute? He wished the ground would swallow him whole.

But she gave him a wide smile, and left.

He thought about how lucky he was to have met her, both her in the present and her in the future. How fortunate he was to be guided by her hand, an anchor amid the currents of his increasingly crazy life, filled with death and secrets and ancient forces—

The realization hit him all at once.

Omega.

The thing—Omega—was let loose during further experimentation, Jacques had said.

Except Stanley had never used the word *omega.* He had never heard anybody call the fail-safe Omega except Maggie, from the distant future.

How had Jacques learned it? How had he known?

The seed of an idea formed in Stanley's head. For some reason, he couldn't get his mind off the whisky—he had had it before, he was sure, but *when?* And another image kept repeating itself: of Jacques picking up a small device from his desk on the way out and turning it off.

There was something about the way he had done it. The way he had acted around Stanley.

As though he had been there before.

Of course.

And as if he were sitting opposite Waldman at chess, everything suddenly fell into place. Every move he had missed, every shifting pawn. It all clarified in an instant. Where had Maggie heard of Omega? From the man she was with in the future, the one helping her with the machine.

Of course, he thought again. *Who else?*

When Jacques realized that his trick hadn't worked, that he couldn't get the full solution from Stanley, he had decided to go through Maggie. She was Stanley's weak point, and he would look to exploit that. For as long as Stanley had the solution in his head, Jacques would come after her.

He would never stop looking for it. Not ever. They would never have the happy life that Maggie had promised him. They would never be free from Jacques's schemes.

But Jacques could never have the full solution, because if he got it, the world would be his. For all Jacques's talk of saviorhood, Stanley knew this was about power. He couldn't allow it.

Pieces upon pieces moved in his mind—multitudes of transpositions, of possible moves, of hinted strategies. The board shifted. The path opened and closed and opened again until he saw it.

There was only one move, one check, one way to stop him.

The only way to ensure that Jacques would never get his hands on the solution was if Stanley didn't have it anymore. He couldn't trust himself to keep it secret, not with Maggie in the game. He'd have to take the solution off the board entirely. He'd have to lay out all the pieces in one go.

Paying for his drinks and stepping out into the cold, he let the plan build inside his head.

He walked straight to one of Sunrise's smaller labs, tucked away in Vauxhall. At his request, Hugo had continued to pay the rent on these places while he was away, keeping them stocked with things he might need. It always made him feel a little more at ease to know they existed close by.

Taking out a piece of paper, he scrawled a letter to Hugo.

*My old friend. Events move quicker than anticipated. The solution
is not safe. I have reason to believe that Jacques will use the memory
spade to access my memories, and that must not happen.*

*Prepare the operations theater in Berlin for a memory wipe.
You will wipe the discovery of the solution from my mind. I want
it erased, as if I had never come across it. I must forget all about it,
or he will find a way to get ahold of it. I do not trust myself.*

He paused, considering his choices.

No. This was too definitive. Too final. There was too much still in play
to make such a call. It wouldn't stop Jacques from experimenting, and
there would always be an outside chance that a real Tokyo event—or
something worse—would get out of control, that someone would actually
need to use the solution one day.

No, there was another move here. Another check, hidden beneath the
first.

He had to know what moves Jacques would make even before he did
them. He could spend his life using Sunrise to keep an eye on Jacques,
working behind the scenes, but even then, that wouldn't be enough. Stanley knew it.

Before Hugo erased the knowledge of the solution from his mind, he
needed to hide it somewhere it could be recovered. Somewhere even *he*
wouldn't be able to access it. Somewhere only someone he trusted completely would ever be able to find it.

And there was only one suitable place: deep in the past, in the distant
recesses of his own memories.

Somewhere no one would think to look, unless they had the right clues.

Even still, Jacques might find a way.

He sighed, shaking his head, picturing the pieces laid out in front of
him. He would have to stay one step ahead, always.

This needed to be foolproof. The final endgame. Moves behind moves
behind moves.

Stanley took a deep breath. He didn't want to add the next few lines, but it had to be done.

> *I leave the protection of my family and my future in your capable hands, with one caveat.*
>
> *You are to monitor me closely and continually. If at any point in the future it appears that someone is trying to gain access to my memories, to break in, you are to erase them all. Everything. Bring me into one of your centers and remove everything.*
>
> *He cannot have it. He must not.*

He sealed the letter, then went to work.

The setup didn't take long—he lit the fire and spread the plants to protect his dive from being seen by Omega. He would need to make several trips to get this right, to leave clues in just the right places, before he wiped the knowledge of this event from his mind.

But there was more: The moment where the solution was, where he was going to hide it, needed to be cut off. It needed to exist independently from other memories, permanently protected from Omega so that it could never be eaten. He needed to use the solution to protect the solution.

He lifted the knife and felt its weight—the weight of a ritual hundreds of thousands of years old. There was no other way.

He clicked himself into the memory spade, thinking of how strange it felt to be back in it after all this time. And as he settled himself in to dive into his memories one last time, he saw her.

She was watching him: Maggie.

Old Maggie, from the future.

She was right in front of him. His brain hadn't registered her as there until she was inches away from his face.

She was younger than when he had seen her before. Not physically, but he could see it in her eyes, a freshness. An innocence. He knew she had only just started traveling back.

He thought on what he was about to do—butcher his own mind to protect them both. He wondered if she would ever understand.

There was confusion on her face—betrayal, even.

"I know," he said, looking deep into her eyes. He understood. "Forgive me."

He took the knife to the top of his chest and sliced diagonally, the pain searing through him just as the spade sent him hurtling into the past.

19

The darkness edges in. It's slow—so slow, like it's just waking up—but it feels inevitable. Stanley is opposite me, and the determination on his face wars with the pain beneath. He sees my panic and my fear, and I can see, as his anger subsides, that he is blaming himself for this.

I know this about him.

He may have had an entire life that was hidden from me, and he may have had a whole chest of secrets that I was never aware of, but this doesn't change the fact that I *know him*.

He cannot take seeing others in pain, and that is amplified with me a hundredfold. It doesn't matter how certain he is, what plans he has made, how iron his will—at the sight of my panic or my tears, his resolve crumbles. It always has. It always will.

"Maggie," he whispers, "I'm sorry."

"There is still a way out of this. There must be. You can't have erased the solution completely."

He runs his hands across his face. "I—I . . ." he stammers. "You don't . . ."

"I won't tell him," I say. "Hassan will not know."

"You can't promise me that!" he shouts, almost in tears. The world around us is black—I cannot see past the next table or two at the hotel. There is nothing there. We are a circle of light in the middle of a black void, and soon we will be no more. "He is *always* watching," Stanley says. "He is *always* there."

I lean forward and take his hand. "Trust me. Please. He will not let me out without something. I need something."

"It's not the right time," he whispers. "These aren't the moves I planned."

I give his hand a squeeze, looking into his eyes. "You told me once that I am not a pawn. I am not a thing to be moved but a player. Trust me, then, as your partner. Let me make some moves. You don't have to do this alone."

"I don't . . . I don't know everything," he says. "I never *let* myself see all the pieces, for precisely this reason. The clues are scattered, but . . ." He sighs. He takes a look at the black and then back at me. "The ninth of July, 1955. Go there. I don't even know why. I only know the date. There might be nothing for you to find, but it's all I have. That's all I've allowed myself."

And that is all he says?

    Yes.

I need you to be absolutely certain. There is nothing else?

    No—just a date. A place to go.

Very well. Continue.

The emptiness is almost at our feet now.

"I have it," I say, praying you're listening. "I have it. Pull me out. Pull me out *now*."

And you do. There is the familiar tug, and the world disappears again. When I wake up, I'm in the bath in front of you, panting.

"What the fuck was that?" I demand, pulling the helmet off my head.

You stare down at me, light glimmering off those marbly orbs you call eyes. "Excuse me?"

I sit up, leaning toward you. "Do you have any idea what you just put me through? You have no right to—"

You bend over, placing a hand on my chest. It's hard as stone. It pushes me back with considerable ease—not suddenly but slowly, definitively, reminding me that whatever you are, you are orders of magnitude stronger than I have ever been.

My back hits the back of the bath, but you keep pressing, like a vise gradually tightening. Your expression doesn't change as you press into me—just a piercing, heartless glare.

I cannot move. I am pinned down, but still, you keep pressing.

Pain sears across my chest. I open my mouth to shout, to scream, but the air is being pushed out of my lungs. I feel my bones creak, about to crack.

"Remember where you are," you say. Your voice could freeze wildfires. "You are in my kingdom. You play by my rules."

I try to breathe, taking in little gasps to fill the depression in my lungs. The pain is unbearable—I twist under your hand, but it presses on. I cannot move.

I have fallen into the trap of thinking you are human, that you are like me, but you are not. That is abundantly clear to me now. You are a monster in human clothes. You are a devil.

"I have been courteous to you," you say, your face inches from mine.

"I have been friendly. But do not make the mistake of thinking that you have power here. You do not question my decisions. You abide by them. Is that clear?"

I manage a small, painful nod.

You smile, but you hold me for a second longer—long enough so the pain will be the last thing that sticks with me—and then you release.

Gasping for air, I put my hand to my chest, trying to feel if you've broken anything.

"You're insane," I manage to whisper through gritted teeth.

Your infuriating smile only grows wider. "When you have conquered mortality, your understanding of sanity tends to shift a little, Maggie. Don't be so closed-minded."

You walk over to Stanley, who eyes us curiously from his chair, the headset from the machine still attached to him. He is aware, but he doesn't seem to really have a handle on what's going on or who we are. This doesn't bother him—he's observes, like he's watching a film.

Slowly pulling up a seat, you sit behind Stanley.

"I think it's time that we drop the pretense. I think you know by now that Stanley is hiding this solution from me, specifically. You may have begun to think that you should not help me out of some misplaced sense of loyalty. But let us be absolutely clear about this: I have waited too long to locate this solution. For decades, I thought it was lost to me. I thought Stanley had, in his arrogance, erased it for good. Only recently did I realize this was not the case. I will not allow it to slip from my grasp again."

Reaching over, you pull a rolling medical cart toward you.

From the instrument tray on top, you lift a scalpel and inspect it, bringing it far too close to Stanley's neck. He looks at you oddly, as if he's trying to work out how you got there.

"I will ask you the questions," you say. "And you will respond to them. You will not argue, or prevaricate, or lie to me. You asked me to pull you out because you had the solution. Tell me exactly: What did Stanley tell you?"

Through stuttering breaths, I tell you about the date he gave me, but

I give you the wrong one. And I leave other bits out. About the clues being scattered. About the moves being unplanned.

You purse your lips. It's a horrific expression, like wax melting. You lean back from Stanley and put the scalpel down. Reaching underneath, you open a drawer and take out a syringe.

"Do you know what this is, Maggie?"

I shake my head, unable to speak. I have never been so terrified in my life.

"It is an analog of 4-hydroxycoumarin, a modified synthesis of a drug sometimes known as brodifacoum. It's an enhanced vitamin K antago- nist anticoagulant. This is an extremely large dose, certainly lethal to a human without treatment, but it will not kill immediately. Instead, it drastically inhibits the reconstitution of vitamin K in the bloodstream; vitamin K is necessary for coagulation. Are you following me?"

I don't reply. I can't take my eyes off the glinting needle.

"In a moment, I will inject Stanley with this agent, and his body will quickly lose the ability to clot blood. He will bleed—slowly at first, then very quickly indeed—out of his nose, his ears, his eyes. Out of his very skin. I will make you watch this, and you will be unable to do anything about it."

"Why?"

"It is important that you understand the consequences of lying to me."

"I haven't lied to you!"

You cock your head, bringing the syringe nearer to Stanley as my heart feels like it's going to leap out of my throat. "You have not told me everything. Not quite. There have been omissions. I do not believe that you exchanged nothing but a date."

"That's all he said!" You shake your head in mock disappointment, the syringe brought closer to Stanley's waiting neck. "Okay!" I shout. "Okay, fine. Just *stop.*"

It is too much. I cannot see you hurt him after everything I have done. I cannot let it happen.

Your hand pauses perfectly in midair, without a tremble. I try to calm my racing heart as I tell you everything. *Everything.* The moment, the conversation, the correct date. Only when I am fully done do you seem satisfied.

And I am utterly ashamed of myself.

I won't tell him, I had said. *Hassan will not know.*

It's a betrayal of everything I promised him. I want the ground to swallow me up.

Stanley is looking at me strangely, like he's trying to work out how he knows me, and I can't meet his eyes.

"Very well," you say. You push the wheeled cart away from you, and it trundles toward me, stopping by my side. I look at the other surgical implements scattered across it and feel ill. I want to throw up. "You will go back into his mind, to the date that he told you, and you will search for any clues you can. You will check in with me as you go, and when you return, you will tell me everything. I hope I don't need to remind you of the unsavory consequences if you deviate."

I nod quietly. It's all I can do. My chest still burns. I feel like a tiny thing—smaller than a mouse or a speck of dust.

You silently prepare the memory spade again, linking me to Stanley's mind, and you turn it on. Before I have time to get my thoughts together, you shove the helmet over my head, and I am plunged back into the past.

When the world returns, I am outside a chapel. The sky is a washed-out gray, like blurry static, and the light is harsh. It must be about midday, but I can't see the sun.

Looking around, I see stone walls and arches leading to distant courtyards—I recognize the architecture, even though I've never been on this part of the campus before. It's Whelton, where Stanley went to school. For me to be seeing this, sharing in his memory, he must be close by.

I turn back to the chapel and notice that people are starting to leave in small dribs and drabs. All of them have solemn expressions and black clothing. It's unmistakably a funeral, though I have no idea whose.

There aren't many people, though—just a handful. They don't talk to one another or stay longer than necessary. As they file out, they do their best to look somber and morose before glancing at their watches and going on with their day. Whoever this person was, they didn't have much in the way of a group of friends. Just acquaintances. Colleagues, perhaps.

The only sound is a conversation that is gradually rising in volume, from just around the corner. I take a few steps in that direction, and Stanley's voice is immediately clear.

"I'm saying you don't need to be a dick about it," he says. I glimpse him now—he is standing round the side of the chapel with his fists clenched, talking to someone. He is trying to keep his voice steady, but it isn't working.

I take another couple of steps to ensure that the full picture is in view, and I almost scream in surprise.

Why?

It's you. I mean—not *you* as you are now. But a younger version of you. A boy. And to be honest, the shock is less about finding you here and more about my mind processing the fact that you *were* a boy once. That you haven't always been, well, whatever it is you are.

"It's not being a dick to tell the truth, Stan," you say. "Maybe if you spent less time hiding from it, you'd realize that."

"Okay," Stanley shouts, throwing his hands up in the air. "Fine. What's your point? What is your *actual* point?"

You take an angry step toward him. "That maybe you should have seen this coming? That if you were going to spend so much time cozying up to the old man, maybe you should have noticed the old man was going crazy?"

"You're saying this is my fault?"

"Er . . . duh!" You smack your forehead. "You spend all that time around him and you miss something like this? How could it not be your fault?"

"You didn't see it either."

"That's because he shut us out!" you shout back. "Because of you! Before you turned up, he was . . . I . . ." You fall short, your face twisting in anger. "These last couple of years, all he ever wanted to do was work with you!"

"You ever wonder why he didn't pick you? You ever wonder why he shunned you toward the end?"

You pause. Your body goes very still. "Every day."

"Because he never thought you were good enough."

You let out a low growl—an aggressive, primal noise that I've never heard from you before. "What, and you *were*? You? The fucking runt of the pack? That's bullshit. Face it, Stan: I'm better looking than you. I'm more popular than you. I'm smarter than you. Hell, I'm *better* than you are. It should have been me. He should have picked *me*."

Stanley laughs at you. "You really think that, don't you? The professor always saw you for exactly what you are: all bluster, doomed to fail at everything you put your hand to. Jacques, he stopped spending time with you because he couldn't be *bothered*. Because he knew that no matter what he did, you'd always be a disappointment. A failure."

"Oh, and look at how well that turned out!" you shout, waving your hands at the chapel behind. "Picking you to be his personal lapdog was clearly such a painful experience that he decided the only way out was to kill himself! I mean, come on—whatever you were doing, he clearly thought hanging himself was preferable to spending another second on it with *you*."

Stanley falls still, reeling like he's been struck. For a moment, I think he's going to stumble backward. He takes a deep breath and looks you right in the eye.

I think he's going to turn away. To walk away. I want him to.

But he doesn't. He is perfectly still, like a statue, for a good ten seconds. Then he leaps at you.

The first punch lands square on your nose, and blood erupts out of it. The two of you collapse to the ground, rolling and hitting and screaming.

I want to jump in, to pull you apart, but I know I can't. I'm frozen in this moment.

It ends before long.

Stanley stands up, brushing himself off. He has your blood on his shirt.

"You're pathetic," he says, then turns away and walks off into the distance.

You scramble to your feet, about to shout after him, but you don't. I watch you internalize the anger, push it down inside of you to simmer and boil.

Stanley doesn't turn. He doesn't even look at you.

You open your mouth again, but nothing comes out.

That's what this is all about, isn't it?

That's not important.

Except it is. It's so painfully clear now. All this talk of controlling time, of overcoming mortality, of saving the world when deep down you're just a jealous, petty little boy trying to control the universe because you still can't get over the fact that Stanley is better than you. That he's always been better than you.

We're running out of time.

And sixty years later, he's still beating you at your own game. God—that must be *so* infuriating. Is it? Is it painful to have to watch?

Oh, now you're not going to talk to me? Now you're going to be silent?

I would be very careful how you proceed, Maggie. You have already remembered what I am capable of. Do not force me to show you again.

Fine. But just know that I see you now. I want you to know that.

I follow Stanley because I must. Despite what I've seen, I'm still thinking about you with that syringe, and about the feel of your hand against my chest. There's a reason I'm here, even if I don't know what it is yet.

He enters the main building and climbs up a long staircase, one that leads all the way to the top of one of the spires. Cracking open an unlocked door, he steps inside. I follow.

I recognize it immediately from my last dive—the office with the old man in it, the place where Stanley was sleeping on the sofa. There's tape on the floor in the middle of the room and around it a half-hearted cordon, which has fallen down.

Suddenly, everything hits me at once: the conversation, the chapel, the office where Stanley was sleeping. I realize what has happened and what it must have meant to him, and I just want to reach out and grab him, hold him tight.

But I can't.

I can't make any more mistakes.

He rummages around the room, like he's looking for evidence of something. It starts quietly. He picks up items and inspects them, putting them back where they were, not wanting to disturb the scene. But as time goes on, he grows more frantic. He drops things on the floor. He throws them. Before long, he's not really looking for anything anymore.

He picks up a chair and chucks it onto the floor; the crack echoes through the small space like a gunshot. There are tears streaming down his face. He grabs books and hurls them across the room in pure, senseless anger.

I just watch. I stand and watch and can do nothing.

You should be looking for the solution, you say in my head. *Don't get distracted.*

I don't reply.

I wait for Stanley's rage and sadness and loathing to come to an end. When it does, he seems emptier, like something has been scooped out of him. He walks right past me, out the door, leaving the wreckage of the office behind him.

I almost follow, but I don't. Because as I gaze over the room, my eye is drawn to a bookshelf. The books he pulled out have collapsed in on themselves, some falling to the floor, others on their fronts, but there is one that still stands with its spine upright.

Plato's *Phaedrus.*

Thamus and Theuth? Stanley had said out in the Australian bush. *From Plato's* Phaedrus?

I take a few steps toward it.

When the time comes, he had said outside our wedding, *go to Thamus and Theuth.*

There's an almost audible click as I feel the decades of pieces fall almost perfectly into place, a lifetime's worth of chess moves clarifying. This is where I'm supposed to be. I have been led here, slowly, cryptic piece by cryptic piece.

My heart is beating fast as I lean down to pick up the book. It's lighter than I expect it to be.

I run my finger down its spine, feeling the foil-stamped lettering.

The reason for all the mystery, all the clues spread across space and time, was to get me here, but to keep it from *you.* Stanley worked long and hard to keep whatever is in here well hidden so that you would never find it. He wiped his own mind so that you wouldn't be able to search for it in his memories. He sacrificed his life to keep this single clue out of your hands, but here I am, leading you right to it.

The image of Stanley bleeding to death in his chair flashes through my mind.

There's nothing I can do.

You have complete control over me. I am your prisoner.

I have to have faith that he's thought of this too, that he's planned for it. I have to believe in him.

I open the book.

What have you found? you ask me.

What is in the book?

The book has been carved out, the pages between the bindings removed but for a single note. Your voice presses into my brain.

What does the note say?

| *Tell me.*

Tell me.

| It says, "There's one more trip to make, my dear, and only you know
| where to go. I'm sorry I never took you. Maybe now you know why. I
| have forgot why I did call thee back."

What does it mean?

| It's a reference to *Romeo and Juliet,* and there's only one thing it can
| mean.

What?

| When Stanley was younger, before we met, he went to see a production
| at the Old Vic on the South Bank. He'd never seen any live Shakespeare
| before, not properly, and he said it was transcendental. He was always
| promising me that next time the play was on at the Old Vic, we would go.
| But we never did. There was always something: Leah was too young; he
| wasn't feeling up to it; we had friends visiting. We never found the time,
| but maybe he was putting it off deliberately.

Why?

| So I'd remember it. "One more trip to make," it says. He wants me to go
| to the time he saw *Romeo and Juliet* at the Old Vic. He's waiting for me
| there—I'm sure of it.

What do you do?

> I go. I let Stanley's mind guide me, and I flitter, maybe for the last time, into his past. I focus on the idea of the play, our favorite play, at the Old Vic. Of Stanley seeing it live for the first time. Reality shifts around me to make a passage, a tunnel leading directly there.

And then what?

> There's nothing here.
>
> *What do you mean there's nothing here?* you ask.
>
> There's . . . nothing. It's black. Empty. There's nothing for me to even put my foot down on. It's just gone. It's been erased, or eaten. I don't know what. But it's gone.

You are sure? No clues? No hints? Nothing?

> Nothing. I almost burst out laughing. All of this—all the chasing, all the clues—has led me here, and it's already been taken. It's pointless. Either Stanley or Omega has removed it. It doesn't matter. The solution was erased long ago.

I don't believe it.

> *I won't believe it,* you say. But believe it you must, because that's all there is. And you know it—somehow, I can feel that you know it.
>
> *You will find out what is there,* you insist. But I can't. There is nothing.
>
> As I wait for you to accept that, I let myself float in the soundless dark. It's vast and empty. There is no sight or smell or taste, but there is *depth.* It continues on forever. I imagine that I am floating in the infinite vacuum of deep space, without even the stars to keep me company. I do not know how long I float there in that total emptiness, but I know you

eventually come to accept that what I'm saying is true, because you pull me out.

I come to in the bath, and you're leaning over me. I'm struggling to parse the expression on your face—I like to imagine that it's disappointment, or fury, or even a tinge of self-loathing because you have failed once again—but whatever it is, your features are too damn alien for it to come through clearly.

I reach over to my left, where the medical cart came to rest after you pushed it away. And in one swift, definitive move that I have been picturing for far longer than you could have known, I grab the scalpel and slash it right across your throat.

Your eyes widen, your hand darting up to the wound. Blood—dark, as though it's been mixed with oil—oozes out of the slit. You open your mouth, and a gurgling sound escapes.

Why? What are you doing?

You raise your other hand to strike me, but I am up. I have already grabbed the syringe you prepared—the poison you threatened Stanley with.

I jab the needle as hard as I can directly into your eye.

You scream.

It's an alien sound: a guttural, gurgling shriek that seems to squeeze out of your sliced throat as much as out of your mouth. I lean forward, pressing on the pump and injecting your eye, your face, full of this poison you have tried to use against me.

You know this will do you no good. I am not so easily killed. What are you hoping to achieve?

You stumble back, falling to the ground. The syringe sticks out of your face, wobbling as you scramble to pull it out. The blood is spreading across your perfect skin and dripping onto the floor. You tug at your clothes, and I glimpse the skin underneath, layered with symbols carved into it like ritual scars, symbols like the ones Stanley put up before our wedding.

Pulling myself out of the bath, I grab a lab coat from the wall and throw it around myself. I give Stanley a hard kiss on the forehead and leave him behind, rushing for the alpha lift. I can't take him with me— there's no time.

No time for what?

As the lift doors shut, I see you still on the floor, wracked with inhuman twitching. You look like a spider or a beetle thrown onto its back, chitinous appendages jerking.

I close my eyes in the lift, breathing, preparing myself for what comes next.

What comes next? What are you doing? What has caused you to do this? I have been interviewing you for hours, and you have not spoken of any of these plans.

When the lift opens, I am back in the Institute's main lab. Staff bustle back and forth, and I hope no one will give me a second look, but even under the lab coat, my wet blouse is covered in the black ichor that spurted from your throat. I am barefoot, my hair scraggly from the fluid. People glance, then begin to stare. As calmly and sensibly as I can, I turn left and walk right down to the end of the hall.

Why are you ignoring my questions?

I walk past the alpha lift, then the beta, gamma, delta, all the way to the final one.

The Omega lift.

I press the button, and it arrives, doors sliding open. There are murmurs of confusion and people pointing now, but I know that they have seen you with me. They know I am your guest. I am hoping their fear of you is enough to keep them back for the time being.

The sign before me just says: *You are in Ω lift. If you do not fully understand the implications of that statement, LEAVE IMMEDIATELY.*

As I get in, one man shouts, and another strides toward me, but it's too late.

Too late for what?

The lift doors close. There's no going back.

20 | Stanley
1958 via 1967

STANLEY REMEMBERED THE EVENING BEING HOTTER THAN THIS. HE'D SPENT the day dipping in and out of the swelter of the Italian summer sun, and he remembered wishing for the cool respite of evening, only to find that he was still sweating.

But after his years in Australia and the Middle East, he had learned to appreciate the soothing touch of an evening breeze and the sweet relief that sunset could bring after a day of oppressive heat. As he watched himself, nine years younger, wiping the sweat off his forehead with his wrist, it was a quiet reminder of how much he had grown. How different he was now.

He could barely remember what it felt like to be the Stanley of back then—a confusing maelstrom of guilt and doubt and hope and ambition. He'd hid it well from others, or at least he thought he had, but every decision he'd made then was laced with second-guessing and self-loathing.

Not so much now.

Not since her.

He wasn't sure he'd be able to explain it to his old self, even if he tried. His old self wouldn't understand. Hell, he wasn't sure he quite understood it now. Perhaps it was the way she looked at him—as if he were capable of anything, as if he weren't bred from cheap stock, destined to be a failure at everything he tried. Perhaps it was the quiet, unshakable faith she had in him, a faith he'd never experienced before.

Either way, Maggie had changed everything.

She had just met him for the first time, mere moments ago in his timeline, at the Merchiston Arms, but already he knew the future they had together.

He wanted to bring her here, to Verona, to this balcony, even though he knew that he never could. She would have to find her own way, if it came to that. Take a longer road.

There was a beauty to its fiction. The building was faded white, belying centuries of age it didn't really have. It wasn't the "real" balcony from the play. Shakespeare's Juliet wasn't based on a real person, and the house hadn't been properly transformed into this state until the 1930s. In fact, almost everything about the house itself was fictional. But the emotions imprinted upon it were real.

The wall beneath the balcony was covered with love letters: desperate messages from people declaring love or asking for guidance in it. There were notes that told stories of visitors' past loves and of their hopes for the future.

When he first came here as a young man, he stood staring at that wall for hours. He had simply never had the *time* for love as he grew up. His mind was always too preoccupied with other things, but his obsession with this wall, and indeed this play, had perhaps always been a quiet sign from his unconscious that he was far more of a romantic than he thought.

Stanley stood just out of sight, watching his younger self—this muddled, tortured twenty-one-year-old Stanley—from a distance. He stared at that wall, lost in thought.

He knew now that he had possibilities ahead of him—chances at hope, at love, at redemption. He wanted to be able to tell his younger self that, to reassure him, but he knew he could not. He needed to protect that timeline, and this meant making sacrifices.

"I never thought I'd actually get to see it," Maggie said, appearing next to him out of thin air. She looked old. Tired.

Still, he grinned at the sight of her. "I hoped I'd see it with you eventually. You found me."

"It was obvious as soon as I saw your note. There was nowhere else you could be waiting. You talked about this balcony for years."

"That's good to know. I haven't actually left the note yet. Some part of me hoped you wouldn't need it, but maybe I was being naive," Stanley said. "What did you tell Hassan?"

She shrugged. "I told him the clue was about a production at the Old Vic, one that you never took me to."

His brows furrowed together. "I never take you to the Old Vic?"

She grinned. "Oh, please, we've been tons. But *he* doesn't know that. This is the moment, isn't it? The moment you hid. The moment he's been searching for."

"Yes."

She nodded. "Good. When I come out, I'm going to tell him there's nothing here. That it's been deleted. After all this searching, that will *really* wind him up."

Stanley laughed, then winced, putting his hand to his chest. He'd bandaged the wound as he traveled, but the cut had needed to be deep. It wouldn't heal for a long time.

Maggie stepped toward him, concerned. "What have you done?"

Stanley took a deep breath and turned toward her. She seemed older now than she ever had before, weathered by conflict and stress. He took her hand. "I'm sorry. It's been . . . so complicated. This meeting—it had to be hidden under layers upon layers. Not just from me but from *it*."

She raised her eyebrows. "Was this all necessary?"

"I think you're starting to get an idea of what Hassan is like," he said. "You will not have been his only attempt to break into my mind, into my past—of that, I'm sure. I have to be so cautious. It wasn't about you—even *I* can't know everything. There is only one version of me who knows the whole plan, who sees all the moves. And I'm here, right now, with you. Once I return to my own timeline, I will erase the memory of this moment. It will be gone."

"You called him Jacques," she said. "In the past."

Stanley nodded. "That was his name, once. He was a friend, I think. Or perhaps not. It's hard to tell."

"And he wants you to stop Omega for him."

"Yes—so that he can control time. If he manages that, a man like him"—Stanley shook his head—"the world will suffer. Everyone will suffer. No one should have that ability. It can't happen."

"He's controlling it somehow, in my present," Maggie replied. "He hasn't stopped it, but he *is* keeping it at bay. How?"

"I don't know," Stanley said, shaking his head. This would always be a guess that he would have to gamble on. "I provided him with a way to slow it, but it should have been only temporary. If he's still using the spade fifty years in the future, he's been keeping it at bay for decades. It shouldn't be possible. I have no idea how he's doing that."

Maggie shuddered. "I'm not sure I want to know."

"I think," Stanley said, "that you're going to need to find out."

TRANSCRIPT NO. 273: Margaret Webb
DATE STAMP: 11 AUG. 2021
0 Hours, 17 Minutes, and 42 Seconds Until Dissolution

The lift barely makes a sound as it whizzes down. There are no flashing lights on the side this time, just the feeling of dropping, faster and faster and faster. For a moment, I think the lift has broken—that I really *am* falling—but then it slows, quietly slipping to a gentle halt.

I need you to tell me what you are looking for.

The doors open and reveal a single large room. It's unlike anything I have seen at the Institute so far. There are similarities: the floor and walls are the same sleek mixture of clinical white and gunmetal gray. There are banks of computers along the back wall, as well as tall screens— at least five feet high—pumping out lines of data and code that I can't interpret.

But in the center of the room, there is a black mass.

An empty.

It sucks in the light nearby, like a black hole. Around it, there are rows upon rows of plants, of essence diffusers and glass paneling. Symbols— like the ones Stanley put up at our wedding—have been carved into the glass in various shapes and sizes.

Right beside it, there is a console and another screen, this one displaying a ticking graph, like an ECG strip, beeping away.

All of the staff down here are in full hazmat suits. When one notices me, he rushes over in a panic.

"What are you doing down here?" he demands, waving a clipboard at me. "You can't be here."

He doesn't reach out to grab my arm or usher me back into the lift. He seems reticent to touch anyone at all.

"I am here to inspect the protections," I say as matter-of-factly as I can. I'm aware that I am barefoot, that under my lab coat, I am in underclothes drenched in fluid and black ichor. Others are looking at us now, staring. "Mr. al-Haytham sent me personally."

He hesitates, blinking, taking in the words. I can see the flicker of fear on his face. "I . . ."

"Do you really think I would be down here if Mr. al-Haytham had not personally sent me? Do you really think I could have wandered here accidentally? Do not presume to second-guess my purpose here. What is your name?"

"Really," he says, "there's no need. It's just that—"

"What," I say, my voice hardening, "is *your* name?"

"Daniel," he replies quietly.

"Daniel *who*?"

"Daniel Nason."

Everyone is watching us now. They have almost all stopped what they are doing. I smile, because you've made a mistake.

What are you talking about?

You've made the mistake of thinking that ruling through power and fear is the way to go. But when the chips are down, your pawns are all too scared to do anything.

"Thank you, *Daniel*," I say, emphasizing his name. "I will make sure Mr. al-Haytham knows how useful you've been. Would you please show me around?"

From behind his plastic screen, he gives a weak, panicked smile. "I don't think I'm best placed to—"

"Oh no," I say, stepping forward. He steps back and away from me. "I think you're exactly the right person. Run me through the containment operation in full detail." I turn to look at all the other faces. "Isn't there some work you should be doing?"

Almost as one, they bow their heads and turn away. How obedient you have made them all. How easy you have made it for me.

Why are you telling me this? It's clear you have been lying to me, hiding things from me. Why now tell me all of this?

Oh, I thought that was obvious.

I know you struggle with human emotion, but this is what we call *gloating*, Hassan. I'm surprised you're not more familiar with it.

"Omega containment has been working at full capacity since that spike yesterday," Daniel says, his voice wavering. "The protections to subdue remain in place, but we've needed to up the number of feeds."

I raise my eyebrows. "Feeds?"

"Sorry," he says. "It's a crude term we use down here. I'm talking about the primary containment procedure. The volunteers."

I blink, glancing across to the other side of the twisting blackness. As I walk with Daniel, the obscured opposite side comes into view.

There are cells—square glass-paneled prison cells that face out to the rest of the room. Inside them, there are people. They are bundled together, pressed tightly against one another, worry and fear and submission plastered all over their faces. There must be hundreds of them.

I take a deep breath, trying not to cry out, trying not to reveal my horror.

"Indeed," I say. "You say you've increased the amount?"

A beep goes off behind me as the graph on one of the screens spikes into the red. I freeze, wondering if it's a message from you. Despite what I did, I am under no illusions that you are not still alive. That you are not coming for me. My time down here is strictly limited.

"See." Daniel pointed at the screen. "Another one already. The last procedure can't have been more than half an hour ago. It's getting out of control."

A tall woman in a hazmat suit presses a button on one of the smaller cells. The people inside all pull back immediately, pressing to hide behind one another, to push to the back of the tiny space. She reaches forward, grabbing the nearest arm, and pulls out a young man.

"No," he says. "Please, no. I'm begging you. Take someone else. T-Take *him*." The man points at another inside the cell, who quickly recoils and tries to hide behind someone else. The protestations are no use. The woman ignores him entirely and drags him to the front.

I am frozen on the spot. I want to dive in, pull them apart, help this man, but I cannot. I have to simply watch.

Daniel looks on impassively. The others are all at keyboards or taking measurements and readings, just going about their jobs.

The man is pushed inside the containment glass around Omega, and a door is closed behind him.

He turns back, his face shivering, his body shaking in panic.

"*Please*," he says. He puts his hand up on the glass. "I just want to—"

He falls silent.

His hands fall to his sides. His face droops.

He is empty, like a mannequin.

His soul has been scooped right out of his skin.

The red line on the monitor above drops back down and turns green again, beeping happily along.

Oh God, Hassan. Is this how you've been keeping it at bay? Is this what you did to protect me from it when I dived? It's hungry, so you *feed* it?

The woman pulls the man back out and places him in a wheelchair. He allows himself to be pulled, like a puppet. There is no will in there anymore. The woman glances at me, seemingly uncomfortable that I'm not suited up like the rest, but she ultimately just pushes the man away.

"Where is he going now?" I only realize I'm whispering as it comes out of my mouth.

"To processing first," Daniel says, "then disposal."

Disposal? I think, hoping desperately that doesn't mean what it must. I want to clarify, but I can't betray my ignorance. "How long will he be processed for?

Daniel frowns. "Oh, it takes minutes. I mean, it's not like anyone is going to remember him."

"I want to see the machine that monitors it," I say quickly, trying to cover up my distress. Trying to distract my mind from the places it's going. "Show me how it works. Now."

"Okay," he says, walking over to it. Underneath the large display with the graph is a wide console covered in buttons and controls, like something from the cockpit of an airplane. Beside it, there are a few computer consoles I recognize. Screens with windows, email servers, web pages. Daniel's glancing at his clipboard, talking about something having to do with "seismic moderation controls" and "relationship of entanglement," and I realize I'm not going to have any idea what he's talking about. But there's one thing I can understand.

What's that?

At the top left of the console, placed far enough away that no one could accidentally go near it, is a large red switch. The label above it says SHUT-DOWN. It doesn't matter what decade you're in or where you come from—a large red switch is always a large red switch. It's behind a metal cage, locked, but the key is just hanging next to it on a hook. It seems that no matter the workplace, over a long enough period of time, people get complacent.

"Is that really enough safety for a switch like that?" I ask.

Daniel laughs nervously. "Um . . . it's not like someone's going to intentionally turn it. We don't employ people who are insane."

I think of you, and I try not to comment on the irony of that statement.

"I mean," he says, with a shrug, "every system has to be shut down occasionally for maintenance. That's basic engineering. But we have to get the temporary measures in place for that kind of procedure. If this shut down without secondary protections, these suits wouldn't do a damn thing. That *thing* has been locked up for what? Almost fifty years now? I don't think it'll just be thanking us if we let it out."

I raise my eyebrows.

He bows his head. "Sorry, I know. I'm talking about the phenomenon like it's a person. Been working down here too long. The lingo, it rubs off. Apologies, ma'am."

"I think you've done enough here," I say, keeping my voice cold. "Go find someone else to assist me."

A mixture of worry and relief flickers across his face, but he backs away and walks over to the main computers.

As quickly as I can, I do the final act that holds me back. Opening one of the email servers, I tap in Leah's address. She may never see me again, but she needs to know.

My darling, I type, *I cannot explain why, but know that everything I told you on that horrible day was a lie. You were the greatest thing to ever happen to either of us. We have loved you from the moment you were born and are so proud of everything you have become. I love you, I love you, I love you. If you ever doubt it, read this again. I love you, and so does your dad. More than you can possibly know. Mum.*

I turn around.

Daniel is talking to someone, pointing over at me, confused why I'm at the computer.

I take a long hard look at Omega, twisting and shaking in its cage. I let the sight of it run through me, sifting through my fear of it. This is the monster that took my wedding from me, that split me from my daughter, that has threatened to take my life, and Stanley's life, and so much more.

And then I look at the people in the cells. Some are crying—quietly so they won't be noticed. Most simply stare off into space.

And I realize I've been telling it wrong.

Omega is not the monster of this story.

You are.

I reach up to the key and pull it off the hook, then press it into the lock on the metal cage.

Four of the screens at the back wall flicker, their data and spreadsheets disappearing. The rest of them follow. They are replaced by a shaking handheld camera stream of you. Your skin is brittle and blackened. Your eye is swollen, and it looks like it's about to pop out of its socket. Your face is pure raging fury, like a tempest at sea. It's repeated again and again across every single screen in the whole room.

"Everyone stop what you're doing," you say, your voice rattling like a set of keys. "Find that old bitch I brought in here and bring her to me. NOW!"

The entire room turns to look at me as I pull the cage door open. Daniel drops his clipboard, and it clatters to the floor.

And do you know what I do next?

Of course I do, Maggie. That's why we're here.

I reach over to the switch and flick it down with a loud, satisfying click.

Stanley
1958 via 1967

"I KNEW HE'D NEVER STOP," STANLEY EXPLAINED TO HER, FEELING THE need to justify all his choices. "I knew he'd come after you. I realized that the moment I met you. I couldn't leave that on you, so I created Sunrise to protect me."

"Protect you?" she repeated. "They were wiping your mind. They were deleting your memories."

"Because I asked them to," he said. "If they were doing that, it means Hassan was trying to get in again, and not just through you. He will try to break into my head. He has all sorts of people under his control. I . . . can't risk him finding out."

"So why keep the solution at all? Why not just delete it from your own mind for good?"

"I hoped—" he started, then stopped, shaking his head. "I was scared that something might happen to you. To us. I held on to it in case I needed it, but . . ." He sighed, looking away from her. "I have caused all of this. Just add it to the list of my failures, I suppose."

"Hey," she said. She put a hand to his face and gently pulled it back. "You have never been a failure to me. Ever. I just wish I could have done more to help you. I wish I could have known more about this life. Why do you never tell me?"

Stanley blinked. "All of this—the experiments, Omega, Hassan—it has caused me too much pain and too much heartbreak. I don't want that in our life together. I want a clean start. A clean break."

Maggie nodded, as if she understood. He desperately hoped that she did. It was so important that she understood.

"There's one thing I still don't get," she said. "I interacted with myself in the past, more than once. Why do I never remember seeing my old self?"

Stanley turned away, his cheeks hot. "That one's easy, I suppose. You can only change the past if the memories are completely objective."

"But I thought that's what the memory spade did—ensure perfect memories."

"That's the idea," he said quietly. "But you were in *my* memories. And it doesn't matter what any technology is supposed to be able to do or not. I've *never* been able to think about you objectively."

"Oh, Stan." She blinked, her eyes wet with tears. "You're such a hopeless romantic."

"Sorry."

She took a breath, getting her emotions under control, focusing on the moment. "Okay—so once I've established how he's keeping Omega at bay, what next?"

"You need to release it."

"What?" She stared up at him. "Why?"

TRANSCRIPT NO. 273: Margaret Webb
DATE STAMP: 11 AUG. 2021
0 Hours, 12 Minutes, and 3 Seconds Until Dissolution

There's a giant shift in the floor, like tectonic plates moving. The glass walls around Omega slide across each other and then retract, disappearing into the ground.

Everyone stares for one second, then two, then panics.

Some run for the lift, shouting and violently pushing one another out of the way. Others just back away toward the wall. I start pressing buttons on the console, randomly mashing at them in the hope that one will do what I want it to.

It does. The cell doors slide open. People come bundling out—stumbling, racing, screaming. The stink of their sweaty bodies permeates the room. One of them grabs a scientist in a hazmat suit and pulls him to the ground, beating and kicking him until the floor around him turns blood-red. Others join the chaos, which washes over the room in a frenzied wave.

And at the center of it all, Omega pulses and grows. It pushes against the plants, withering them as it passes, testing the walls of what was once its cell. As it grows, it becomes less and less black. The swirling mass turns gray, then almost transparent, and before long, it just . . . disappears.

It disappears?

As though it has stretched itself too far and just dissipated, dissolved into thin air. There's no sign of it anymore. Everyone slows, confused. Even the prisoners attacking the scientists pause midblow.

Silence envelops the entire room.

The calm before the storm.

Then it begins.

What begins?

It starts with a blond middle-aged woman halfway between me and the back wall. She is half-crouched, about to run, when it hits her. Her body falls slack and droops, her past flickering out of existence. She is *erased*.

Then two more follow, then four. It spreads across the room indiscriminately. Through a throng of screaming and fury and panic, a tidal wave of *nothingness* sweeps. It's taking all of them. It will take me too.

I press myself back against the wall as staff rush past me, trying to get out of the room, to get away, but they are dragged to the floor by prisoners, turned berserk in their fury. People are smashing the consoles with chairs, with tables, with pieces of metal—sparks fly and catch, the acrid smell of burning plastic cutting through the stench of unwashed human flesh.

A man collapses by my feet, a shard of glass in his back. Just as he looks up at me, reaching, begging, his face goes blank. His arms fall to his sides.

Oh God.

I have done this, I think. *I have made this happen.*

My stomach heaves, and I cough, feeling the bile rise into my throat.

Three men—three of the lab-coated staff—dash to a large metal chest some twenty yards to my right. Frantically opening it, they pull out guns. I wonder, for a moment, what the hell they plan to do, how on earth they expect to fight this with weapons.

That's not what the guns are for.

I see one of them—oh God, it's Daniel—pick up a pistol and put it to his temple. He splatters his brains all over the wall. It makes sense: Death is better than being erased from time, than having your loved ones forget you ever even existed. The crack of another gunshot follows, and others scramble toward them, climbing over the bodies to pick up their dropped weapons.

One woman puts a pistol in her mouth, but she is too slow. Before she can pull the trigger, her face goes blank. Her arm falls and dangles by her side.

The room is all screams now, all fire and madness. I have made this happen. They have died because of me.

A door flies open behind me with a clang of metal.

I jump, jerking round feverishly.

You hobble into the room. Your body is crooked—your left arm curls back on itself, bending at the elbow in the wrong direction. Your head is improperly fixed onto your body, sticking out at an odd angle, as if whatever you have done to extend your body's natural lifespan is disintegrating beneath you. Your clothes are ripped open, tattered, and your whole body is covered in carved symbols and blood.

"You!" you utter, starting toward me, even as everyone around us turns to puppets. I back away, but you dart forward. You are still impossibly quick, scuttling like a twisted spider.

I do not know why I haven't been taken yet.

Maybe it knows I set it free, I think. *Maybe it's thanking me.*

But I don't have time to take the thought further, because your hand is tight around my neck. The symbols carved into your skin must offer you some brief protection.

"You're not getting away that easily," you say, and tug me forward, your hand a leash. I stumble after you, choking.

I struggle for breath. I feel my vision starting to go black as you lurch me forward, my feet scrambling to keep up.

You pull me through the door and into another lift, one that I didn't know was there. I'm about to pass out. The world swims.

Just before the door closes, I catch a glimpse of the devastation behind me. Nobody is moving anymore. Over a hundred people. They are either dead or just standing or sitting there, gone.

Empty.

Never to be thought of ever again.

Stanley
1958 via 1967

STANLEY TOOK A SEAT ON ONE OF THE BENCHES ON THE STREET OUTSIDE that faced the house. Maggie placed herself gingerly next to him. She winced a little as she sat, and Stanley wondered just how difficult an experience she had endured.

Younger Stanley was still looking at the wall beneath the balcony, reading the hundreds of names inscribed and pasted there, professing their love for one another.

"I know what he's going to do next," Stanley said.

"What do you mean?"

"Jacques—Hassan—he's always had the same problem. He reveals himself too early. He thinks he's won in the middle game, so he gets showy and signposts his endgame. He thinks I didn't notice what he was doing to me the other day, but I did. It took me a while to figure it out, but there's no other way."

Maggie frowned. "What are you talking about?"

"He has developed a way to repeat moments. To replay them again if they don't go the way he wants them to. Everyone in the moment forgets—they go back to the start of the timeline—but *he* remembers."

"That sounds terrifying."

"It is," Stanley said, nodding. "He is a terrifying man. And yet there must be limits. I've been thinking about what he did to me. There must be a time limit of some kind on how long the moment can be isolated, and I would imagine that it's not particularly long. There must be a geographical limit as well. There's no way he's putting the whole universe on repeat." He paused, mulling it over. "And I think he needs to start the machine at the beginning of the moment—he can't just go backward."

"Like recording a TV show," Maggie said. "You need to press record first."

"Exactly."

Stanley fell quiet, looking at his feet. Neither of them said anything for a few seconds.

"What is it?" Maggie asked.

"I don't want to have to ask you to do this."

Maggie took his hand, squeezing it tightly. "I think we've come a bit far for that."

"By releasing Omega, you'll force his hand. He'll have other protections in place—I know him—but they won't last for long. He'll get desperate. This is about more than just control for him. If Omega wipes him out, he will be forgotten for all time. He will be wiped from history. No one will ever remember his existence. That's just about the worst thing he can possibly imagine. If he suspects you have the solution, he'll use the machine to trap you in a loop until he finds out what he needs. Until you give the solution to him."

"But I don't know the solution."

"Not yet," he said. "No. But you will. Because I'm going to tell you."

TRANSCRIPT NO. 273: Margaret Webb
DATE STAMP: 11 AUG. 2021
0 Hours, 6 Minutes, and 15 Seconds Until Dissolution

> The last thing I remember is passing out with your fist tight around my throat. When I come to, I'm in this pool, in front of you.

Yes.

> What is this place?

It's not really a swimming pool. It's a carved-out basin underneath the Institute. It is our last protection. After you unleashed Omega, I was forced to retreat here. Outside this room, there are lines of fire, of symbols, of plants. I have spent many years studying the few protections Stanley shared with me. The shape of the basin acts as a conduit for the energy created. But it's not perfect. It is never perfect. Omega always finds a way through.

> Oh God, all those people down there. They were all erased completely. They don't exist anymore. They never existed.

You did that, Maggie. That was your choice.

> Oh, fuck off. How many people have you fed to that thing over the years? Thousands? Tens of thousands? I will not be guilt-tripped by a mass murderer, Hassan.

It will take you too. And Stanley.

> Where is Stanley?

He is nearby. He is safe, for now, but he won't be for long. Not unless you tell me how Omega can be stopped for good.

| And what makes you think I know?

Don't play coy with me, Maggie. You know it. I know you know it. You've been lying to me. Over and over again.

| How many times have we done this?

More than you can possibly know. We have been here for a very long time, you and I, and we will continue to be until you give me the solution. As long as I keep repeating the loop, we have all the time in the world. Only when it stops will Omega enter, and by then, you will have told me how to stop it.

| You're crazy.

No—I am determined. Let me make you a promise, Maggie, right now. If you help me, if you give me the solution, I will do everything in my power to save Stanley. To bring his memories back and to bring you back together. I will ensure that whatever happens next, you two will live as long and as happy a life as I am capable of making for you. And I am capable of many wonders.

| And if I don't?

I will find the solution, Maggie. It's not a question of *if*—it's a question of *when*. And if I deem that you have been more of a hindrance than a help, I will roll Stanley in here and slice open his throat in front of you. I will make you watch him die, and then I will kill you myself. That is my promise.

Stanley
1958 via 1967

SLOWLY, AND IN STAGES, HE TOLD HER EVERYTHING. HE STOPPED AT POINTS, checking to see if she had any questions. Sometimes she did; sometimes she simply nodded for him to continue. He ran through the various rituals and blood rites he had learned, the correct use of the plants and the interplay between fire and life. He explained the exact procedure, in perfect detail, for stopping Omega once and for all. He explained how to switch off the failsafe. How to open up the past to manipulation, to meddling, to control.

And when he was done, he lay back. It was the first time he had ever spoken it all out loud—all he had learned from his years in the outback, from his studious travels throughout other parts of the world, from distant caves and ancient archaeological sites. He let out a deep breath. It was done. The solution that only he knew: It had been passed on.

They sat in silence for some time, and he could see that Maggie was processing what he had just told her. Eventually, she spoke.

"If I give it to him," she said, "he'll leave us alone?"

"Maybe," Stanley replied. "It's easy for him to make promises he has no intention of keeping."

"But I might be able to get you back." She leaned forward. "The other option is that I lose you."

"I know," he said. "And, yes, he'll probably let you stay alive, maybe me too. He may do that for you. But in doing that, we give him complete power over time itself. That is what he wants: to remove the strictures of cause and effect, to have power over all things. He will be unstoppable. He will remake the world as he sees fit, and everyone in it will be subservient to him. The human race isn't meant to live like that. It's not right."

"So what do I do?"

"You tell him the wrong thing."

She blinked. "What?"

"Don't tell him the full solution. Change a few things—I can tell you what to change so that it doesn't work."

"Hold on," she said, putting her hand in the air. "Didn't you already try that?"

Stanley nodded. "It didn't work because it was the wrong time. There was no urgency. He had time to consider it cautiously, to test it. He is nothing if not meticulous in his approach. But if I can predict his final move, we can trap him in it. Once you unleash Omega and he locks you in a loop, we're going to have two things going for us. One, he'll be desperate. Whatever protections he has will be temporary at best. Sure, he's maybe safe in the loop with you; maybe it can't get him in that bubble. But the moment he stops the loop, if he doesn't have the solution, Omega *will* get to him. He knows it will. It's waiting for him. Two, he still thinks he's the one in control. He thinks that because he can keep looping you, he'll be able to control you. That way, when you eventually give him the false solution, he'll believe it. He'll try it. It won't work. His protections will fail, and Omega will do its job."

"Its job?"

"Cauterizing the wound. Cleaning up. Wiping from existence everyone and everything that was involved. Hassan, the Institute, you, me. When that is done, it can stop again, but only then. The rest of the world will continue as if none of us had ever existed."

Maggie stared back at him. "And Leah? What will happen to her? Oh, Stan—you've never met her, but Leah . . ." She fell quiet, unable to bring the words to her lips.

Stanley sighed. It was the one question he didn't want to answer. "She'll forget us. We will stop existing—in the past, present, and future. Her memories will make up the deficit, invent a story, but she will never remember a thing about us."

"That's . . ." Maggie looked up at him, desperate. "I don't know if I can do that, Stan."

"It's a lot to ask."

Tears fell down her cheeks. "I don't want our daughter to forget me. She's the best thing I've ever done."

"I know."

"But wait," she whispered. "I don't understand. Why even tell me the solution? If the plan was always to get him here, and to give him a false one, why tell me the real one?"

TRANSCRIPT NO. 273: Margaret Webb
DATE STAMP: 11 AUG. 2021
0 Hours, 4 Minutes, and 1 Second Until Dissolution

> Why all this? Why the interview? Why the trawling through my memories? Either I'm going to tell you or I'm not.

People aren't that black and white, Maggie. Whatever their intentions, there is always a way to get them to talk. You just need to try enough times.

> So, what? You're hoping that one day you'll just charm me enough to give in? I *remember* all the things you've done, Hassan. I'm not an idiot.

No—but you are a liar. You have lied to me. You know the solution. Stanley has shared it with you. I am sure of it. He always was a sentimental fool. You have lied to me. And still, you lie every time. I know that your story about visiting the theater was a lie. You've come back to that one a few times, but it often changes. Last time it was a gallery in Paris. The time before that it was a church in Sicily.

> I see. This isn't the first time we've done this.

Far, far from it.

> Okay, so you have proof that I am lying to you. So what?

I also know what you are lying about. The more times we do this, the closer I get to isolating the lies. I study these transcripts every time, before we reset again. I identify the discrepancies. You are not perfect, Maggie. You will make mistakes. Slowly, by process of elimination, I will arrive at the truth. All it will take is time.

Stanley
1958 via 1967

STANLEY STOOD UP. HE TOOK A FEW STEPS OVER TOWARD THE BALCONY, where his younger self was just packing up and getting ready to leave. From this distance, he could see the pain and loneliness in every movement, in every step.

"A good friend of mine once told me I was obsessed, back before I met you, and he was right. He said the source of my obsession came from 'trying to heal the wound that never heals.' I never really understood that. Not until I met you." He turned to Maggie, taking her hands and lifting her up off the bench. "You healed it," he said. "I see that now. You made me whole."

"I don't understand," she said. They were so close that he could feel her breath against his skin.

"The choice is up to you," he replied. "You can either give him the real solution and try to save us both or give him the false one and sacrifice our lives to save everyone else. It has to be your choice."

"Why?"

"Because nothing made sense until you came into my life. Because I trust you more than I trust myself. Because for all that I think I know what the right thing to do here is, I've been wrong before. I've been wrong a lot. The only thing I've never been wrong about is you."

TRANSCRIPT NO. 273: Margaret Webb
DATE STAMP: 11 AUG. 2021
0 Hours, 1 Minute, and 43 Seconds Until Dissolution

> What are you hoping to achieve by doing this? At least be honest with me if you want me to make a decision. What's your endgame?

Ever since I was a child, I saw the path that humanity was treading. I tried to tell Stanley—to explain it to him—but he never believed me. But I was right, Maggie. Look at what the world has become: the climate crisis, a dying planet, an oncoming extinction. People live in bubbles now, coddled by the internet, raging blindly at whatever conspiracy theory they are fed, while the world destroys itself. Just think, Maggie, of the wrongs that I can right with control over the past. I would have the power to do anything.

> And what would you do?

Take the world by the reins. Show it the right path. Fix it. Perfect it.

> By perfect it, you mean control it, don't you? There's a saying about power and corruption that I think you're probably familiar with.

It will be different with me. I am different.

> Did it hurt that much?

What are you talking about?

> The fact that your old professor picked Stanley over you. The fact that he rejected you. That's what all this is, isn't it? All this death, this destruction—it's just a desperate desire to control everything you can so you can prove that you're not the failure he thought you were. But he's dead, Hassan. You're not proving anything to anyone.

You're being ridiculous.

| I don't think I am.

It doesn't matter. You are as blind and stupid as your husband was. You will give in eventually.

| And what if I just stop talking? What if I don't tell you anything?

Then we will go again. And again. And again.

| The same loop? You make me relive the same memories?

Yes. Always. Until you give in. This only ends when I want it to. You are not fighting against time here, Maggie. You are fighting my force of will, and that, I assure you, is indomitable.

Stanley
1958 via 1967

HER EYES WERE WET. HE HELD HER GAZE, BRINGING HER CLOSE.

"What happens if I can't choose?" she whispered.

"Then Hassan will make you repeat the same loop over and over again, forcing you to relive those memories eternally. If you release Omega, then you've backed him into a corner. It's his last defense. He has no choice—if he can't stop it, he knows that ending the loop will let it in."

She blinked. Letting go, she took a few steps back from him. A strange expression crossed her face, a light switching on. Stanley frowned as he watched an improbable smile appear on Maggie's lips.

"The same loop?" she repeated.

He nodded. "The same memories."

"And I get to see you again," she said, her voice almost shaking. "I get to be held by you at our wedding again. And, for all of the horrors and mistakes, I get to see Leah's birth again, and I get to watch her as she grows up. I get to see the first time we meet again. I get to experience our entire life over and over."

Stanley shook his head, trying to work out what she was saying. This didn't make any sense. "In segments, yes, I suppose. In flashes. But no more than that."

"Oh, Stan," she said, taking a step closer to him again. "It's *so much* more. It's so much more than I ever hoped for."

"I don't . . ." He took her hands in his, looking at them. "You can't just live your life in a loop, Maggie."

She laughed. "Can't I? What do you think I've been doing for the past ten years, Stan? In that house on my own, without Leah, visiting you at Sunrise—at least in this loop you'll actually recognize me! You tell me that if I do this, we will be erased, disappear into nothingness, but I already *did that*. I have been nothingness for years. Hassan threatens to kill me, but I *already died*."

"But you'll be locked in there with *him*. Over and over and over again."

"But Leah won't forget us. She'll live on, and she'll remember. If there's one thing I've learned through all of this, it's that the most important thing we have is our memories. I won't make her give those up."

Stanley shook his head. "She won't know what's happened to you. To either of us."

"I will find a way to tell her. And even if I don't, she'll be okay. She'll have a life. I choose that over living my own life. I already *did* choose that. I'm happy with the memories I have, Stan. Let her hold on to hers. Let her make some new ones. At least in my memories, I still have you."

"So you just . . . repeat?" Stanley asked. "In a loop with him? Forever?"

The smile on her face grew wider. "Forever."

And then she burst out laughing.

He frowned. "What's so funny?"

"Each time I restart the loop, I forget, yes?" She wheezed between breaths, putting her hand to her chest. "I forget all the previous ones?"

"I . . . I think so."

"But he doesn't. He remembers them all. Every single one."

Stanley cocked his head. "I think that's how it works. So that he can try different tactics. So that he can—"

"But he doesn't have anything," she insisted. "His genius plan is to trap me in a loop of my own life, over and over again, until he gets what he wants. But I'm not stuck in there with him, Stan. He's stuck in there *with me*. At least in that loop, I've got you. I've got Leah. I've got more vivid memories of my entire life than I could ever hope to relive, and I relive them anew every time. All he's got is his own ego and a batty old woman with endless questions whom he has to placate for all eternity. Christ, if there's a definition of hell, that's got to be it. What an idiot!"

Stanley stared at her—this crazy, wonderful, fantastic woman—and could think of only one more question to ask.

"Is it worth it?"

"Oh, Stan, there's never been anything more worth it in the entire world."

Leaning forward, she kissed him. And all the age between them, all the time, all the distance—it dissolved into nothing. For a brief respite amid the madness of his life, all that he could think about, all that he could remember, was this moment.

She took a step back so that she could look him right in the eye.

His heart throbbed.

"And I'll still stay," she said, "to have thee still forget, forgetting any other home but this."

And in a flicker of light, she disappeared.

TRANSCRIPT NO. 273: Margaret Webb

DATE STAMP: 11 AUG. 2021

0 Hours, 0 Minutes, and 18 Seconds Until Dissolution

What is it, Maggie? What is the solution? Let us end this madness—just tell me.

| You know what?

What?

| For the life of me, I can't remember.

HALF-LIFE COMPLETE. DISSOLUTION ENGAGED.

[END TRANSCRIPT]

TRANSCRIPT NO. 274: Margaret Webb
DATE STAMP: 11 AUG. 2021
11 Hours, 0 Minutes, and 0 Seconds Until Dissolution

Hello, Maggie. We've got eleven hours until it resets.

I   Where am I?

That's not important, Maggie. The only thing that's important is that you focus on me.

Acknowledgments

When I sat down to write this story, my Grandpa Joe and my Grannie May were in their early nineties, and after a long lifetime living together in a multitude of countries across the entire globe, they remained still the very picture of absolute love: completely devoted to and utterly inseparable from each other. As I sit to write these acknowledgments, Joe has passed and May, tragically, has all but forgotten him, clutched by a similar dementia I saw my Grandma Vera go through some years before. This book, in many ways, is an ode to their over seventy-year relationship, and to the warmth of the memories that live on beyond them in the people lucky enough to witness their love.

But it is also, primarily, a love letter to my wonderful wife, Allys, without whom none of my achievements would be possible. And, yes, I'm aware that she married a man whose idea of a love letter includes violence, murder, and dismemberment, but there's not much I can do about that. Here's to many more decades of beautiful memories and to chiseling away at the sculpture so we can find out what's underneath.

My deepest thanks go to my agent, Alex Cochran, who had the wisdom to make me remove *that* scene from this book, even if I fought him on it. And also to both Alexandra Machinist and Dan Milaschewski for all their